MOTHER
OF THE
BRIDE

BOOKS BY SAMANTHA HAYES

The Reunion

Tell Me A Secret

The Liar's Wife

Date Night

The Happy Couple

Single Mother

The Trapped Wife

The Ex-Husband

The Engagement

The Inheritance

MOTHER
OF THE
BRIDE

SAMANTHA HAYES

bookouture

Published by Bookouture in 2024

An imprint of Storyfire Ltd.
Carmelite House
50 Victoria Embankment
London EC4Y oDZ

www.bookouture.com

ISBN: 978-1-83790-967-4
eBook ISBN: 978-1-83790-966-7

This one's for all my amazing readers!
Thank you for turning the pages...

fresh and clean look. The bride is smiling, but it's the glow from within that shines the brightest.

The wedding party begins the slow march down the aisle as the organist plays on. But almost immediately, there's a hesitation. The bride stops walking, her expression changing – at first a blank look, then a flash of concern, worry, fear... Then the maid of honour whispers something to her and the bride is moving again, gliding down the aisle with her arm linked through her father's – her smile back in place.

The reverend, holding his ceremonial leatherbound book in two hands, stands in front of the altar, smiling as the bride approaches, waiting as her father hands her over to the groom. The best man watches on, his eyes flicking between the bride and the maid of honour, a slight twitch under one eye as he wonders, thinks, sizes up. All the guests are enraptured as the couple join hands and stand side by side, ready to begin the rest of their lives together.

The organ music subsides, and the reverend begins to speak... welcoming everyone to his beautiful church.

'Dearly beloved...' he says, his voice reaching even the furthest corners of the building.

The bride looks around to her maid of honour, then back to the reverend, giving her groom a warm smile. The groom, unobserved by anyone else, gives his bride's hand a fond squeeze. In just a few moments, they will be married.

'Therefore, I ask...' the reverend continues solemnly. 'If any person can show just cause why this man and this woman may not be joined together in holy matrimony, let them speak now or forever hold their peace.'

Silence.

Someone coughs.

Something rustles.

More silence.

PROLOGUE

The church is packed full of guests, and the bells are ringing. Sprays of white blooms decorate the end of each pew, and the altar is adorned with huge bouquets of roses, hydrangeas, hollyhocks and eucalyptus. The organist plays Wagner's bridal chorus, the music filling the entire church, setting the scene for the most beautiful wedding – the most wanted and anticipated union between two people very much in love.

The bride stands just inside the old oak doorway, her father beside her – his eyes glistening with proud tears, dressed in his smart suit and pale-pink tie as he prepares to give his daughter away to the man she adores.

Behind them stands the maid of honour in her cream satin dress, her simple spray of flowers in one hand, her other hand fussing over the bride's veil so it falls perfectly around her shoulders.

And the bride – a picture of perfection in a white and cream lace dress that enhances her slim shape without being too fussy. Her dark, wavy hair is held back in a pretty chignon, decorated with simple daisies, and her light make-up gives her a

Then a voice echoes throughout the church – crisp and clear. One single syllable.

'No!'

A woman's voice.

Slowly, the bride turns, fear slicing down her spine as she realises who has spoken.

Then her mouth drops open as she stares straight into her mother's cold, black eyes.

ONE

TWO WEEKS EARLIER

'*Darling!*'

The single word seems to fill the entire driveway – no, the entire *village*, as it trills from between my mother's bright-red lips.

'Dar*ling!*' Mum repeats, as though the first time wasn't enough. But the expression on her face is blank, and I can't tell whether she's pleased to see me or not.

I give Owen one last look as he grabs our weekend bag from the boot and we head across the drive and up to the front door where Mum is waiting.

Perhaps the last look we'll share while he still has any love or respect for me, I can't help thinking.

I never wanted to come here in the first place, but now that we're engaged, Owen was naturally keen to meet my family. Though I've not yet revealed the news of our upcoming wedding to my mother. Besides, our being crammed into Peter's tiny flat in London, outstaying our welcome ever since we've returned from working overseas, isn't ideal. This is a chance to give him some much-needed space. Peter is one of my closest friends and has been very patient putting us up. We never intended to stay with him for so long.

I take a deep breath as I draw closer to my mother, reminding myself it's only for a couple of days – a pleasant weekend in the Cotswolds – and nothing will go wrong. I also have to convince myself that I'm not a child any more, that I'm not a victim or responsible for dealing with Mum's erratic outbursts, should she have any, and neither is it my job to soothe or placate her if she goes *brain bad* – the name my father gave her more turbulent moods when my sister and I were growing up.

'Hello, Mum,' I say, making sure I stick close to Owen as we approach the front door, my fingers tightly entwined with his. My mouth is dry and my heart galloping.

A quick glance around tells me nothing much has changed here. Medvale House is an idyllic Cotswold home that deserves to be between the pages of a homes and interiors magazine – honey-coloured stonework, pretty leaded windows with rippled glass, old rosemary tiles on the roof and well-stocked flower borders in the large garden. The old place is far too big for Mum and Dad now, but I know for certain there's no way Mum would ever agree to sell it. Owning a house like this is part of her identity – impressive, desirable, expensive.

Though I'm more intent on sizing up my mother's state of mind than the pink roses around the door, or the tubs of scarlet geraniums either side of the gravel path. What happened last summer has only made me more anxious and uneasy about being in her company.

'Mum, this is Owen,' I announce, though my tone falls flat. It feels as though I've already lost him, just by introducing him on the doorstep of my old family home – the entryway to what I've already convinced myself is our demise as a couple.

'How lovely to...' Mum pauses, casting her silver-blue eyes up and down Owen, her stare ending on his face again as she scrutinises him, her lips tensing into a tight line. '...To meet you,' she finally says, extending a hand that's heavy with gold jewellery.

My mother is dressed entirely in black – loose-fitting trousers and a long-sleeved tunic top, and her fingers are glittering with chunky antique gold rings, her wrists jangling with all manner of bangles and chains. I'd bet that what she's wearing on her hands alone is worth more than the car we turned up in – a seen-better-days Volvo that Owen promised was just a stopgap until we're both earning again and are able to afford something better for when the baby comes.

I smile to myself as my hand automatically rests on my stomach. I'm nowhere near showing yet, and it's only me and Owen who know I'm pregnant. For now, we're keeping it that way.

But the most startling thing about Mum – and it might be my imagination, my deep desire for things to be normal, at least for the next two days – is that she doesn't sound quite as confrontational as usual. A little *subdued*, even. Which makes me concerned about what's really going on in her mind.

'Come in, come *in*, both of you,' she says, still shaking Owen's hand as she stares him down. It seems to go on forever, as though she's downloading a secret armoury of weapons to use against us simply by making physical contact. I know she's judging every minute detail about him, gauging his suitability as my partner. Until a few days ago, she didn't even know Owen existed.

In Mum's eyes, no one will be good enough for her daughters, and I have no intention of telling her we're engaged. As soon as she hears that wedding bells are in the air, whether she approves of him or not, she'll want to take control of everything, making everything about her.

'It's a lovely place you have here, Mrs Holmes,' Owen says as we step over the threshold. I whisper that he should just leave our bag by the door for now. *In case we need to make a quick escape.*

'Thank you, Owen,' Mum says as she leads the way down the long, flagstoned hallway. She flicks a glance back over her shoulder. 'And please, do call me Sylvia.'

Familiar smells sweep me back in time as I breathe in the cool, still air within Medvale House. As we pass the creaky oak staircase, I almost catch sight of myself scampering upstairs to hide in my bedroom, trying to escape the fallout from whatever Mum's latest drama was. I've since wept for that poor little girl – helpless and afraid as she ran away and hid, spending much of her childhood cowering. Little did I know back then that my mother's unpredictable moods were the least fearful part of her.

'Here, these are for you,' Owen says, producing a slightly battered and wilted bunch of flowers that we picked up when we stopped off at a service station for me to go to the toilet.

'Oh. How lovely,' Mum says, accepting them with a small smile. I brace myself, waiting for the inevitable comment about *garage bouquets* or *how cheaply you can buy chrysanthemums these days.*

But none comes.

Instead, Mum busies herself finding a vase and arranging the pink blooms in water.

'There,' she says, 'lovely.' And she sets them down on the kitchen table.

Mum's pleasant reaction makes me feel almost as unsettled as if she *had* kicked off.

'How was your journey?' she asks, filling the kettle.

'Traffic was bad getting out of London, but after that it was fine,' Owen replies, giving me a wink. 'Lizzie kept needing to stop for—'

'Garden's looking great, Mum,' I almost shout. Anything to prevent her train of thought going down the obvious route if Owen had continued. *Stopping regularly for the toilet must mean pregnancy...* It would be an easy (and correct) leap for my mother's alert mind to make, but by not telling her that we're having a baby, I feel as if I'm protecting my unborn child from her. For the time being, anyway.

'That's Preston's work,' Mum says, coming over to where I'm peering out of the window. 'Look at the roses. Aren't the colours adorable? And still in bloom even in September.'

Adorable, I think. Never in my life have I heard Mum use such a fanciful or frivolous word to describe anything. Dreadful, abhorrent, disaster and catastrophe would be at the top of her most-used words list. Something inside me unknots just a little, though I'm sure Mum's mask will slip soon enough.

'Preston?'

'My new *man*,' Mum crows. For a fleeting moment, I catch sight of the woman I know best – duplicitous, dangerous and deranged. 'By new man, I mean gardener, of course.' Then comes a girlish laugh, the likes of which I've never heard before. 'Whatever he does to the roses, they simply love him for it.'

'They're a gorgeous shade,' I say, treading carefully. Sticking to conversations about the garden, Mum's church and fundraising work and topics such as the weather are, I know from experience, safest.

'Yes indeed,' Mum says, getting on with making the tea. 'They're such a deep red. Just like the colour of blood.'

TWO

'I'm dying to hear how you two met,' Sylvia begins, once the three of us are seated at the kitchen table. Several plates of triangular sandwiches sit on a red and white gingham tablecloth, and, arranged on a tiered cake stand that I remember from my childhood, are some shop-bought almond slices. Mum hands us each a floral china plate before pouring the tea, telling us to dig in. 'I want all the juicy details,' she adds, eyeing Owen.

I look at my fiancé, feeling goosebumps break out on my arms. Instinctively, I slide my left hand under the table so she can't see my ring, making a mental note to take it off later. Since I left home for university aged eighteen, I've kept Mum on a need-to-know basis about my life. It's just been easier like that, especially after what happened that first winter I was away.

I never got to find out all the details, with Shelley, my older sister, protecting me as she'd always done, though on this occasion I don't think she knew much more herself. She did let slip something about a visit from the police and Mum suddenly leaving her job (though she had no idea why), not to mention the stress our father was under and what had happened to him subsequently. But I'd effectively blocked my ears to it all, choosing my new-found freedom over getting involved.

Looking back, I should have been here for my dad and sister, but I was young and intent on relishing my first taste of freedom – freedom from my *mother*. I'd been trying to run away my entire life and, having finally done it, nothing short of a murder would have drawn me back.

Since then, I've kept visits to just once or twice a year, mainly to catch up with Dad and Shelley. And I only return Mum's phone calls occasionally. Infrequent contact has meant that I've managed to keep any 'juicy details' about my life secret from her – which is why I jump in to answer her question before Owen has a chance to reply.

'I was private tutoring two children in Dubai,' I begin, giving Owen a glance. We share a look, making me stifle a smile at the thought of what really happened the afternoon we met. But I want to keep the story as brief as possible for my mother. 'The children's father, who happened to work in the same industry as Owen, had a party for clients and business associates. Owen was invited and that's where we met, Mum.'

Flaunting yourself half-naked by the pool, were you?
Whore...
Having an affair with the children's father, I expect.
Disgusting...

I try to silence the voice in my head, but, strangely, Mum replies, 'How romantic. Just like that time when your father and I...'

As she talks, I zone out, allowing the memory of Owen's proposal just six months after we first met to drift into my mind. Now *that* had been romantic – a meal in a skyscraper restaurant in the centre of Dubai, a view of the stunning coast with its endless beaches, yachts and twinkling lights. It was the perfect setting. He'd dropped to one knee after we'd shared a dozen oysters, presenting me with the most beautiful ring – a solitaire diamond in a white gold band. I'd felt giddy from happiness.

Until I remembered my mother.

'Gretna Green, here we come,' I'd joked, feeling awful as the happy expression on Owen's face dissolved.

'You don't want a proper wedding?' he'd asked. 'A beautiful village church back home, with six bridesmaids and you in a gorgeous dress? I'm imagining a marquee on the lawn of a country hotel, a live band, caterers. The works.'

He was literally describing what I knew my mother would start organising the second I told her we were getting married. Whether she approved of Owen or not, I knew she'd instantly take control of everything. Mum had always believed in keeping her enemies close.

'Of *course* I want a proper wedding,' I'd replied, trying to sound upbeat. 'But...'

Owen's puzzled expression forced me to explain a little about my mother, though I'd kept the details extra light. I didn't want to spoil the evening. Spoil our entire *lives*.

'Mum is...' I've never known quite how to describe her. 'Thing is, she's...' I continued, still struggling to find the right words.

'She's what?' he'd replied with a laugh, though I sensed the apprehension in his voice. I'd paused while the waiter served the champagne Owen had ordered.

'Mum's... well, she's a *lot*,' I settled on with a smile. 'But she means well,' I added, seeing the slight frown on Owen's brow. I didn't want to put him off me altogether.

Even though we'd only been together a few glorious months when he proposed, I knew he was 'the one' almost immediately. And he'd said the same about me. Fate had brought us together in the most unlikely of places, and now that we've returned to the UK, I'm damned if my mother is going to ruin it. I'd put three and a half thousand miles between us for a reason.

'Well, she gave me you, so I love your mum to bits already,' Owen had said across the table in Dubai, making me wince inside as he raised his glass.

I'd forced another little smile, gazing out across the cityscape below. It was far too romantic an evening to be tarnished by talk of my mother.

'Here's to the mother of the bride,' Owen had then said, chinking his champagne glass against mine.

Now, sitting in my mother's kitchen with Owen by my side, I smile to myself, knowing at least Mum can't take those memories away from me.

'It was indeed a very romantic meeting,' Owen says, snapping me back to the moment. 'While Lizzie was sitting under a parasol playing word games with the kids, I was discussing a multinational green energy deal the other side of the pool. Our eyes kept meeting across the water.'

Mum clasps her hands under her chin. 'I can just imagine it. Oh, but the heat wouldn't suit me. Must have been terrible for your fair skin, Elizabeth.' She turns to me.

You get your pasty colouring from your father...

So unattractive...

'Everywhere is air-conditioned out there, so it's easy to escape the heat if you need to,' Owen tells her. 'And Lizzie was always sensible with sunblock.' He nudges my leg under the table, giving me a fond look.

'You should have told me you'd met such a handsome fellow, darling. Not even a postcard from her, Owen,' my mother directs across the table. 'But I know how busy my girl is, what with all her jet-setting around the world.'

'It's not exactly jet-setting, Mum. It was a six-month tutoring post that I got through an agency because I really needed the work.'

She has no idea that I was penniless, left paying off debts that weren't even mine with my credit rating in tatters through no fault of my own. And I have no intention of telling her. The gloating and 'I told you so's would be off the scale.

'If you hadn't answered Lizzie's phone for her the other day, Owen, I might never have known about you two, let alone found out that you're engaged to be *married*,' Mum says in an unnervingly calm way as she plays a trump card. I'm certain she'll have more of them up her sleeve. 'Daughters, eh?' she says to Owen again as if they already share a private joke.

I almost choke on my sandwich, watching as Owen squirms in his chair, giving me an apologetic look.

One–nil to Mother...

'Oh, no, he told me all about the phone call, Mum,' I say, not wanting her to think she's got Owen into trouble. I knew he'd taken a call from her but hadn't realised he'd told her we were engaged. He must have forgotten to tell me that bit, perhaps realising afterwards he'd made a mistake. I make a mental note to ask him later, though I can hardly blame Owen. He has no inkling of how my mother's scheming mind works.

'Let me see your ring, then,' Mum says, grabbing hold of my left hand. 'Well...' she continues, taking my fingers firmly in hers. She gives the solitaire diamond a quick look. 'Plain and simple must be the new trend these days. On the plus side, I suppose going for the cheaper option means you have more to save for a house deposit.'

And there she is...

'Mum!' I begin, horrified, but Owen squeezes my leg under the table, giving me the courage not to take the bait.

'I have Mummy's antique gold wedding band for you to wear on the big day. But I'm afraid it's going to clash horribly with your silver engagement ring.'

'It's not silver, it's white gold,' I shoot back, feeling the heat building inside me.

'No matter,' Sylvia continues, ignoring me. 'I've got Mummy's engagement ring, too. You'll have to wear that instead. It's not like your sister needs them any more.' She mutters that last sentence. 'Anyway, how exciting. Another wedding to organise. I'll have to buy a new hat. I can't possibly wear the one I wore to Shelley's... *fiasco*. No, that simply wouldn't do at all.'

THREE

'What do you mean, *she's nice?*'

I pace up and down the wonky floor of my childhood bedroom. Being back at Medvale has made me feel about nine years old – powerless and childlike. And we only arrived an hour ago.

Despite the room finally being clear of all the boxes I'd packed up a couple of years ago (Dad only put them in the loft last summer, before his health went downhill), I can still see everything so clearly, just how it always was. I can almost *smell* my childhood in here – the fear, the misery, the uncertainty. I knew Mum's reluctance to get rid of mine and Shelley's childhood possessions several decades after we'd left home was because she'd been clinging onto the past. A past she didn't get right.

'I think she's nice, your mum,' Owen repeats, reclining on the new double bed that has since appeared in my old room – apparently now the guest room, not that anyone ever comes to stay. 'Harmless enough,' he adds. 'I can tell she's trying really hard.'

I keep pacing up and down the creaky boards, stopping

briefly at the small paned window to stare out at the view. Why the hell did I ever agree to this weekend away? I curse to myself, thinking back to last night at Peter's flat when Owen and I had planned a quiet evening with a takeaway and a movie, followed by a weekend of flat hunting.

'Unmarried, pregnant *and* homeless,' I'd groaned from the sofa, eyeing Owen's glass of wine longingly.

'Hormones?' he'd replied with a wink.

'Unhelpful.'

While I'd wanted to thump him for the remark, I had to admit he was probably right. But I'd welcomed the hug that followed, even if it meant having to smell his wine breath on a Friday night and watch him sink a bottle of our favourite Rioja alone.

'Sorry,' I'd said, resting my head on his shoulder. 'I can't help worrying about our situation.'

Owen stopped scrolling the property website and gazed at me, that warm look in his eyes being part of the reason I'd fallen for him in the first place – deep yet dreamy; serious but boyish.

'We're in this together, Lizzie,' he'd replied, touching my engagement ring. 'And you being pregnant has been the best news anyone has ever given me.' Then he'd leant over and kissed me, making me wilt from relief.

I hadn't been sure how he'd feel about my pregnancy when I'd broken the news a week earlier, but I suppose it was the same initial shock that I'd felt, given we've only been together six months.

But the intimate moment last night had been interrupted when Peter, my best friend from university, had arrived home. To *his* home. His *tiny* home where we've been staying. Or, rather, *over*staying. It was only meant to be for a night or two when we first arrived back from Dubai, but there we still were, taking up space – literally most of it with all our possessions shoved in boxes and suitcases – eight weeks later.

Peter had started sneezing then, four times in a row before he'd even had a chance to take his jacket off.

'Minnie is shut in the bedroom,' I'd told him, feeling guilty for foisting my cat on him along with us and all our stuff.

While I'd been working overseas, Minnie had been staying in a cattery. Not ideal and it had cost me a fortune – another drain on my already battered finances. But I love her, and she'd got me through some hard times after my last relationship ended two years ago, when I'd been left with a lot more than a broken heart.

With debts I knew nothing about taken out in my name, my savings account emptied without my knowledge and a gambling problem the size of a planet, David had left me in a financial mess that I'd only just dug my way out of thanks to regular agency tutoring work, culminating with the job in Dubai.

'I promise we'll be out of your way soon,' Owen had said to Peter, navigating his way around a pile of our boxes to grab a glass from the cupboard. 'Good news is that I may have just found us the perfect flat. Most of them get snapped up before I can even call the agency. Join us for a spot of red to celebrate?' he'd asked Peter. 'You can have Lizzie's share.'

Peter's head had whipped up. 'Oh?' he'd said, eyeing me. 'That's good news indeed about the flat. But you're not drinking, Lizzie?' I knew his train of thought was heading in the right direction.

'Not for the moment,' I'd replied vaguely. Owen and I have decided to wait until I've reached the three-month mark to tell people about my pregnancy. Until then, we don't want anyone to know. I'd been thinking about combining our baby news with a 'save the date' type of announcement for our wedding – which we also haven't begun planning but probably should.

Truth is, I've been torn, not knowing whether to go the whole nine yards with a big white wedding, or slink off somewhere romantic, just the two of us, and grab a couple of witnesses off the street. Everything has happened so fast – from us meeting, to our engagement, the pregnancy, and now looking for a home together.

But the thought of my mother's reaction to an announcement was enough to make me veer towards the latter option – a quiet wedding, just the two of us. As far as Mum is concerned, no man will ever be good enough for either of her daughters, though even that wouldn't stop her interfering and taking over my wedding plans. Mum has to be in control.

'Not preggers, are you?' Peter had asked as he sat cross-legged on the floor in front of us.

I'd glanced at Owen then, but he was scrolling through more flats on his phone and wasn't listening. 'Um, no. Antibiotics,' I'd said, jumping as the incoming call on my phone saved me from a grilling.

Though when I saw who it was, my heart sank.

My mother.

I usually let her calls go to voicemail, taking a few days to reply to her ensuing texts, but to avoid an inquisition from Peter, I answered her call this time.

'Hi, Mum,' I'd said flatly, catching sight of the pictures on Owen's phone. A flat to rent – a very *nice* flat, from what I could see. 'Yes, I'm fine, thanks. How are you? And... and how's Dad doing?' I'd swallowed down the guilt at the mention of my father. I should have been to visit him.

'I'd be all the better for seeing you...' came my mother's shrill voice down the line. No mention of Dad. She was talking so loudly, I was sure Owen and Peter could hear her, too.

'I know, Mum, I'll come and see you soon. I've been busy looking for work since I've been back in the country and—'

'Do you need money, is that it?'

'No, no, I'll be fine,' I'd replied, not revealing that she was right. I *did* need money. To tide me over until I could find work, anyway.

Owen is due a big consulting fee from his contract in Dubai any day now, and as soon as that's paid, we'll be grand. He's been so generous, telling me many times that he's happy to support me while I hunt for a new tutoring job, especially as we're soon to be married.

'So will you?' my mother had said. 'Lizzie?'

'Sorry, Mum. The line broke up.' It didn't. I just wasn't listening. And that's when she insisted we come and stay.

After I explained to Owen about the invitation, a hopeful expression had lit up Peter's face. 'Brilliant idea!' And I knew immediately that was his way of asking for space, that he wanted to spend time alone in the flat with his partner.

Owen had then said, 'I hope you told her we'd come,' followed by, 'If your mum is even a tiny bit like you, then I already know I'm going to love her.'

Silence then, until I'd uttered a feeble, '*But...*' By which time, Owen was calling the letting agent, leaving me feeling too selfish to refuse the invite.

I told myself it was natural for my fiancé to want to meet my family. Besides, Peter had been sleeping on the sofa for weeks, giving up his bed for us, and it was time we gave him a break.

'Sure,' I finally whispered, though I felt chilled that Owen had compared me to my mother. We couldn't be more different.

To begin with, I haven't killed anyone.

FOUR

Still staring out of the little window in my bedroom, I shudder, reminded of when I used to sit here at my desk, trying to focus on my homework, chin in hands, praying that Dad would arrive home from work so that the atmosphere in the house would lift. But he commuted to London most days and wasn't back till late.

'When do I get to meet your dad?' Owen asks, lying on the bed and beckoning me to join him. I lie down next to him, resting my head in the crook of his shoulder, wondering if he's read my mind. So far, I've been careful not to say much about my father whenever my parents have come up in conversation – but then, I never expected to be plunged back into life at Little Risewell quite so soon, where the truth about him will inevitably come out. I haven't prepared any clever excuses so decide basic facts are the safest option for now.

'Dad doesn't live here at the moment.'

Owen lifts his head, peering down at me. 'Are your parents separated... or divorced?'

'No,' I say, though I don't mention that they should be. 'Dad's in... he's in a care... a sort of care facility not too far away.' I'm relieved Owen can't see my eyes. He'd know I'm lying.

'I'm sorry to hear that. I had no idea. Why didn't you tell me?' Owen shifts position so he's sitting up, forcing me to do the same.

I shrug. 'No particular reason.'

'Does he have dementia or something?'

I shake my head.

'A stroke or a heart attack?'

I shake my head a second time.

'It's probably easier if you just tell me.'

I sigh, hugging my arms around myself. 'Dad's not been well since...' I trail off, not ready to tell him the full story – either about what happened last summer at Shelley's wedding, or the winter after I'd left for university. Both events lead back to my mother. 'He's in a place called Winchcombe Lodge about five miles from here. It's... it's a private hospital and—'

'A *hospital*? Oh, Lizzie, I'm so sorry. Can we visit him? Take him anything? When will he be home?'

I'm not sure where to begin with all the questions. 'Yes, we can see him,' I say. 'But I don't know when he'll be home.' I swing my feet off the bed to get up, but Owen catches me by the arm.

'What's wrong with him, Lizzie? Is... is he going to be OK?' The slight wobble in Owen's voice tells me he's assuming Dad must be in end-of-life care.

After what happened to his own family, I know he's triggered by the thought of losing a parent. I could hardly contain my shock when, not long after we'd met, he told me about the motorway pile-up that had killed his mum, dad and brother three years ago. The drunk driver was sent to prison, but, of course, no punishment would bring them back. And financially, Owen was left with nothing as his parents' modest assets were only just enough to cover their debts. There's not a day he doesn't mourn them.

I know I need to put him straight about Dad. Just not now.

'Oh, and you could have told me that you'd mentioned our engagement to Mum when you took the call on my phone from her that time.' I get up and walk over to the window again, feeling bad for confronting him, but I also want to change the subject from my dad.

'I'm so sorry, Lizzie. I... I guess I forgot,' Owen admits. 'I didn't mean anything by it. And I figured you'd have already told her.' He gets off the bed, slipping his feet into his navy loafers, and joins me at the window.

'Right,' I say, feeling miffed. 'It's kind of a big thing to forget to tell me, though, isn't it? I've explained to you what Mum's like, that she can be *difficult*.' Though I didn't give him the full-fat version when we'd talked about my mother. No, I'd given him Sylvia Lite.

'Sorry, love, it really wasn't on purpose. You were in the shower one evening soon after we got back from Dubai, and I thought it was a good chance to introduce myself and tell her our good news. We were in a rush to make the cinema on time, so it slipped my mind.'

I nod, checking myself. I don't want anything coming between us. And certainly not my mother. He'd only been trying to help. And unless I cut my family out of my life completely, then telling Mum about our engagement was going to have to happen at some point. At least this time tomorrow, we'll almost be on our way back to London again. I hold onto that thought.

'Sorry,' I say, my shoulders dropping. 'It's just being here... it makes me feel...' I hesitate, unsure how to finish. I'm not sure Owen will understand what I'm trying to explain – it would take experiencing my entire childhood for that to happen. But, more importantly, I'm not sure I *want* him to understand. I'm quite content being Dubai Lizzie, London Lizzie, pregnant and wife-to-be Lizzie.

Not Sylvia Holmes's daughter Lizzie.

Suddenly, I swing round. 'Did you hear that?' I whisper, my eyes darting to the door.

'Hear what?' Owen says, wrapping his arms around me and nuzzling my neck, almost as if he knew it was prickling.

I listen, holding my breath. 'A noise. On the landing.' I put my finger over my lips, as I listen again. But there's nothing. 'Sorry. Being back here makes me on edge...'

'I know, I know,' he says softly into my hair. 'I'm right here with you. Everything's going to be OK.'

I nod, tilting back my head and giving him a kiss in return.

Then he whispers in my ear. 'Though it won't be in a moment if I don't get to the bathroom.'

I laugh, telling him it's just across the landing, and he heads off, but stops abruptly as soon as he opens the bedroom door.

'Oh, Sylvia!' he says, shocked to see her standing right outside our door.

'Hello, Owen.'

I whip round, my heart speeding up at the sound of my mother's voice.

It's time for school, darling!

But Mummy, it's the middle of the night...

Or,

Get down there and think about what you've done...

No... no, please, not the cellar again...

When I was a child, she'd spy on me – day or night – listening outside my door, opening it a crack without me realising as she stood there, silently watching me, before dishing out a punishment for absolutely no reason apart from believing I deserved one.

Mum's mouth twitches into a little smile as she stares up at Owen, then she strides into the bedroom carrying a pile of soft white towels which she places on the end of the bed.

'I forgot to put these out earlier, what with it being short notice and all that.' She looks over at me. 'If you'd told me you were coming, darling, I would have been able to prepare.'

'But, Mum, you invit—'

'Now, what do you think about getting dinner down at the local pub? They do the best steaks in the area but get very busy on Saturday nights, so I'll need to phone for a table.'

'I think that's a fine idea,' Owen replies, frowning and shaking his head at what just happened. 'Saves the trouble of cooking. OK with you, Lizzie?'

I know there's no point arguing or chastising Mum for lurking outside the door instead of knocking. Besides, her behaviour is usually reasonably normal when we're out in public, and it will cross off a couple of high-risk hours, at least – especially as evenings are always a danger zone when she gets the wine out.

'Fine,' I say, daring to look directly into my mother's eyes.

There's something smug and self-satisfied about what lies behind the icy blueness – yet something equally sad and tragic too. As a child, I noticed how they seemed to change colour depending on her mood or whatever drama she'd created, like an early warning system I'd learnt to read from a young age. Right now, they're the colour of still waters, a lagoon, which, frankly, terrifies me more than anything. The calm before the storm.

FIVE

'So, tell me, Owen, what exactly is it that you do for work?' Mum says once we've sat down at a table in the busy pub restaurant. The Golden Lion is the most popular place to eat in the surrounding villages with its old-world charm, thatched roof, beams and log fires.

I'm still in shock from our arrival a few minutes ago, and so embarrassed that Owen had to witness the scene. Before we'd left home, Mum had called the restaurant three times, borrowing my phone as hers had run out of battery, demanding they give us a table. She'd refused to listen when they told her they were fully booked, insisting we were coming anyway.

'Do you want to keep your job or not?' Mum had barked at the waiter as we'd stood at the restaurant entrance. Customers turned and stared, and I remember 'parish council' being bandied about, as well as something about being good friends with the pub's owner, plus Tripadvisor reviews if we didn't get a table immediately. But I'd stepped a few paces away by that point, trying to block out my mother's nonsense.

'Don't worry,' Owen had whispered to me, seeing how mortified I looked when the poor waiter finally gave in. We'd followed him to the table, watching as he swiped away the reserved sign that was already set out on it. No one said 'no' to Sylvia Holmes.

'My work is quite mundane day-to-day,' Owen says now, holding the menu. His eyes flick down to Mum's hand as she fiddles with her cutlery – an annoying habit she's always had. 'Basically, I'm a consultant in the energy industry trying to strike up new deals between partners, so lots of meetings. It's all about the green these days.'

'Remarkable,' Mum says, now tapping her serrated steak knife on the table. 'How clever you must be. I shall make sure to tell all my friends that my son-in-law-to-be is an eminent scientist and a key player in saving the planet.'

As Mum stares at Owen, her knuckles tightening around the knife handle, I'm tempted to remind her that she doesn't have any true friends, but keep quiet, convincing myself that this is still very much Sylvia Lite. I don't want to trigger the next level.

The waiter comes back to take our drinks order, and Mum jabs at a bottle on the wine list with the tip of the knife. He goes off to the kitchen again with a big sigh.

'I'm just the middleman. The go-between,' Owen says of his work, glancing at Mum's hand. 'It's... it's nothing special, and I'm certainly not a scientist, but it pays the bills.' He gives me a smile. 'Well, it will when we have a place of our own and actual bills to pay.'

'Talking of bills,' Mum says, reaching out and clasping my hand, the knife still gripped in her other one. 'I absolutely insist that I pay for your wedding, darling.'

'Oh, Sylvia, that's an incredible offer,' Owen says before I get a chance to reply. 'But we can't possibly...' he adds, trailing off as he gives me a look.

'No, we definitely can't,' I reply, sensing Owen doesn't

really mean what he said, whereas I do. There's no way I want to be beholden to Mum for the cost of our wedding.

Tap... tap... tap... goes the knife on the table again.

'Nonsense,' Mum shoots back. 'It's just that... after what happened to your sister's fiancé last year...' She pauses, wafting her free hand in front of her face, visibly shuddering as tears fill her eyes.

'*Mum...*' I say in a warning voice. I don't want her talking about Shelley's wedding right now, not in front of Owen. He's the last person who needs to hear about that. He knows my sister lost her husband, but I haven't told him the details.

'It's a very kind offer,' Owen says, suddenly jolting as I give him a sharp nudge under the table. 'But as Lizzie says, we couldn't possibly let you foot the bill.'

'Last year ended in such tragedy,' Mum goes on, her gaze set on the far wall of the restaurant. 'I'll never get over it, you know, what happened to poor Rafe.'

Tap... tap... tap...

'Mum, I don't think now's the time to—'

'On his wedding day of all days,' Mum continues in a whisper as she leans in towards Owen, her knuckles white around the wooden knife handle. 'It nearly killed me, you know.' Spittle collects in the corners of her mouth.

Then suddenly, she lifts her hand and brings the blade of the knife, point down, hard onto the table, stabbing it into the wood.

Instinctively, Owen yelps, whipping his hand away, inspecting his fingers.

'Oh my *God...* Are you OK?' I ask, grabbing his hand and glaring at Mum.

'Fine, I'm fine.' Owen laughs nervously, giving me a look.

'For Christ's sake, Mum, be careful. You missed him by a bloody millimetre!' I snatch the knife from her and drop it down beside my cutlery. 'Anyway, I think last year was pretty hard for Shelley, too, if you recall.'

God, I just want this meal to end and be back in my bedroom so I can vent to Owen and, hopefully, sleep off my anger. When I wake, we'll be that much closer to going back home... or rather, to Peter's place. As things stand, there is no home.

A ringtone suddenly trills through the restaurant.

'Oh, sorry, that's me,' Owen says, retrieving his phone from the inside pocket of his jacket. He glances at his screen. 'I'd better get this,' he says. 'It's the letting agency,' he adds in a whisper to me.

'Really?' I reply, but then Owen is darting across the restaurant to take the call outside. I pray it's good news.

Before we left London this morning, we'd squeezed in an early viewing of the flat Owen had called about last night – Flat 3, Belvedere Court.

'Oh my God, it's *gorgeous*,' I'd said as we parked outside, peering up at the Victorian building. 'Look at those sash windows!'

Inside, it was everything we'd hoped. I'd followed the agent around, imagining where the furniture would go in the spacious living room as Owen's fingers linked with mine.

We both knew the flat was perfect. Just like we knew there was a queue of potential tenants wanting it.

'I can transfer a holding deposit first thing Monday to secure it,' Owen had said after he'd offered twenty per cent over the advertised rent. Meanwhile, I'd crossed my fingers that his invoice would be paid very soon.

The agent had then explained about all the other viewings booked in, suggesting we fill out an application form and email it to the office by Monday morning. We left and drove to Medvale feeling less than hopeful about getting it.

'He's... well, he's... lovely, darling,' Mum says now with

Owen out of the room, reaching out to touch my hand with a kind of pitying expression on her face. Her skin feels warm and surprisingly soft for someone I once believed to be, as a child at least, reptilian.

I smile. Or rather, after what she just did with the knife, I *force* a smile. 'He's a keeper, that's for sure,' I admit, instantly wishing I hadn't. Need-to-know basis is the rule with Mum. Give her no ammunition to be stored for later use. And I'm certainly not about to mention our housing problems to her.

Mum's eyes flick over towards the pub door. 'But are you certain about marriage?' she asks, a frown pulling her brows together. 'I mean... isn't it all rather quick?'

Here we go, I think. I glance over my shoulder to see if Owen is coming back yet.

'When you know, you know, I guess,' I reply as a place-holder. Clichéd, meaningless phrases have been very useful in the past. Mum simply wouldn't understand how I feel about Owen, that he's different to all my previous relationships. It's been two years since I ended things with David and, if nothing else, the scars in my heart tell me what to avoid. It might only have been six months since I met Owen, but I know I've finally got things right.

'He'd literally lay down his life for me,' I tell Mum, again wishing I hadn't. Though I'll never forget the time he did actually save my life – jumping into the pool to rescue me when I'd embarrassed myself at the party by falling in. Luckily, I wasn't hurt – just a clumsy step backwards. The children I was tutoring thought it was hilarious.

Concerned I'd hit my head, Owen had dived in and grabbed me around the waist, our bodies flailing in slow motion underwater.

'You didn't need to do that,' he'd said after we'd surfaced, his arms around me. 'You'd already got my attention.' And then he'd introduced himself.

'Well, you be careful, darling,' Mum says after she's droned on at me for another five minutes. 'I'm not one for interfering, but I had a dream about you the other night. A dream that you'd met someone. Call it a premonition if you like, but it didn't end well for your fiancé—'

'Sorry about that,' Owen says, suddenly rejoining us at the table, just as I half choke on my lime and soda. I grab a napkin to wipe my mouth. 'Did I miss something?'

'Nothing,' I say, staring at my mother, wondering if I just heard her correctly. 'Nothing at all.' I take a breath and turn to Owen. 'What did the agent say? Did the landlord take our offer on the apartment?' I cross my fingers under the table.

'You've got a flat?' Mum says. 'This calls for champagne!' She picks up the wine list again.

'Actually, there's no reason to celebrate,' Owen says, shifting in his chair. 'I'm afraid the flat has already gone to someone else, love,' he says quietly, letting out a sigh. He takes my hand, giving it a squeeze. 'But there'll be others.'

'Oh no... well, never mind,' I reply, trying to hide my disappointment. 'Though I'm annoyed we didn't even get to submit our forms.'

Owen gives me a quick nod, then pulls a pained face that tells me there's something else on his mind. 'While I was outside, I gave Peter a quick call to check how Minnie is doing. I know how much you worry about her.'

I sit bolt upright, my eyes wide. I grab Owen's wrist. 'Is she OK? Nothing's happened to her, has it?'

'Who on earth's Minnie?' Mum asks, but neither of us replies.

'Relax, she's absolutely fine,' Owen says. 'Thing is, love...' He takes a deep breath and leans close to me, whispering so Mum doesn't hear. 'There's no easy way to say this, but...' Owen closes his eyes briefly. 'Peter has asked us not to come back.'

SIX

'I still can't believe it,' I say when we're back at Medvale.

The first thing I did once we were alone upstairs was hurl myself onto the bed and pummel the pillow. If I hadn't felt like a little kid in this room when we first arrived here, I certainly do now as I act out a mini tantrum that two-year-old me would be proud of. 'It's so unlike Peter to let me down like this. And so sudden, too.'

After we got back from the pub twenty minutes ago, Mum had put the kettle on, fussing around Owen when she overheard him complaining to me about a slight headache.

'It can't have been the wine,' she said, rummaging in the kitchen cupboard for some painkillers, despite Owen protesting he didn't need any. 'I chose the most expensive bottle on the menu.'

'It's fine,' Owen had said, giving me a look that told me he wished he'd not said anything. 'I just need a good sleep,' he added when Mum wouldn't let up about finding the tablets.

'Ah, *here* they are,' she finally said after plucking a brown bottle of pills from the back of the cupboard, squinting at the faded label, frowning. 'I'm fairly certain these are paracetamol.'

She handed him a couple along with a glass of water, watching as he reluctantly swallowed them.

'I can't believe it either,' Owen says now, dropping down beside me onto the bed. He rubs my back gently. 'I didn't want to say too much in front of your mum, but Peter has received some bad news of his own. I think he's got family coming to stay... or something like that. Poor chap, he was very upset and gabbling quite a lot.'

I roll over onto my back, sitting up. 'Oh no, that's awful. Did he say what happened? I must call him.' I reach down to the floor to grab my phone from my bag.

'Not really, and I didn't like to pry. He was very emotional and I could tell he hated having to break the bad news to me. He asked that we give him some space for the time being, so I told him we understood entirely. I hope that was the right thing to do.'

'Yes, yes, of course,' I say, hesitating, phone in hand. 'Maybe I won't bother him tonight, then. I'll give him a call in a day or so,' I say, pressing the home button on my phone to check if I've got any notifications.

But I freeze, staring at my screen.

'What the *hell*?' I say, flashing Owen a look. 'My background picture was set to a photo of us, so where on earth has *this* come from?'

Owen takes a look. 'Blimey, that's a bit... creepy,' he says, pulling a face.

I stare at the image again in case I'm seeing things, but the old gravestone half-covered with ivy is very much still there, the yew tree canopy overhead casting eerie, twilight shadows on the graves in the background.

Quickly, I change the image back to the selfie I took of Owen and me in Dubai, checking my camera roll for the churchyard image. 'Look, the photo was added earlier this evening, at 6.40 p.m.'

'And you definitely don't remember doing it?'

'No! Why would I swap our photo for a grave, for heaven's sake?' I shake my head, inhaling sharply. 'But I think I've got a pretty good idea of who did it and, believe me, I'll be having words with her in the morning.'

As I drop my phone back into my bag, Owen gives me a hug. Then I'm thinking about the phone call from Peter again. I have no idea what on earth could have caused my oldest, dearest and most reliable friend to have a change of heart, but I know it wouldn't have been an easy decision for him. We've been friends for close to twenty years. 'It's *so* not like Peter. Something awful must have happened.'

'I think we're doing the right thing by not bothering him tonight. We'll check in with him soon.'

'Oh God, what if it's because of *us*?' I get up off the bed and pace over to the window, leaning on the sill. 'We've been so selfish these last few weeks, haven't we?' I swing around but stop when I see Owen sitting with his hand over his mouth. All the blood seems to have drained from his face. 'Owen, are you OK?'

He shakes his head, closing his eyes. 'Don't feel so great all of a sudden,' he says in a choked voice. I scan around the room, grabbing the little waste bin from beside the dressing table.

'Here,' I say, holding it out. He looks as though he's about to be sick.

For a few moments, he sits there, his head cradled in his hands and down between his knees. I rub his back as I sit beside him on the bed.

'I feel really strange,' he says, clutching his stomach. 'Dizzy and sick.'

Then the blood drains from *my* head, but it's not because I feel ill. 'You don't think it was those pills, do you? Mum didn't seem too sure they were paracetamol.'

Owen takes a deep breath, covering his mouth again as

another wave of nausea hits. 'I... I don't know... I'll be OK,' he says, reaching across for the glass of water I put beside the bed. He takes a few sips then lies back down again, holding his stomach. His forehead feels cold and clammy.

'What a mess,' I whisper, dropping my head into my hands – now concerned for Owen as well as worrying about Peter and whatever bad news he's received. Then I wonder if his problems are to do with that new guy, Jacko, he's been seeing. He's been absolutely smitten these last few weeks.

'Darling,' Owen says through a weak smile. 'I love that you care so much – about me *and* your friend – but Peter didn't sound annoyed or angry with us. He was just a bit weary and preoccupied. We'll give him the space he needs and take it from there.' He reaches out for my hand.

I sniff, nodding. 'You're right. You're always right.' I smile back at him, glad to see he has more colour in his cheeks now. 'But where the *hell* are we going to live? And what about all our stuff?'

'I can't answer the first question, not while I feel like this, but when we spoke on the phone, I arranged with Peter to fetch our belongings tomorrow afternoon. And Minnie, of course. Everything should just fit in the Volvo with the back seats down.'

'OK,' I say, mulling things over, though I have no idea where we're going to go, especially with a cat.

'I'm checking my bank account hourly,' Owen says, taking a few more sips of water, resting his head back down again. 'As soon as that money drops, I'll get us an Airbnb. Somewhere decent to tide us over until we find a flat. And meantime, if we have to, we'll spend a night or two in a hotel. My new credit card might have arrived in the post at Peter's after we left yesterday.'

I nod, wondering where we'll find a cat-friendly hotel at such short notice. My stomach knots from anxiety – especially when I think about Owen being pickpocketed on the tube last week. He had to cancel all his cards.

'I'd put it on my own credit card, if only I had one,' I say, rolling my eyes. Owen knows the full story about David, how he destroyed my credit rating by taking out loans in my name – loans that I knew nothing about, the money blown on his gambling addiction. 'How are you feeling now?' I ask, more concerned about Owen than anything else.

'I'll live...' he says weakly, closing his eyes again. And for some reason, my stomach knots even tighter at the thought of that not being true.

'Morning, both,' Mum trills when we come down to the kitchen after showering and dressing. She's always been an early riser – in fact, when I was growing up, I used to wonder if she ever actually slept at all. But, despite her insomnia, her skin is flawless for a woman in her mid-sixties, and her lack of dark circles or puffiness beneath her eyes, in comparison to me, makes me feel about a hundred today. I hardly slept a wink, tossing and turning with worry, keeping an eye on Owen.

'Good morning, Sylvia,' Owen says, wiping his hands down his face. I know he didn't sleep well either, and we were woken early by the thunderstorm – an ominous rumbling rattling the old leaded windowpanes, and fat raindrops pelting down the glass. He's wearing his old joggers and a T-shirt and, despite claiming he feels better, I can tell he's still not right.

Mum stops in her tracks and stares at him for a moment, a glimmer of a smile on her face, but then she gets on with making the coffee.

'Morning, Mum,' I say flatly, dropping down into a chair at the kitchen table. 'Do you mind telling me why you put a picture of a grave on my phone yesterday?' I fold my arms, staring up at her.

'Did you not sleep well, darling?' she says, looming over me in her long black kaftan. 'Is that why you're in such a grumpy mood?' She leans forward to get a better look at me, tilting up my face with a finger under my chin. 'You look like death.' But when she says it, she's staring directly at Owen.

'Answer my question.' I hold up my phone, shying away from her as I show her the picture of the grave in my camera roll. I don't tell her that I've been thinking about it most of the night.

'Oh *that*,' she says as a small smile creeps over her mouth. 'When I borrowed your phone yesterday, I thought you'd like to see a photo of the local church. I got it off the village website. With all this talk of weddings, I thought it might inspire you.'

'Mum, it's zoomed in on a picture of a *grave*. You can barely see the church behind it.'

'I'm so useless with technology,' Mum says with a laugh. 'I can never get pictures to line up properly.' She rolls her eyes and taps the side of her head. Then she stops, her face falling serious again as she shoots another look at Owen. 'Right, who's for coffee? Owen, you look like you need it. Did you not sleep well either?'

'Not really, if I'm honest, Sylvia. We're just a bit stumped about where to go after we leave here later,' Owen blurts out. I whip around, glaring up at him. 'Since Peter turfed us out of his flat.'

What is he *doing*? While I hadn't explicitly told him to keep quiet about our housing predicament, I'd have thought it went without saying that there's no way I wanted it broadcast to my mother. Owen knows how I feel, after all – and what our home-lessness will mean to her. *Control*.

'What a shame that Peter let you down,' Mum says. I can almost see her salivating, her mind whirring through the opportunities this presents. 'I never much liked him. Anyway, there's no "stumped" about it. You must both stay here with me until you're back on your feet.' Mum puts a pot of coffee on the table, followed by some freshly popped-up toast as well as various jams, marmalades and spreads. 'I won't take no for an answer. If you think about it, it couldn't have worked out more perfectly.'

'Mum, that's kind, but—'

'No, no, listen. You two move in here with me – I rattle around this place like a marble in a bowling alley anyway – and Lizzie, you and I can get on with planning your wedding. We could even have the reception in a grand marquee on the lawn—'

'Mum, stop! There's no way—'

'I bet if we put our minds to it, we could have it all sorted in just a few weeks. No time like the present, eh?' She goes up to Owen and, to my horror, drapes her arms around his neck. 'And it's less than an hour and a half to Paddington from the local station here, so you can still commute and do your business, Owen. I really won't hear otherwise.'

'Mum, please. You're jumping the gun massively here...' I feel the blood drain from my head, unable to understand why she's done a hundred-and-eighty-degree turn since her concern last night about me rushing into marriage. Now she can't seem to plan my wedding fast enough.

But it's what else she's planning that worries me most.

This is history repeating itself, I think in a panic. *And it's not even history yet... what happened to Rafe was only twelve months ago.*

Mum tightens her hold around Owen, and I notice the uncomfortable look on his face as he peers at me over her shoulder. *Sorry...* he mouths through an embarrassed smile.

Then an image of what I found on my sister's wedding day flashes into my mind – Mum's scarlet corsage the colour of freshly spilt blood lying barely a foot away from Rafe's dead body.

SEVEN

The rain has finally stopped, though Mum insisted we take one of the huge umbrellas in the old iron stand by the front door. She'd fussed over us before we left, worrying that we'd be too cold, too hot, too wet, too *everything* until I placed my hands firmly on her shoulders.

'Mum, stop. I'm thirty-nine. Owen is thirty-six. We're going for a walk to Shelley's house, not taking a trip to the dark side of the moon. If the weather turns bad again, I'm sure Shell will drive us back. It's only a couple of miles away.' Then I'd felt guilty for being snappy.

'She knows exactly how to make me feel wretched,' I say now as Owen and I trudge along the lane, the first leaves of autumn fluttering to the ground, making a slushy mess on the verge. 'Yet it's so hard to describe to anyone else.'

'Don't be too hard on her,' Owen says with a laugh. 'She's just being a mum. I can see how pleased she is to have you home. I like her.'

The tinge of sadness in his voice doesn't go unnoticed. A few days after we arrived back from Dubai, we'd travelled north on the train to see his parents' and brother's graves at the cemetery – a black marble family headstone with their names, dates of birth and a few words chosen by Owen carved in gold lettering.

'Mum, Dad, Luke... I want you to meet Lizzie,' he'd said as we sat on the grass beside them. 'She's so special to me, and I know you'd have loved her as much as I do.'

We stayed for an hour, pulling a few weeds from the little patch, arranging the flowers we'd brought, with Owen telling me all about them, how he'd looked up to his big brother so much, regaling me with stories about their childhood in the North East, how his dad, an engineer, had been so proud of both his sons.

'Mum was a nurse and doted on her "three boys", as she called us all,' he'd told me with a tear in his eye. 'I still can't believe they're gone.'

Now, as we walk, I try not to feel rankled by Owen's comment about liking my mother. He's bound to be reminded of his own mum, wanting to become part of my family now we're going to be married. I sigh, holding back my real feelings for Owen's sake.

'You're right,' I say, staring at my phone screen as we walk. 'But I still wish she wouldn't make me feel like a little kid.' I decide to leave it there as I wait for the browser on my phone to load.

'Families, eh?' Owen laughs, giving me a squeeze. 'Don't jump down my throat, but have you considered taking your mum up on her offer to stay with her for a while? It would solve all our problems for now.'

'Ha!' I shriek. A bird flaps out of a nearby oak tree. 'I'm not sure that's a great idea.' I don't tell him that I'd rather sleep in a ditch. 'Come on, *load*, dammit.'

'What are you looking up?' He peers at my phone.

'Rental agencies in London. We're going to be homeless in

exactly eight hours and I don't know about you, but I'm a bit concerned.'

There's a slight hesitation in Owen's step, causing us, linked arm in arm, to fall out of kilter as we walk.

'I doubt any agents will be open today. It's pointless, love. Besides...' He hesitates for a moment. 'I'm afraid the funds still haven't come in from Dubai. Even if we found a place tomorrow, we're not going to be able to pay for it yet. I'm sorry.'

I scuff the ground, taking on board what this means. I know Owen's invoice will eventually be paid – but that's not much good to us right now. If I hadn't had to pump all my earnings from Dubai into paying off the debts my ex had left me with, I'd happily get us an Airbnb or hotel for as long as we needed. I thought I'd been doing the right thing at the time, trying to get ahead of myself financially, clear up the mess David left behind.

In fact, Owen had encouraged me to do so, agreeing it was best to build up my credit rating again. After the financial mess his parents left behind, he's very against borrowing and debt, and I know he won't take out an overdraft himself, however temporary. There's nowhere near enough in my bank account now to cover a deposit and rent up front. Probably not even enough for a night in a hotel, if I'm honest. We've been counting on this invoice being paid.

I jab at the phone number on my screen and wait for the line to connect. 'Answering service,' I say a moment later, leaving a quick message. I try four other rental agencies, but it's the same story. The next attempt, someone answers, but it's fruitless. Prospects are dismal – all decent rental properties or house shares are being snapped up within hours of going online (if they even make the listings), and landlords are being stricter than ever about tenants having reliable incomes.

'I'm going to hit up a couple of friends, see if they can let us couch surf for a few nights. I could ask Shelley, of course, but after what she's been through lately, I don't want to put upon her if I don't have to.' I call several numbers in my contacts list, but only one person answers.

'Lizzie?' the voice says. 'Oh... *that* Lizzie,' the woman continues. 'God, it's been ages... It must have been that alumni party about five years ago when we last saw each other.'

When the call ends, I shove my phone back in my pocket. 'Well, that sucks. Neither of my closer friends picked up and the last one barely remembered me. She's on holiday with her new partner, apparently.'

'Look, let's just enjoy a couple of hours with your sister, eh? Put all this out of our minds for now,' Owen suggests, pulling me close. 'And enjoy this stunning scenery.'

I nod, knowing he's right as we carry on down the lane towards Wendbury, the village where Shelley lives. The last time I saw her was at the end of February, a couple of weeks before I'd taken the job in Dubai, though I was thinking about her the entire time I was away.

Shelley had turned into a ghost of herself since her wedding day the previous August. It was hardly surprising. Instead of leaving the church in a ribbon-festooned Rolls-Royce with her new husband, she'd left in the back of a police car with a rough brown blanket wrapped over her wedding dress because she couldn't stop shaking from shock.

'It's this way,' I say, indicating a little lane shortly after we pass the village sign for Wendbury. Several planters of brightly coloured flowers decorate the approach, still vibrant from the summer.

'Has your sister lived here long?' Owen asks. 'She's chosen a beautiful village.'

I can't help the snort, but manage to hold back what I really want to say. That Shelley didn't exactly *choose* Wendbury – rather our mother chose it for her. 'She's been here since she completed her training in Bristol years ago,' I tell him. 'She's forty-four, five years older than me, so that's—'

'And she works locally?' Owen asks, interrupting my calculation.

'Yes, at the practice in Stow a few miles away.' I've already told him my sister is a vet – as was her late fiancé, Rafe – and that they met at work when Rafe joined the team. But I haven't bothered regaling Owen with the story of how my mother had bought the little cottage for Shelley straight after she'd finished veterinary school, or how she'd paid off her student debt. Mum was quite happy spending our father's money, and it suited her to keep Shelley close by. She'd tried the same with me, of course, but I'd chosen a different path – to get away from the area at the earliest opportunity.

'And you two sisters are close?'

'Very,' I say, smiling, though I don't tell him how, as kids, Shelley, being the eldest, had had to protect me from Mum's emotional outbursts on many occasions. One of my earliest memories is hiding in Shelley's bedroom in a fort she'd made from blankets pegged between several chairs. She'd stocked the inside of the tent with biscuits, books and a pair of scissors.

'Let's play *hide from the monster*,' I remember her whispering to me one dinner time before Dad was home. My stomach had flipped from excitement. Now, looking back, I know what we were really playing was *hide from our mother*.

'Shelley loved being the big sister,' I say, trying not to get upset at the memory. 'But we went to different schools. Shelley was at the grammar in the nearby town. She's always been smart.'

I can almost laugh about it now, but back then it had stung. As a kid, all I'd wanted to do was follow in her footsteps, but Mum had told me I wasn't clever enough to take the eleven-plus exams.

'Which grammar?' Owen asks.

'St Lawrence's,' I tell him. 'And I went to Filbert Comprehensive.'

'I *see*,' Owen says thoughtfully, raising his eyebrows as though he's impressed by Shelley's capabilities.

'I think she had a bit of a hard time at St Lawrence's, truth be known. She was always the more academic one out of the pair of us, but because...' I hesitate, wondering if I should tell Owen about my mother being a teacher at the same school. It might lead to more questions about her career and, more specifically, her retirement. I never knew the exact details of what happened because I was at university by then, and Shelley didn't know much either, but I know Mum left her job under a dark cloud.

'Oh, that's a shame,' he says pensively. 'How come?'

It's natural he wants to find out about my family, but the more I reveal, the more I'm scared he'll have second thoughts about *us*. I couldn't bear to lose him.

Finally, we reach Shelley's house, but I stop before we go up the front path, turning to face him.

'Mum taught biology at St Lawrence's, and she was... well, she had a reputation for being very strict and not the most popular with the pupils. Shelley got loads of stick for it. It was hard having her mother teach at the school she went to.'

Especially a mother like ours, I think, deciding to leave it at that.

EIGHT

I barely recognise my sister. In fact, when she opens the front door, I briefly wonder if I've got the wrong address.

'Shell...' I say before lunging at her to give her a hug. 'Oh, *Shell...*' But I also know I mustn't make a thing of it, that she won't appreciate being grilled or told off about why she's not eating properly or getting enough sleep, especially in front of Owen, who she's never met in person before.

'What's up with you, you sentimental old thing?' Shelley replies, reciprocating with as tight an embrace as her skinny arms will allow. 'Let me see you, you jet-setting world traveller, you.' She holds me at arm's length, looking me up and down.

We both laugh, hovering on the doorstep staring at each other and not knowing quite what to do. There's so much to catch up on, yet so much that we don't want to talk about, too. And I know that with Owen present, Shelley will put on that brave face of hers – the one she wears to work every day and faces the world with. Although since I last saw her, the veneer has worn even thinner, confirming what I already suspected – that Shelley is still deep in the clutches of grief. She looks empty and dead behind her eyes.

'I've made some lunch,' she says in the kitchen, after I've introduced her and Owen officially.

Shelley and I FaceTimed often while I was living in Dubai, and she'd seen him in the background. They'd said a few light-hearted words in passing, though I didn't reveal how serious we were about each other. I'd mulled over how to tell my sister that I, the woman who had sworn off men since my break-up with David, had finally met the man of my dreams, deep in the shadow of Shelley's loss. In the end, I'd decided to save the news of our engagement for when we'd returned to London.

Even on the morning of my sister's wedding last year as we were all getting ready, Shelley had joked about my permanently single status.

'Always the bridesmaid and never the bride, Liz,' she'd said to me, sipping her second glass of champagne as I curled her thick, dark hair into soft waves. Though it wasn't strictly true as I'd never been a bridesmaid before, and anyway, I was maid of honour. But still. The situation now felt cruel.

'How have you been, sis?' I ask once we've slipped off our coats and muddy shoes. Owen has gone upstairs to the bathroom, so we have a few moments alone. 'I worry about you. You're not eating properly, are you?'

'Never mind that.' Shelley glances towards the kitchen door and lowers her voice. 'I had a call from the police a week ago,' she whispers. 'From a detective, DI Lambert. He's new to the local force, apparently, and he's reviewing old cases. He wants to talk to me about Rafe.'

I touch my sister's arm as she stirs the soup. 'Oh, Shell, do you know why?' My heart rate quickens as I imagine what it could be about. The last thing she needs is everything being dragged up again.

'I think it's because the previous detective had his doubts about the coroner's conclusion and made it known before he retired. It's set me back a bit. I was just coming to terms with

everything, starting to accept the inquest results, and now this.'
Another quick glance to the door.

'I can imagine. Did he say anything else?'

She leans down to taste the soup, spilling some onto the
hob. I squeeze her arm just as we hear the toilet door open and
close above us, followed by Owen's footsteps as he comes down
the stairs, bursting through the door just at that moment,
preventing Shelley from answering.

'Soup smells delicious,' Owen says a short while later as we sit
down at the tiny kitchen table. At six foot two, he makes the
little cottage seem like a doll's house.

Like most of the old houses in the area, Shelley's home is
built from Cotswold stone and is filled with beams, flagstones
and a cosy inglenook fireplace. The end terrace two-up two-
down has a small front garden and a bigger patch at the back
overlooking open fields, but my sister hasn't inherited our mother's talent for growing things.

'We're rewilding,' Rafe had once joked about their overgrown garden when I'd come to visit in spring last year, bringing
a few wedding canapé menus with me for Shelley to choose
from. I'd been taking my maid of honour duties seriously,
although Mum had pretty much overruled everything Shelley
and I had picked. At least she didn't get a say in the hen night
arrangements – that was purely down to me.

'I made up the recipe myself,' Shelley replies to Owen about
the soup. 'It's kind of an Indian lentil dhal sort of concoction.
Great in winter if I've been working late.'

'Shelley is master of soup. Except... remember last year?
The mushrooms?'

My sister smiles. 'Well, I thought it was nice, even if you lot
turned up your noses.'

I fill Owen in quickly about the hen party I'd organised.

'Think guided foraging, campfire cooking and sleeping in tents, basically.' And no Mum. We'd kept the activity a secret, not wanting her to ruin it. 'Shell collected a ton of stuff from the woods to bring home. Did you ever cook with it?'

'I did. I made some amazing mushroom pâté,' Shelley says. 'Though Mum somehow got wind of the hen do not long after.'

I imagine her wrath at being excluded. 'Maybe someone told her about the Instagram post you put up,' I say, though as soon as I'd seen it online, I'd suggested Shelley take it down. Rubbing Mum's nose in it would only cause drama.

'She decided to do some of her own foraging after that,' Shelley tells me with a wry smile. 'To make a point. She even bought a book about it and left it lying around so I'd see it.'

'Sounds about right,' I reply.

'Well, I can confirm that the soup also tastes delicious,' Owen says. 'Are you a vegetarian?' He tears up a piece of crusty bread.

'I am indeed,' Shelley admits.

'She's a *vet*, Owen,' I laugh, pleased to see a reciprocal smile on my sister's face. Though what she told me just before Owen came down is still playing on my mind. I have no idea why the detective would want to talk to her a year after Rafe's death. The case was concluded and closed by the coroner.

'Saving animals for a living then eating them doesn't really sit well with me,' Shelley explains. 'Rafe felt the same.' She inhales a breath at the mention of his name.

'I'm so sorry about what happened to your—'

'Can we not do this?' Shelley asks, gulping down a mouthful of the white wine she's poured for her and Owen. Thankfully, she hasn't questioned my abstinence. 'You know, all the apologising and sympathy. It's like the whole world has heaped it on me this last year and while I'm appreciative, it also feels like a weight. As though I'm not allowed to move on.' Shelley has never been one to mince her words.

'Of course, of *course*,' Owen replies, staring down at his soup again. 'I completely understand.'

'How's Mum?' Shelley asks me. Then she laughs. 'Or should we swerve that topic too?'

'She's fine. Same old, same old. More to the point, how's Dad?' I chime back, sliding my hand on top of hers with a knowing look. 'We've not been to visit him yet. Though perhaps that's another no-no subject. God, what do we have left to discuss – the weather?' Shelley and I laugh in sync, just as we used to.

'Are you quite sure you want to marry into this madhouse, Owen?' Shelley says. 'You seem pretty normal to me.'

'*Very* sure,' Owen replies solemnly, sliding his hand on top of mine, which, in turn, is still resting on top of Shelley's.

'Seriously, though,' I ask again, 'how is Dad? Have you seen him recently?'

'Liz, I visit him at least three times a week.' She pulls back her chin and shrugs as if I should know that – or at least I would do if I'd been around these last few months. 'There's not much change.'

I'm aware of Owen tuning in to our conversation, which, actually, is what I want. The chances of him working out that he *is* marrying into a dysfunctional family are increasing the more he finds out about us, so facing this in the company of Shelley is a good way of diluting the impact. Seeing that my older sister has a respectable career and had been about to get married to a decent man until tragedy struck, might show him that some shred of normality exists within the Holmes family. That we ourselves might follow the same path.

Though it's that *same path* that's concerning me most.

I glance down at the flagstones, reminded of what I discovered on the morning of Shelley's wedding. I'm sitting just a few feet away from where it happened – from where I found Rafe's lifeless body slumped on the floor with my mother's scarlet corsage lying beside him.

The blood has long since been scrubbed away, but in my mind's eye, it's still there, the panic still as real as it was back then.

The same panic that made me do something so stupid, I can't possibly tell a soul.

NINE

Keeping my attention focused on our conversation at lunch is hard. I'm still haunted by what I found the morning of Shelley's wedding, despite trying to convince myself that there must have been a rational explanation. There was an inquest, after all, plus a post-mortem, and the coroner's conclusion was unequivocal.

But the police didn't know about the corsage... screams my guilty conscience. *Or what I did with it.*

I shudder at the memory.

'Anyway, Dad still barely says a word to anyone,' Shelley continues, making me realise that there isn't much chance of Owen being spared my family drama after all. 'How long are you guys staying with Mum?'

I'm about to reply, grateful for the subject change, but Owen gets in first.

'A while longer,' he says, smiling across the table. 'Your mother has very kindly offered us a room for as long as we need. Long story, but for now we're... well, we're a little bit homeless.'

'It's not quite that dramatic,' I say, glancing longingly at the wine bottle. 'Timing's just been bad. We're not hinting, by the way, Shell. I know you've got enough to deal with,' I add, though I'd much rather stay here than at Mum's.

'I'm sorry to hear all that,' Shelley says with a frown. 'And of course, you know I'd offer you my spare room, but I literally just let it out to a lodger a few days ago. I figured it was about time I had some company around the place.'

'A lodger?' While I'm pleased my sister is finally taking steps to move on, I'm concerned that this might not be the right way to do it. A stranger in the house might be too much, too soon. 'I'm pleased for you, Shell,' I add, wanting to sound supportive. 'I don't like to think of you here all alone. Did you advertise the room?'

'Word of mouth. Jan at the pub said she'd overheard him saying he was looking for a place to stay around here, and she put us in touch.'

'*Him?*' I don't want any more heartbreak for my sister.

Shelley laughs. 'Yes, it's a *him,*' she scolds, waggling her finger at me. 'You may remember him. He's from Little Risewell and went to the same school as me, though he's a few years younger. More your age.'

'Go on, who is it?' I cast my mind back. I can barely remember anyone from my own school, let alone the grammar school kids. There was a divide in the village, with those who went to the comprehensive, like me, often looked down upon by the others.

'Jared Miller. Computer nerd extraordinaire. Think shock of sandy red hair and about two feet taller than the rest of us and you'll be close.'

At the mention of his name, I try to remain poker-faced, pretending I don't recall. But of *course* I remember Jared – he's one of the few people that has stuck in my mind over the years – though I never expected for a minute that *he'd* be Shelley's lodger. I saw something on social media ages ago about him living in the States, the West Coast, but I'd heard nothing since.

Jared was my first ever crush. And me his. We got to know each other when I'd sneak out to the village playground to hang out with the local teens. Mum used to think I was upstairs doing my homework. A few times, Jared had called round to the house when the coast was clear. Our first kiss – more a nervous peck somewhere on the face (each missing our mouths in fright when my mother, who'd come home unexpectedly, had yelled at us to get the hell out of the potting shed) – has stuck with me all this time. It had been my very first kiss, and Jared gave me butterflies just being in his presence. There'd been something about him that had aligned with my soul; something on a cellular level drawing us together. Though we never found out what that was as the universe had other ideas and our paths had diverged. I never told Shelley about our short-lived relationship, and I haven't seen Jared since I was eighteen.

'Jared... Jared...' I say, shaking my head and feigning ignorance.

'Oh, come on. Lanky Jared. Geek boy. Too-short trousers guy. Starey-eyed Jared with the crooked teeth?'

'Oh *him*,' I say, vowing to keep my teenage crush to myself if that's how everyone saw him. All I'd seen at the time was a kind, intelligent, generous person who, while not one of the most popular kids in the village by a long way, had understood me. He'd tuned in to my unstable home situation and respected my need to spend most of my life in my bedroom hiding, while also being there for me if I needed a friend. He was kind, gentle and a good listener. He even wrote me a few letters, hand-delivering them in the hope that my mother didn't intercept them. And he was never once mean to me like some of the other local kids had been.

'Yeah, I think I know who you mean,' I add for good measure. I don't want Owen getting jealous. Though really, he has nothing to worry about.

'Turns out he's back in the area permanently now. House

hunting for a place to buy, which is why he needs a temporary place to stay in the meantime.'

'He has my sympathies,' Owen chips in. 'Finding a decent property of any sort at the moment is nigh on impossible. Especially on a budget.'

Shelley smiles, reminding me of how she used to be. Perhaps it isn't all broken inside her – the sister I used to know is still in there somewhere.

'I don't think budget is his problem,' Shelley says with a wink, getting up to clear the empty bowls from the table. 'I've heard that he sold his tech company in Silicon Valley for an absolute fortune.'

Owen insists on washing up. Shelley and I protest that we should help, of course, but we relent at Owen's insistence and retreat to Shelley's cosy living room with cups of tea.

'He seems really... nice,' Shelley says quietly, dropping down beside me. 'Sort of... dependable.'

I stare at her. 'Is that it? *Dependable?*'

'Give me dependable any day.' Shelley curls her legs up underneath her, cupping her mug with both hands. 'Your usual type wasn't exactly working.'

'I guess,' I reply, knowing she's right.

In the past, I've gone for unstable men, unreliable men, emotionally unavailable men. I've always been attracted to the *un*-anything men, as though I had a sign on my head stating that I want to be treated badly. It's what I've been used to all my life, after all. Running away and bailing out was always an option for me if things got too intense – a familiar drill when the going was tough.

When I finally found the courage to break up with David – the man who'd promised me the world yet stolen it away from me – I paid the ultimate price. A broken heart as well as broken finances. Five years we were together, the longest relationship I'd ever had, and after I'd moved a hundred miles away from him, I swore it would be the last time I ran away.

It wasn't. Two years later, I'd met Owen at the bottom of the swimming pool in Dubai.

'He's a good 'un, that's for sure,' I say. 'It all happened so quickly, but—'

'Yes, about that,' Shelley says, glancing at the door that leads to the kitchen. It's slightly ajar. 'It's not like you to plunge into something head-first. Like *marriage*. Normally you run a mile from the first sniff of commitment.'

'I know, I *know*,' I say, nudging Shelley with my foot as I also curl up on the sofa. 'This time it feels... *different*. Being with Owen just feels right. Like I've known him forever. We've slotted around each other so perfectly. Like an old slipper that I'd lost and then found again.'

'An old slipper?' Shelley hoots but quietens as she glances over her shoulder again. 'Fuck sake, Liz. This is the man you're spending the rest of your life with, not a stinky old shoe. You're *sure* you're sure?'

'Very,' I say. 'He's funny. Kind. Clever. Ambitious. Perceptive. And I can be myself with him – vulnerable and open without a scrap of judgement. *And* Minnie loves him. Besides, I want kids, and time is... well, it was running out.'

Shelley doesn't seem to pick up on my mistaken use of the past tense, nor does she notice that my hand instinctively slips down to the top of my jeans. Rather, it's the mention of Minnie that lights up her face. 'How's the kitty doing?'

It's because of Shelley that I came to be Minnie's owner. Several years ago, a young cat was abandoned at her vet practice and needed a home fast. I'd just broken up with David and, being a cat lover, had volunteered to take her in, even though I'd just moved down to north London and had no garden.

'Minnie's fine. A little darling still. Owen is going back to

London this afternoon to collect her from Peter's place, along with all our belongings.'

'So you really are moving in with Mum?'

'We're not *moving in*. But I suppose we'll have to stay an extra night. Then it's a hotel or Airbnb until we sort a proper flat rental. It's all going to be fine.'

'Why not just go to a hotel tonight, then?'

'Owen's still waiting for his last invoice to be paid. He has a big client in Dubai, and they've not coughed up yet. They will pay, of course. Any time now, in fact. They don't really understand about our pathetic housing problems and cash flow issues.'

'Liz, your issues are not pathetic. Do you want me to lend you a few quid?'

I hold up my hands, shaking my head. 'That's so kind,' I tell her, knowing I can't possibly take her up on the offer. When the full horror of David's betrayal hit me in the form of declined credit cards and court summonses, she'd lent me two thousand pounds to tide me over. I still owe her the money. 'But we'll be fine. Like I said, any day now the funds will drop into his account. It's just the way his line of business works.'

'I hope so,' she replies, reaching out and grabbing my fingers. 'It's so good to have you back, Lizzie. I've missed you. These last few months have been really shit without you around.'

I bow my head. 'I'm so sorry, Shell. I shouldn't have taken the Dubai job and left you, but at the time it just seemed like a good way to make a dent in my debts...' I trail off, not wanting to make it all about me. 'After Rafe died, Mum just got too much. And then with Dad going into hospital...' I shake my head as it dawns on me just how selfish I *have* been by working overseas. 'I should have been here for you both.'

'It's OK,' Shelley whispers, squeezing my fingers. 'I just miss him so much... Rafe. Every day that's passed since he died feels like he's slipping further and further from me, as though the tide is taking him out to sea and I'm standing on the shore squinting at the horizon. Each day, my memories become a little more faded, the smell of him on his clothes lessens, and I'm gradually packing up his possessions and storing them away or taking them to charity shops. Not even any mail arrives for him any more.' She sighs. 'Though—'

'Oh, Shell...' I shift closer to my sister, wrapping my arms around her. Then I stop, pulling back. 'Though what?' The look on Shelley's face has turned almost... *fearful*.

Again, Shelley checks the kitchen where Owen is just visible drying up the last items on the draining board. 'I had a phone call the other day,' she whispers.

'From the detective, yes, you said.'

'No... no, I don't mean that. I don't know who this was. It was from a withheld number.'

'Oh?' I sit up straighter. 'What did they say?'

'That's the thing. It was really hard to tell, and the more I replay it in my mind, the more I twist it into something sinister-sounding. It was probably just a spam call.'

'Shelley...' I say in a worried voice. '*What*?'

'I'm not even sure if it was a man or a woman, to be honest. They spoke in a sort of growling whisper about someone getting what was coming to them. Then they hung up. Maybe it was a wrong number. I don't know. It all happened so quickly.'

'Christ, that's unsettling,' I say, seeing how upset Shelley is just recalling it.

But the strange expression on her face tells me she hasn't quite got everything off her chest.

TEN

Later that afternoon, I watch Owen drive off, the wheels of the Volvo carving wet grooves in the slushy leaves that have settled on the hospital's long driveway. When we arrived at Winchcombe Lodge after our lunch at Shelley's, he'd wanted to come inside – *just a quick hello*, he'd suggested – but the thought of it made my throat tighten.

'Dad's not great with... with new things. New people. Not a good idea.' I blushed. I was gabbling, mainly because I was ashamed of what my mother had done to him. Who he'd turned into.

'When *do* I get to meet him then, Lizzie?' Owen had said as the car idled outside the entrance.

I'd bitten my lip, looking up at the soft, honey-coloured facade of the place where my father had been admitted once before, not long after I'd left home for university – though back then, he'd been held in the secure unit of the building. I had no idea of the seriousness of the situation at the time. Guilt surged through me that I'd never visited him back then. And now, not wanting to suggest a time that Owen could meet him gave me similar feelings. Besides, arranging an introduction felt too much like we were moving in with Mum for longer, not simply tolerating the one extra night I'd probably have to agree to.

'Well, say hello from me, and...' Owen had said when I'd remained vague, 'and tell him that I hope he gets better soon.' His eyes flicked around the grounds as if he were trying to ascertain exactly what kind of place this was, and if it was the sort of facility that you got better in.

While Owen was making the trip back to London to get our stuff, I also planned on finding us a budget hotel. I'd even thought about trying to get a payday loan or similar to cover it. I don't want to ask Owen to foot the bill, what with him buying our flights home, giving rental money to Peter these last few weeks, as well as forking out for our car and other expenses. Until the money comes through from Dubai, I know he's maxed out, too.

After the tail-lights of the Volvo disappear, I imagine him back in London gathering up all our belongings, hurriedly shoving everything into the car. I never even got a chance to say goodbye to Peter or thank him properly for having us. Similarly, I feel bad I didn't manage to help Mrs Baxter, the old lady who lives in the flat across the hall from Peter. Everyone in the building looks out for her, and I'd promised to take her to the bank when I bumped into her on Friday evening.

'Let me help you with your shopping bag,' I'd offered as I spotted her shuffling home from the bus stop across the road.

Mrs Baxter had peered up at me from under the brim of the burgundy felt hat that she always wore. 'Such a wonderful morning,' she'd said, looking up at the darkening sky.

'It's evening now, Mrs B,' I'd told her gently, but she didn't hear. Once inside her flat, I'd put her shopping on the small kitchen table and had been about to leave when something caught my eye.

'You ought to put that in a safe place,' I'd said, pointing to a wodge of cash beside the kettle. It looked like a few hundred pounds at least.

'Oh!' the old woman said, squinting at it. 'Thank you, dear. That's the proceeds from selling a couple of old paintings I've had for years. Peter kindly helped me. I've labelled the money with my name, so don't worry.' One of the twenty-pound notes had 'Betty's' written on it in black felt pen. 'And you're right, I suppose it does need to go in my bank.'

'We could give you a lift there tomorrow, if you like,' I'd suggested. 'Owen, my fiancé, can take us in the car.'

'No need, duck,' she'd replied, shuffling over to the worktop. Then she'd picked up the money with a shaking hand and, after several attempts to get the lid off, she'd dropped it into an old-fashioned tea caddy. 'All safe in the bank now,' she added with a laugh. 'The Bank of Betty.'

I'd stared at her for a moment, wondering whether she had any relatives we could contact, then I'd gone across the hall with the takeaway I'd been out to fetch. I later told Owen what had happened, and, after a thoughtful nod, he agreed that we should indeed let Peter know the situation.

Now, as I walk up the stone steps at Winchcombe, checking in with the receptionist, I head for the communal living room, praying that I'll see an improvement in Dad. I last saw him nine months ago in late January and, even since Shelley's wedding the previous August, he'd deteriorated noticeably.

'Dad...' I sing out from the lounge doorway when I spot him, though quietly enough not to disturb the other patients. Something loosens inside me at the sight of him – a knot of tension unravelling, similar to when I saw the lights of his car arcing onto the drive when I was a child, desperate for him to come home, not understanding that him being on the board of a major bank meant long hours at work. Now, a part of me wonders if he stayed away from the house for as long as he could, perhaps taking a detour via the pub on the way home, or simply sitting in the car, the engine idling, in a lay-by... thinking, waiting, delaying.

My father doesn't hear me or, if he does, he doesn't turn to acknowledge me, so I head across the plush carpet. A cricket match is showing on the large TV, but no one seems to be watching it. There are clusters of comfortable armchairs set around shiny coffee tables adorned with sprays of flowers and glossy magazines that don't appear as though they've ever been read.

'Dad, hi, it's me, Elizabeth.' I skirt around him to approach him from the front so as not to give him a fright. He's sitting in the bay window with its floor-to-ceiling glass, staring out across the striped lawn. 'It's good to see you.'

When he doesn't respond, I crouch down and take his hands in mine. He feels cold, though the room is warm enough.

'How have you been, Dad? I'm back from Dubai now. I'll be able to come and see you more often.'

Slowly, as though his eyes are trying to focus through honey, my father turns his head, his gaze gradually connecting with mine. He lets out a little sigh as though it's taken all his effort just to do that. But there's nothing else.

I beam a smile at him in the hope of eliciting some kind of response.

'You're looking well, Dad,' I say, thinking the opposite. 'Have they been looking after you?' Another smile and a glance over his shoulder as I catch sight of one of the nurses passing through the lounge.

I drag a chair close to Dad's, sitting down so our knees are almost touching. 'Some of the roses at Medvale are still in bloom, can you believe?' I notice the nurse heading our way. 'Everything is fine back home. Including Mum,' I add, though it feels strange to say those last two words – mainly because I have no idea if they're really true or not.

'How are you doing, Mr Holmes?' the nurse asks. She's

young and keen with full lips set in a round face that pout out the words in comforting puffs. 'Is this your daughter?'

When Dad says nothing, I introduce myself. The nurse tells me she's called Billy.

'He's a quiet one, your dad,' Billy goes on. 'But a demon on poker nights.'

Poker? I think. That doesn't sound like Dad. But then seeing him sitting here in a private psychiatric hospital isn't much like the man I remember, either. Where is the vibrant, fit and capable father I once knew?

'I think the straight face helps his game,' Billy laughs as she marks something off on her clipboard. 'Meds are coming soon, Frank,' she tells Dad. 'And the tea trolley is on its way.' She beams a doughy smile and pads off, her sensible black shoes sinking into the deep pile of the burgundy carpet.

'She seems nice,' I say to Dad, wondering what might trigger a response from him. Before I went to Dubai, he'd at least acknowledged me and said a few words. 'I've got some news, Dad. I'm engaged to be married.' I hold out my left hand so he can see my ring. 'My fiancé's name is Owen and you're going to love him. We're so happy.'

I recall my mother's predictable reaction, how her first thought was that she'd be organising our wedding, paying for it, taking it over. There's no way that's happening. My wedding is going to be on my terms and it certainly won't be around here.

'Here, this is him.' I tap on my phone and pull up my favourite photo of the pair of us standing together on Owen's hotel balcony in Dubai, the crimson and purple sunset the perfect backdrop to our happy faces.

Dad glances down at my phone. *There...* his eyebrows rise just a little. No one else would have noticed, but I do.

'Owen's gone back to London this afternoon to... to get some of our stuff,' I say, not wanting to explain why. 'He's promised he'll come and visit you soon. You'll like him. He's so good to me.'

That's when my father looks up. He stares straight at me and shakes his head, slowly at first, but then faster and faster until I wonder if he'll ever stop.

ELEVEN

While Dad gets given his medication, I go in search of the toilets, puzzled by his reaction to my news. When I get back, Billy, the young nurse, suggests we go for a walk in the hospital grounds. 'Take your daughter down to the river, Frank,' she says, helping him slip on his coat.

I link my arm though my father's as we head out of the patio doors and onto the terrace. It isn't that Dad doesn't engage or understand, or that he refuses help or treatment, because he does as the nurses say, eats his food, goes to bed and listens to me chattering away about my time in Dubai as we walk. But there's something... *missing* in him. As though his soul has been stripped out and he's an empty shell just waiting for a new person to step in.

The only person I want to do that is *him*. My lovely old dad.

'This reminds me of when I was little,' I say, giving his arm a squeeze as we head across the lawn. 'When we used to go on hikes, just you, me and Shell.'

It's true – the three of us had trekked all over the area when Shelley and I were still at school. 'Done your homework, fair lasses?' Dad would ask. Shelley and I both knew this was code for *Let's escape...*

Mum always despised us going off as a trio, leaving her behind, and she did everything in her power to stop us. Us being out of the house left her with no audience, which, I now know, was exactly Dad's aim. It allowed him to protect us and neutralise her. By the time we returned, she'd usually burnt herself out.

'Frank, if you leave, something bad will happen,' Mum shrieked one time. 'I *swear* it. I *feel* it.' Her hair was matted with sweat and her eyes wide and staring. Her skin was twitching on her bones. 'Be it on your head if I'm dead when you return.' She'd paraded around in her flimsy dressing gown shaking a bottle of pills like a maraca in one hand, and swigging neat Scotch from the bottle she held in the other. 'Fra-*ank...*' she'd screamed over and over until her throat bled. Her episodes came out of nowhere and were caused by absolutely nothing. It was just Mum's way.

Dad ushered us out of the front door, turning back to face her.

'Be safe, Sylvia. And be calm when we return. Nothing bad is going to happen unless you make it so.'

By the time we'd got to the post office in Little Risewell, Shelley and I would have mostly forgotten about the day's outburst – the pair of us giggling together, sharing the packet of sweets Dad gave us. It was one of many such walks that occurred on a regular basis, whatever the weather. Nothing out of the ordinary on a Sunday afternoon. Or ten o'clock on a Wednesday night.

'Pay no attention,' Dad had often told us, though I saw the worry on his face. 'Toddler tantrums is all it is.' Other times, he blamed it on our mother's fluctuating hormones, alcohol, a new medication that the doctor had given her, and once he'd even considered that she might be possessed by an evil spirit and thought about seeing the vicar for an exorcism. No one had known about our mother's *affliction*. A closed door was a closed door.

At the end of our walks, Dad always said the same thing as we tramped back up the garden path.

'Let's show your mother how much we love her, fair lasses.'

I was never sure what loving my mother entailed, and, when we returned, our cheeks rosy, our noses dripping and our fingers numb from the frost, Dad made us hot chocolate and planted us beside the fire.

'Chestnuts!' he'd announce, bringing over a wooden bowl brimming with brown nuggets. It gave us something to do while he dealt with Mum and cleaned up any mess she'd made. That particular time, we'd found her collapsed on the kitchen floor with a kitchen knife in one hand and blood oozing from her wrist. Shelley and I had been ushered from the room to sit by the fire.

As I carved an X in the tough outer shell of the first chestnut, I wondered how hard my mother had to press to get the knife to pierce her skin. I almost wanted the blunt little paring knife to slip as I gouged, to see what it felt like on my own flesh. To see if I could understand my mother's pain.

By understanding how she felt, I figured love might follow.

We popped the prepared chestnuts into the old brass roaster and laid it on top of the embers in the fire. Dad had instructed us to give it a shake every five minutes or so to ensure they were cooked evenly. Then, half an hour later, the three of us had sat peeling the crisp, blackened shells away from their creamy hot flesh, dipping it in a little salt before popping the chestnuts in our mouths whole.

It was at this point our mother usually joined us, silent and contrite.

. . .

'There's a bench – look, Dad. Let's go and watch the river.' I lead him down to it, the ground getting soggier underfoot the closer we get to the bank. Dad gives a little nod as we sit down, keeping hold of my arm.

'Mum seems...'

I trail off, not sure whether I should talk about her. While I'm certain she's the reason that Dad's mental health has suffered, I know he still adores her. He was once so full of zest and ambition, a hard-working man with a top-of-the-ladder career, but gradually he's become a silent and stooped shell of a man. At seventy-four, he's nine years older than Mum, but it's still no age to be living such an empty and unfulfilling existence, not when he's physically still in good shape.

'Well, Mum seems OK,' I settle on. 'You know. There's been no trouble.'

Another little nod from Dad.

'Maybe you'd like to visit home one afternoon?' I suggest, instantly wishing I hadn't. That would mean being around to oversee it, which, in turn, means staying at Medvale even longer. Shelley will be too busy with work to mediate and, like me, she'd be happy if our parents never set eyes on each other again. Any notions that one day things might get back to normal between them – visions of Owen and me bringing future grand-children to visit Grandma and Grandad in the countryside, for example – have long since gone.

Dad sneezes loudly three times in a row.

'Here,' I say, pulling a packet of tissues from my bag. He takes one and blows his nose, balling the used tissue up in his fist. His knuckles turn white.

'I missed you so much while I was away,' I say, resting my head on his shoulder. 'But London's not far, and there's our wedding to look forward to now.' My stomach churns as I recall my mother's reaction to the news. 'Mum already thinks she's going to be organising it, of course. She wants us to get married in the village church and have the reception at Medvale.'

Fleetingly, I wonder if it wouldn't be such a bad idea, knowing how much Owen wants a proper occasion, rather than the two of us hotfooting it to an impersonal registry office. But I quickly shut down the intrusive thought. Mother of the bride Sylvia might be, but experience screams at me that it's a terrible idea to involve her. It will be my wedding on my terms.

Suddenly Dad's head whips round to face me, his watery eyes locking onto mine, his lips parting.

'*Don't,*' is what I think he says. Though I really can't be sure.

TWELVE

An hour later than expected, Owen pulls onto the drive of my childhood home. Shelley picked me up from the hospital, popping in to see Dad briefly before dropping me back at Medvale. Since then, I've been sitting alone, thinking about my father's strange reaction to my happy news.

'Hey,' I say to Owen now, slipping on a pair of wellies by the door and crunching across the drive to greet him. 'Missed you.' I give him an overly long hug before flinging open the passenger door of the Volvo, seeing the pet carrier strapped to the seat. 'Minnie!' I ring out. 'I missed you, too.'

Owen laughs. 'She's been good as gold all the way here,' he tells me. 'I think she knew she was coming home.'

'This isn't our home,' I say, giving him a poke. 'And wait, I don't think we should unpack anything.' I go round to the back of the car as he's about to take out the first suitcase. 'I've found a motel near Oxford that's not too pricey for a night or two, and they allow cats. It's nothing special, but that doesn't really matter.' I take a deep breath, hating that I have to even ask this. 'It's my treat, of course, but is there any way you could cover it for now, until I can get some online tutoring work?'

'Wait... you'd rather go to a grotty budget motel than stay here in this beautiful house with your own mother?' Owen looks puzzled. 'That makes no sense, love. Your mum's enjoying having you here, and I'm not at all fazed by her, so don't you worry about that.'

But I *am* worried. I stare up at him, remembering what Dad said.

Don't...

I'm still not sure I even heard him correctly, but it certainly sounded like a warning, and came right after I mentioned that Mum wanted us to get married in the village. I asked him what he meant, of course, but Dad had remained silent for the rest of my visit.

Standing here now on the drive with Owen, each of our hands on the suitcase handle, I'm torn over what to do. Seeing Shelley looking so gaunt and thin earlier, still consumed by grief, and then visiting my father, witnessing his deterioration, has churned up so much guilt.

'OK,' I say, closing my eyes for a beat. 'You're right. Why waste money on a hotel, eh? One more night here won't hurt.'

'Sylvia, this is absolutely delicious,' Owen says as he tucks into the Sunday roast dinner Mum has made. And I'm inclined to agree. She's outdone herself with the roast chicken, stuffing, crispy roast potatoes and vegetables. And best of all, there was no drama preparing it. 'I certainly missed food like this in Dubai.'

'Talking of Dubai,' I whisper to him when my mother goes to fetch more wine, 'any sign of the money? I really want to get looking for another flat.'

Owen shakes his head. 'Not since you last asked about an hour ago,' he says, winking. 'And it won't happen on a Sunday, Lizzie,' he replies in a low voice. 'It'll be tomorrow now.' He gives my hand a squeeze then holds up his glass for Sylvia to refill it when she returns to the table.

'What's that about a flat?' Mum says, her hearing as sharp as ever. 'Tell me you're not leaving already.'

'No plans as yet,' Owen replies, sending a jolt of panic through me. *We do have plans*, I want to scream, but Owen seems confident the money will be in tomorrow, so I bite my tongue, determined to be patient.

'Well, whatever place you end up getting in London, make sure there's room for a little one,' she says, eyeing me over the rim of her wine glass. 'And for a doting granny.'

I can't help the sudden cough, and a piece of chicken shoots from my mouth back onto my plate.

'You OK, love?' Owen asks, patting my back. 'And don't worry, Sylvia. We're looking for somewhere with two bedrooms.'

'I'm fine,' I croak, wiping my mouth.

Does she *know*? Can my mother somehow sense I'm pregnant? Or was she listening outside the bedroom door when we were discussing baby names last night? I do *not* want her knowing about our unborn child. Not yet. I can't deal with her controlling tendrils sinking into my uterus as well as everywhere else.

'Anyway,' Mum continues, 'I don't know how you can stand to live in the city these days. It's overpriced and overpopulated, if you ask me. Give me the countryside any day.' Then she grabs my phone from where it's lying on the table beside me, flashing it up to my face to unlock it before I have a chance to stop her.

'*Mum*, what are you doing?' I reach out my hand to take it back, but she jerks it away.

'Photo time!' she sings out, angling the camera lens towards me and Owen. 'Get in closer you two, that's it.' She beckons us with her free hand.

Owen puts down his knife and fork and slings an arm

around my shoulder, pressing his cheek close to mine as he goes along with her. I force down the food in my mouth and fake a smile, watching as Mum snaps photo after photo.

'There,' she says finally. 'Happy memories for you to look back on one day.' She locks my phone again and places it back down next to me, giving it a tap. I don't give her the pleasure of looking at them right now, knowing I'll probably delete them all anyway.

'Right,' Mum says, after we've finished the roast and the empty plates are cleared away. 'I've made you a special treat for dessert, Owen.'

She opens the oven and takes out what looks like a small, individual pot. Just enough for one person.

'A forest berry crumble, especially for you,' she announces, placing the ramekin in front of him. 'I foraged for the berries myself. There's custard coming.'

I look down at the dessert, seeing the deep reddy-brown juice oozing from the sides. Why has she only made one?

My heart speeds up as I watch her stirring the custard on the hob. She glances at me over her shoulder, giving me the faintest hint of a smile.

'You picked the fruit yourself?' I ask, trying not to betray my concern.

'I did,' she says, still eyeing me. 'The berries are just ripening at this time of year. My foraging book was very helpful in identifying the different types. And what to avoid, of course.'

Suddenly, I'm right back in the village hall – aged nine at the only birthday party I was ever allowed to have. Mum had lit the candles on the birthday cake that she'd made – a lopsided sponge dripping with pink icing and a crown of red berries.

At first, no one in my class at the village primary school had replied to the party invites. But then Mum bragged that there was going to be a magician, pony rides, a bouncy castle *and* an ice cream van, and the acceptances had poured in. For a few magical days, the classmates who usually shunned me let me join in their playtime games.

Everyone came to that party, arriving with armfuls of gifts, but it soon became clear that Mum's promises were false. There was no bouncy castle and no pony rides, and the magician was just Dad plucking ten pence coins from behind children's ears. All the kids moped about, bored, while I spent the afternoon hiding in the corner.

Then, after the sandwiches and crisps, Mum had brought out the cake as my classmates sang a lacklustre rendition of 'Happy Birthday'.

'None for you, Elizabeth,' Mum had whispered, patting my tummy after she'd handed out all the slices. I'd watched everyone scoffing my cake, hating the tears in my eyes.

On Monday at school, virtually all the desks in my class were empty, with the teacher telling me that everyone was ill with a stomach upset. The local doctor even called by our house that evening to check what Mum had fed them at my party. I'll never forget her shrill, indignant voice, followed by hysterical sobbing after the doctor had left.

'Well, that's very kind of you, Sylvia,' Owen says now, giving me a wink. 'But aren't you or Lizzie having any crumble?'

'Oh, I have to be careful of my waistline,' Mum says, patting her stomach. 'And Lizzie's always had to watch her weight, haven't you, darling?'

'Mum, I—'

'Anyway, I'm afraid my meagre harvest only ran to one portion, and as you're the guest, Owen, it's all yours.' Mum turns back to the stove, taking the pan off the hob. The custard is ready to serve.

Knowing I have to do something, I reach across the table for the water jug, knocking the ramekin off the table and sending it to the floor. Pieces of china skid across the tiles, leaving a burgundy puddle of stewed berries and sugary crumble topping lying at Owen's feet.

'Elizabeth!' Mum shrieks. 'You *stupid*, clumsy girl!'

Then I swear I hear her sending me to my room, yelling that I'll get no food for a week because of how naughty I've been.

'I... I'm so sorry,' I say, scraping back my chair and standing up. I stare at the mess, hearing Owen telling me not to worry, that he'll clean it up, that it was only an accident.

Then I rush off to the downstairs toilet, sliding the bolt on the door and panting as I lean back against the wall. Tears well up in my eyes, eventually rolling down my cheeks. Just as they had done when I was nine years old at my party.

THIRTEEN

I wake the next morning to find Owen straightening his tie in front of the full-length mirror.

'Sorry if I disturbed you, darling,' he says, sitting down on the bed beside me. 'I made you tea.'

I glance at the bedside table and see a steaming mug waiting for me. 'You're an angel,' I say with a smile. 'You're dressed smartly. Are you off somewhere?'

'Work beckons,' Owen replies. 'After you went to bed last night, I brought in all our stuff from the car. Your mum said I could put all the boxes we won't need up in the loft, but when I opened the hatch and looked, it's rather full up there.'

He gestures to some of our clutter, reminding me of how much space we took up at Peter's place. I must have slept like a log because I didn't hear him bringing it in.

'The rest is on the landing as I didn't want to wake you. Anyway, after I'd finished unloading, your mum offered to drive me to the station this morning so I can get the train to the office. That way you get to keep the car today in case you need it. I won't be late home.'

Home.

The word makes me sit bolt upright in bed.

'I thought you were in between contracts.'

'The big bosses at the London branch of the company want to discuss more consulting work with me,' he announces. 'They've bought my train tickets. Sorry, I thought I mentioned it.'

I sip my tea, trying to recall. 'I don't think you did.'

'Hormones,' he jokes, which I hate, but have to admit that he's probably right. My mind has been all over the place since I found out about the baby.

'Anyway, it'll give me an opportunity to chase up the money they owe me. I won't be doing any more work for them until they've paid up.'

'Do you want me to drive you to the station instead?'

Just at that moment, there's a knock on the bedroom door.

'*Coo-ee...*' a voice outside says. 'Ready to leave when you are.'

'No need,' he says, leaning forward to give me a kiss. 'I'll see you tonight, darling.'

And with that, Owen is gone, leaving me sitting in bed with my tea, and Minnie curled up beside me, oblivious to all the questions swirling around my head.

It's a long shot, but if Shelley isn't home, I'll go and visit Dad again. Anything to get out of the house and avoid being alone with my mother while Owen is at work. I don't want to listen to her talking about wedding plans or us moving in with her, longer-term, and I don't think she's best pleased with me after I destroyed her dessert.

I park the Volvo outside my sister's cottage, looking up and down the street for her battered old four-wheel drive. I smile at the thought of it, remembering how Shelley had once put down a plastic bag for me to sit on when she'd given me a lift.

'Sorry, dog puke,' she'd said. 'Or it might have been a cat. Or a lamb.' While she doesn't have any pets of her own because of her irregular hours, I know she often ferries animals between different veterinary facilities. The inside of her vehicle had smelt like a farmyard and looked like one too, with bits of straw in the footwells, dog harnesses and leads strewn about, medical equipment bags and various other detritus typical of the busy life of a country vet.

While her navy Jeep is nowhere to be seen, I decide to knock on the door anyway, in case she's had to park around the corner.

'Oh!' I say as the front door opens before I've even had a chance to knock. 'I just called by to see—'

'Shelley...?' the man says. 'She's at work, I'm afraid.'

He stands in the low doorway, his head almost reaching the lintel and his broad shoulders spanning the width.

'That's a shame,' I reply, staring up at him, something stirring in my mind. He's wearing pale jeans with a black shirt on top, and clean Adidas trainers. He has a dark padded jacket slung over his arm and a small backpack hooked on his shoulder as if he's on his way somewhere. But he makes no move to come outside. 'I wasn't sure what shift she was on today.'

The man, around my age, smiles, sweeping his hand through thick hair that's on the cusp of auburn but mainly a rich brown. It's a colour that reminds me of polished mahogany, but then I notice the copper highlights in his neatly clipped beard lit up by the sun.

When the man clears his throat, I realise that I've been gawping at him far too long.

'She had an early call-out to a farm. I'm Jared, by the way,' he says, holding out his hand, his mouth curling into an amused smile. 'Shelley's new lodger. I can tell her you stopped by.'

'Oh my God, *Jared*,' I squeal. 'Yes... of *course*!'

Another smile showing his straight, white teeth.

'It's Lizzie.' I beam up at him as I try to work out how the lanky, geeky teenager I once knew has turned into this very good-looking man. I'd never have recognised him in a million years if he hadn't said who he was. 'Lizzie Holmes, Shelley's sister. You remember?'

Jared plants his hands on his hips and shakes his head slowly. 'My *God*,' he replies, his pale-green eyes growing wider. 'It's *so* good to see you.' He holds his arms open to embrace me. 'How *are* you, Liz?'

It hadn't taken much persuading for me to get into Jared's BMW and go with him to a house viewing. 'It's only a fifteen-minute drive,' he says as we set off. 'It'll give us a chance to catch up.'

'Nice wheels,' I tell him, mentally comparing it to the old Volvo estate Owen bought for us. But I can't grumble – it's been reliable so far, despite its mileage and age.

'I'm still a bit of a nerdy petrolhead,' Jared confesses, taking the twisty lanes steadily. He glances over at me, his smile making me hold my stare for a heartbeat too long.

A few minutes and lots of catch-up questions later, Jared says, 'Right, I think it's somewhere down this lane.' He shifts down into second gear as we make a turn in the centre of a pretty village about five miles from Shelley's house.

'This place is gorgeous,' I say. Chocolate box-style cottages with low-fringe thatches are arranged around the village green, complete with a pond and ducks at its centre. 'I'd forgotten just how pretty this area is.' *And with a price tag to match*, I think.

'Ah, there it is,' Jared says, pointing at a 'For Sale' board further along the lane. He indicates right and pulls into the driveway of an old stone cottage with a sagging roof that's missing most of its tiles. Several of the windows are boarded up, and the front garden is so overgrown that I'm almost attacked by brambles as I lever myself out of the car.

'It's certainly a project,' I say, hands on hips as I stare at it. 'But lots of potential.'

A woman wearing a smart suit appears at the front door. 'Mr and Mrs Miller, welcome to Cherry Tree Cottage,' she calls out, picking her way over the weedy path to reach us.

'Oh my God, even the name is adorable,' I whisper, giving a little tug on Jared's sleeve. 'I insist you buy it for us right now, darling,' I add in a silly voice.

'Actually, it's just me looking for a house,' Jared informs the agent. 'This is my friend, Lizzie. A very old and *dear* friend,' he adds, glancing at me and smiling.

I ignore the fluttering feeling inside me and follow Jared to the front door. I'm not much of a property expert but, back at Shelley's place, when he'd told me he was on his way to a house viewing, he'd said, 'A second opinion would be very welcome. Then a coffee afterwards to catch up properly, if you have time?'

Indeed, I *did* have time. With Owen unexpectedly in London, the whole day stretched ahead, empty. I'd left my mother a note on the kitchen table simply stating 'Back later'.

'So will you put in an offer?' I ask after the viewing has finished. We've driven on to Stow-on-the-Wold, finding a little café with a picturesque courtyard out the back, which is where we're now sitting in the dappled sunlight, waiting for our lattes.

'I'm tempted,' Jared says. It feels as though he's not taken his eyes off me since we sat down. 'I just can't get over that it's *you*, Liz. After all this time.' He shakes his head again. 'Shelley mentioned you were in the area. It's so great to see you.'

'Are you in touch with anyone else from school or the village?' I ask as the waiter places our drinks on the wrought-iron table.

Jared shakes his head. 'Sadly not, apart from Shelley, of course.'

'You're back from the States for good?'

He nods. 'It was never my plan to stay out there forever. Silicon Valley is... well, it's a bit too full-on for me. I'm an English country boy at heart.'

Jared had explained during the drive here how he'd sold his tech company earlier in the year – something to do with software and AI.

'Selling up has given me financial freedom to pursue other avenues,' he tells me. 'I want to put down roots, have a place to call home, and as long as I've got a decent internet connection, I'm happy. Mum and Dad still live in Little Risewell, so it'll be good to be near them as they get older.'

'I knew I should have listened more in IT classes,' I joke. 'I'm just a twenty-pound-an-hour private tutor.' I tuck a strand of flyaway hair behind my ear. 'But I love it. I did a PGCE after my degree then taught at a primary school for a few years. Since then, I've been tutoring through an agency.'

'Following in your mother's footsteps?'

'God, I hope not,' I say with a laugh. 'Luckily, my fiancé's work pays well, so we're not totally broke.' I swallow down the lie.

'Congratulations on your engagement, by the way,' Jared says, giving me a look.

I explain the falling-in-the-pool story, telling him how Owen and I met in Dubai. I leave out the bit about me needing to pay off debts that weren't even mine. 'I never used to believe in love at first sight, but here we are.' I feel a blush creeping up my cheeks.

'And your parents, how are they keeping?'

'Dad's not been so good lately,' I confess, though I hesitate, wondering whether to tell him more. Then I decide I can trust Jared, knowing he's not judgemental. 'He's actually staying in

Winchcombe Lodge for a bit.' Everyone in the area knows it's a psychiatric hospital – the type of place that holds mentally ill criminals in a secure wing, as well as those needing a break from life, or rehab and recovery from drugs and alcohol.

'I'm so sorry to hear that. I always liked your dad.'

'And Mum... well, she's still Mum.'

'She was always a force, was Sylvia. It must have been hard for you and Shelley growing up.'

'You have no idea,' I reply. 'Though it's Dad who's paying the price now. It's so sad. I mean... why didn't he divorce her decades ago? That's what I don't understand. He could have had such a different life.'

'From what I remember, your mum had some mental health issues. And things were different back then. No one talked about that sort of stuff, especially the older generation. It was put up and shut up.'

'You're right. But it's awful seeing Dad in hospital. And Mum's now desperate to organise my wedding, of course. But after what happened last year...' I trail off. 'Let's just say I'd rather have a quiet registry office ceremony.'

'Shelley has already filled me in,' Jared says in a way that shows me he understands. 'I was so sorry to hear about Rafe. Just tragic. Maybe you and Owen should run off somewhere to tie the knot.' He leans in closer, his eyes latching onto mine as he speaks in a low voice. 'Then at least your fiancé will be safe from the mother of the bride.'

I stare at him for a moment, wondering what he means. What he *knows*.

'I'd happily do that, but Owen wants the whole works.' Then I check my phone to see if he's texted. He hasn't, but my heart sinks when I see the screen. I had my phone on silent for the house viewing. 'See what I mean?' I flash Jared a look.

'*Nine missed calls from Mother*,' he reads. 'Feel free to call her back.'

'No need to do that, look.' Another quick glance shows him that my mother is calling me for the tenth time.

'Hi, Mum,' I say as I answer. '*What?*' I glance at Jared, pulling a face. 'No, not really. I'm with someone right now. Can't it wait?'

I listen to her, convinced Jared must be able to hear my mother's increasing volume.

'OK, OK, look, give me half an hour and I'll be there,' I reply in a resigned voice. 'Bye.'

'Trouble?'

'I don't believe it. Mum has only gone and made an appointment with the local vicar at midday to discuss Owen and me getting married at St Michael's church in the village.' I sigh, closing my eyes for a second. 'Apparently, there's been a wedding cancellation and they have a Saturday afternoon slot free in two weeks. I mean, does it even *work* like that with weddings? I literally have no idea.' I tuck my phone back in my bag.

Jared laughs as he drains his coffee. 'You're asking an eternal bachelor,' he says, 'who has absolutely no knowledge of such things. I'd just play along with her for now. It'll satisfy your mother's need to—'

'Interfere?'

Jared nods. 'And then in a few days you'll be back in London moving into your new flat, and you and Owen can sort out your own wedding arrangements. I shall look forward to my invitation,' he adds with a smile.

'That's assuming we even find a flat,' I reply, knowing the odds are against us. 'But you're right. I'll just humour Mum for now and hopefully when Owen gets home later, there'll be good news about us moving back to London.' By that, I mean hopefully the money will have come in.

We continue with our catch-up on the short drive back to Shelley's house in Wendbury, where I go directly to my car.

'Thanks for the coffee,' I say, unlocking it. 'You must meet Owen, though I'm not sure when as we'll be leaving soon.'

'How about coming round here for some food tonight?' Jared suggests, catching me by surprise. 'Shelley says I'm welcome to have guests any time, and you being her sister, she's hardly going to object. I'll whip something up for us to eat. Seven o'clock suit you?'

I smile, keen to introduce Owen to one of my oldest friends. 'We'd love that, thanks.' Then I have an idea. 'Here, let me show you some photos of him. Mum snapped some of us last night at dinner.'

I go onto my camera roll and pull up the last few pictures, quickly scrolling through the ones she took. Then I frown, swiping back further in case I'm mistaken.

'That's odd,' I whisper as Jared peers over my shoulder. I check through the photos she took again – eight of them, all from last night, and all taken at the kitchen table because there I am, a forced smile on my face and my roast dinner in front of me.

Except in each of the photos, it's just me.

In every single one, Mum has cut Owen out.

FOURTEEN

'So, wait... your mother has arranged the actual *day* for our wedding?' Owen says with an incredulous laugh as we tramp along the lane that evening. We decided to walk to Shelley's house, both of us wanting the exercise and fresh air.

'Yep. I spent two hours with her and the vicar this afternoon, listening to her organising our entire wedding. I'm literally counting down the hours until we get back to London.' I decide not to mention the photos she took, knowing he'd be upset that she didn't include him. If he asks to see them, I'll just have to say I deleted them by mistake.

Owen hadn't been keen on going out tonight when I picked him up from the station earlier, but as soon as he saw how disappointed I looked, he changed his mind. I've never had that before – someone considering what I want, putting my needs ahead of theirs.

When we were first dating in Dubai, he booked a week's impromptu holiday from his work to fit in with my tutoring schedule. 'How else will I get to see you otherwise?' he'd said, turning up with a picnic basket full of delicious food and a beach umbrella. He'd planned a different activity every afternoon for when I finished work at three – a beach walk followed by a sunset dinner, horse riding in the desert, tickets to the opera, a cruise. And now, since life has taken a more mundane turn, he's still here for me, always wanting to make me happy.

On the drive back to Medvale, I'd tentatively asked him about the invoice. He'd wiped his hands down a tired face, turning to me. 'My bill is like petty cash to them, love,' he sighed. 'But I've been chasing it, don't worry.'

I didn't think that a £23,000 invoice for five months' consulting work was petty. Anything but. It was more than I'd put on my last tax return for an entire year's work. And I *was* worried.

'Anyway, Mum was smarming up to the poor vicar, insisting the wedding *had* to be soon,' I say now as we walk along the lane. I don't mention that she told him she was undergoing tests for a potentially fatal illness, how she wouldn't die happy if she didn't see her youngest daughter get married. Of course, Mum revealed afterwards through a smug smile that none of it was true, but that's more than Owen needs to hear.

'She's certainly determined,' Owen says, clasping his fingers through mine. 'When is this wedding of ours, then? Be good to get it in the diary.' He laughs again.

'Oh, a week on Saturday,' I reply in an exasperated voice. 'Apparently, another couple had booked for that day but then they split up and cancelled the service, along with everything else.'

'Shame for them.'

'Yeah, but Mum pounced on the opportunity. She was even talking about booking their caterers and florist.'

'I wouldn't worry. There's a load of paperwork that will need sorting, including banns being read out at the church. There simply isn't time.' He looks at me, giving me a wink.

'Though I can't lie, the thought of marrying you so soon *is* appealing.'

I rest my head against him briefly, giving his hand a squeeze. I feel the same way too, yet the thought of Mum controlling our special day fills me with dread.

'This is my mother we're talking about,' I say. 'She's done her research. Apparently, there's something called a common licence that we can get pretty quickly. We'd have to provide some ID documents and then meet with someone from the church who's authorised to issue it. Because I lived in the village and was a regular at St Michael's growing up, none of this seemed to faze the vicar at all, especially once Mum had got her teeth into him. She's been phoning marquee companies all afternoon. She's exhausting, but I guess it's kept her occupied.'

'Think about it from her perspective though, love,' Owen says as we finally enter Wendbury. 'Her husband is in hospital, so she must feel quite alone. It'll be giving her something to focus on, especially after her eldest daughter's wedding day ended in such tragedy, and her other daughter ran away overseas to—'

'Hey, it wasn't like that,' I say in a jokey way, though his comment stings. I slide my hand from his, instinctively fiddling with my engagement ring – a habit I've formed partly to check it's still there, but also something I do when I'm stressed.

I freeze.

The ring isn't on my finger.

But then I relax, remembering that I'd taken it off when I had a shower before fetching Owen from the station, leaving it on the edge of the basin. I decide not to mention it as I don't want him to think that I've been careless. Rather, I make a mental note to put it back on as soon as we get home later.

'Your mum just wants to see at least one of her daughters happily married. It means a lot to her. I don't think it's *that* unreasonable.'

As we approach Shelley's house, I wish Owen could see what I see behind Mum's facade – not a mother who cares, rather a woman who needs to be in control. A woman who will stop at nothing to protect her daughters. Then one of my earliest memories flashes into my mind, perhaps triggered by the smell of woodsmoke from someone's log fire as we walk through the village.

I was only four and Shelley had just turned nine. My mittened hand was slotted into my sister's as we watched the flames licking up the huge pile of wood that had been collected for the village Bonfire Night celebrations. The local Scout group had made the guy, his straw-and-newspaper-stuffed body sitting on the top of the fire.

'Want to go over *there*,' I'd whined to Shelley, who was engrossed in her toffee apple. After more pestering, I dragged her over to the other side of the bonfire to get a better view of the fireworks, weaving through the crowd. Mum and Dad were nearby, or so we'd thought, but they soon weren't. Adult bodies towered over us, everyone *ooing* and *ahhing* at the display – kids yelling, rockets popping overhead, the squeal of bangers and squibs.

I'd spun around, staring up at the night sky as explosions of colour rained above me. I'd never seen anything like it.

At some point, my hand must have slipped out of Shelley's grip. I was swept along in a sea of people, my eyes flashing with flames and fireworks, and the grisly face of the guy as he collapsed into the inferno, the heat of the flames on my cheeks.

And then the man was talking to me, crouching down. His hand was big as it wrapped around mine, leading me away from the crowd as he promised me sparklers and sweeties.

As he opened the car door, I'll never forget the scream as it shredded the night sky louder than any fireworks.

I knew instantly it was my mother.

It all happened so fast, I don't recall all the details, but I know there was more screaming and then the man was howling and bent double in pain when Mum slammed the car door on his hand. Then she kicked him, yelling obscenities.

As Mum picked me up, cradling me to her body as we walked away, I felt her shaking to her core. She was so alight with adrenaline, she was hardly able to speak as she pressed her face into my hair.

'*I nearly lost you... I nearly lost you...*' came her wails.

When we found Shelley and Dad, she set me down next to my sister and knelt in front of us.

'I *promise*,' she said solemnly, her mouth quivering from fear. 'I will never let *any* man take you from me as long as I live.'

And I knew she meant it by the way she crossed her heart.

Now, as we head to Shelley's house, my mother's words from all those years ago still ringing in my ears, I have no idea if she approves of Owen or not. Either way, I'm not taking the risk by allowing her to have anything to do with our special day – especially not after what happened at Shelley's wedding last year.

I tug on Owen's jacket sleeve, pulling him to a stop.

'It just feels rushed, that's all,' I say, turning to face him. I don't want him to think I'm not keen to get married – I just don't want to do it here. 'Mum has a tendency to... to take over,' I say, not knowing how else to put it.

'Is it *really* such a bad thing?' Owen says, tilting up my chin. 'We're in love, we want to get married. Maybe your mother is doing us a favour by helping. Not to mention kindly offering to pay for it all, too.'

I close my eyes for a second. He doesn't understand. How *could* he? I know Owen is set on a traditional ceremony, and the beautiful church in my childhood village makes perfect sense. I feel so selfish resisting, but after what happened to Rafe, I just can't do it. Though it's no secret that he and Mum hadn't seen eye to eye. She'd taken an instant dislike to him.

'She bloody well asked him how *tall* he is,' Shelley had once told me, mortified on Rafe's behalf. 'Then she told him he was too short for me.' My sister, seething, then recounted how Mum had grilled Rafe about his parents and what they did for a living. She did not like that Rafe's father was a taxi driver and his mother a cleaner, despite them working all hours to support their son's ambitions of becoming a vet. 'And she virtually caught fire when Rafe informed her that he voted Labour.'

As Owen knocks on the door of Shelley's cottage, I screw up my eyes, trying to get rid of the image that still haunts me even a year later.

The cream and red mother-of-the-bride corsage – delicate freesias with a single rose at the centre – was chosen by Mum (of course) to match the bride's bouquet, and I'd found it lying on the flagstone floor beside Rafe's body.

There was no mistaking that it was the same corsage my mother had been wearing earlier that morning – it was the only one like it in the wedding party. It had been fixed to the lapel of her peach-coloured jacket with a pearl-topped pin, and she'd been fiddling with it in the car on the way to the church, complaining that it wouldn't stay in place.

I'll never forget the staring, vacant expression on Rafe's face as he lay lifeless, twisted on his side on the cold stone floor. He was wearing his morning suit with a single red rose pinned to his dark-grey jacket, and a cream satin waistcoat underneath. The knees of his pale-grey trousers were scuffed and dirty, and a burgundy pool of blood had spread around his head. It surprised me that his feet were completely bare, despite him being dressed for the wedding.

After he'd failed to arrive at the church – he was due to be there forty minutes before the ceremony – we'd begun to get concerned. It wasn't like Rafe to be late. The bride was sent around the village several times in the cream Rolls-Royce that Mum had hired, stalling for time. When, eventually, Shelley demanded that the car stop and she and Dad be let out, it was me, her maid of honour, and George, Rafe's best man, she called upon for help. We'd set about hunting for the lost groom.

Never in my life, after phoning him dozens of times and searching around the churchyard in case he was having second thoughts or necking a swig of Dutch courage behind a grave-stone, had I expected to find him dead on the floor of his own home.

And never in my life had I ever done anything so reckless as hiding potential evidence of a crime from the police.

On impulse, I'd grabbed the corsage from where it lay beside Rafe, fixing it to the bodice of my long cream dress with a hairpin – hiding it in plain sight. I'd planned on dealing with it later, wanting to ask Mum how it had come to be there, giving her a chance to explain, terrified for our entire family that she'd had something to do with Rafe's death.

Except, as it turned out, I never did ask.

By not knowing the truth, my panicked mind convinced me that I was somehow protecting Shelley, protecting my father, protecting *myself* from the fallout I knew would destroy what was left of our family.

Then I'd called 999 with trembling hands.

Once the police and ambulance had arrived, the corsage completely slipped my mind, and, with the shock of everything going on, no one had noticed that I hadn't previously been wearing the flowers pinned to my dress. As maid of honour, I had my own small bouquet to hold, along with a basket of petals for the flower girl, but I'd left those back at the church on a pew.

It was only later that day, after I'd returned from the police station with Shelley, that I remembered the corsage. Alone in my bedroom at Medvale as I slipped out of the dress, I unpinned it. I stared at it for ages, as if the flowers might reveal a secret, eventually shoving it deep inside a box of my childhood possessions that were due to be stored in the loft. No one would find it there. No one would know what its discovery at the scene of Rafe's death might mean.

FIFTEEN

'Here's to the happy couple,' Shelley says half an hour after we arrive, raising her glass across the dining table. I can't help noticing how tired she looks today. More so than yesterday.

We all join in the toast, Shelley's glass clinking rather too hard against Owen's. She follows up the gesture by knocking back the contents of hers in several glugs, and then she pours herself some more.

'Shell, it's OK,' I say to her quietly. 'We don't need to talk about weddings and stuff. Not tonight,' I add, patting her leg under the table, but Shelley shies away, scowling at me.

''Course we do,' she says. 'Couldn't be happier for you guys.' I can tell by her eyes that she's tipsy already.

At that moment, I've never been more grateful to Owen, who suddenly decides to regale us with a monologue about wind versus solar energy. I notice how Jared seems engaged at first, though after a few minutes, his attention wanes as Owen moves on to the future of hydrogen.

'Either way, it keeps me gainfully employed,' Owen eventually says, wrapping up his speech. I pass him more of the vegetable curry Jared has made, in the hope it might steer him away from talking about work now that the topic has thankfully moved on from weddings.

'That new detective came to see me at the practice earlier,' Shelley suddenly pipes up, making my stomach knot again. Owen's distraction hasn't worked. 'DI Lambert.'

'What did he say?' I ask.

'It was weird,' she replies, laying down her knife and fork. 'He implied there was new evidence, though... though he didn't say what.' She takes a sip of her wine, a look of anguish on her face. 'He wanted me to go over a few details again, but I was basically repeating everything I told them last year.'

Everyone falls silent for a moment.

'I hope it's not someone stirring again,' I say.

Rafe's death had been all over the local news, mainly because a groom dying on the day of his own wedding made for a good story. When the police initially released a public statement, they couldn't rule out suspicious circumstances. Then came the prank calls and nasty messages on social media.

The police, while used to dealing with such things, had to follow up every instance, diverting their attention from the main investigation. The inquest took several months, but the coroner eventually concluded that Rafe had died of a heart attack – although the detective on the case at the time, DI Waters, had always made his doubts known, still maintaining his belief that there was more to the story. But late last year, he'd retired and that had been that. Shelley was left with a hole in her heart and a feeling that something wasn't right.

'Whatever it is, DI Lambert is taking it seriously,' Shelley replies, pouring herself more wine.

I stare at my plate, pushing my curry around with my fork. Despite having had all-day morning sickness, I was enjoying Jared's tasty cooking until Shelley mentioned this development. Now, the thought of eating anything else makes me feel queasy again.

Then I'm reminded of Mum last year, how she'd foisted wedding canapés on us the evening of Rafe's death, not wanting the expensive wedding food to go to waste. But it had been Shelley vomiting that night, not me – my sister still wearing her wedding dress while I held back her hair as she let out her pain. There'd been nothing to come up, but she couldn't even keep sips of water down.

'Mum, Rafe has *died*,' I'd snapped at her once we were all back at Medvale and my mother was bustling around with the silver platters. She was still wearing her peach mother-of-the-bride outfit – minus the corsage – despite me trying to coax her to change so as not to remind Shelley of how the day *should* have gone. 'Canapés are the last thing on our minds right now.' While Shelley and I had been making statements at the police station, Mum had been cancelling and dismantling the wedding with as much efficiency as she'd organised it.

Almost *too* efficiently, I've since pondered. At the time, I'd been grateful that she'd dealt with all the practicalities – informing the guests that the wedding wouldn't be going ahead, letting the reception venue know what had happened, cancelling the live band, DJ and hog roast that had been organised for the evening's celebrations. Dad had tried to be of use, but as the day had worn on, he'd become even more upset and overwhelmed, following Mum around, trying to talk to her, asking her questions that she didn't seem willing to answer. It made me wonder if he knew something.

In the end, George, the best man, had taken care of Dad, ushering him upstairs to rest, although I remember George looking rather fragile, too. It had been Rafe's stag do the previous night, having been cancelled the week before because of Rafe being on call. A few of the guys looked decidedly ropey and hung-over.

Later that evening, after everyone had left, the four of us sat together at Medvale, mostly in silence, but also picking over events as if that might somehow rewind the day and bring Rafe back. Shelley's stifled sobs had been our soundtrack.

It was clear Dad was struggling with what had happened, though in a different way to the rest of us. After he'd come back downstairs, he'd remained silent, staring at the wall and refusing to engage with anyone, and actively avoiding Mum.

'The way Dad is right now, it reminds me of how things were when you went off to university,' Shelley had told me later in private when we were getting ready for bed. We both knew neither of us would sleep.

It was a tough time for all of us – everyone giving statements to the police, all of which were followed up by the detectives over the coming days with further interviews, as well as a forensics team spending a day at Rafe and Shelley's cottage. Seeing her home invaded by officers traipsing in and out wearing disposable coveralls was so upsetting for my sister. They even had a team up at the Airbnb rental where the groom, the best man and four others from the stag night had all been getting ready. At the time, until it was proven otherwise, his death was being treated as suspicious.

Now, sitting around the dining table eating the food that Jared has prepared, I can't help wishing that Owen and I were back in London at Peter's flat, that Mum had never invited us here and that I hadn't been persuaded to come. It's turning into a lot more than two days in the countryside.

It's turning into our *wedding*.

No, scratch London, I think, suddenly consumed by an overwhelming urge to get on a plane. *I wish we were back in Dubai...*

'You've got yourself a good man there, Liz,' Jared says as we wait for the kettle to boil. Owen is flicking through Rafe's record collection in the living room – Shelley can't bear to get rid of his beloved vinyl – and Shelley, while she isn't on duty this evening, has stepped outside to take a call from a local farmer wanting advice about a cattle problem. She's never been good at switching off from work.

'I know, I'm lucky,' I reply.

'*He's* lucky,' says Jared, at which I smile.

'I'll keep an eye on her, don't worry,' he continues, his eyes flicking to the back door. Shelley is just visible as she paces about outside, suddenly acting very professional and sober on the phone to the client. 'I don't know the full story, but it sounds as though Rafe's death was very unexpected.'

'He had a heart attack,' I tell him in a low voice. Shelley will be back inside at any moment. 'It was such a shock. He was mid-forties, so it wasn't entirely impossible, I suppose. Thing is, he played rugby for the local team, swam regularly, had never smoked and ate healthily.'

'An underlying genetic heart condition, perhaps?'

'That's exactly what Shelley told me after the inquest. The coroner requested a forensic pathologist for the post-mortem and they found that Rafe had a congenital heart problem.' I pause, trying to remember what she'd said. 'Hypertrophic some-thing or other.'

Jared instantly nods. 'Hypertrophic cardiomyopathy. Someone I knew in California had it. Or rather, their younger brother did. Early twenties, also fit, but he dropped dead on the sports pitch. Utterly tragic. Apparently, it runs in families.'

'God, how awful.'

'I sense there's a "but" to follow in Rafe's case, though?'

I wish I could answer that question, but another glance at the door tells me that Shelley has just hung up from her call and is heading back inside.

'Maybe,' I say, sounding deliberately vague. 'If you're free, we could meet tomorrow?' Though I can hardly explain to him that the original detective had a hunch something wasn't right, and that his investigation might have taken a very different path if I hadn't hidden evidence from what could actually have been a crime scene, rather than the unfortunate tragedy it appeared to be.

'I'd like that,' Jared replies, slipping me a card with his phone number on.

I take it gratefully, desperately wanting to tell someone about my suspicions – that I'm concerned my mother was at the scene of Rafe's death. But to do that would mean tightening the noose around my own neck.

SIXTEEN

The look of hurt and dismay on Owen's face when I tell him I've misplaced my engagement ring was to be expected, though I'm grateful that he's not angry.

'Oh, Lizzie,' he says once we're back at Medvale. 'It must be somewhere. You last saw it here?' His eyes flick around the bathroom as he stands, hands on hips, looking as puzzled as me.

'It was on the edge of the basin. I swear it was...' I cover my face, utterly distraught that it has seemingly vanished into thin air. We've replayed my movements of earlier this evening over and over, creeping back downstairs so as not to wake Mum and checking the kitchen and living room thoroughly. Owen even went outside to search in the car, while I rummaged through my handbag and make-up bags for the third time.

'It's not your fault, darling,' he says as we get into bed. Though I can tell by his voice he's upset. 'We're living out of boxes. Everything's in chaos. We'll check with your mother in the morning, but if it doesn't turn up then I'll look into making an insurance claim. Of course, we'll need to report it to the police. There might have been an intruder.'

I nod, folding myself against him as I listen to the sound of him dropping off to sleep. Usually, I love the way his breathing turns into slower, gentle rasps as it helps me doze off, too, but not tonight. I'm lying here with my heart thumping, anxious that someone has been in the house and stolen my precious ring, as well as feeling troubled by what Shelley revealed earlier – that the police possibly have new evidence in Rafe's case. I don't think I'll be able to sleep at all. Instead, I'm counting down the minutes until my mother wakes so I can ask her if she found my ring and put it somewhere safe.

But in the morning, the news isn't what I was hoping for. Bleary-eyed and exhausted from dozing in and out of bad dreams all night, I pad into the kitchen where I find Owen already up and dressed for the office again, and my mother at the stove stirring porridge.

'Morning, darling, how did you—'

'Mum, have you seen my engagement ring? I left it on the side of the basin after my shower last night.' I hold my breath as I wait for her reply, smiling over at Owen. He's sitting at the table, peering at the newspaper, which is open on the crossword page. Mum's glasses and pen are lying beside it.

Mum turns, wooden spoon in hand, that same barely-there smile on her face as when she was stirring the custard on Sunday evening. My eyes flick to the saucepan, then back to her. 'No, I'm sorry, I haven't seen it,' she says. 'You've lost it?'

I nod, my heart sinking. 'Yes. Or someone has stolen it.'

'But no one's been in the house, darling. How could that be possible?' Mum serves out a bowl of porridge for Owen, putting it in front of him, along with a cup of tea. I only relax when I see her tasting some from the wooden spoon after she's served out two more portions for me and her. 'You did lock the door before you went to Shelley's, didn't you?'

'I'm one hundred per cent certain of that,' Owen says. 'Plus, I checked for signs of a break-in last night, and unless someone was very skilled at picking old iron locks, then no one got in the house while we were out. Oh, and I'm not sure you've got four down right, Sylvia,' he adds, picking up the pen and tapping it on the crossword.

'Perhaps your ring fell down the plughole and is stuck in the basin trap,' Mum suggests. 'I'll call Ned to come out and take it apart. My handyman in the village,' she adds for Owen's benefit. Then she peers over his shoulder at the crossword, a glimmer of a smug smile appearing on her face again. 'No, I think my answer is perfectly correct,' she tells him.

'I'd appreciate that, Mum,' I say, staring out of the window. Preston is on his knees at the edge of a flower border, the drizzle that returned overnight soaking his back as he pulls out weeds. 'You don't think it was...' I gesture out of the window to where the gardener is working, feeling bad for making accusations.

'Good God, no,' Mum replies immediately. 'He wouldn't steal so much as a seed from the garden, let alone come in the house and take your ring. Let's see what Ned finds later. But meantime, I have something that will make you feel better.'

She passes me the bowl of porridge, and I'm about to tell her that I'm not really hungry – without alerting her to even the vaguest whiff of morning sickness – but she dashes out of the room.

'Lizzie,' Owen says. 'You're the crossword genius. "Scarcity in the heart of dessert". Six letters, first one is D.'

'Oh, um...' I say, racking my brains, but then Mum returns with a small velvet box in her hand. She sits down at the table, turning her back to Owen.

'This, darling, is your dear grandmother's engagement ring. It belonged to her mother before that. It's Edwardian. She and I would be absolutely honoured if you wore it.' Mum opens the little box to reveal a gold, slightly scratched, antique-looking ring. There's a central emerald with several much smaller diamonds arranged around it.

'Mum, I—' I gasp, not meaning to sound as though I'm delighted, but that's how she interprets it.

'Oh, I'm *so* pleased you love it, darling. Here...' She removes the ring from the box and lifts my left hand from my lap. Then she puts the ring onto my engagement finger, forcing it hard over my knuckle. 'It fits perfectly!' she says. 'Like it was made for you.'

'Mum, I really can't—'

'Nonsense, darling. You really *can*. I'm giving it to you. It's a family heirloom.'

I sigh, trying to remove the ring, but it gets stuck. 'Mum, you gave this to Shelley when she got engaged. You can't just give it to me after everything that's happened. Anyway, I have my own ring from Owen, and I'm determined to find it.'

'What do you think, Rafe?' Mum says, turning round and ignoring my protests. 'Doesn't it look beautiful on her? I think gold suits her much better.'

'Mum!' I say. 'For God's sake, watch yourself. It's *Owen*, not Rafe.'

'Yes, yes, oh, I'm so sorry, *Owen*. Force of habit.' Sylvia taps the side of her head. 'Silly old brain is so forgetful these days.'

I sigh, getting up to head to the sink. I'm going to need soap and water to get the ring off. But first, I quickly peer over Owen's shoulder at the crossword clue he believes Mum has got wrong. I stare at it, a chill slicing through me when I see what she's put.

'The answer is "dearth",' I whisper to him, picking up the pen and filling in the missing letter. For some reason, my mother had written *death*.

'Can you *believe* it?' I rant later that morning, recounting the story about my ring to Jared as we walk along the lane. The rain has let up for a bit so we've decided to get some fresh air while we can. 'I'm so worked up I could scream!'

Jared laughs. 'Then why don't you? No one will hear you out here.'

'*You* will,' I say, scuffing the tarmac. I need to let the anger out somehow. 'You must think my family is bonkers enough without me adding to it.'

'Everyone's bonkers in their own way,' Jared replies calmly. 'If I learnt nothing else about the human race when I worked in Silicon Valley, I certainly learnt that.'

I smile across at him, wishing I could feel as composed. He walks beside me, his hands shoved deep into his black puffer jacket pockets and a dark-green beanie covering his head. The weather feels particularly autumnal today.

'When I took Owen to the station earlier, he said I should just wear the ring for now to humour Mum, then swap it over without making a fuss when we find mine. He's also convinced it's fallen down the basin waste trap. Though it turns out the handyman can't come until tomorrow.'

'I'd say Owen's advice is right,' Jared replies. 'And he's probably right about it having gone down the plughole, too.'

'Like my entire life,' I grumble. 'Worse is,' I go on, thrusting my left hand out in front of him, 'I can't get the bloody thing off!'

Jared stops walking for a moment, taking hold of my hand. 'At least it's a nice ring to have stuck on your finger.' The wink he gives me does nothing to allay the feelings fizzing up inside me.

'Ring aside, Mum is steaming ahead with *my* wedding plans! There's no way I'm getting married in Little Risewell on her terms, I should add. She's got the vicar sorting out all the legal and church stuff at top speed, and she's even sweet-talked Owen for his signature and ID documents. She pulled that little stunt behind my back when she took him to the station yesterday. But the thing that's disturbing me the most is... is that she's acting so *normal* compared to usual. That alone is making me really on edge. Like there's a massive explosion of *Mum-ness* about to erupt. But then again, this isn't normal behaviour by most people's standards, and—'

'Elizabeth Holmes,' Jared suddenly says, grabbing my arm and pulling me to a stop. 'I think you're getting more worked up than is necessary. I insist you calm yourself down immediately and allow me to accompany you back to your mother's house and dismantle the offending basin forthwith. I'm a whizz with a spanner, don't you know.' He gives me a wink.

My shoulders slump forward, and I feel as though I'm either about to burst into tears or laugh hysterically. 'Thank you,' I say, looking up at him. 'That's so kind.'

But an hour later, I'm really, *really* wishing I hadn't accepted Jared's offer of help.

SEVENTEEN

'Thanks for trying,' I say as I perch on the edge of the bath. Jared is tightening the waste trap collar after reassembling it.

'No bother,' he replies. His head is inside the wooden cupboard beneath, and his back is twisted at an awkward angle as he peers up at what he's doing. 'It needed a good clean out, anyway.'

'It's a total mystery where my ring has got to,' I say, crestfallen that it wasn't in the basin trap. I'm concerned it's been washed away down the drain completely.

I make us both a coffee after Jared has finished, and we sit at the kitchen table.

'I only came inside this house a couple of times when we were teenagers, but nothing much seems to have changed,' Jared says, glancing around.

'*Boys* were a dirty word as far as Mum was concerned,' I say with a laugh. 'She liked to keep them well away from her daughters, swearing she'd beat off any potential husbands with her broomstick.' A shudder spirals through me as an image of Rafe fills my mind. This is what I want to confide in Jared about, though I've been putting it off. In the cold light of day, telling him that I'm worried my mother had something to do with Rafe's death doesn't seem like such a good idea – not when it means admitting that I hid evidence from the police. 'Do you think you can ever really know someone?' I ask instead, skirting around what I really want to say. 'Or more to the point, do you think people are capable of doing things you'd never imagine?'

'Bad things, you mean?'

I nod.

'God, yes. Who knows what goes on in people's minds? Does this have anything to do with what we were talking about last night?'

I nod again. 'Kind of.'

While finding my mother's corsage isn't definitive proof that she had anything to do with Rafe's death, it does mean that she must have been back to the cottage at some point after we'd arrived at the church. I recall there was a window of opportunity when she went off alone before the service was due to start, perhaps telling me she needed to phone the caterers... or speak to a relative. I can't quite remember.

'The detective in charge of Rafe's case last year, DI Waters, had a hunch there was some missing information in the last hour of Rafe's life. But given the lack of evidence and the inquest being closed by the coroner, that was that. It was so hard for Shelley.' I feel my cheeks flushing at the mention of evidence. I need to change the subject.

'No wonder she's finding it so hard to move on.' Jared sips his tea, mulling over what I've just told him.

I nod, remaining silent for a moment. 'Anyway...' I sigh heavily. 'What were we talking about before?'

'The old days, and me visiting you here when we were teens,' Jared replies with a smile. 'I think the last time was the summer before you went off to university. Didn't you have a few friends over to celebrate the end of exams?'

'I did. Mum didn't know about it. She and Dad were away on holiday.'

Jared grins again. 'There was a lot of alcohol, I remember.'

'You took a gap year before uni, right?'

'I wouldn't exactly call it a gap year,' he says. 'I wanted to make it sound like I was doing something exciting with my life, but really, I just stayed in my bedroom at home with my computer. Though my parents insisted I do a few shifts at the petrol station in the next village to earn a bit of cash.'

'Jackson's. I remember that place.' I smile fondly, though it's long since closed down. 'Which uni did you go to?'

'I never made it,' Jared admits. 'When I wasn't pumping petrol, I was programming. My first business was up and running by the time I was nineteen.'

'Clever you,' I reply. Then I have an idea. 'I've got a few old photo albums up in the loft, if you fancy a laugh.'

'Oh God,' Jared says, following me upstairs to the landing. 'Are you sure this is a good idea?'

'What, crawling about in the attic, or seeing our teenage selves?'

'Both!' he says with a laugh, not even needing to stand on a chair to slide the loft hatch open because the ceiling is low and Jared is tall. He makes clambering up into the roof space look easy, using the staircase balustrade to stand on.

'Be careful,' I call up. 'There's a light switch just to the left.' I remember how Shelley and I would sometimes hide from Mum up there.

Jared's face appears at the open hatch above, looming above me. 'What am I looking for? There's a ton of stuff up here.'

'There are a few boxes labelled with my name,' I tell him. 'They're probably the nearest to the hatch as Dad only put them up there last summer.'

It had been Mum's way of clinging onto the past, of not letting go, of keeping a shred of control by keeping mine and

Shelley's bedrooms just as they had been when we were kids. But it wasn't healthy. Nothing had changed until I was well into my thirties, and even then, she was reluctant to let me sort through my stuff and pack the special bits away for safekeeping.

'Everything has slipped away from me,' she'd said forlornly as she watched me tape up the final box. 'First your sister left for veterinary school, and then you went. Things completely fell apart when your father had his breakdown and was put in *that* place. You never even came to see us in the holidays, Elizabeth. I felt so *lost*. So *alone*.'

That place, as Mum has since referred to it, was Winchcombe Lodge, which, Shelley later told me, had literally saved Dad's life. He'd been admitted to the secure wing of the psychiatric hospital just before my first term at university had ended, as the nights were drawing in and Christmas approached. I was eighteen years old and had barely been away from home ten weeks.

'Your father is in hospital, and it's all your fault, Elizabeth! It's because of *your* selfishness that this has happened,' Mum had barked down the phone at me as I'd stood shivering in the corridor of my halls of residence. My young mind had tried to form a link between Dad needing urgent care for his mental health and me studying for an English degree. But it couldn't.

'Just when he needed you, when *we* needed you, you abandoned us.'

I'd even ended up agreeing that it was all my fault just to get some peace. But I still didn't go home that Christmas, even though Mum begged and had a meltdown on the phone. This time, her *brain bad* was at a distance and I was able to hang up on her. It had made all the difference, and I suddenly understood why Dad used to take Shelley and me out on those long walks to escape. The thing was, as kids, we always had to go back.

That first term away from home, I'd saved up a bit of money

from a part-time job and used the spare cash to buy an Interrail ticket. I travelled around Europe for the four-week winter break enjoying every minute of my freedom. My first holiday season alone. If I didn't like a place, or met someone who irritated me, I simply hopped on a train and went to a different city. Running away came naturally to me. By then, it was in my DNA.

When I returned to campus, I found a stack of letters waiting in my pigeonhole – all from my mother. She was incandescent with rage that I'd been away, and not only was she blaming me for Dad's poor mental health, but she was also blaming me for having to leave her job.

'*My career has ended in the most life-shattering way because of you and your selfishness… Life as I know it has ended… Curse you, Elizabeth…*'

Even though I threw it away, the contents of that handscrawled note have stayed with me. I still struggle to understand how Mum could have blamed me for never working again. I know there was some kind of drama – probably her upsetting someone – and she'd been forced to take early retirement. Truth was, by then I didn't *want* to know about her drama, refusing to be caught up in whatever had happened. The less I knew about it all the better.

But even to this day, I still do blame myself for it. Just like she intended.

'Here, grab this box if you can.' Jared suddenly appears at the hatch, snapping me out of my thoughts. 'It's labelled "*Liz books, photos etc.*", so I think we've struck gold.'

A few moments later, the box is on the kitchen table and I'm peeling off the brown tape. It comes away easily, almost as if it's been opened and resealed again, not quite sticking properly, but that could be from its having sat in the loft for a year.

'Oh God,' Jared says with a grin when I pull out a couple of plastic-bound photograph albums. 'I'm not sure I dare look. Am I going to see evidence of my spiky mullet?'

I laugh. 'Can't be any worse than that perm I got just after A levels. Mum went ballistic. She threatened to sue the hairdresser for abuse.'

A smell wafts out of the box – a musty tang mixed with something floral-scented, but with a dark, decaying undertone. It makes me wonder if my old make-up is in here, perhaps gone mouldy. Though I'm certain that when I packed up my stuff, I'd have thrown away things like that.

'I swear there were more photos than just these couple of albums,' I say, lifting out a few school exercise books and my battered old pencil case, complete with my favourite band names scrawled in Sharpie marker on the side.

Then I see Jared's name encircled by a love heart with an arrow through the centre. I shove it out of sight, but it's too late – he spots it as well. We share a glance and a smile.

'It's like a time capsule in here,' I say, lifting everything out. Though I can't help wondering if someone has been though the contents. It's all jumbled up, which isn't like me. It was only last year, a short while after Rafe died, that Dad finally put the boxes up in the loft.

'What the *hell*...' I whisper under my breath, digging deeper. I glance over at Jared, but he's busy leafing through the photograph album, grinning to himself, and doesn't notice what I take out next.

Flower petals. Just a couple – dried and crisp and brown around the edges, but well-preserved. *Rose* petals, to be precise. And I know exactly what they're from. I shoved the corsage in a box the evening after Rafe died. *This* box, as it turns out. The rest of the corsage must be in here somewhere, too.

I push my hand deeper inside, working my fingers under more clothes. 'Oww!' I cry, whipping out my hand. A bead of blood oozes from the tip of my forefinger.

Jared glances up. 'You OK?'

I nod, hurriedly pulling out more items.

'Oh my God,' he goes on. 'Take a gander at this photo. It's Gavin and me, look, in your back garden. Those huge shorts make my legs look like spaghetti.'

But I don't look. Instead, I'm staring down into the now empty box, focusing on the pearl-topped silver pin lying at the bottom. And there's no sign of the rest of the corsage it was once attached to.

'Liz, you've gotta see these photos,' Jared goes on.

I lift out the pin and stare at it. Then I quickly tuck it inside my handbag, not wanting to have to explain what it is or why it's in this box. I turn to look at the photo Jared is waving in front of me.

'Who's this other guy in the background?' he asks. 'Was he at your school or mine?'

'Let me see,' I say, taking the album from him, being careful not to get blood on it. I smile when I see us all standing there, grinning at the camera. 'What *were* we thinking?' I say. 'I'm clearly obsessed with Avril Lavigne, look, in my camo pants and vest top. And you look like Eminem with your baggy shorts and bandana.'

We both burst out laughing, but the sting in my finger reminds me again of what I did last year. What I should have told the police about at the time but didn't.

'So go on, who do we reckon this chap is?' Jared points at the boy standing a few feet behind Gav.

'I'm not sure,' I say, holding the photo closer. 'I do kind of remember his face, but I don't think he went to my school. Maybe he was at the grammar with you. Shelley might know...'

But I trail off at the sound of the front door opening and the jangle of car keys on the hall table. Followed by Mum's almost hysterical sobs, taking me right back to the age I was in the picture.

EIGHTEEN

'Bottoms up!' Mum says, raising her champagne glass as the three of us sit in the bridal boutique. She's wearing a pale-blue cashmere sweater with loose cream trousers, and her silvery hair is held in place behind her temples with two mother-of-pearl combs.

No one would ever guess that just over an hour ago, my mother was wailing inconsolably in the kitchen with Jared (shocked) and me (not shocked) watching on.

'Cheers,' Shelley says flatly, pulling her legs up under her on the cream velvet chaise longue, being careful not to spill her drink – orange juice, like me. Our mother is the only one drinking alcohol. The shop owner had asked Shelley, as politely as she could, to take her muddy wellington boots off at the door, which she did, but she failed to notice that her thick socks and jeans were also caked in mud from a morning at work.

'She's an eminent veterinary surgeon,' our mother had explained to the boutique owner as we arrived at the impromptu wedding dress fitting, at which only one of us wanted to be present.

'Will this take long?' Shelley had asked, rolling her eyes as we were shown through to a plush lounge area where everything was either cream or white. 'Tuesdays are a busy day for me, and I've got a hundred head of cattle to vaccinate this afternoon, followed by evening clinic.'

'That all depends on our bride here,' the boutique owner, who'd already introduced herself as Pattie, said through a sparkling grin.

'Everything in this place is so... *weddingy*,' Shelley had said in a low voice, giving me a nudge. 'Just pick the first halfway decent thing,' she whispered in my ear. 'I need to get going.'

'So, Mother of the Bride,' Pattie trills in a high-pitched voice, 'if you sit over here, you'll get a fab view in all the mirrors when our bride-to-be twirls out of the changing room.'

Pattie guides our mother to a cream leather chesterfield sofa, where she sits down obediently, grinning and lapping up all the attention. 'How exciting,' she croons. 'Isn't it, girls?'

'I'll choose any old dress and then phone up to cancel later,' I whisper back to Shelley. 'Mum won't be any the wiser for a while.'

'Come on, come on, Elizabeth,' Mum says, and when I look up, Pattie is standing right in front of me with a tape measure dangling in her hand. She leads me over to a rail crammed with dozens of bridal gowns.

'What sort of thing do you have in mind?' the assistant asks.

'Pick a gown that will complement your new ring, darling,' Mum chimes in. 'Something with a classic feel.' Then her phone rings, and she makes a show of fishing it from her bag. 'Hello, yes, hello...!' she says, in a shrill voice.

Pattie sets to work, plucking some gowns off the rail in a puff of silk, lace and long, billowing skirts. 'Follow me, then,' she says, hanging up the dresses in the changing room before whipping the curtain closed.

I stare into the mirror, hearing my mother's loud voice as she talks on the phone – clearly gossiping about someone, as occasionally her tone drops lower. I strain my ears to hear when she hisses something about a man. I stand there, bristling, still wearing jeans and a sweatshirt – the first thing I'd grabbed out of a jumbled suitcase this morning before meeting with Jared for a walk. I'm reminded of the photos we were looking at, laughing our heads off at our questionable fashion choices, how easy it felt to be with him. Then I'd found the corsage pin – minus the actual corsage – and soon after that Mum had returned home in hysterics.

'Is she OK?' Jared had asked when I'd escorted her into the kitchen and sat her down. Experience told me that coddling her went some way to alleviating the drama. A kind of first aid. But then, as I made her sweet tea, I saw myself as a four-year-old, a ten-year-old, a sixteen-year-old performing the same ritual, how I'd been terrified back then that she was on the verge of death or possessed by an evil spirit.

Give it to me... I used to pray in my head. *Whatever she's got, dear God, give it to me... I'll take her pain instead...*

Because that's what it looked like on the outside. Pain. Cell-deep agony.

'Mum, what's wrong?' I'd asked in a tone that probably made Jared think I was cold and uncaring. I'm not. I've just seen it countless times before.

'It's nothing, darling,' she'd finally said, flapping her hand and looking at Jared with eyes that would melt even the toughest of souls. 'I'm sorry. And I'm so sorry to your friend, too,' she said, almost convincing me that she meant it. 'Sometimes things are sent to try us, and today is one of those days.' It was the only explanation she gave, and I knew from experience that it meant she'd not had any attention today.

And there we were, giving it to her by the bucketload.

'Maybe your mum knows who this chap is,' Jared had suggested when she'd calmed down, showing my mother the photograph of us all in the garden at the start of the Summer of Freedom, as I'd called it back then.

Before I could stop her, Mum had whipped the photo from him, studying it intently. I held my breath as I waited for her to comment on the illegal gathering I'd arranged all those years ago, but because of Jared's presence, she managed to bite her tongue.

'This boy here,' Jared said, pointing to the lad we couldn't identify. 'Any ideas?'

I doubt Jared noticed my mum's face turning pale or her fingertips blanching as they gripped the photo. But I did.

'Yes, yes, I remember him,' Sylvia said in a voice that didn't sound like hers. At first, her tone was dreamy, wistful almost, as though she was lost in a memory. Then her expression turned sour, and her top lip curled upwards. I noticed how the tendons in the backs of her hands stood proud as she fought to contain whatever was simmering inside her. She was visibly shaking.

'Did he go to the grammar school?' Jared asked, unaware of what I saw brewing inside my mother. My aim was to usher him from the house before it exploded out of her. A proper *brain bad* episode.

'Yes,' she said pointedly. 'Yes, he did.' Then she looked up, staring straight at me. 'And something terrible happened to him.'

I pull back the changing room curtain and step out of the cubicle to a flurry of *oohs* and *aahs* from Mum, who briefly covers her phone with her hand. I turn to look at myself in the full-length mirror and instantly hate the over-frilly dress.

'I can't talk now,' I hear Mum hiss into her phone again, catching sight of her in the mirror as she turns her back. 'But yes, he'll be got rid of, you can be sure of that. I'll let you know when it's done. Bye.' Then she drops her phone back in her bag again.

'Who were you talking to?' I ask as she comes up to me, fussing around and fluffing up the skirt, pulling the bodice higher.

'No one that concerns you,' she says in the tone she always uses when she wants no more questions. Then she taps the side of her nose, giving me one of her piercing looks.

Slowly, I turn back to the mirror with the words *he'll be got rid of...* playing on my mind. I stare at the dress. 'I don't think it's really me.'

'I agree, it's not the most flattering look,' Mum says, tugging at the bodice again. 'If you had a little more up top, it would suit you better.'

I close my eyes and take a breath, before disappearing into the cubicle again.

When I step out next time, Shelley takes one look at me. 'Nope,' she says. 'Awful. Haven't you got anything that doesn't look as though it's come directly from nineteen eighty-two?' she asks Pattie, which surprises me given her desperation to get out of here.

Without even looking at it, I grab the alternative dress that Pattie hands me. When I emerge from the cubicle for the third time, Shelley gets up slowly from the chaise longue and pads over to me in her mucky socks.

'Bloody hell,' she says. 'Liz, you look... you look *stunning.*'

Slowly, I turn towards the mirror, taking in my reflection. OK, so my hair is windswept and needs a good trim, and I'm not wearing any make-up, but the *dress...* Shelley's right. It *does* look stunning. Elegant without being overly fussy. I glance down at my belly, making sure there's no sign of a bump. I think I've got a few weeks to go before that happens.

I can't help the smile as I turn sideways, gazing at the strap-less, vintage-style lace bodice. It fits perfectly, flattering my shoulders, and the simple layered skirt drapes naturally to the floor.

'My, look at *you*,' Mum says softly, lifting up my left hand and holding it in front of the lace. 'See how beautiful Grandma's ring looks with it? Elizabeth, this dress is perfect. I *have* to get it for you. If you love it, that is,' she adds, surprising me by even considering my feelings.

'I do love it,' I whisper, staring at myself as I hold up my hair in a kind of messy updo. I imagine fresh flowers in my hair – daisies, perhaps. But then all I see in the mirror is me bending down and picking up the blood-red corsage lying next to Rafe's lifeless body.

I gasp, letting my hair fall as I step away from the mirror.

'She's all overcome,' I hear Mum say to Pattie. 'Do you think it needs any alterations?'

But their words float around my head as a sick feeling grows inside me.

What if this new detective, DI Lambert, wants to speak to *me* while he's reviewing Rafe's case? Being the one who discovered him, I was put through the wringer last year, making several statements down at the police station. They took DNA samples for their files – *elimination procedure*, they'd told me. *Nothing to be worried about*, they'd insisted.

And back then, I wasn't worried. I wasn't responsible for whatever had happened to Rafe. I'd been the unfortunate person who'd discovered him. It was a tragedy, of course, and I was desperately concerned for Shelley, but not worried about myself. I'd done nothing wrong.

Until later that day, when reality hit me and I became concerned that I *had* done something wrong. Taking something from the scene of an unexplained death probably *was* a crime. No, *definitely* a crime. Hiding evidence. Perverting the course of justice. Obstructing the police in their duty. Or whatever else they'd call it if I was found out. I was terrified I'd go to prison for what I did.

That's why I'd shoved it in the box heading for the loft. By then it seemed too late to confess.

But now the corsage is gone. Someone knows I took it.

NINETEEN

The first time I ran away from home I was five. I'd packed a little bag, counting out seven pairs of underpants, three vests, as many socks as I could find, plus a few skirts and tops, a spare pair of jeans and a pretty dress in case I got invited to a party at my new home. The bag was so full, it was hard to close. And even harder to carry. I said a last goodbye to all my books and toys. No room for them.

In my imagination, my new home was modern and comfortable, and my mother was a kind woman with a face that lit up when she saw me. My bedroom would have a soft pink carpet and a four-poster bed with pretty drapes that my new mummy would close around me when she kissed me goodnight.

She'd bake cakes, and she'd give me a thick slice of lemon sponge with a glass of milk when I got home from school, and she'd make spaghetti hoops for tea with apple pie for dessert. All my clothes would be clean, as would I, because she wouldn't forget to run me a bath or wash my uniform, and my new father... well, I didn't really mind if he was the same as my old one.

I crept out of the house and walked down the front path, closing the metal gate behind me. Once out on the lane, I headed towards the village shop in Little Risewell to buy some sweets on the way. I'd need food for my journey, after all.

The shop lady, who knew me, smiled at me from behind the counter as she gave me my change.

'Off on an adventure, are you, Elizabeth?' she asked. I saw her eyes flick out of the window to see if my mother was waiting for me.

I'd just nodded, not wanting her to snitch on me. I pocketed my chocolate bar and Polo mints and headed off before she could say anything and continued my journey along the road. The lane suddenly seemed big and wide and scary. I trudged past the primary school where I'd been going for a few weeks now, and finally came upon the sign indicating our village.

'Bye-bye, Little Risewell,' I told it. 'See you never again,' I added, feeling a lump in my throat. I opened my Polo mints and popped one in my mouth, hoping the lump would go away, but as I walked on, it didn't. It only got bigger, especially when I had to walk on the bumpy grass verge to keep out of the way of cars, and I kept twisting my ankle. Then it started to rain, and I remembered I hadn't brought my coat.

That was when I realised I didn't know where I was going, that I didn't have another home with another mother who didn't wail and shout and pretend to die when she was too drunk to know better. It had all been make-believe, just like me running away. Just like the stories in my books.

A car slowed down and stopped beside me.

My heart flapped so hard I thought I was going to pass out, like I'd seen happen to my mother so many times.

The man in the car made me get in. And then he took me home.

'Thank you, Doctor,' was all my mother said to him when

he presented me at the front door. Only when he'd gone did she haul me upstairs by my collar, refusing to let me out of my bedroom for three whole days. It was enough time for me to figure out that one day, I'd run away for real, that I'd never come back. Then she'd be sorry.

'*Lizzie?*' I hear a voice say, my ears still buzzing from the past. 'I said, it's good news and bad.'

'Sorry?' I turn back to Owen, giving him a smile. 'I was miles away.' Since I fetched him from the station twenty minutes ago, he's changed into his running shorts and a T-shirt. I give his hand a squeeze across the kitchen table as he munches on a protein bar.

'The invoice for the work I did in Dubai. They want me to reissue it. Apparently, there's been some kind of internal hiccup with the purchase order.'

'*What?*' My mind gallops through what that means. 'So, we'll be waiting another thirty days, then, is that what you're saying?'

'Geoff said he'd try to rush it through when he gets a moment, but dealing with this sort of thing is way below his pay grade.'

In a dramatic display, I allow my head to bang onto the kitchen table as I let out a long groan. Then I sit up, ashamed that I'm verging on Sylvia Lite.

'How's your Tuesday been?' Owen asks, chucking his protein bar wrapper in the bin. Then he stretches out his calf muscles. 'Did you have much luck with the temping agency?'

I look at him sheepishly. 'I haven't contacted them today,' I say. 'I assumed your money would be in by now. I'll call them tomorrow.' It seems this invoice is never going to get paid.

'Thanks, darling,' Owen says, giving me a hug. 'We just need a bit under our belt to tide us over. I mean, we can't impose on your mum forever, can we?'

With perfect timing, Mum walks in at that precise moment.

'Nonsense,' she trills. 'You're both welcome to stay as long as you wish. I mean, there's literally no point you moving out before the wedding now, is there? That'll virtually take us up to the end of September. Then before you know it, it'll be Christmas – a terrible time to be looking for a new place and moving. Then spring will be upon us, and we all know what that means!' Mum clutches her hands under her chin, grinning.

I stare at her, my blood running cold. Slowly, I turn to Owen, but his face remains blank, as if he doesn't know what she's talking about. Though, deep down, something tells me he does.

'By then, Elizabeth will be far too huge to be bothered with all the effort of moving and settling into a new place. You don't want to put baby at risk, do you, darling? I'll have the small bedroom decorated and we can turn it into a nursery. Everything's going to work out just great, you'll see!'

Mum's outpouring sends shivers through me as I play out the scenario in my mind – Mum taking my baby over from the moment he or she is born, dictating my daily routine, bottle-feeding when I want to give breastfeeding a good try, her strict rules imposed upon a new little life. I will not have my baby brought up anywhere near this woman. It's bad enough that we're here now. I'm concerned my unborn baby will become infected simply by being in this house.

'Baby?' I blurt out, shocked. 'I appreciate the offer, Mum, but none of that will be necessary,' I add as calmly as I can manage without actually confirming I'm pregnant. I shoot Owen a look, praying he backs me up.

'Don't be like that, Elizabeth,' Mum says, giving Owen a conspiratorial glance, and it takes all my strength not to rise to her bait, to start a showdown. I have no idea how she found out I'm expecting, but I'm not about to admit it. Anyway, a part of me doesn't *want* to know how she found out, because there's only one person who could have told her.

'I'm so, *so* sorry,' Owen says ten minutes later once we're alone. I've stalked him to the front door as he laces up his running shoes.

'What the *hell*, Owen?' I spit at him in a low voice, my hands on my hips as I loom over him. I hear Mum singing in the kitchen, sounding as if all her Christmases and birthdays have come at once. 'We agreed we wouldn't tell anyone about the baby yet.'

Least of all my mother.

'I *didn't* tell her... not in so many words,' he whispers, standing up. He grabs an ankle and hoists it behind his thigh, stretching out his quad muscles. 'She sort of tricked me,' he adds in a low hiss.

Finally, I think. *He's getting the measure of her.*

'What? *When?*'

'When I was at work in the middle of a bloody meeting with Geoff. My phone rang and her name came up. Naturally, I thought something had happened to you, so I excused myself from the boardroom to take the call.'

I sigh, imagining the scenario. I can't blame him for answering – I'd have done the same, though I have no idea how she got Owen's number. She must have prised it out of him when she asked for his ID documents. 'What did she want?'

'She told me...' he hesitates, checking down the hallway to make sure we're still alone. 'She told me that she was worried about you, that you didn't seem yourself, and asked if everything was OK.'

'For God's sake,' I say, leaning on the staircase balustrade. 'And you told her I was pregnant based on that?'

'No!' he retorts. 'I told her you were fine, that you were a bit stressed, what with trying to find a flat and everything, but otherwise you were fit and healthy.'

'There's no way she deduced I'm pregnant just from that. What else happened?'

Owen sighs. 'She found the pregnancy and childbirth book I bought for you. She asked me outright if you were expecting, and I couldn't lie.'

'Yes, you could have!' I spit back, instantly regretting my harsh tone. 'Jesus,' I say, sitting down on the bottom stair. 'But hang on... that book is packed up with all our stuff. It's in one of the sealed boxes you brought back from Peter's.'

Owen looks down at me, nodding.

'So she went through our things?' I ask, stating the obvious.

'Seems like it. But don't be cross with her. She was probably just rearranging and tidying our bedroom and—'

'And what? My pregnancy book happened to fall out of a sealed carton?' I shake my head. 'I want to go ho— I want to leave, Owen. I don't care where we go, but I *have* to get out of this place. Mum dragged Shell and me to a bridal boutique earlier and it virtually killed my sister, being in there. She's a thoughtless old—'

'Dinner in half an hour!' Mum calls out from the kitchen.

I silence myself as Owen crouches down and takes both my hands in his. 'Did you find a beautiful dress?' he asks, smiling.

I know he's only trying to cheer me up.

'As it happens, I did, yes.' I can't help the smile. 'Mum insisted on paying for it.'

'There you go, then,' Owen says. 'A productive day, after all. And listen, your mum's going to find out about our baby soon enough, anyway. What do a few weeks matter? Before you know it, the money will have come in, we'll be married and settled into our new place in London. And your mother will be at arm's length again.'

I nod. He's right, and I need to wind my neck in. After all, without Mum's hospitality right now, we'd be homeless. 'I know how much you want a church wedding here in the village...'

'I do,' he says solemnly. 'But I'd marry you anywhere, darling. Whatever makes you happy.'

'In that case, you may kiss the bride,' I tell him, the sadness in his voice preventing me from admitting that I really want to wait until we're back in London to get married.

While Owen is out running, I take the chance to have a quick lie-down before we eat. When I go into my old bedroom, sure enough I see my pregnancy book sitting on top of a moving box. Owen had to pack everything up in such a hurry, the box is bulging. No wonder it had burst open. The book must have been right at the top for Mum to have seen it. I'm now wishing Owen had managed to find room up in the loft for all our stuff.

Then I'm reminded of Peter, how we took over his flat for so long, hoping he's OK after what he told Owen. It's not like him not to contact me, so I grab my phone and open WhatsApp, typing out a quick message. Despite saying he wanted some space, at least he'll know that I'm thinking about him, that I've not abandoned him in his time of need.

'Pete, just to say I'm here if you need me and...'

But I stop. In our message thread above the text box are the words *'You blocked this contact. Tap to unblock.'*

'What the *hell?*'

Never in a million years would I have done that to Peter. My hand shakes as I check the list of numbers I've blocked in the past – mostly spam calls or messages, and a couple of guys I dated ages ago who refused to take no for an answer.

'Oh *Peter*,' I say, seeing his name on the list. I immediately unblock him and go back to WhatsApp to complete my message before sending it. I wait for the two grey ticks to make certain he receives it, but for ages there's only one tick, showing me the message hasn't gone through. 'Odd,' I say, going over to the window to get better reception in case the Wi-Fi isn't working, though that doesn't seem to be the problem. And there's a decent 4G signal here too.

And then I notice that Peter's profile photo has completely disappeared, replaced with a grey head icon, which means only one thing: that he's blocked me too.

TWENTY

'I was thinking right about here for the marquee,' Mum says after we've eaten dinner. She strides across the lawn, spreading her arms wide and drawing a huge imaginary circle. 'We'll get the evening sun, which can be absolutely glorious in September.'

'Sounds perfect,' Owen says, standing next to her. He doesn't notice when I tug on his arm, trying to warn him off getting too embroiled in her plans. There's a balance between making her believe we're going along with her, and not getting too invested.

'I'll have Preston mark out the spot with some wooden stakes. The events company people are coming out in the morning to talk about catering. There'll be a separate tent for cook—'

'But Mum,' I say, 'won't they be booked up months ahead? I think we also need to consider the possibility of a wedding next spring. I don't want you wasting your money with all this planning.'

'You underestimate me, darling,' she says, winding a wiry but strong arm around my back. Then she does the same to

Owen the other side of her, so we're joined in a line. 'Reverend Booth put me in touch with the bride who cancelled her service, and she gave me the details of all the companies she was using. Naturally, they had her slots to fill and were more than happy to give me a good rate. Money isn't an issue. There are florists, musicians, a chauffeur, even the cake... it's all worked out perfectly!'

Never in my wildest dreams would I have imagined, four days ago, that I'd be standing on the lawn at my childhood home with my mother arranging my wedding, now less than two weeks away. And neither would I have ever imagined that Peter would have blocked my number.

'I just don't understand how it happened,' I'd said to Owen as we were clearing up from dinner. Mum had gone upstairs to the bathroom. 'I'd never cut him off like that. We've been through so much together.'

'It's definitely odd,' Owen replies, drying up a plate. 'If he saw you'd blocked him, perhaps he did it in return?'

'The whole point is, I *didn't* block him. Though...' I stop, a shiver running down my spine. 'Oh my God, *Mum*,' I whisper, remembering how she'd borrowed my phone before we left for the restaurant on Saturday night. 'Her phone had run out of battery, so I lent her mine, remember?' I say. 'She was using it while I went upstairs to grab my jacket. *She* must have done it.'

'Really?' Owen had replied, incredulous. 'Why on earth would she do that?'

I was about to explain how Mum had never liked Peter – for no good reason, of course – but fell silent as I heard her coming back downstairs from the bathroom.

'Shelley will be your maid of honour, Elizabeth,' Mum announces as we head off down the lane from the house. She wants to visit the church to work out where the flower arrangements will go, as well as orchestrating a brief rehearsal of who will stand where on *the happy day* as she's taken to calling it.

Thankfully, it's only a short walk through the village. I'm feeling tired and want nothing more than to put my feet up.

'I'll get my sewing machine out tomorrow and alter her wedding dress to make it more flattering and less *bridey* for her to wear. I never much liked it, anyway.'

'Mum!' I say, shocked she's even considering such a thing. Owen squeezes my fingers by way of warning, which I don't heed. 'You can't alter her dress! There's no way she'll want to wear it to my wedding. If I'm honest, we shouldn't be having this ceremony in the first place. It feels too much like rubbing Shelley's nose in it. I'd got a quiet registry office do in mind until—'

'Your sister is tougher than you think,' Mum says with authority. 'She's not going to dissolve in a puddle of grief. Look how happy she was for you at the bridal shop earlier. Besides, you can't be unmarried and pregnant.'

I bite my tongue as we walk up the churchyard path, grateful that Owen is present. Without him here, I'm not sure I could be held responsible for my actions. Yew trees line the entryway and ancient graves lie beyond, some of them hundreds of years old with their lichen-covered headstones. Mum turns the old iron latch of the arched oak door of the church, and we go inside.

'It's beautiful,' Owen says, his voice echoing as he gazes around. He pulls me closer, and I can almost feel the excitement dripping off him.

I can't deny that he's right. There's an air of stillness and calm in the cool, quiet church. Something safe about being in here that soothes my mind. All the history and memorable occasions stitched into the fabric of the old building – the weddings, christenings, even funeral services all contributing to the feel of the place, the coming together of a community. I'm not a particularly religious person but being here makes me want to believe that someone is watching over us.

But before we even get a chance to look around properly, a voice speaks out from behind the altar, making me jump.

'Good evening,' the vicar says, and my mother strides down the aisle to where he's attending to some hymn books. 'I'm so glad you came, Mrs Holmes.' He flashes a look to where Owen and I are standing.

'We'd better go and say hi,' I say to Owen. Reverend Booth is a kind man and well loved by his congregation. He was a regular fixture in my childhood, running the Sunday school that Shelley and I attended each week.

'Elizabeth,' the vicar says warmly, taking both my hands in his. 'It's so good to see you again.'

'This is Owen, my fiancé,' I say, grinning. 'We're both so grateful to you for accommodating us so quickly. I know it's all a bit sudden.' I hear my words floating around me, but they don't sound like mine; they don't reflect what I'm really thinking – that I have absolutely no intention of getting married in this church in eleven days' time. The only reason I'm seemingly going along with it all is to make life slightly more tolerable while we have to stay with Mum.

Owen and the vicar shake hands and exchange a few pleasantries, while I stand in a kind of bubble as though the world has gone soft around the edges. Nothing feels real.

'Will your parents have far to travel for the special day?' Reverend Booth asks Owen.

'Sadly, they won't be coming,' Owen says with a calmness that I admire. It can't be easy telling people. 'I'm afraid my family passed away.'

Mum's gasp fills the entire church.

'No parents at the wedding, Owen?' she says, frowning as she processes what this revelation means. 'How very unfortunate.' She pauses, the skin beneath one eye twitching as she thinks. 'Family is *everything* to me,' she says, leaning in closer to him and lowering her voice. 'And I want you to know that I protect mine at all costs.' She stares at him for a moment, her lips stretched into thin lines. Then she whispers, 'I've done it before, and I'll do it again if I need to.'

Owen hesitates, his eyes wide as we exchange a look. I take a deep breath, about to say something to Mum, to rein her in and make her apologise, but Owen gets in before me.

'I understand, Sylvia,' he says, far more good-naturedly than she deserves. 'I have a couple of second cousins and their families in Northumberland, but we're not particularly close so I doubt they'd make the journey down.'

'I'm so sorry to hear all that,' the vicar says, bowing his head for a moment. 'I just want you to know that I'm very happy to be marrying you both in my church.'

I press myself closer to Owen's side – not because I'm nervous, but rather to offer some kind of protection from Mum.

'I appreciate that,' Owen says, shifting from one foot to another.

'But what of your poor parents?' Mum says, clasping her hands under her chin, her eyes seeming to turn a thunderous grey. She's not going to let this go. 'What on earth happened to them?'

'Mum, not now,' I warn, sensing an inquisition brewing.

'They died in a car accident along with my brother,' Owen tells her.

'But you must invite your remaining family members to the wedding,' she continues, deaf to my caution. 'Your side of the church will be empty otherwise, and we can't have that.'

Owen smiles awkwardly, giving a noncommittal nod.

'Anyway, I've already sent out the main invite list,' Mum directs at the vicar. 'But I can easily add more names to it. Of course, I had to do it by email at this late stage, but we've had a good number of acceptances already.'

Owen senses I'm about to flip out at this news, and is probably thinking that standing in front of the altar with the vicar present is not the best place to do it. He tugs on my arm, shaking his head slowly and mouthing *count to ten* through a smile. I pull him aside.

'*What* bloody invite list?' I hiss. 'And I'm so sorry about what she just said.' Though he doesn't know how much her words have riled me... no, *scared* me.

I've done it before, and I'll do it again if I need to...

'Try not to get too upset, love,' he replies quietly.

'It would have been nice to have a say in who comes to this fantasy wedding of ours,' I whisper, while Mum is talking to the vicar about flowers.

'If you really don't want to go ahead with it, I think you have to let her down gently,' Owen says wisely. 'And stop her blowing a load of money on arrangements. But when we *do* get married, the only person I'll be focused on is you. It doesn't matter who else is there as far as I'm concerned.'

I smile, looking back at the pretty altar with its ornate carvings and candles and autumnal flowers, imagining us standing there on our wedding day, me in my gorgeous new dress, Owen smart in his morning suit, saying our vows as we stare into each other's eyes, preparing to spend the rest of our lives together – wondering if, for Owen's sake, I could actually go through with it at the end of next week.

But then the image is shattered as, in my mind's eye, I picture my mother running down the aisle, screaming out how she won't let anyone steal her daughter away from her and stabbing Owen in the back with her big kitchen knife.

TWENTY-ONE

My mother was supposed to have died by the time I was eight. Then when I was twelve, and again a few weeks before my fifteenth birthday. The first time she got terminal cancer she arranged her own funeral, describing in detail what music she wanted at the ceremony. She'd summoned Shelley and me to her side, where she was sitting in the dining room with her sewing machine set out and swathes of black velvet in front of her.

'"The Lord is my Shepherd" will be sung first,' she'd told us, showing us a handwritten order of events. 'And then I want you to recite this poem together. One line each. You must wear these matching black dresses that I'm making for you.' There was no mention of Dad in the proceedings.

Then she insisted we listen to Chopin's funeral march, which she'd chosen for the committal, and explained how a curtain would close around her coffin and that would be the last trace we'd ever see of her.

'Except when you scatter my ashes, of course,' she'd said, describing how we must sprinkle her into the sea because that's where she felt most at peace. We'd never been to the seaside with our mother, and her affinity with the water came as news to us. As had the news of her imminent death.

I'd burst into tears when she explained how the cancer was poisoning her blood, that there was nothing any doctor could do to save her. A week later, when Dad arrived home with a brand-new Jaguar for her to drive, she announced that she was cured. She told us it was a miracle.

My phone pings with a message as I pull up outside Shelley's cottage the morning after our church visit. Before I check it, I sit for a moment, bringing myself back to the present. Since I've been at Mum and Dad's house, so many memories have been stirred up, most of which I'd long since buried away. Bringing Owen to the place where I grew up is a strange collision of a past that I've spent years trying to forget and a future I can't wait to get started.

And in the middle lies a wedding that I don't want.

'*Discuss menus NOW!!!*' Mum's text says. I put my phone back in my bag and rest my head back, closing my eyes for a moment. I don't have the mental strength to reply just yet. Instead, I get out of the car and head up the front path, but it's not my sister I've come to see – though I do need to have a chat with her about being my maid of honour – or rather *not* being my maid of honour, given that I have no intention of getting married in Little Risewell next week.

When Owen and I left for the station half an hour ago, Mum had her sewing machine out, wasting no time in setting to work butchering the beautiful wedding gown that Shelley had worn last summer. The scene seemed chillingly familiar, and I was suddenly eight years old again, seeing her sitting there with her sewing kit, remembering her piecing together two black velvet dresses that Shelley and I were to wear to her funeral. She never did finish them. Just like she never did die.

'I managed to scrub the blood out of it,' Mum had said earlier, looking up from Shelley's gown. My mind was filled with the horror of last year when Shelley had first learnt the news about Rafe – the worst phone call I'd ever had to make. She'd come rushing back from the church to find him lying on the floor of their kitchen. As we waited for the emergency services to arrive, she'd dropped to her knees, cradling his head on her lap, blood and tears all over her white gown. I'd had to step outside for some air, unable to watch her pain.

'The stain is hardly visible at all now,' Mum had continued, popping a pin between her lips as she hacked at the lacy layers with her fabric shears.

I turned to go, already sensing Owen's shock at the mention of blood on the wedding dress, ushering him out to the car to take him to the station. He'd promised me that today would be the last day at the London office for a while. And he also promised that he'd kick up a stink about the unpaid invoice.

'Coffee?' Jared says now once I'm inside Shelley's cottage.

'Do you need to ask?' I like how our friendship has fallen back into the easy companionship we had as teenagers – minus the awkward kisses, of course. Jared is a rare breed who somehow manages to make me feel safe and at ease. Never have I needed that kind of company more than I do now.

My phone pings again.

Jared raises his eyebrows as he hands me a mug of coffee. 'Do you need to check that?'

'It'll just be Mum harping on about menus again. Honestly, I'm running out of steam with her and this bloody wedding. And it's only been a few days.'

My phone pings again.

'She's persistent, I'll give her that,' he grins. 'Anyway, I've got some news. I did a bit of digging.'

Another ping from my handbag.

'Sounds intriguing,' I say as yet another message comes in.

'For heaven's sake,' I mutter. 'I'd better check she's not got some medical emergency or other disaster,' I add, wondering if I'd even believe her if she had.

But when I take my phone from my bag, I see the last few messages aren't from Mum at all.

They're from Peter.

'Oh, heavens,' I say, not expecting that.

'All OK?'

'Not sure yet,' I say, opening the WhatsApp messages. Peter must have seen that I'd unblocked him, and then unblocked me in return.

'*I don't get it, Lizzie. Why shut me out?*' reads his first message.

Followed by, '*I was hoping to see you before you left.*'

And finally, '*Just return the money and I'll say no more.*'

'What the *hell?*' I stare at my phone, wondering if it's a joke.

'Trouble?'

'Yes! No! I... I don't know. I'm completely baffled.'

'I'm a good listener if you need to vent.'

So as succinctly as I can, I explain about Peter, that we'd met at university, how Owen and I had been staying with him for the last few weeks, and how Peter had asked us to move out, hence us being stuck at Mum's now.

'But I literally have no idea what money he's talking about.' I shake my head, racking my brains. 'Maybe it's a veiled hint that we should have paid him more rent,' I say, mulling over every possible explanation. 'Or maybe he's mislaid some cash and assumed the worst, though he surely knows I'd never steal from him in a million years. I just don't know.'

'Text messages are frustrating,' Jared says. 'Call him. Ask him. Easy, right?'

'Yes, yes, I will. But later. I need to think what to say first.' I tuck my phone away, not wanting to foist my drama onto Jared any more than I already have, whining on about my wedding, my mother, my homelessness. 'It's probably nothing. Or a misunderstanding,' I add, knowing it won't be either of those things. Peter is straight down the line and has always valued our friendship. He wouldn't accuse me of anything if he wasn't one hundred per cent certain of the facts – and that's what's making my stomach knot. 'Anyway, you said you had news?'

'Ah yes, I did some digging.' Jared's eyes sparkle as he reaches over to a stack of papers on the kitchen counter, plucking a photograph from the top. 'Hope you don't mind, I borrowed this,' he says, holding out the picture we'd found in my box of belongings from the loft. He must have taken it without me noticing, when I was preoccupied with Mum's mini meltdown. 'I figured that since I'm moving back into the area, it'd be nice to catch up with a few people from the past. Facebook was my friend,' he says. 'I managed to find Gavin, my mate in the photo. He still lives locally with his wife and kids.'

'I don't mind at all,' I say, taking the picture from him, pleased he's building a new life for himself in the area. I can't help the smile when I see the picture again. Normally, I'd take a photo of it and send it to Peter, who'd be in hysterics to see me wearing those clothes, my hair like that, but... now, for some reason, things have changed. And I don't know why. 'I'm really pleased you're back in touch with Gav.'

'We had a drink last night in the pub,' Jared says. 'It was good to see him. I showed him this photo and he remembered who the other boy was.' He taps the picture. 'It's Danny Wentworth.'

'Ah, yes – *Danny*! I remember now.'

'And you know how your mum said she thought something terrible had happened to him?'

I nod slowly, tensing up.

'Well, Gavin confirmed it. Apparently, Danny died.'

'Oh my God, that's *awful*. What happened?' I take the

photo and place it on the table between us, staring at Danny's grinning face.

Jared shrugs. 'Gav wasn't sure of the exact details, though he seemed to remember it was all kept hush-hush by the family and the funeral was a private affair. It seems poor Danny passed away the summer after our A levels. It can't have been long after this photo was taken.'

'How tragic.' I stare at Danny's face again. 'He looks so happy here. Wasn't he really clever and hoping to get into medical school?'

'Yes, that's the guy,' Jared says. 'Gavin told me that he had a younger brother, too, though I don't remember him.'

'Me neither,' I say, casting my mind back. I pick up the photo again and touch Danny's face. 'It's hard to believe he's dead.'

'It is indeed. Gav did mention one other thing, though,' Jared says, staring right at me. 'He'd heard rumours that Danny died just before some scandal at the grammar school. Something to do with a teacher who worked there. I vaguely remember it myself since Gav mentioned it. He thought the two events were linked.'

'A *teacher*?' I ask, my voice suddenly weak as my blood runs cold.

TWENTY-TWO

Jared drives carefully along the narrow lanes as we head back to the house that he's interested in buying for a second viewing. I'm happy to tag along with him, and it'll take my mind off everything else that's currently racing through it – Peter's strange messages, my mother and her unstoppable wedding plans, and now the news about poor Danny. Mum has already admitted to knowing 'something terrible' had happened to him, but I can't help wondering what else she knows, and if she had anything to do with the scandal Jared mentioned.

'It was a stroke of luck when Gav told me that he's a builder,' Jared says as he parks on the property's drive. 'I showed him the sales details and we talked over renovations. I can't lie, I rather like the old place, but it needs a lot of work. It's the beautiful views that sealed it, rather than the caved-in roof.'

I agree with Jared about the views and, as I get out of the car, I see that Gavin's white van is already here.

'Gav, mate, thanks for coming,' Jared says as we greet him at the door. 'I feel another session at the pub is on the cards by way of thanks.'

The men pat each other on the backs in a semi-hug, and the

pair couldn't look more contrasting – Jared, tall and skinny, dressed entirely in black with his LA Angels baseball cap, and Gavin, much shorter and stockier, wearing heavy-duty combats covered in cement dust, a torn T-shirt and work boots.

'Hi, Gavin,' I say, shaking his hand. If I didn't know who he was, I'd never have recognised him. But then, he was at the grammar school, not the comprehensive, and Mum didn't really allow me to hang out at the park to socialise after school. She didn't make it easy for me to have any friends at all.

'Lizzie Holmes, my God,' Gavin says with a sturdy hand-shake in return. 'You've not changed one bit!'

'You remember me, then?' I say with a laugh, suddenly wanting to question him on everything he recalls about me. Was I shy, happy, sad, angry? But I keep quiet, just as I had back then. Having other people know what life was like behind closed doors would have made it seem all the more real.

''Course I do, *'course* I do!' Gavin says. 'Frank's lass,' he says, shifting from one foot to the other. He has an enthusiastic air about him, with crooked teeth and ruddy round cheeks that look as though they've seen a lot of fresh air as well as many pints of beer.

I smile, thinking it's better than being called *Sylvia's girl*.

'I heard that your dad's not been well lately,' Gav goes on. 'Sorry to hear. My mum gets all the news from your mum. They used to be in the WI together back in the day, I think,' he says, spraying out a laugh. 'Jumble sales and cake stalls. Good stuff!'

'Yes, growing up in Little Risewell was all a bit jam and Jerusalem,' I reply, echoing his laugh. 'How is your mum?'

'Struggling on, but not too well since Dad died. She still lives in the same house, and Lynda visits her most mornings, makes sure she's up and washed and gets a meal.'

'Lynda?'

'My wife,' Gav says with a twinkle in his eye. 'A right gem, she is. I think Mum's heading for a care home soon, though,' he adds. 'She's getting quite forgetful now.'

'I'm so sorry,' I reply, following the two men into the house, after the agent has opened it up. I mind where I tread on the old, rotten floorboards, brushing a few cobwebs off my face from the doorway. Conversation then turns to Jared's plans for an extension to enlarge the kitchen, taking advantage of the countryside views, and I'm about to offer up my thoughts when I feel my phone vibrating in my bag.

I step outside the back door and find myself on a weed-covered terrace overlooking fields and rolling hills. When I glance at the screen, I have second thoughts about answering, but whatever misunderstanding there's been, it needs to get sorted out.

I take a deep breath.

'Hi... Peter,' I say, walking further away from the house. 'How are you?'

'Lizzie,' comes the familiar voice down the line, though his tone is cool. 'I'm fine, thanks.'

'I... I honestly don't know what happened with my phone,' I begin to explain. 'It must have been a glitch or something, because I never blocked you and—'

'When I saw what you'd done, I blocked you back,' he retorts, confirming my suspicions.

'Whatever it is that's upset you, Pete, I'm *so* sorry.'

'It's not me you upset, for God's sake, Lizzie,' he continues, 'though by default, you have.'

'I literally have no idea what you're talking about. You said something about some money? I know Owen and I should have contributed more to living costs and honestly, it was my full intention to give you some extra cash just as soon as Owen got paid. But then us having to leave happened in such a hurry and—'

'Convenient timing, don't you think? A bit obvious of you –
leaving just after you stole the cash.'

'*What*?' I turn back towards the house and see Jared and
Gavin coming out, so I walk further down the garden. 'I did not
steal any money, Pete. What the hell are you talking about?'

'Mrs Baxter's money. You know exactly what I'm referring
to. Hundreds of pounds. Seriously, Elizabeth, I know you're
struggling a bit financially right now, but taking from an old
lady is beyond low.'

My heart sinks when I hear his words, but I also feel relief. I
can fix this because I know I didn't do it. 'Oh my God, I did *not*
take Mrs Baxter's money, Pete. Surely you of all people know
I'd never do that to anyone, let alone a vulnerable old woman.'

There's an unnerving silence on the line for a few moments,
as if Peter knows what I'm saying is correct, yet he has some
kind of evidence to prove otherwise.

'But you were in Mrs B's flat the other day, weren't you?'

'Yes, and—'

'And did you see she had a pile of cash on the kitchen
counter?'

'Yes, I did! But—'

'And you told her she ought to get it in the bank before it got
stolen, didn't you? Yet you were the one to take it.'

'Yes, that's exactly what happened, apart from the bit about
me stealing it. I even said that Owen and I would take her to the
bank so she could deposit it. But she insisted it was fine and put
it in the tea caddy. She called it the Bank of Betty, for heaven's
sake.'

'There you go. You even admit to knowing where she hid it.'

'I'm sorry, Pete, but I'm not listening to this. You know
better than anyone that I'd never steal. I'm insulted you're even
thinking this way.'

Another silence. Then a sigh. 'Lizzie, I want to believe you,
I really do, but...'

For a moment, I hear the old Peter – the Peter who I know inside out, and who knows me in the same way, the man who's held my hair back many times in my life, metaphorically speaking as well as literally after our drunken nights out at uni.

'Then believe me, for Christ's sake, Pete. Someone else must have taken it because it sure as hell wasn't me. Do you want me to speak to Mrs Baxter and see if I can jog her memory?'

'I'm afraid that's not possible,' he says, sounding cold and solemn again.

'Why? It would clear this up and—'

'You can't speak to her, Lizzie, because she's dead.'

TWENTY-THREE

After we left the house viewing, I declined the offer of a pub lunch with Jared and Gavin, not feeling in the mood for socialising after my call with Peter.

Mrs Baxter. Dead. And she died believing that *I'd* stolen her money.

'In that case, why don't you and your fiancé join us for a game of pool at the Bull tonight?' Gavin had suggested. 'I'd love you to meet Lynda.'

I thought about it for a moment, deciding it would be a good chance to introduce Owen to Gavin and his wife, as well as an opportunity to get out of the house for a few hours. So I told him we'd be there.

Before we'd driven off, Jared made an offer on the house, and the estate agent promised to get back to him later with a response from the owner. I left them to discuss the details and wandered back to Jared's car to wait. By then, my thoughts were all over the place, going over and over what Peter had told me.

'I let myself into Mrs Baxter's flat with the spare key,' he'd said on the phone. 'I hadn't seen her for a couple of days and was worried. And that's when I found her in bed, dead.'

As the call with Peter drew to a close, with him sounding slightly less accusatory about me taking the money, though still uncertain about what had happened, I only just remembered to ask him about the other news he'd received, the reason Owen and I had to move out of his flat in the first place. I braced myself for more bad news.

'Oh *that*,' Peter replied. 'Jacko and I are planning on moving in together. Things between us have been going really well. We're taking the next step.'

'Right,' I'd said, not quite understanding. From what Owen had said, I'd been expecting something terrible – an illness or another death, or that he'd lost his job.

'I've even introduced Jacko to my mum, so it must be serious.' He'd managed a laugh then, seeming to forget he was cross with me, but again, I was confused.

'Did your mum come and stay with you, then?' I ask, remembering Owen said that Peter had family coming.

'Heavens, no,' Peter said. 'We went to Hastings for the day and called in at hers for lunch. She was happy about our big announcement.'

'I see,' I said, trying to work it out in my mind. Maybe Peter wanted to move Jacko into his flat right away, which would explain why he'd wanted us out. But it suddenly didn't sound as urgent as we'd been led to believe. I was about to ask, but Peter changed the subject back to the missing money again, grilling me about the evening I was in Mrs Baxter's flat.

'Look, I can't return the money if I didn't take it in the first place, can I?' I finally snapped.

After we hung up with a terse goodbye, I felt guilty for being so short, but also furious with him for thinking I'd steal from an old lady. I can only assume his accusation was based on what Mrs Baxter told him before she died. But then, I can hardly blame her, knowing how muddled she used to get.

But now that I've cooled down a bit, I figure I'll leave it a few days and send Peter a message. Perhaps by then whoever *did* take the money will have either owned up or been found out.

Back in my car after Jared dropped me off, I drive to Winchcombe Lodge to pay Dad a visit. If nothing else, being with him while I'm in the area is time well spent – even if it does mean another one-sided conversation.

'He's resting in his room,' one of the nurses tells me as I sign in, pointing me in the direction of room twelve. I head down the carpeted corridor, passing several more nurses accompanying patients of varying ages.

I think back to the first time Dad was admitted – the phone call from a panic-stricken Shelley sticking in my mind. She'd been away from home doing a vet placement, and I'd not long left for university. My first taste of freedom interrupted.

'Dad's been sectioned!' she'd screamed down the line, as though I might know what to do. At the time, I had no idea what being sectioned even meant – let alone anything about the secure unit at Winchcombe or what this all meant for my family – and while I felt desperately sorry for my father, returning to Little Risewell would have also meant returning to my mother – the person I'd finally managed to escape. I'm ashamed to say that my eighteen-year-old self left Shelley to cope alone.

I knock on the door to Dad's room and, when there's no reply, I go in.

'Hi, Dad.'

My father is sitting in an armchair staring out of the French doors that lead on to a little terraced area with pots of flowers. It's a pleasant view, and his room is comfortable enough with its single bed, veneer wardrobe and TV mounted on the wall, but it's still not any kind of a proper home for him. All I want is for him to get better, but then my concern would be that returning to Medvale would only set him back again.

'How are you today?'

I look at his hunched shoulders, his gaunt face, and suddenly I'm overcome with guilt, wishing I'd come back to help him all those years ago. According to the almost daily updates I received from Shelley back then, various types of medication were tried, but nothing seemed to help. Nothing changed my father's low mood or behaviour, and the doctors never gave us a reason for what they described as an 'emotional breakdown', with Dad 'presenting as a danger to himself as well as others', which I found hard to believe. It was only the passing of time that brought him back to us, as though he'd plugged himself back into life and, finally, the doctors were happy to release him. And now here he is again, back in hospital soon after Rafe died, detached from life once more.

Dad stares out at the beautiful grounds, seemingly oblivious to my presence.

I pull back the net curtains and turn the lock on the door, opening it wide for some fresh air. A strong breeze floods the room, billowing one of the curtains right up over me. For a moment, I stand there with the white lacy fabric covering my head and face, imagining myself at the altar of St Michael's church with Owen standing beside me, and Reverend Booth joining our hands as he prepares to marry us.

Then the curtain is gone – but it's not the wind that's blown it off me. It's Dad, his hand reaching up and whipping it away.

'Dad!' I say, delighted that he's reacted to something. 'What do you want to do today? We could go for another walk if you like. It's nice outside. I can tell you all about my morning.'

Dad nods, so I fetch his shoes and lace them up – tearing up when I remember him doing the same for me many years ago – then I get him into his coat and tell one of the staff we're going out. This time, instead of heading to the river, we amble down the driveway of Winchcombe Lodge towards the lane.

'It feels like we're making a run for it,' I joke, linking my arm through his. We're not exactly walking fast, but his pace seems sprightlier than when I saw him three days ago. 'If we could go anywhere, say hop on a train, where would you go?'

I glance across at Dad as we reach the end of the drive, not expecting him to answer and, indeed, he doesn't. His gaze is fixed firmly ahead, neither taking in nor ignoring the stunning countryside views as we continue our walk along the lane.

He just *is*. This is Dad existing. One breath in. One breath out. And repeat.

'I'd go to the north-east coast,' I tell him, thinking I could meet Owen's remaining family. 'Bamburgh Castle. It always seems so romantic, those moody skies and windswept beaches. Or maybe the Dorset seaside. We could go fossil hunting, like you and I used to do in the garden when you were transplanting your cabbage plants in the spring. I found all sorts of treasures. Do you want to come with me to Dorset?'

No amount of fantasy travel is going to lure Dad to talk.

'Remember when Mum pulled out all your lettuces, thinking they were weeds?' I laugh at the memory, feeling Dad's arm stiffen against mine. 'She swore she didn't know what they were.' I shake my head, feeling bad for bringing up that particular memory, so I change the subject. 'I found a beautiful wedding dress,' I tell him. 'It's got this amazing lace on—'

'Lizzie, *stop*,' Dad suddenly says, pulling on my arm and spinning me round, his voice as clear as glass, his face close. 'You need to leave. You need to get as far away from here as possible and don't ever come back. Do you hear me? I'm serious, Elizabeth. Just get away from here and go. *Now*.'

TWENTY-FOUR

I lurch to a stop, my feet refusing to move.

Dad stares at me through wide eyes, and I feel the warmth of his breath on my cheek.

'*Dad?*'

'Elizabeth,' he says solemnly.

'Oh my God... you... you just *spoke.*'

'You need to listen to me.' He shakes his head, his whole demeanour suddenly changing – as though a fire is igniting inside him. I see it in his eyes – a spark of the father I once knew. A strong, competent man who had a successful career, a man who devoted himself to protecting Shelley and me with his life – literally, sometimes. Once, when Mum was cooking dinner, he'd had to defend us against the pots, pans and cutlery she was hurling about. He'd ushered us out, getting us safely upstairs. I was only ten and Shelley was in her teens. Later that evening, he'd brought a tray of soup and toast upstairs to us.

'Brain bad,' he'd confirmed calmly with a nod. 'Not a good day at work for your mother.' He'd sat with us as we ate, helping Shelley with her maths homework while I got ready for bed. Later, as I'd tried to sleep, I heard our parents arguing downstairs, Dad's final comment before he went to bed ringing in my ears.

'For God's sake, Sylvia, if you detest your job that much then just leave!'

I'd spent the rest of the night worrying about what would happen if Mum gave up work – if we'd be poor and forced to move house, or not have enough money for food. Back then, I hadn't realised just how senior Dad's job at the bank was or, indeed, how much money he earned. Of course, it's that same money that's paying for his stay at Winchcombe Lodge now, though this time his admission is as a private patient, whereas his first hospital stay was enforced, paid for by the health service.

Dad stands with his feet apart, planting his hands on my shoulders with that same look of kind determination on his face that I remember so well from childhood.

'Dad... I...' I can't stop staring at him. 'I mean, are you OK? Should I call the hospital? Get someone?'

He shakes his head. 'No, Lizzie. Who would you call anyway? Some useless doctor who knows nothing? A nurse who treats me like a five-year-old?' He breathes in deeply and huffs it out in a doleful sigh, striding over to a nearby gateway. He leans on the wooden bar, one foot on a rung, staring out across the fields.

'It was never meant to turn out this way, you know,' he says, beckoning me over. I stare at him in bemusement. 'Ever since I was a young man, I'd always dreamt of having a family, being a good husband and father, keeping us all safe and happy. I feel like I've failed.'

'Oh, Dad,' I say, moving to slide my arm around him. 'You *are* a good Dad. You haven't failed at anything.'

He makes a strange noise in the back of his throat. 'See that farm down there in the valley?' he says, pointing into the distance. 'These days, it's eight hundred acres of prime Cotswold pasture and arable land. Worth an absolute fortune.'

'Dad, wait, stop,' I say, confused. 'Can we just back up a little bit, please? You're... you're talking like nothing's happened. You... you sound... *fine*. I don't understand.' I try to turn him around to face me, but he shrugs me off, still staring out across the fields. '*Are* you fine?'

'Of course I'm bloody fine,' he says gruffly, making me take a step back. 'There's nothing wrong with me, and there never has been, either. Not with *me*, anyway.'

I frown, trying to take in what he's saying, trying to believe what my own eyes and ears are telling me: that the man who's been in a psychiatric hospital for the best part of a year is acting as though nothing has happened. 'Do you want me to call Shelley?' I ask, thinking that she'll know what to do. She's always been good in a crisis, the one to stitch our parents' relationship back together time and time again. 'Or... or do you want me to phone Mum?'

I scrabble for my phone, knowing I need to call *someone*, but Dad grabs my wrist.

'It'll be over my dead body if you tell your mother. She knows nothing about this,' he says as a grain lorry thunders past on the lane, its metal container clanking and groaning, making the earth tremble. '*Please*. Don't do that, Elizabeth.'

'Dad, have they put you on some new meds or something? Is that it?' I stare at him, still incredulous. 'I understand, really, I do. I'll talk to—'

'I haven't been taking my medication.' Dad suddenly looks concerned, shaking his head. 'But... but the nurses don't know this. I've got all the tablets hidden.' He sighs, blinking away the tears as he stares at the ground.

'*What?*'

'Just let me tell you about that farm.' He composes himself

and points across the fields again, a wistful look on his face. 'I nearly bought it once. A long time ago now.'

I join him beside the gate. None of this conversation seems real, and I wonder if it's me who's delusional or suffering from some kind of psychotic episode. Perhaps triggered by pregnancy or low blood sugar.

'It was nineteen-eighty, and the small, tumbledown farmhouse came up for sale.' Dad points towards a building in the distance. 'It only had a few acres of land at the time, and I imagined it being the perfect home for us – plenty of space for a family to enjoy, perhaps keep a small herd of cows. I was keen to buy it, but your mother wouldn't hear of it. She didn't see herself as a farmer's wife or want me to give up my London job. She didn't share my dream.'

He stares out across the land again, wiping a finger under his eye.

'I was ready for a change. I was still young and wanted a decent place to bring up my family. I'd done all right for myself financially, even before you and Shelley were born – *better* than all right, especially with my parents' inheritance coming in – and I often wonder how things would have played out if I hadn't listened to your mother and had bought the farm anyway.' He laughs then – a contemplative chuckle. 'I guess she liked the money I earned at the bank too much, as well as the prestige of being a director's wife. The farm had its own wood. And a river,' he adds wistfully.

'Oh, Dad...' I lean my head against his shoulder.

'She might have always had her sights set high, your mother, but you wouldn't have recognised her back then. She wasn't like she is now, you know. In the early days, we used to have fun together. We'd go out, have good times, a laugh, share private jokes. It was us against the world. A real team. Can you believe that?'

I shake my head. I really can't.

'But over the years, there was a gradual... a decline in her, I suppose. The truth is, I don't know why her personality changed so much. It was as though she lost herself and found someone else entirely to put in her place. She became bitter, resentful, controlling, and, at first, I blamed myself.' He turns to me, shaking his head. 'Though I must admit, there was something almost dangerous about her when we first met, though I chose to overlook it. It was like she had an itch inside her. A bloody great big itch of the soul. Perhaps that's what drew me to her. The excitement, the challenge. I believed I could save her from herself. And she was beautiful, you know. Turned heads everywhere we went.'

Dad smiles, that wistful look in his eyes again.

I try to take all this in, but on top of hearing my father talking as if nothing is wrong with him, it's too much to absorb. Just like that, he's turned into the man I've wanted back for so very long. And he was here the whole time.

'I did love her, you know, Lizzie. Bone-deep love. And honestly, I still do. I made my wedding vows to her, promising I would never leave her, and indeed, I've stuck by her. Even after that boy's death that awful summer. Then, with what happened shortly after that...' Dad trails off, his face crumpling into a frown. He leans on the gate again, bowing his head.

'Dad?' I say, sensing there's something else. 'What is it?'

He shakes his head.

Another grain lorry rumbles past, making a din.

When it's gone, Dad looks sideways at me. 'Just before they put me in Winchcombe for the first time – and I'm not proud of myself for this – I finally lost it with your mother. After all the years of protecting you and Shelley, after holding our family together, it all got too much. I was exhausted. Always living on a knife edge around Sylvia. Never knowing how she was going to be one minute to the next. She needed help, and I wasn't strong enough to give it to her any more. I was broken. I needed a rest.

Then, when it came out what she'd done, what they were *saying* about her...' He stops, taking a cotton handkerchief from his pocket, blowing his nose. 'It was unthinkable. A scandal. Let's just say it was the final shove that sent me over the edge. At least you and Shelley had left home and were getting on with your lives by then. It made it easier to keep the sordid details from you.'

'Dad, I have no idea what you're talking about.' I think back to my first term at university, Shelley's hysterical phone call about Dad being sectioned... me not being there to help.

Then I freeze, grabbing hold of the gate for support as my mind tries to join dots that, until a short time ago, I didn't even know existed.

Dad sighs. 'I don't want to go into it, Lizzie. It's too upsetting. And I still don't know what's true or not. All you need to know is that something bad happened and your mother had to leave her job. And I, temporarily I might add, lost my mind because of it. It was my own *brain bad*, if you like.' He stops, huffing out an ironic laugh. 'I'm not proud of it, but I finally cracked. I smashed up the house, the cars, tearing apart our lives. I'd learnt from the best, after all. I saw no point to anything after that, not if what they were saying was true.'

'What *who* were saying, Dad?'

He shakes his head, looking away. 'I can't, Lizzie. It's been too long. I don't want to talk about it. But that's why they sectioned me. They believed I was a danger to myself and to others.' Dad looks up. 'Ironic that after all those years of living with your mother, they made *me* out to be the mad one.' He laughs, kicking the gate. 'It was for the best, I suppose. Under the circumstances. Your mother had her own thinking to do.'

I stay quite still, staring out over the patchwork of green fields, not wanting to press Dad if it upsets him, but then wanting to shake the truth out of him as well.

'So, let me get this straight. Some people were saying bad

things about Mum – but you won't tell me what – and she had to leave her job because of it, and then you smashed up the house and were sectioned?'

Dad nods. 'That's about the size of it, Elizabeth, dear.' He takes my hand and gives it a squeeze.

'But I don't understand why... why you've been at Winchcombe for most of this last year if you're saying there's nothing wrong with you now?'

Dad takes me by the shoulders and stares right into my eyes. He sucks in a breath. 'Rafe's death last year triggered a lot of old feelings in me, love. It stirred up emotions I thought I'd dealt with. I was terrified that I was losing control again, that I'd take my frustrations out on other people – namely your mother. It was just safer this way, me admitting myself for a break. Think of it as me leaving your mother without *actually* leaving. She'd never have let me go otherwise.'

My mind races, trying to see things from Dad's point of view, but also through a practical lens. Both times he's been a patient at Winchcombe have been preceded by an upsetting event. And both upsetting events have a common denominator.

My mother.

But this time, no one apart from me knows that she was present at the scene of Rafe's death.

'I... I heard about a pupil at the grammar school who died a while back. A boy called Danny. Is he the one you're talking about?' I hardly dare ask.

'Yes,' Dad says matter-of-factly. 'And ever since I was admitted shortly after that, it's as though I've been in a self-imposed prison.'

'Oh, Dad—'

He puts a finger over my lips, a tear rolling from his eye. 'I tried, Elizabeth, I really did. I want you to know that. And now... what am I left with? Cooking skills class on a Monday, hourly observations by well-meaning nurses, and enough medication hidden away to fell a carthorse. I can't stay here forever, I know that, and I do want to go home. But also, I'm scared of the prospect. I feel stuck. If your mother finds out I've been lying to her...' He shudders, making a strange noise in his throat again.

I give him a hug, resting my head on his shoulder. 'Oh, *Dad*... I'll support you. I'll help you however I can.'

'I'm so very sorry,' he says, his voice choking up. 'I did my best, I want you to know that. But sometimes, even that wasn't enough.'

Then he points across the valley again.

'So, you take a good long look at that farm down there, Elizabeth, my darling. One day, when you have children of your own, you sit them on your knee and tell them stories of what it was like growing up. Make up happy tales of two fair lasses loving life on the farm. Tell them tales of how wonderful it was feeding the lambs in spring, and how you and your sister rode on a tractor trailer with your old dad bumping along at the wheel. Tell them how their grandad loved you very, very much.'

TWENTY-FIVE

'So, are you up for it?' I ask Owen as we pull onto the drive at Medvale later the same day. 'A drink with Gavin and Lynda in the Bull? Jared might be there too.' It's taking all my effort to sound enthusiastic, trying to put what happened with Dad out of my mind so I don't blurt it out.

I still can't believe it: Dad – *pretending* to be ill all this time. But what's bothering me most is the apparent coincidence between his two hospital stays and Rafe and Danny's deaths. I have no idea what else happened the summer that Danny died – this so-called scandal – but, for Dad's sake, I need to find out. Whatever it is, he's been blaming himself for it this whole time, and I can't stand the thought of him spending his older years eating himself up, his mental health deteriorating. He might claim that there's been nothing wrong with him this last year, that it was easier for him to be away from Mum by admitting himself to Winchcombe Lodge – she'd never have let him leave her without good reason – but he was the one to call it a self-imposed prison.

My *poor*, dear father.

'You know what?' Owen says in an upbeat voice, surprising me with his answer to my question. 'I'd love to meet your old friends. I'm enjoying the deep dive into your past.'

I shudder, praying he stays at surface level. I have a terrible feeling that there's a lot even *I* don't know about my past. I slide my arm around Owen's waist as we go inside the house, thankfully not encountering Mum on the way upstairs.

'I've never met Lynda,' I explain to Owen, 'and Gavin wasn't exactly a friend. More an acquaintance.' I don't want to reveal that I didn't have many friends growing up, thanks to Mum. And it doesn't seem right to mention that Jared was the closest thing to a first boyfriend that I ever had. I don't want Owen feeling uncomfortable. 'But it'll be nice to have company to hang out with. Plus, it gives me an opportunity to thrash you on the pool table.'

Owen lunges at me, grabbing me playfully before planting a kiss on my mouth. 'Not a chance,' he says. Then he goes off to shower while I rummage through our suitcases for something to wear. I pull out a pale-green floral wrap dress that doesn't seem too crumpled. It'll have to do, and I won't be able to wear it in a few weeks. I'm not showing yet, but it won't be long before a little bulge begins to restrict what clothes I can fit into.

'You look lovely,' Owen says when he comes back wearing nothing but a towel around his waist.

'Good job you didn't bump into Mum on the landing,' I say. 'You'd give her a heart attack.'

He pauses for a moment, one eyebrow rising, before letting out a brief laugh. Then he quickly towels off his hair and pulls open the wardrobe to find something for himself to put on.

Minnie saunters into our bedroom, licking her lips, having just eaten the food I put out for her, and jumps up onto the bed. She settles down to have a wash before, no doubt, taking another three-hour nap.

'What the *hell*...' Owen shrieks, yanking one of his shirts from the wardrobe. 'What in God's name has happened to this?' He holds out his favourite designer white shirt that he bought in Dubai – the one he likes to wear with his Levi's and tan brogues.

'Oh my *God*,' I say, taking the hanger from him. 'Someone has cut the sleeves off.'

'Not meaning to sound rude, Lizzie, but I can bloody well see that. The question is, who?'

We stare at each other for a moment.

'Mum,' I whisper. Not a question, more a statement of fact.

'But why?' Owen asks, a puzzled look on his face. 'I mean... I know it's just a shirt, but it was one of my favourites.'

I stare at the frayed edges where the sleeves have been hacked off just below the shoulder seam, reminded of when Mum did something similar to all my dresses. *You're nothing but a slut, Elizabeth...* still rings through my mind occasionally from when she accused me of showing off my legs in my school skirt, thinking I'd hitched up the waistband on purpose.

As punishment, she'd gone through my clothes and cut the skirts off all my dresses. *There... see how the boys stare at you now...* was what she'd said when she'd found me sobbing in front of my already scant wardrobe. I didn't dare tell her that my school skirt was so short because it was too small, that I really needed a new one but was too afraid to ask her, that I could barely fit into it any more and everyone made fun of me for still wearing the skirt I'd had at primary school. She'd never have understood.

I swipe the shirt from Owen and march downstairs, heading to the dining room where I heard my mother at her sewing machine when we came back. Still butchering Shelley's wedding dress, no doubt.

But when I go in, she's not there. What I do find, though,

are Owen's shirt sleeves cut into even smaller pieces, with sections of the white fabric pinned inside the bodice of Shelley's dress ready for sewing. It looks as though she's making the lacy neckline higher and less see-through. Apart from ruining an expensive shirt, the dress now looks hideous. I know Shelley won't be seen dead wearing it.

'Mum!' I call out, striding into the kitchen. Owen has caught up with me, now wearing jeans and a T-shirt, and we find my mother chopping onions. She looks up.

'Hello, darling,' she says, a startled smile on her face.

'What do you call this?' I spit, chucking the remains of Owen's shirt at her so it lands on the chopping board. She puts down the chef's knife and holds up the fabric, feigning ignorance.

'It... it's a shirt,' she says quietly. 'Why are you asking me?'

'It's not a bloody shirt now, is it? Why have you cut it up?'

I see familiar cogs turning inside my mother's mind. 'I... well... Owen said I could use it for the dress alterations. He heard me muttering about needing extra white material and he suggested this. He said that he didn't want it any more.'

I laugh. A proper belly laugh. 'Oh my God, Mum. You are incredible. And here's me thinking that you'd mellowed a bit.' I shake my head, staring at her in disbelief. Then I turn to my fiancé, not even needing him to answer because I know he'd never have said that. It's his favourite shirt. It cost over a hundred pounds.

Owen squirms a bit. 'Sorry, Sylvia, but I don't remember saying that to you. Do you think you might be... a bit confused?'

'See?' I snap at her. 'You're just plain thoughtless. You'll be buying him a new one.' Owen's fingers slide around mine as he takes my hand, giving me a squeeze.

'Come on, love. It was clearly a mistake. I'm sure your mum didn't mean any harm,' Owen says, sounding uncomfortable. He's never heard me shout like this before.

Mum stares at me, then drags her gaze across to Owen. 'No, I really didn't mean any harm,' she says in a cold, steady voice. Then she returns to chopping the onions, the stainless-steel chef's knife coming down onto the wooden board... *chop... chop... chop...* in a slow, deliberate action. And all the while she keeps her stare firmly fixed on my fiancé.

TWENTY-SIX

'What you need to know about my mother,' I say to Owen as we walk down to the Bull, one of two pubs in our village, 'is that she's a master manipulator. If there's a slight chance that she's not believed or can't get her own way, she'll turn on the drama.' I don't mention that I didn't like the look Mum gave Owen one bit – the same look I've witnessed many times over the years.

That's as far as I'm going in terms of explaining what she's like. If I tell him everything, he'll run a mile, wondering what kind of genetic cesspit he's marrying into.

'It looked to me as though she was confused and trying to hide her mistake because she was embarrassed,' Owen says, holding the door for me as we head inside the pub. I decide not to correct him.

'Liz, over here!' I hear a voice call out as we approach the bar. I turn and see Gavin with a pool cue in one hand and a pint of beer in the other signalling to me from the back room, where about half a dozen other customers are milling about.

The Bull is very different to the Golden Lion. While the latter boasts fine dining, fancy wines and has a month-long waiting list for a reservation, the Bull is a good old-fashioned pub with real ales on tap and pork scratchings behind the bar. Plus, they do a fine plate of pie, chips and gravy. There's an old jukebox in the corner behind the pool table, where I see a woman browsing the songs, jangling some coins in her hand. Owen and I order drinks and go round to the games room, where all the action is.

After I've introduced Owen to Gavin, the woman comes over from the jukebox to join us, bobbing her way over as Coldplay's 'Clocks' starts playing. She's shorter than me, with wild curly blonde hair flecked with grey threads. She's wearing skinny jeans and ballet flats, with a bright-pink and white tunic on top. She exudes warmth and gives us a big grin. 'Hello, hello, I'm Lynda,' she says, almost shouting, despite it not being necessary. The music's not that loud. 'Lynda, Gav's wife. Gav's filled me in. Filled me in, he did.'

Filled me in? What is that supposed to mean? My heart clenches at the thought of the village grapevine following me through the years.

'Sounds ominous,' Owen laughs, shaking the woman's hand.

'No, no,' Lynda says with a loud laugh. Her body shakes, and I'm not sure if it's because she's still sort of dancing or because she finds something funny. I won't find it funny if I have to explain to Owen exactly what everyone in the village thought about Mum. 'All good. All good,' Lynda continues, seeming to say everything twice. But I already like her. She seems genuine, warm, and a crack shot at pool as she grabs the cue from Gav, swings around and pots a stripe at an almost impossible angle with barely a second glance.

'Hey up, Lynda,' Gav says, walking behind her and patting her on the hip as she leans forward over the table, lining up another shot. 'Don't show me up.'

'Oi, oi, cheeky!' she says. 'Stop putting me off. Putting me off.'

The pair laugh in the kind of synchronised way that

married couples do, which makes me press myself closer to Owen, giving him a smile.

'Your go next, mate. Winner stays on.' Gavin gives Owen a nudge.

'Oh, I'm not sure—'

'Nonsense, nonsense,' Lynda says, potting another ball. Then she sinks two more in a row and, finally, slams the black into a corner pocket with a ricochet shot off the cushion.

'Nice work, missus,' Gav says, giving her a squeeze. 'Come on, Ow, rack 'em up.'

I can't help the giggle as Owen half chokes on his pint. 'It's OK,' I whisper up at him. 'You'll be fine. I'll show you how to set up the game.'

Lynda puts more money in the slot, and I hear the familiar clatter of balls as they tumble down from the innards of the table.

'God, that sound takes me back,' I tell Owen. 'When I was seventeen, I sometimes used to sneak out of my bedroom window and come down here on a Thursday night. The landlord allowed teenagers in the games room, but Mum would have flipped if she'd known.'

'You and Jared, remember?' Gavin says, overhearing me. 'Him on a half of cider one of the older lads bought for him, and you with your tonic and bitters.'

I give him a look, trying to indicate that it's not a good idea to mention that Jared and I came here together in case Owen gets the wrong impression.

'Good times,' Gavin continues. He has no idea how much I wish they had been. I was always waiting for Mum to find out I wasn't in my bedroom. If she'd discovered that I'd sneaked out, she'd have burst into the Bull to drag me home and put me under house arrest for a month. All I'd wanted was a bit of fun, to make some friends, and perhaps get a snog from Jared.

'Did I hear my name mentioned?' a voice says and, when I

turn, Jared is there with a pint in his hand. I can't help the double-take, seeing him in his denim jacket and black jeans – he's still the boy I once knew, as well as the adult man that I don't. I give Owen's arm a squeeze.

'Good luck,' I say to Owen as he chalks up his pool cue.

'Ow's just about to take on the missus at pool,' Gavin tells Jared, hitching up his knee-length shorts. 'Come on, mate, take one for the guys!'

Lynda tosses a coin and Owen loses, so she breaks, smashing up the triangle of balls with two spots flying directly into pockets. She continues to play, winning the next couple of turns, but ends up giving Owen a free shot when she accidentally pots one of his stripes on the rebound.

'Go on, show 'em how it's done, Owen!' I say, watching as he ponders the angles of the balls. Then I sidle up to Gavin. I don't want the evening to slip away before I've had a chance to ask him what he knows about Danny and his family. If his parents are still alive and living in the area, I want to pay them a visit. For Dad's sake, I need to know if Mum was their son's teacher, and what happened to Danny. I don't intend breathing a word to anyone about this, especially Dad, given how upset he seemed about it. But equally, it doesn't feel right not to do anything.

'I wanted to ask you about Danny Wentworth,' I say quietly to Gavin. 'Remember Jared showed you that photograph of us when we were eighteen? You said Danny died.'

'Yeah, he did. Very sad.' Gav touches my arm, drawing a long sip from his pint glass.

'Do you know how he died?'

'Ooh, now you're asking. It was so long ago.' Gavin wipes his lips on the back of his hand. 'It was during the school summer holidays, not long after we got our exam results back. All sorts of rumours went around – might have been an accident, or an illness. Or worse.' He gives me a look, making a pained face. 'I don't think any of us knew the details. It was all a bit hush-hush. Tragic. He had his whole life ahead of him.'

'Do his parents still live in the area?' I watch as Owen walks around the pool table, squinting and crouching low as he stares at the ball he's aiming at. It's sitting about three inches from the centre pocket, directly lined up with the white cue ball.

'You could ask my mum about that,' Gavin says. 'Fount of all local knowledge, she is. When she can remember.' Gavin laughs. 'Poor old thing. Though it's the more recent things she forgets, so you might have some joy. Lynda will be at her house in the morning. Why don't you pop round when she's there? Ask Mum a few questions.' Then he takes a pen and a small grubby notebook from the back pocket of his shorts and writes down an address, tearing off the page and handing it to me. 'She enjoys having visitors,' Gavin says with a wink.

'Thanks, Gav,' I say, moving out of Owen's way as he comes back around to our side of the table to get into position for another shot. Then he jabs at the ball from an almost standing position and the cue tip gouges straight into the baize, ripping a hole in it.

'Ahh, *man...*' Owen says, stepping back, pushing his fingers through his hair. He leans the cue against the table and folds his arms, shaking his head. I go up and give him a hug.

'How about a game of darts instead?' Jared suggests, heading over to the board.

TWENTY-SEVEN

The next morning, I feel as though I'm about to burst out of myself, and it's not because of my pregnancy, or what happened with Mum and Owen's shirt last night, or even what happened with Dad. It's because I've just lied to my fiancé.

While I'm relieved Owen isn't going to the office in London today, it would have made what I'm about to do a whole lot easier if he *had* been on the early train to Paddington. I don't want him thinking that I'm obsessed with the past, needing to find out the truth about Danny and what happened after he died, but it's not an easy thing to explain given he doesn't know the half of everything about my mother.

But I'm also close to bursting point because of all the other secrets I'm harbouring. I'm terrified that I'm going to forget what I'm keeping from whom and that something will eventually spill out.

For starters, it was only meant to be Owen who knew about my pregnancy, being such early days, but now that Mum knows (even though I've tried to deny it), it's only a matter of time before everyone gets to hear about it. I feel bad not telling Shelley and Dad in person, and Shell will hate finding out second-hand, but then she's got enough on her plate as it is, what with that new detective sniffing around about Rafe's death.

In turn, that reminds me of the corsage – or should I say the now *missing* corsage. I know I should confess to the police about what I did, face whatever punishment I might get for withholding evidence. But that will unleash a whole load of things about Mum, how I was trying to protect Dad's fragile state, hold my family together, not upset Shelley any more than she already was. Which leads me on to my family's past – another secret I'm trying (but gradually failing) to keep hidden from Owen. The less he knows about all that the better. Things are too perfect between us to jeopardise our relationship now.

I feel as though I'm about to explode.

I try to put everything from my mind as I walk up the front path of the bungalow in Long Aldbury, a large village a couple of miles away from Mum and Dad's house. Despite being neatly kept, the property has a sad feel about it. There's a low box hedge edging the path, a clean and weed-free block-paved driveway to the side and a small patch of lawn at the front. But for some reason, there's a desolate air surrounding it compared to the other bungalows in the close. As if a dark cloud is looming overhead.

A man answers the door. He's tall, late sixties, and casts a disapproving glance up and down me. I didn't tell him I was coming, and have no intention of explaining who I really am. I hug my jacket around me – partly from the chilly morning air and partly because of the man's grim expression. I rehearsed what I was going to say as I was getting ready to come out.

'Hello, sir,' I say, pretending not to know who he is. 'Sorry to bother you, but I'm interviewing local residents for a piece I'm writing for a history society in... in Oxfordshire.' I'm hoping this is just enough detail so as not to arouse suspicion, but also interesting enough to engage him. I would have preferred his wife to have answered the door – perhaps a softer touch – but a moment later I hear a woman's voice chime out in the background. *Who is it, John?*

'No one, Mary,' he calls over his shoulder. 'What kind of interview?' He tugs down his navy cable-knit cardigan over his rounded belly. The skin on his hands and face appears waxy, mottled with age spots and moles. Not exactly ugly, but not appealing either. There's a stern, wearisome look about him.

'I was wondering if you have any interesting memories of the village that you might like to share, depending on how long you've lived here, of course.'

Forty-seven years, I think, already knowing the answer to that, thanks to Gavin's Mum, Ada, when I paid the old lady a quick visit first thing this morning before coming here. Gavin was correct when he said that she liked visitors – she didn't stop talking the entire time I was there. Going over the past seemed to help her memory, which made it half an hour well spent.

Lynda had been in the kitchen, preparing Ada's breakfast and making sandwiches to put in the fridge for her lunch later, and the old lady, while occasionally a bit confused, was happy to tell me where Danny's parents lived – well, which street, at least, saying it was the last property on the left – the same house the family had always lived in. There didn't seem to be much wrong with her long-term memory.

'I can't help you,' the man says.

'It'll only take a few minutes,' I say, surprised by my own tenacity. 'The history society is compiling an anthology of local stories… think jubilee celebrations or the annual church fete,' I tell him. 'Or maybe you remember a time when villagers rallied together or faced adversity. Its aim is to help local dementia patients.' I just made that last bit up, feeling quite proud of myself for my acting performance. But then I realise that I'm actually *lying*, not acting, and flying too close to Mum's skill set for my liking. I bite my lip, suddenly feeling ashamed.

The man lets out a huff – a cross between a laugh and a cough.

'Like I said, not interested.' He's about to close the door, but just before he does, a small woman slips underneath his arm and stands in front of him, beaming a smile up at me. She's barely five feet tall and has a pale-blue pinafore tied around her waist and a grey, short-sleeved sweater on top. Her hands are covered in flour, and she keeps blowing upwards trying to get rid of a strand of grey hair that's come loose from her bun.

'What is it, dear?' she asks.

I explain to her what I just told her husband.

'Oh, you'd better come in, then. She'd better come in, John,' the woman says, twisting round to look up at her husband. 'We've lived here most of our lives.' She grins, shuffling aside and pushing him out of the way even though he towers over her. 'Lots of stories to tell.'

Ten minutes later I'm sitting beside a hissing gas fire sipping on milky tea and biting into a digestive biscuit. The place seems as sad inside as it does on the outside, as if it's stuck in a time warp.

'We bought this place when it was new,' Mary tells me. 'This is the original carpet, can you believe? Worn well, hasn't it?'

Yes, I can *believe it*, I want to tell her as I stare down at the orange and brown swirl-pattern carpet, but instead I compliment her choice of decor. The rest of the room screams nineteen-seventy-something and would likely fill an entire history society anthology all by itself, if indeed there really was a history society.

'Did you raise your family here?' I ask, having already spotted the framed photographs on the wooden shelf above the gas fire. I try not to stare or show too much interest in them, but most are of a boy in his mid to late teens – the same boy that was in the photo with Jared, Gavin and me. *Danny*.

As yet, the couple haven't recognised me as one of Danny's peers. I can't say *friend* because Danny and I barely knew each other, what with going to different schools. So I doubt they'll realise who I am, especially since twenty years have passed.

In three of the pictures, Danny is alone – posing by a tree in one, sitting astride a bicycle in another and lying on a lawn in the third. There's also a family shot of Danny with his parents – a man and woman recognisable as John and Mary – but for some reason, the picture seems a bit odd. Unbalanced, as if... as if part of it is missing. Someone else's shoulder is just visible off to one edge of the picture, pressing up against a much younger John as if they've been cut out, but I can't be certain.

'We did so,' the man, John, replies in a full-stop kind of way. 'Raised a fine boy, we did.'

'Is that him?' I ask, pointing at the photos.

John nods and folds his arms across his cardigan.

'*Boys*,' I hear Mary whisper, emphasising the plural.

'You had another son?' I ask, remembering Jared had mentioned this fact.

From the corner of my eye, I see John tense in his armchair. It's clear he doesn't want me here.

'She said *boy*,' John snaps before Mary can reply. 'One son.'

I try not to appear taken aback by John's gruff tone, but I am. 'Does your son still live in the area?' I gesture to the photographs again, knowing I'm pushing my luck, but I have to ask them about Danny, what happened to him, and this is a way in. 'Perhaps he might have a story he'd like to share.'

'Too late for that,' John says just as Mary opens her mouth to speak. 'Our boy killed himself a long time ago.'

TWENTY-EIGHT

Suicide?

I never imagined for one minute that would have been the cause of Danny's death. I pause a moment, trying to recall how he'd seemed the day the photo was taken of us all in the garden at Medvale. We were all so relieved that exams were over, and I was also relieved because my mother had gone away. Shelley was home for a few days to help look after the house in their absence, but she didn't mind me having a few kids from the village round; wasn't bothered that we'd got our hands on some Lambrusco and beer. I think back to how Danny had seemed – if he was as happy and carefree as the rest of us, looking forward to the next stage of our lives – but it was a long time ago and I barely recall him being there.

'Oh, I'm so very sorry to hear that,' I say, bowing my head out of respect. 'I... I can write a few words about... in his memory, if you like.' I take a breath, having almost slipped up by saying his name. 'Maybe share a special memory. He looks like a lovely boy.' I glance at the photos again, hating myself even more for spinning lies to these poor people. But I need to know what happened.

'Daniel took his life soon after he turned eighteen,' Mary says quietly. 'We have another son, too, Joseph.'

Biblical names, I think, wondering if they're religious people. Then it occurs to me that Joseph might be the best person to answer my questions, rather than the parents. They're not exactly forthcoming, although I get the impression that Mary wants to open up to me, if only her husband would let her.

'No, we do not have another son, Mary,' John says, lifting his foot and placing it firmly down again. As if to literally put his foot down. 'He's dead to us.'

'*John...*' Mary says, wringing her veiny hands together. Then she looks at me. 'We don't see Joseph any more. He didn't cope well, losing his brother like that.'

'Enough, Mary!' John booms, suddenly standing and looming over the pair of us.

'I'm so sorry to hear that, too,' I tell Mary, reaching over and wrapping my hands around hers.

Like me, it seems as though she's bursting with secrets. And if I've sussed her husband out correctly, then she's not allowed to tell them. Her face is twisted from pain and her shoulders hunched and tense. As I glance at the family photo again, I realise the cut-out person is probably their other son, Joseph.

'Is there anything you want to share for the local history anthology?' I rummage in my bag and pull out a notebook and pen so that I vaguely look the part. My hands are shaking. 'You say you bought this place when it was new. Tell me about that. Are any of your neighbours also original residents?'

John mutters something about *waste of time* and *nosy reporter*, then strides out of the room, making it suddenly feel a whole lot easier to breathe.

'He won't speak to us,' Mary suddenly says in a hushed voice, leaning close to me. 'Our Joseph. He won't have anything to do with us now. Not after what happened.'

'That's really tough for you,' I say, glancing at the door, hoping her husband doesn't come back.

'He thought it were our fault, you see. Danny dying.'

I tilt my head to the side to show her I'm listening, hoping she continues. She does.

'Our Danny... he... he wasn't a happy boy. Not after what went on that summer.' Mary crosses herself quickly. 'It was our Joseph who found him hanging in the garage. The poor boy never got over finding his brother like that. None of us have.' She takes a deep breath. 'They were very close, you see. My two boys. There was only three years between them, but our Joseph looked up to Danny like he were a father.'

A shiver runs through me as I try to piece together what I know. Which is basically not much. But I have to find out if there's a connection between Danny and my mother – and whatever else Gavin said happened that summer. The so-called scandal.

'That's so awful, Mary. I'm very sorry. And I'm sure it wasn't your fault.'

Mary wrings her hands again. 'He wanted to be a doctor, our Danny. He was so bright. Much too clever for this family. That were all down to John, though. Being strict. Making him do his homework. Doling out consequences if he didn't get top marks. John went to every single parents' meeting at school, making sure our boy made the best of himself, getting him extra help from the teachers if he needed support.' Mary takes a breath. 'Though John was a bit free with his fist when it came to discipline with the boys,' she whispers, leaning closer. 'He was determined our Daniel would be the first in the family to go to university, to make something of himself. Do us all proud. He told him he'd get a good hiding if he didn't pass all his exams. Not that John were anything special himself, mind. He was a driving instructor until he retired three years ago. And he was in the army before that.'

I imagine the pressure poor Danny must have felt to succeed. I can't help thinking that Danny's father and my mother have a lot in common.

She gives another glance to the door to check the coast is clear. 'But then Danny failed his biology A level exam and didn't get offered his place at medical school. They insisted on a top grade in that subject. I suggested he try again and retake it the next year, but you can imagine how angry John was. He didn't accept failure.'

'*Biology?*' I say with a gasp. My mother's subject at St Lawrence's. 'Oh, poor Danny,' I add, trying to keep my voice from betraying my worst fears. 'I'm sure he tried his very best.'

Mary looks at me and nods. 'He really did. If it wasn't for that terrible woman, our Danny would have got his grades. He'd still be alive. Danny was so ashamed that he'd let us down and failed an exam, he took his own life.' Mary dabs at her nose with a tissue. Then she glances at the door and, when there's still no sign of John, she continues. 'That teacher taught the wrong syllabus for an entire term. The whole class suffered, with most failing their exams or getting poor grades. But Danny was the one who took it the hardest. He was the one who paid the ultimate price.'

I try to imagine the shock of sitting such an important exam, realising you'd been taught all the wrong things, not knowing any of the answers. And with Danny's father already strict and piling on the pressure, it was too much for him to bear. I can hardly stand to ask who the teacher was, although I'm certain I already know.

'That's so awful, Mary,' I say. 'I'm so sorry.'

Mary looks at me and nods again. 'Those boys – *my* boys – they had a special bond. They loved each other. They were my life. But now I've lost them both.'

'And you have no idea where Joseph is?'

I'm suddenly filled with a compulsion to find him and bring

him home, orchestrate a reconciliation for Mary, but then I imagine how I'd feel if someone did the same to me if I'd completely cut my mother out of my life – which I have come very close to doing many times.

Mary shakes her head. 'No, we have no idea where he is. Not after what that... that teacher did to him, too. Though...' She pauses, as if she's considering revealing something to me, but changes her mind. 'As if she hadn't already caused enough damage to our family.' Her face takes on a pinched, disgusted look. 'I hope she rots in hell, carrying on like that with an inno-cent boy.'

'Oh no...' I say, unable to help myself. 'What... what do you mean, *carrying on like that*?' I clasp my hands together, resisting the urge to cover my face as I brace myself for what she's about to tell me.

'You'd think teaching the wrong syllabus would have been enough to get her the sack, but no. She kept her job. Then, during the next autumn term, Joseph confessed everything. He found the courage to report her for the way she'd been carrying on. All the terrible things that she'd done to him, how she'd groomed him over the previous two years, bribing him by saying he'd get top marks, that he was her favourite pupil, getting him alone and taking advantage of him. He was so worried about getting into trouble, the poor lamb. The school tried to cover it up, of course, but we knew the truth. We reported it to the police, but by then our Joseph was too scared to press charges, and there wasn't enough evidence for them to proceed. It was his word against hers. That evil bitch failed *both* our sons.'

Mary stands up and paces about, clutching at her chest. Her legs are shaking and her face turns a deathly shade of grey. 'Do you know what punishment she got for doing those things to our boy, Joseph, who hadn't even had his sixteenth birthday?' She leans on the mantelpiece for support.

'I... I don't know,' I say, trying to take all this in, praying harder than I've ever prayed before that what she's telling me has nothing to do with my mother. That this isn't the scandal Dad claimed had sent him over the edge.

'She got a big fat redundancy pay-off and was told to take early retirement. The whole matter was swept under the carpet. A disgusting outcome, and there was nothing we could do about it.'

For a moment, I feel a flood of relief. I don't recall Mum getting any kind of pay-off – but would she have told me? Then a chill runs through me when I remember the end of my first term at university. When Mum wrote to me after I'd been travelling, and she blamed me for having to leave her job.

My career has ended in the most life-shattering way because of you and your selfishness...

The only thing I know for certain is that I must find this Joseph and speak to him about my mother. For Dad's sake, I need to know if she was responsible for what happened to *both* of the Wentworth brothers. If she's guilty, then she needs to be punished, however many years later it now is. It might go some way to giving Mary and John some peace, but, more importantly, if my mother is sent to prison for her crime, it will allow Dad to return home without fear of falling victim to her behaviour again. He's suffered enough.

I take a deep breath, plucking up the courage to ask Mary the teacher's name, but I don't get the chance as a booming voice suddenly approaches.

'Right, get out!' John yells, striding back into the living room. I'm half expecting to be dragged out by the arm, such is his anger, but I'm up on my feet and walking briskly to the hallway before he can manhandle me.

'Sorry, I'm going,' I say, fumbling with the catch on the front door. 'I didn't mean to upset you both.' I rush out of the bungalow and hurry back to my car, only allowing the tears to fall once the door is shut and I'm safely locked inside.

TWENTY-NINE

When I get back to Medvale, the house is empty, which is not what I was expecting. 'Owen?' I call, going into the kitchen. Mum doesn't seem to be home either, which makes me nervous, wondering if they've gone out somewhere together. I check my phone, but there are no texts, and, when I ring Owen, it goes straight to voicemail.

'Hi, love, it's me. I'm back at the house. Where are you? Is... is Mum with you? Call me back.'

I hang up. My concern is that she's taken him somewhere, that she's inflicting her nonsense on him, filling his head with lies or forcing his hand about this wedding – a wedding I don't want.

Then I freeze, holding my breath. Was that a noise – is someone here?

I listen, straining my ears, but there's nothing, so I shrug and head upstairs, knocking on Mum's bedroom door – she might be having a nap, even though it's not lunchtime yet. When I was a kid, she'd sometimes stay in bed for days on end for no other reason than not to have to partake in family life. Shelley and I took it in turns to bring her up trays of food at Dad's request.

Once, when I came in to collect her empty dish, I saw she'd thrown the bowl at the wall. Tomato soup dribbled down the plaster like someone had been shot in the head. It took me ages to clean it up.

But Mum's bedroom is empty. The bed is neatly made, the little paned window behind her dressing table open a few inches. The room smells of her – that sweet floral perfume she's always worn that seems to stay in my nose for days, plus fresh laundry and country air. A gentle breeze ripples the cream-coloured curtains.

My eyes flick around, and I feel guilty for being in here, almost as if Mum is watching me. I'm about to leave, perhaps head outside to check if she or Owen are in the garden, when something on her dressing table catches my eye. It's a small, framed photograph that I've not seen before. I go over and pick it up, smiling when I see a young Shelley and me grinning at the camera, both dressed in our Sunday best and each of us holding a bright-red balloon. Shelley is about twelve and I'm around seven. We look as though we've just been to a birthday party, though I don't recall whose it would have been.

'Oh, Mum,' I whisper, staring at it. I shake my head. Is this what she believes our childhood was like? Is this how she remembers those years – captured by one seemingly happy photograph? More like, it's what she's forcing herself to recall – a snapshot in time where we both happened to be smiling – recalibrating her memories, conning herself that things were really like this. It wouldn't surprise me if this picture had been staged for this very reason – *say cheese!* I place it back on her cluttered dressing table, accidentally knocking the lid off a porcelain trinket pot. I grab it, hoping it hasn't chipped, and I'm about to replace it on the pot, but I stop.

'What the *hell?*'

I stare at it for a moment, wondering if my mind is playing tricks. The delicate floral pot contains a couple of silver chains, a few safety pins, some hair clips and a charm from one of her bracelets. All normal things to put in a little pot on a dressing table. But what makes me gasp, my eyes grow wide, my hand slowly reach out to make sure I'm not hallucinating, is the white gold and diamond engagement ring sitting on top.

I pick it up and study it, turning it round and round. 'My ring. It's *my* bloody engagement ring!'

I slam the porcelain lid back on the pot, not caring if it chips or cracks, and head straight to the bathroom to have another go at getting my grandmother's ring off my finger – it's been stuck there all this time. It's not that I don't like it or want it or don't appreciate the history attached to it – it's just not *my* engagement ring. Not the one Owen gave me.

I run my hand under hot water, cold water, use squirt after squirt of soap as a lubricant, then I hold my hand above my head so that the blood drains out of my finger, but the antique ring remains stuck fast.

I sit on the edge of the bath and let out a sob.

My mother has some explaining to do.

It's as I'm going back downstairs that I hear the noise again. *Thump... thump... thump...* At first, I think it's my feet stamping on the wooden treads – I'm so angry at my mother, I could burst – but it's not. The sound is coming from somewhere else.

I stop, listening out – at first hearing only the whoosh of blood pulsing in my ears.

But *there*. The noise again. And something else, too... something that sounds like... like a muffled voice calling out.

'Owen?' I yell, running down the remainder of the stairs. I dart between the rooms – hallway, kitchen, living room, dining room, back through the kitchen to the utility area. But the thumping is loudest when I'm in the hallway.

I fling the front door open to see if he's locked outside, but there's no one there – only Preston in the garden, bent double over the roses as he deadheads them. When he hears me calling out Owen's name, he glances up, giving me a toothless grin and a lazy salute.

I rush back inside, standing at the bottom of the stairs where I heard the noise, listening out, wondering if I'm going mad.

'*Shit!* Owen...!' I call out when I hear the dull *thud-thud* again, realising exactly where it's coming from.

The cellar.

I run to the door under the staircase, turning the old wooden knob, but it's locked fast. Think, *think*... I tell myself, suddenly remembering where Mum keeps the key – in a drawer in the utility room. 'Oh, thank God,' I say, when I see the familiar key ring made from an old champagne cork and string with the iron cellar key attached to it.

My hands fumble with the lock as I turn it, shoving open the old door. A musty damp smell instantly hits me as I feel around for the light switch, my eyes taking a moment to adjust as I tread carefully on the worn stone steps leading down into the cold, dank space under the house. 'Owen!' I call out. 'Are you down here?'

The thumping is louder now, coming from another chamber at the back of the cellar – the small, locked room where Mum keeps her coveted wine collection.

'Owen?' I yell again, brushing a cobweb off my face. I bow my head as I pick my way over the uneven bricks, squinting in the dim glow of the single bulb fixed to a joist above.

Thump... thump... thump...

'Lizzie!' comes a muffled voice.

'Oh my God, Owen!' I cry out, seeing the small door rattling in its frame as he thumps it. 'What the hell are you doing in there?' I slide the top and bottom bolts to the side, yanking on the old iron latch and opening the door.

'Thank *God*... at *last*,' Owen says, his face panic-stricken.

He's as white as a sheet and I feel him shaking as he gives me a hug. 'Where's your mother gone? I thought I was going to bloody well die in there.' He lets out a relieved laugh, but I can tell he's really upset. 'I tried calling you, but there's no reception down here.'

'I've no idea where she is,' I say. 'Come on, let's get you upstairs.' I take his hand and lead him back towards the steps. 'What the hell were you doing down here, anyway? And how on earth did you get locked in? The bolts are on the outside of the door.'

But when I look back over my shoulder, the expression on Owen's face tells me all I need to know.

THIRTY

'I'd been sending emails all morning,' Owen says when I ask him to recount what happened. He's standing at the kitchen sink, washing his hands. 'So when your mum asked me to help her with some lifting, I didn't mind the break. She wanted me to fetch some cases of wine up from the cellar. She told me they were "from her special collection".'

I roll my eyes at him as he glances round, drying his hands.

'Anyway, she unlocked the top cellar door in the hallway, telling me which cases she wanted brought up. They were going to be for the wedding – for the important top table guests, apparently.'

'Sounds about right,' I say, bracing myself for what's coming.

'I went down the stone steps, through the main cellar and into the back room. It was very dark in there, so I used my phone torch to read all the labels. I was hunting around but couldn't see the Malbec she wanted and was going to come back up to ask her – and that's when I realised the door of the back room had shut behind me. And it appeared to be locked. It must have closed itself somehow, maybe in a draught, but I swear I didn't hear any banging. I figured there must have been a latch of some kind that had locked from the outside.'

I'm shaking my head. 'No. There are only two sliding bolts on that door, Owen. There's no way they locked of their own accord. I was out, so there's only one person who could have trapped you down there.'

Owen and I stare at each other, both knowing what the other is thinking. I decide not to tell him that the door at the top of the stairs was also locked, and that the key had been put back in the drawer.

'But *why*? Why would she do that?' Owen finally asks. 'Kind of goes against what she wanted me to do in the first place – fetch the wine.'

I sigh, trying to control the anger that's already steaming out of me since I discovered my ring in Mum's room. I really don't want to let it out in front of Owen, or be forced to explain fully what she's like, but with each hour that passes, it's getting harder and harder to contain everything.

'You're... you're right,' I say, forcing a shrug. 'It's weird. Maybe she thought you'd already come back up and locked the cellar, not realising you were still down there.'

'Maybe,' Owen replies, though I can tell he's not convinced. 'You don't think she did it on purpose, do you, to freak me out... or worse?'

I swallow, hating that I'm about to lie to my fiancé – again. I just need to keep a lid on everything until we escape back to London. 'It... it was probably just a misunderstanding.' I clear my throat, turning away. I can't bear to look him in the eye. My mother did the same thing to Shelley and me many times when we were children, punishing us for simply existing.

'Anyway,' he says, 'did you enjoy having coffee with your friend?'

For a moment, I wonder what he's talking about, then I realise it's the other great big lie I spun him earlier when I went out first thing to see Gavin's mother, and then on to Mary and John's house. There's no way I'm telling him the truth about *that*, or what my next task is – to find Joseph. But given that he has nothing to do with his parents any more, that's going to prove tricky.

'Yeah, I did, thanks,' I reply, watching Preston from the window. 'It was... pleasant.'

Owen comes up beside me, giving me a squeeze as we stare out across the lawn. 'Look, why don't we go and get some bits from the shop for lunch?' he says. 'We can eat in the garden. Make the most of this September sunshine.'

I agree that's a good idea – anything to get out of the house – so I grab my keys and we head for the car. But as I put out my hand to open the driver's side door, I can't help the scream, recoiling when I see what's lying on the roof.

'Oh my *God*!' I cover my mouth, holding in a retch.

Owen rushes round to my side. 'What the *hell*...?'

I stare at the two dead rabbits, tied together by their back legs. There's a trickle of blood running down the paintwork to the top of the door, their blank eyes staring at the sky. I bury my face in Owen's shoulder.

'Aye, sorry 'bout that,' a voice says. 'Mrs Holmes told me to leave 'em there.'

'The rabbits?' Owen says, swinging round.

Preston comes over, pointing at the car roof with a pair of secateurs. I look up to see him giving us a slow nod.

'Maybe you could... you know, get rid of them? We're going out,' Owen says, frowning and shaking his head.

But Preston just stands there, staring between the pair of us, a small smile creeping over his face, exposing black teeth, several of them missing.

'Give you a fright, did they?' he says, followed by a croaky laugh. Then he shakes his head, sweeping up the poor creatures by their hind legs and dropping them onto a bench at the edge of the lawn. Then he goes back to work.

On the short drive to Long Aldbury, after we've both calmed down, Owen chats about his work – though I don't dare ask if there's any news about the invoice. I haven't mentioned that I've found my ring yet, and he's not noticed that it's now on my finger, next to my grandmother's gold ring. I'm putting off telling him because, unless I spin more lies, that would mean explaining who took it – and therefore revealing that my mother is a thief and a liar, as well as a vicious old hag who likes locking people in the cellar.

'You wait here,' he says, getting out of the car after I've parked outside the small supermarket. 'I'll dash in and get some crusty bread and other bits. Won't be a mo.' He grins and strides off, with me resting my head back and closing my eyes. *What a morning...* I think, processing everything that's happened.

He's only been gone a few minutes when a phone rings – and it's not mine. When I look down, I see it's Owen's phone vibrating in the central console where he left it.

I pick it up, knowing that it will probably be someone from his work, but then I see *'Tara – letting agent'* lit up on the screen, so I take the call.

'Hello, Owen's phone,' I say, crossing my fingers in the hope that she's got another flat to offer us, that we're the first on her list to call, and we'll have an offer accepted by the end of today. Hell, I'll even take something without viewing it, I'm so desperate to get away from here.

'Is that Lizzie?' she asks, and I confirm it is. 'Sorry to bother you, but I was just wondering if you and your partner were going to officially offer on Flat 3, Belvedere Court. I've not had your form back yet.'

'*What?*'

I imagine Tara whipping the phone away from her ear, my shriek was so loud.

'I never received your official offer form back on Monday as you promised. Without that, I'm afraid nothing gets submitted to the landlord.'

'But... but you phoned and told us that the flat had already gone.'

'Sorry?' Tara says, sounding confused. 'No, I didn't call you.'

'Well, someone from your office called Owen on Saturday evening and told him the flat had been let to another couple.' My heart thumps wildly at the possibility that, for some reason, the deal has fallen through and the flat has become available again.

Tara is silent for a moment. 'I'm sorry, but it wasn't me who called your partner. There must have been a mistake. The landlord is still in the process of collecting offers, so if you want to submit your form, you still just about have time. He'll be making a decision by the end of today.'

I can't help the air punch, even though I'm confused. 'OK, look, I'm so sorry for any mix-up. We'll get the form off to you in the next half an hour. We are extremely keen to secure this flat!' I can hardly contain my excitement as we say goodbye.

But as I wait for Owen to return to the car, I puzzle over who phoned Owen on Saturday night if it wasn't Tara. It had been a double whammy of bad news, what with the call to Peter as well. But at least the flat is still up for grabs now, though it all depends on his invoice being paid soon. I wonder if I dare ask Mum to lend us the money in the meantime, though after what's just happened, I'm not sure I can even bring myself to speak to her.

A few minutes later, the car door opens and Owen gets in, dropping a bag of shopping into the footwell, the top half of a baguette poking out. 'Hey,' he grins, buckling up. 'Got some chicken and avocado. Your favourite.'

'Great,' I say, starting the engine. Then I look across at him. 'While you were gone, a call came in on your phone.'

'Oh?' Owen says, picking up his handset, checking the screen.

'It was Tara, the agent who showed us round the flat at Belvedere Court. Apparently, it's still available.' I pause, watching his expression change as his head whips up.

'Wait, what... *really*?'

'Yeah. It was weird. Not only that, but Tara said she didn't call you at all the other night when we were at the pub.'

Then Owen turns to face me – each of us sharing the same concerned look again as we try to work it out in our minds, not wanting to believe it had anything to do with my mother.

THIRTY-ONE

'Very strange,' Owen says a few moments after I've explained how we're still in with a chance to get the flat. But I can't help my suspicions, and I can tell Owen is thinking the same. I watch closely as he checks back in his call log, drumming his fingers against the car door. 'It was a mobile number that called me on Saturday evening.'

In my head, I replay what happened at the pub restaurant. Owen's phone had rung at the table, and he'd gone outside to take the call, leaving me alone with Mum. While outside, he also took the opportunity to call Peter to check on Minnie for me. When he came back, he'd delivered the bad news: that the flat had gone to someone else, and Peter had had a change of heart about us staying with him.

If Mum was involved in this, then she must have had an accomplice.

'Before you went to take the call, you seemed certain it was the letting agent's number,' I say, giving him a glance as I pull out of the car park.

'I *assumed* it was them, love,' Owen admits. 'And I was right. Besides, who else would have been calling me from an unknown mobile number on a Saturday evening? Whoever it was definitely told me the flat was off the market. I just assumed it was Tara.'

'I don't know,' I say, hating where my thoughts are now heading as I concentrate on the road. 'I guess it must have been someone else who works at the agency, then. Someone who made a mistake about the flat.' I give him a sideways glance.

'Possibly,' Owen replies, 'though it doesn't look good on them, does it?'

'It doesn't,' I say a few minutes later, pulling onto the drive at Medvale and yanking up the handbrake.

'Here, this is the number that called me,' Owen says, flashing his phone at me.

'In that case, I want you to call them back. Right now.' I fold my arms, making no move to get out of the car.

Owen stares at me, shocked by my harsh tone. 'OK, OK, love,' he says slowly, a frown creasing his forehead as he taps on the number, looking at me as he waits for it to connect. 'Straight to voicemail,' he replies with a shrug, getting out of the car to go inside. I follow him, slamming my door hard.

'How convenient,' I mutter, immediately realising that I've overstepped the mark.

Owen takes hold of my arm and pulls me to a stop, turning me round to face him. 'Here, I'll call it back and you can listen to the recorded message yourself if you don't believe me. It was the same woman's voice who called me on Saturday.' He dials the number again.

I take a deep breath, staring up at him, mumbling an apology for mistrusting him as I hear a woman's voice indeed introducing herself as an agent from the agency.

'It's still weird,' I say, feeling awful for implying that he was lying as we go into the kitchen. Though at least we both agree that we need to get our application form in as soon as possible. And there's still no sign of Mum. 'Also... look what I found,' I say, deciding I should come clean about where I found my ring. I thrust my hand out for him to see.

Owen is unpacking the groceries, but he stops, staring at my fingers. 'You found it!' He pulls me in for a hug. 'Thank God for that. I didn't want to make too much of a deal of it, but I was pretty upset it was lost.'

Right on cue, before I even get a chance to explain about the ring, Mum appears in the kitchen.

'That's the wedding menu and the cake taken care of,' she announces with a grin, brushing her hands together in a chopping motion. 'Right, where's my to-do list?' Her eyes flick around, settling on an A4 notepad on the dresser. She grabs it and crosses a few things off on what looks like a very long list. 'There's still so much to get done.'

Owen and I share a look.

'I've gone for a three-tier sponge with white and pink icing, and the roast lamb for a main course,' Mum tells us. 'And there's a salmon option for the vegetarians.'

Owen snorts quietly to himself, while I take the bait.

'Mum, vegetarians don't eat salmon. And don't *we* get a say about the menu at our own wedding? But more to the point, why the *hell* did you lock Owen in the cellar?'

My mother freezes, every muscle in her body tensing as she glares at me. 'What are you talking about?'

'When I came back, I found him down there in the back chamber. Both bolts were locked. From the *outside*. *And* the top cellar door was locked.'

Mum then stares at Owen for a moment, swallowing and licking her lips. She puts a hand on the back of the kitchen chair, looking unsteady. 'He was not in the cellar when I locked it. I don't know where he was.'

'I don't believe you, Mother. Unless we have a poltergeist in the house, then it can only have been you. You *knew* he was down there. It was a rotten bloody trick.'

Mum does a good show of looking crestfallen. 'There's no reasoning with you sometimes, Elizabeth. But look, we need to talk about dessert menu options. We're stuck with this caterer's cancellation slot as no one else in the area is available at such short notice for a hundred and twenty people. Their menu was limited, to say the least.'

'A hundred and twenty?' Another pained look shared with Owen. He just shrugs. 'We don't know that many people, Mum.'

'Well, *I* do. There are your father's old banking colleagues and their families, for a start. Then there are all the WI members, plus their husbands and families, and most people in the village know me and will be expecting an invite. There's bridge club to think about, and the church congregation – they come from all the surrounding villages, you know, and—'

'Mum, stop!' I grip onto the back of a chair. 'Literally none of those people mean anything to Owen and me. You might as well hire a bunch of extras from a casting agency. I don't know what to say to you right now.'

She hasn't even mentioned any of our *actual* family on her list, not that they'd even fill one pew. And as for Dad being involved with plans, I'm guessing he's far from her mind in that regard – though he's not left my thoughts since his shocking revelation. The fact is, he lied to me. He's lied to *all* of us – and while I understand that his mental health has suffered, it's making me wonder what other secrets he's keeping – and how long he's planning to keep up the charade.

What a mess, I think, listening to Mum drone on about canapés and tablecloths.

'Well, if that's all the thanks I get,' she finally says, turning her back on me and slamming the notepad back on the dresser. She's about to head out of the room, but I'm not having that. Not after what she did to Owen.

'Mum, wait.'

She stops. Turns.

'Look.' I show her my left hand.

She stares at it, her top lip turning up in a sneer. 'That silver looks tacky next to Mummy's gold ring.'

'Wait, *what*? You're not even going to ask where I *found* my engagement ring?'

'Is there any need, Elizabeth? I have a feeling you're about to tell me.'

'Oh my God,' I mutter, making an exasperated face at Owen.

'Who wants a cup of tea?' he says, hand on kettle, probably thinking that will defuse the situation. I love him for it, but it won't help.

'My ring was in your bedroom, Mum. On your dressing table. In your blue and white china pot.' I fold my arms, standing my ground. Staring at her. Waiting for her confession.

Mum's mouth opens wide, and, for a horrible moment, I think she's going to scream. But then she starts to sway, touching her temple as her eyes roll back in their sockets.

'Mum... *stop* it...' I hiss, hoping Owen won't see her.

'Oh, Elizabeth, I feel strange,' she says, her fingers dragging down her face, 'Maaahhh...' she bleats.

'*Mum!*' I snap, glancing over at Owen, who's now busy making our sandwiches. 'Why was my ring on your dressing table?'

'I don't know.' Another sway, her head lolling.

I flash a look at Owen, who has turned round again, and is watching the scene unfold with his mouth hanging open.

'Did you take my ring, Mum?'

Before I can react, she suddenly drops to the floor, her body buckling sideways. She goes down with a thunk, though she's careful not to hit her head on the flagstones.

'Oh... oh... gosh, where am I?' She looks up at me, pouting, touching her temple as she gazes around, pretending not to know where she is.

'Oh my goodness, Sylvia, are you OK? Let me help you up.' Owen rushes to her side, dropping down beside her.

'There's nothing wrong with her, Owen. She does this.'

He glances up, shooting me a look that says *Don't be so unsympathetic...*

'Come on, up we get,' Owen says, lifting my mother from behind. After a bit of a struggle, he gets her into a kitchen chair. 'Let me fetch you some water.'

'Thank you, Owen. I... I just came over all dizzy. It's my blood pressure.' She takes the water, smiling up at him. The glass rattles against her teeth as she sips.

I go over to the sink, staring down into it with my shoulders hunched up around my ears. *Count to ten*, I tell myself. *Count to a hundred. A fucking thousand.*

'I'm so sorry, darling,' I hear Mum say in a breathless voice. 'I do not know why your ring was in my bedroom. Anyway, what were you doing in there in the first place?'

'Looking for you!' I say, spinning round to see Owen with his arm around her shoulders, giving me a dirty look for being mean to her. 'OK... OK...' I say, backing down, knowing there's no point arguing. 'I'm just pleased to have it back.'

But not pleased to have my grandmother's ring stuck on my finger, I think, knowing I'll probably have to get a jeweller to cut it off.

'I'm going upstairs to send off the letting agency forms,' I say, using all my strength to stay calm. I give Owen a smile, but when he doesn't look up from comforting Mum, I make a hasty retreat to my old bedroom and drop down onto my bed, punching the pillow. Just like I used to do as a child.

THIRTY-TWO

Thank God for my sister. Her text arrived half an hour ago, just after I'd scanned and emailed the completed form to the letting agent, and it couldn't have come at a better time – asking if I wanted to hang out because she had the afternoon unexpectedly free. I was in the car within minutes, poking my head into the kitchen on the way out to let Owen know where I was going, pretending that Shelley wanted to discuss wedding stuff. This appeased Mum as she sat with Owen, chomping on the chicken and avocado baguette that was meant for us, the pair of them deep in conversation. I didn't wait around to find out what about, though I doubt it involved Mum apologising.

'Intense is an understatement,' I tell Shelley now as we sit in her kitchen, having explained to her about my ring, the cellar incident and how Mum is still full steam ahead with wedding plans. 'I feel like my head is in a vice. And I swear she's trying to cause trouble between me and Owen.' Then I explain about the flat, the misunderstanding, how we've been offered a second chance but probably can't afford to secure the place even if we do get accepted.

Shelley listens, watching me as I rant on.

'God, sorry, Shell. I'm being so bloody insensitive. My worries are nothing in the scheme of things.'

'Nonsense,' she says kindly. 'I don't know how you can stand to stay with her, to be honest. You're made of sterner stuff than me.'

'We don't have a choice at the moment.' Then I summarise our dismal finances, making them out to be slightly less embarrassing than they really are. 'So, we're kind of stuck for a bit.' My stomach knots at the thought.

'I wish you'd let me lend you some more money,' Shelley says calmly. 'I know you've refused my offer once, but honestly, it's no problem.'

I stare at her, so grateful the offer still stands. 'I couldn't possibly accept,' I say, but only because it's the done thing, not because I really mean it.

She waves a hand at me. 'Don't be stupid. I have savings. Might as well be put to good use. And I know you'll pay it all back.'

'OK... then yes, yes, oh my God, yes! A hundred per cent I'll pay you back. With interest. Owen's being treated so badly by this company. Just knowing that we can at least put down a deposit and the first month's rent will literally save our lives.' I'm almost in tears. 'Thank you a thousand billion times over, Shell.' I lunge at her for a hug, feeling, for the second time today, like a little child who can't manage her own life.

'On another note, when were you going to tell me your big news?' she asks as she gets up, grabbing a loaf from the bread bin. A quick glance over her shoulder with one eyebrow raised is all I need to know what she means.

'I wondered how long it'd be before Mum broadcast it.'

'The post lady told me. And Angie a few doors down told her. God knows where Angie heard the news.'

I shake my head slowly, though none of this comes as a great surprise. 'We weren't going to tell anyone until I was three months. Thanks,' I add when she hands me a sandwich. 'But you know how Mum has a way of sniffing things out.'

'Indeed, I do. Now eat up. Can't have you going hungry, not in your condition.' The added wink ensures she doesn't get a sisterly thump. 'But...'

'I sensed there was a *but*.' I sink my teeth into the soft bread.

'But... was this a planned pregnancy, Liz? I mean, getting married after knowing each other for such a short time is big enough news, but a baby too?'

I stare at my sandwich, my appetite fading. She's right. Of *course* she's right, but I'm not about to admit that. 'We'll be fine,' I tell her. 'We're excited.'

'I know you better than anyone, Liz. Accidents happen. It's OK to admit that you had one.' She sits down beside me.

'Fuck you,' I say flatly, and she knows I'm joking. But she also knows I'm not joking. 'Anyway, I was ready for something to happen in my life. Something that didn't just consist of me running away constantly.'

There's an unspoken exchange between us. She's thinking *idiot*, and I'm thinking *shit*.

'I do want the baby,' I tell her, though it's probably to convince myself more than her.

'Just as long as you know you have a choice.'

'And I'm exercising that choice, aren't I?'

A slight widening of her eyes and a silent bite of her sandwich as she stares at me.

'Owen's happy,' I say. 'He was overjoyed when I broke the news.'

I put down my sandwich, concerned that the bread may get stuck in my throat if I take another bite because of the big fat lie blocking the way.

Are you certain, Lizzie? I guess we'll manage... We'll have to deal with it... Not ideal timing... These are some of the things I remember Owen saying moments after I'd told him I was pregnant. There'd been a pause before he'd said anything at all, presumably as he took the news on board. I was fresh from the bathroom, standing there, holding my breath. That single word 'Pregnant' showing up on the stick in my hand. Two syllables that changed the course of our lives.

Shelley is still staring at me, chewing slowly.

'What I mean is... I guess he was a bit shocked. We both were. It's... it's not ideal timing, but we'll adapt.'

Then I burst into tears and Shelley wraps me up in her arms.

THIRTY-THREE

'Right. Hen do,' Shelley says after I've had a good sob. While we now have an understanding that she won't question my choices, I know that she's got my back. And that's a huge comfort. I've missed her so much.

But what she doesn't know is that I haven't got hers, not truly, and I haven't had since her wedding day. Though I can't possibly tell her why.

For a start, if I'd had her best interests at heart, I wouldn't have run off to Dubai, deserting her when she needed me most – leaving her to cope with her loss alone, as well as Dad's admission to hospital. But more importantly, I would have told her what I'd found beside Rafe's body – Mum's corsage – and what it could potentially mean.

Now, blowing my nose in Shelley's kitchen, I deeply regret not leaving it where it was for the police to deal with – and who knows, perhaps they'd have found Mum completely innocent. But it's the alternative explanation that's got me worried.

What if Mum killed Rafe?

I wish I had the courage to tell the detective what I did, how stupid I was for taking the corsage, but the more time that passes, the harder it is to confess and the more trouble I'll be in. All I've succeeded in doing is making things worse. They'll never believe me that I panicked, that I wasn't thinking straight, that I wanted to give my mother the chance to explain, but never did. Then my mind fast-forwards to me being arrested for my crime, having to go through a court case, a prison sentence... my baby being born behind bars.

And now the corsage has gone missing from the box where I hid it.

My stomach knots from all the lies.

'Hen do?' I reply to Shelley, snapping back to the moment. 'I'm hardly going out on the piss in my condition, am I? Besides, I'm not getting married here in the village church. Final answer.'

'Good luck with telling Mum that,' Shelley laughs. 'But you'll be getting married at some point soon, right? A bit of planning won't hurt. Anyway, it doesn't need to be a pub crawl with a male stripper, does it?'

'Worst. Nightmare.'

'I'll never forget what you did for my hen do. It was so thoughtful.'

It was indeed a success, mainly because Mum didn't know about it and therefore didn't come. In secret, I'd organised a midweek girls' bonding camp at an adventure centre in Wiltshire a couple of days before the wedding. The other hens were under orders not to breathe a word about it, and I knew I could trust them.

The couple of days consisted of camping, climbing, wild swimming and rafting, as well as an afternoon of foraging for food in the woods. It was right up Shelley's street, especially when we got to cook our own harvest on the campfire.

After we got home, Shelley posted a picture on Instagram of the wild mushroom pâté she'd made from the leftover ingredients she brought back – #hendo #wedding #foragedfood #lovemytribe, among other giveaway hashtags – but I'd quickly phoned her and told her to take it down in case word somehow got back to Mum.

'Thing is, Shell, if Owen and I get this flat, I doubt we'll be getting married until next year anyway. We'll be busy moving, getting settled in, having the baby. Wedding arrangements have only got this far because I've been humouring Mum to keep the peace.' I stop, suddenly feeling selfish despite Mum's behaviour today. 'Although I must admit, Owen *is* rather keen on the idea of a church wedding. Anyway, I can't imagine how all this must feel for you.' I haven't dared tell her that Mum is ruining her wedding dress.

'People are going to keep getting married the world over, and whether they do or don't isn't going to bring Rafe back. But more to the point,' she goes on, 'do you really *want* to get married?'

'Yes! Just not here and not with Mum organising it.'

Shelley's the last person I need to explain to about our mother's overbearing ways, but admitting that I'm growing fearful for Owen's safety would mean revealing my suspicions about Rafe's death. And now, with the police reviewing the case, I'm just praying that whatever new evidence they have doesn't lead them directly to me.

Then Mary's words burn through my mind – *if it wasn't for that terrible woman* – which reminds me to ask Shelley about the family. 'Jared and I spotted someone in an old photo the other day, and I've been trying to find out about him,' I say. 'Danny Wentworth. He's my sort of age, went to the grammar school. Do you remember him?'

Shelley takes a moment, thinking, shaking her head. 'No, no I don't think so. If he was a few years below me, I might have left for university.'

'He had a brother called Joseph. Ring any bells?'

She shakes her head. 'Why are you asking?'

'No reason,' I reply, unconvincingly.

'But you said *had* a brother? Which probably means one of them is dead. Am I right?'

'Jesus, Shell,' I say. 'You're in the wrong job. But yes, you're right. Danny died a few weeks after his A level exams. He killed himself.'

'Oh shit, that's really sad to hear.'

Perhaps it's because I feel so guilty for not telling Shelley about the corsage, or perhaps it's because I think she might know more if I jog her memory, but I can't help myself from blurting out, 'And I think Mum had something to do with it.'

THIRTY-FOUR

When I arrive back at Medvale later that afternoon, Owen is walking up to the front door with a small bag of shopping. I lock up the Volvo, give him a kiss and we go inside together.

'Your mum is feeling a bit better,' he says, when I ask why he's been out for groceries again. 'She wanted me to fetch a couple of things from the little village shop. Tea, milk, the newspaper. I didn't mind helping.'

'She's got you right where she wants you,' I say with a sigh, though I'm also keen to tell him my news. 'Shelley's offered to lend us some money to secure the flat if we get accepted,' I whisper as we go into the kitchen.

Mum is standing at the sink, washing vegetables, so that's the end of the conversation, but I sense that Owen is... well, to be honest, he looks a bit dubious about the idea. I suspect he's feeling his pride about taking money from Shelley, even if it is just a loan.

'Here's the stuff you wanted, Sylvia,' he says, dumping the bag on the table. 'And here's your twenty-pound note back. Don't worry, I paid for it.'

Which illustrates exactly what I was thinking – even

though every penny counts for us right now, Owen is too proud to accept a few pounds from Mum.

'Thank you, Owen, that's kind. Just leave the money on the table,' Mum replies, scrubbing potatoes in the sink.

Owen tucks the twenty-pound note under the salt shaker and, at first, I don't realise what it is that makes my heart speed up. Then I see it, gasping when I realise what it means.

'*Betty's*' is scrawled in black felt pen on one corner of the note.

I grab it, staring at it, unable to believe my eyes. Owen isn't paying any attention; rather, he's busy putting the tea in the cupboard and the milk in the fridge, before picking up the newspaper and glancing at the headlines. 'Owen?' I say quietly, holding the money out at him. 'Look.'

'Yeah, it's your mum's,' he says, giving it a casual glance. Then he shakes his head quickly as if to tell me, *Don't worry about it... I didn't mind paying.*

'No, no, *look*,' I insist, flapping the money in front of his face so he has no choice but to see it. I point at Betty's name, written in her scrawly writing.

Owen frowns, looking at me quizzically, then mouths, 'What?' as if I'm mad.

I beckon him over to the window, further away from Mum, who has just put some music on. She turns up the volume, giving us a lingering look from across the room, interrupting my train of thought. Suddenly, goosebumps break out all over me.

'You OK, love?' Owen asks when I fall silent.

'Listen,' I hiss. 'The music.'

Owen shrugs, giving a quick shake of his head.

'It's Mozart... it's called "Dies Irae",' I tell him.

Another shrug. 'It's a bit sombre and depressing, but I don't mind listening to classical.'

'No, *no*...' I whisper. 'It's a requiem mass for funerals. It's all about judgement day and casting souls into hell. It literally means "Day of Wrath".'

I take a deep breath, knowing I'm not going to get Owen to understand. At least the doleful music has given me cover to ask Owen about the money.

'This is *Betty's* money,' I whisper, waving the note around again. 'The money that Peter was certain *I'd* stolen!' He already knows my suspicions about the strange blocking incident, and how Peter has since called me, making horrible accusations about the cash. Naturally, Owen was sad to learn that Betty had passed away, but his advice about Peter was to do nothing, that it would all soon blow over.

'Really?' Owen says, sounding shocked. We look over at Mum as she turns up the volume even further, the doleful chanting filling the room.

'I'm totally certain...' I pause, flapping the note about again. 'I saw a load of cash in Betty's kitchen when I helped her inside with her shopping. I told you about it, remember?'

Owen nods, looking perplexed.

'I remember seeing this exact banknote on the top of the pile. She told me she'd labelled it with her name and that she was putting it in the "Bank of Betty", aka her tea caddy. As if I'd ever...' But I trail off, my entire body suddenly turning cold as it dawns on me.

'I know you wouldn't steal, darling.' Owen slips an arm around my waist, but I instantly pull away.

'Oh my God, it was *you*, wasn't it?' I stare up at him, my eyes wide and panicked.

'What? *No!*' Owen protests, looking mortified by my accusation.

'Well, Mum hardly went to London to steal it, did she?' I hiss. 'You... you must have given her back a different twenty-pound note from your wallet for the groceries just now. Otherwise, how would *she* have had Betty's money in her purse to give you in the first place?'

Owen stares at me, then at the twenty-pound note, slowly taking it from between my fingers. 'Oh no, love, you've got this all wrong,' he whispers, reading the shaky writing on the banknote.

'You *knew* I'd told Betty that we'd take her to the bank to pay in the cash. And you *knew* she'd got at least five hundred quid stashed away, if not more.'

Owen is about to defend himself, but we're suddenly interrupted.

'What are you two whispering about over there?'

When I turn, Mum is approaching us, a large chopping knife in her hand, eagerly trying to see what Owen is holding.

'I... I think this is yours, Sylvia,' he says, handing the money back to her. 'Groceries are all put away.'

What is he doing? I want to scream, but I keep my mouth shut until I get a chance to talk to him alone. I do not want Mum gloating over the possibility that Owen is a thief – though I can hardly believe I'm thinking this way.

'Oh, you're a sweetheart, Owen, dear,' Mum says, staring directly at him. She takes the money and goes to her handbag hanging on the back of the kitchen door, taking out her purse. When she opens it, I see that it's bulging with a stash of twenty-pound notes. And all the while she's mouthing 'dies irae' over and over, not taking her eyes off Owen.

THIRTY-FIVE

'Owen, you need to explain,' I say once we're alone upstairs in my old bedroom, the door firmly shut. '*Now!*' I hate accusing him, but there's no other explanation for him having Betty's money.

'Whoa, Lizzie, stop,' Owen says, almost laughing, but looking more hurt than anything. 'Just calm down, will you?'

Thankfully, we managed to escape the kitchen without any drama from Mum, with her chiming out that it's home-made leek and potato soup for dinner as we came upstairs.

'You've jumped to a horrible conclusion.' He shakes his head, hoisting up one of his small suitcases – the cabin bag he used in Dubai – and drops it onto the bed. He opens it and pulls out an envelope from inside a zipped-up compartment. Then he lifts up the flap and takes out a wodge of cash.

'Where the hell did all *that* come from?' I squeak. 'Jesus Christ, Owen, tell me this isn't Betty's money? *Please* say you didn't steal from her?'

I can't help backing away from him, my heart thumping. This *can't* be true... not the man I love, not the man I'm going to marry.

'Is *this* why Peter kicked us out – because you stole the money? Owen, I want you to be totally honest with me. You owe it to me and the baby.'

'What the *hell*, Lizzie?' Again, he laughs, but I doubt I'll ever be able to forget the look of hurt and shock that whips across his face. 'You really think that I *stole* this?'

Owen grabs a handful of the money, waving it in the air. A few notes flutter to the ground.

'Is that the kind of man you think I am? The man who's sticking by you, working every hour God sends to make a good life for you and our baby – and now you think I'm capable of stealing a measly few hundred pounds from an old lady?' He lets out a sigh and shakes his head. 'Yes, this money belongs to Mrs Baxter and that's *exactly* the reason that I haven't dipped into it to pay for the hotel you've been so desperate to go to.'

'No, no, I don't think you stole it, it's just that Peter said on the phone—'

'Oh, yes, and about that. You went behind my back and contacted Peter after he made it quite clear that he wanted to be left alone. Full marks for making a fool of me, Lizzie.' He drops down on the bed, looking crestfallen and hurt.

'Oh, God, Owen, I'm so sorry. No, no, of course I don't think you stole anything. After everything that's been going on, I'm overly sensitive. If I've jumped to the wrong conclusion, I apologise.' I sit down beside him and wrap an arm around him, but he pulls away. 'I'm so, so sorry...'

I'm so sorry... Oh God, I'm begging you... Sorry, sorry, sorry...

Suddenly, I'm right back there, aged fourteen, when Mum jumped out of our moving car on a country lane. Dad jammed on the brakes, causing the car behind us to also skid to a stop as he leapt out to find Mum. The passenger door was wide open, and I was in the back of the car, sobbing. Shelley was trying to comfort me, but I was inconsolable.

'*Sorry, sorry, sorry...*' I'd wailed a thousand times or more, not daring to look out of the window. It was my fault that she'd flung herself from the car. I should never have called her a mean bitch. But I'd wanted to go on that school trip to France so very, very much – I was sick of being the odd one out in my class, the one always excluded – and while it was only two nights away from home in Boulogne, a chance to practise our language skills, it felt as though I'd be escaping home for an eternity if I was allowed to go.

'Please, Mum, *please*. I'll be good forever and wash up every night if you let me. I'll even clean all the windows and weed the garden. Anything. Just let me go. Mum, please, can I?'

I'd gone on and on like a broken record, until she swung around in her seat and pulled a face so terrifying, I'd had nightmares for months after. She hissed at me, her teeth bared and her bony fingers hooked into claws as she lunged at me. The look in her eyes was demented as she lashed out, and it was only when I swore at her, called her a mean bitch, that she unclipped her seatbelt and opened the car door, hurling herself out onto the grass verge.

Ever since, I've never been good at sticking up for myself, or voicing my opinion, or stating my needs. It would mean risking a similar outcome, having to face the horrible consequences. As it happened, my mother was unscathed, though she didn't speak to me for a week. Instead, it was me who'd come away with the injuries – mental wounds that had healed over with painful, fibrous scars.

'Like I've been trying to tell you, I did not steal the money, Lizzie,' Owen says now. 'When I went back to Peter's flat to get our belongings on Sunday afternoon, he wasn't there, but I met Mrs Baxter in the communal hallway, and she beckoned me into her flat. She told me about the cash and then *gave* it to me, entrusting me with it so I could pay it into the bank for her, just like you'd suggested. With everything that's been going on since, I completely forgot to mention it.'

'So why didn't Mrs Baxter just give the money to Peter, then?'

'I asked her exactly the same thing. She told me Peter had gone away for a couple of days with his partner and was always too busy to do it. After everything Peter's done for us, I figured that saving him the trouble was the least I could do. And I put his flat keys through his letterbox after I'd locked up.'

'Owen, I—'

'I've literally not had a moment to take it to a bank yet. And if I *had* stolen the money, Lizzie, don't you think I'd have done a better job of hiding it?' He shakes his head and sighs. 'I know how uncomfortable you are staying here, and I feel wretched that I can't afford for us to stay elsewhere right now. I'm not being a good provider.'

'Yes, I understand, and I'm so—'

'What I think we need to be asking ourselves, Lizzie,' Owen continues, in a quieter voice, 'is why your mother had Betty's twenty-pound note in her purse in the first place. I was humouring her downstairs, of course, especially given she was brandishing a chef's knife in my direction and playing that creepy music, but I think you're right. Something's off with your mum. She seems a bit... I don't know, unhinged?'

'I know, I *know*... it's just so awful...' I trail off, watching as Owen gathers up the rest of the money and begins counting it out, laying it in stacks.

'I think this tells us all we need to know.' Owen points at the piles of cash on the bed, tapping each one in turn, plus showing me the three twenty-pound notes he's holding. 'There's three hundred and sixty pounds here. Do you know how much Betty gave me to pay into the bank?' He grabs the envelope that the money came from and shows it to me. 'Six hundred and twenty, look. I made a note of it.'

I see the same figure written in Owen's handwriting on the back of the envelope. And below it is a sort code and bank account number that he's printed alongside Betty's full name. We stare at each other, my mouth hanging open as it dawns on me.

'Mum's been in here again,' I whisper, looking over at the door. 'She's gone through your suitcase and taken the money.'

Owen nods once, making me feel even worse for accusing him, but even more angry at my mother. 'Yes, I believe so.'

'How *dare* she.' The rage inside me reaches boiling point as I swipe up my jacket, shoving my arms into the sleeves. 'Right. That's it. I've had enough. We're leaving.'

I fling open the wardrobe doors, grabbing a load of Owen's clothes off the hangers. I only just manage to stop myself from blurting out what she was like when I was a child, how I had no privacy, how she'd barge into my room, searching through my belongings, looking for *clues*, as she'd called them. Mum was always convinced that I was up to no good, or taking drugs, or that I'd got a secret boyfriend hidden away, sneaking him in through the window. Once, when I was sixteen, she even accused me of being pregnant. She was about to throw me out of the house, until she forced me to prove to her that I was on my period.

'Nothing was ever bloody private,' I say, panting as I grab a load more stuff. But then my phone chimes on the bed. It's an email alert. A quick glance at the screen tells me that the sender is the lettings agency. I'd put my email address on the application form, rather than Owen's.

I dump the clothes down and unlock my phone, praying for good news. With the flat secured and Shelley's generous offer, it will mean we can get the hell out of my mother's house once and for all. I don't care if we have to sleep in the car for a few days in the meantime.

But it's not good news.

'Fuck,' I say after I've read it. Then I thrust my phone at Owen.

'Oh no, Lizzie,' he says, wrapping me up in a hug. 'We fought so hard for this place. I guess it wasn't meant to be.'

'No matter,' I say, shoving my phone in my back pocket and grabbing more clothes. 'I'm still packing up our stuff and we're getting out of here before Mum does any more damage.'

'Hey, love, stop. Calm down and have a cup of tea before you do anything too hasty.'

'I don't want a bloody cup of tea, Owen! I want us to get as far away from my mother as we possibly can. Maybe we can sleep on Shelley's sofa for a night or two. I don't know.' I charge around the bedroom, grabbing random items and stuffing them into any old box or bag. I don't care if things get broken, creased or squashed. I just want out.

Then I swipe up the car keys, attempting to zip up the big suitcase. 'Help me,' I say, indicating for him to squash it down. But instead, he just flaps his arms by his sides, clearly not happy about my decision.

Finally, I get the case shut and lug it out of the room onto the landing. Getting our stuff out of the house without Mum seeing or hearing is going to be a challenge, but she can't stop me leaving. As I bump the case down the stairs, I don't care if she kicks up a fuss or throws a tantrum. By the time she's at full force, we'll be gone.

When I get to the hallway, sweat is dripping from me, my face is bright red and my back hurts. But that's the least of my worries compared to what happens after I open the front door to leave.

THIRTY-SIX

Everything seems to happen in slow motion. Owen is still trying to dissuade me from packing up the car and leaving, telling me that he'll have a word with my mother, see if he can smooth things over.

'Lizzie, wait. Don't hurt yourself carrying that outside. I can't have my pregnant fiancée sleeping in the car or on a sofa. *Please...*'

'My mind is made up, Owen,' I say, shoving my feet into my trainers by the front door.

Then he says something about *reasonable explanations* and *silly misunderstandings* about the money that Mum stole. I don't know why he's defending her after what she's done, but he doesn't know who or what he's dealing with and is scared that we'll be homeless. He takes hold of my shoulders, turning me round to face him.

'Listen, love,' he says quietly, both of us aware that Mum is not far away in the kitchen. 'How about we use the remainder of Mrs Baxter's money for a hotel tonight? Then hopefully by tomorrow, the invoice will be paid. The accounts department told me the new one is being fast-tracked and will be processed soon. They even mentioned something about an advance payment on account being possible after I got stroppy with them.'

I stop in my tracks, one hand on the old front door handle. Using poor Mrs Baxter's money is an idea I don't like at all, virtually making me the thief that Peter accused me of being, but I admit that it's tempting. 'I'm not sure that's very... ethical, is it? Under the circumstances. That money is not ours to do what we want with.'

'I'm sure Mrs Baxter would totally understand,' he says. 'As soon as the lump sum comes in from Dubai, I'll make sure the full six hundred and twenty pounds gets paid straight into her bank account. I'll even let her executors know.'

'I don't like it,' I say, 'but yes, OK. Let's do it. Anything to get out of this place. I can't stand to have *her* going through our stuff all the time.' I jab my finger towards the kitchen. 'Not after everything else I've found out about...'

I stop. I don't want Owen knowing what I suspect my mother has done. After learning about Danny's death and the scandal that drove her from her job, I'm almost certain that she was involved with not one but *two* deaths, though what part she played exactly, I'm not yet sure. I'm convinced my mother is capable of anything, and the longer we stay here, the more danger I'm concerned Owen is in. But until I find Joseph and confirm that she was the teacher involved, I can't go throwing accusations about.

'Will you help me get this in the car?'

'Of course, love,' Owen says, lifting up the suitcase. 'And try not to worry. I have a good feeling everything will work out just fine.'

Hearing his comforting words makes me feel a little better, but that quickly changes when I pull open the front door and come face to face with a uniformed police officer – his hand raised to ring the bell – and another, older man in plain clothes standing beside him.

'Oh!' I can't help the gasp.

'Miss Holmes?' the man in plain clothes says, holding out his ID. I give it a glance. A detective.

'Yes... yes, that's me.'

Owen comes up beside me, his fingers slipping between mine. 'Lizzie?' he whispers.

'My name is Detective Inspector Doug Lambert.'

The officer continues talking though I'm not entirely sure what about as all my senses suddenly seem to stop working. I feel numb and frozen, unable to process what's happening.

'What do you mean, police station?' I hear Owen saying a moment later.

The detective's lips are moving, but my brain won't pick apart his words to allow me to make sense of them. I feel as though I might pass out.

'What's... what's happening?' I look up at Owen, pressing myself against him for support.

'Miss Holmes, like I said, we'd appreciate it if you would come down to the station with us for a voluntary interview. In the light of new evidence, we're reviewing the Rafe Lewis case, and we'd like to ask you a few questions.'

'Interview?' I grab Owen's arm. 'But... but we were just about to... to get away.' As soon as I say it, I know it sounds suspicious, as if we're fleeing the scene of a crime. I glance behind the officers, noticing the marked police car sitting on the drive – a luminous beacon to anyone passing by.

Then I hear noises from the kitchen as my mother clatters about. Whatever happens, I can't possibly allow her to witness this scene. The drama would be on a nuclear scale.

'Are you saying my fiancée is under arrest?' Owen says sternly. 'She has rights, you know.'

'We're well aware of her rights,' DI Lambert says wearily. 'And no, she's not under arrest. Of course, if Miss Holmes was unwilling to come with us right now, that may change our procedure.'

Owen sprays out a laugh and puts his hand on the door as if he's about to close it in their faces. Then I hear Mum's voice, calling out to us about dinner and wine, wanting us to set the table.

'Owen, distract Mum,' I whisper. 'Tell her Jared picked me up for an opinion on his house or that Shelley wanted me for something. Just keep her occupied for a bit. I'll go with them, and I'll call you soon. It'll just be a chat about what happened to Rafe last year.'

'OK, if you're sure, darling. Should I contact a solicitor?' He follows me out onto the drive as I'm led to the police car. I duck into the rear seat when I'm instructed, and the two officers climb into the front. Nothing feels real.

'No, and please don't tell Mum about this,' I say, praying she hasn't spotted what's going on. 'I... I don't think I'll need a solicitor,' I say weakly through the open window, but secretly I'm wondering if I do. I force a smile so that Owen doesn't worry. I can't imagine what he's thinking as the officer starts up the engine. 'Why don't you finish packing up the car so we can leave when I get back? And phone around some cheap hotels, too.'

'I will,' Owen says with a concerned look on his face. 'And I'll fetch you just as soon as you're finished. Keep in touch.' He leans in through the window and gives me a kiss and, for some stupid reason, I wonder if it's the last one he'll ever give me.

Then the car reverses and turns around, heading off down the drive. I stare back at Owen through the rear window, watching him standing on the drive, hands on hips as he mouths *I love you* before I'm driven away, leaving him and Mum alone.

THIRTY-SEVEN

The interview room is just like the ones I've seen in the cop dramas that Owen and I watch on TV – a small, drab space with a laminate-topped table, several plastic chairs, fluorescent lighting, everything monochrome. DI Lambert settles himself opposite me after I'm shown where to sit. A female plain-clothes officer, about my age and wearing black trousers with a grey shirt, is already sitting at the table. Her blonde hair is pulled back in a tight ponytail and her face is make-up free. She looks fit, as though she runs or goes to the gym, and her eyes are keen and alert, sizing me up as they flick over me.

DI Lambert puts down his paper coffee cup, having asked me in the reception area if I wanted one (I refused, opting for water instead), then he says something quietly to the woman beside him. She nods and taps a large file set out in front of her.

'No need to look so worried, Miss Holmes,' DI Lambert says with a smile that's probably meant to put me at ease. It doesn't. 'Just a bit of a fact-finding mission for us at this point. I'm the new kid on the block around here,' he says in a dry tone that makes any intended humour fall flat. 'And lucky me, I've been handed this closed case to review after a... development. It might be nothing, but it's pricked up our ears. I know my prede-cessor, DI Waters, had his own opinions about the Rafe Lewis case before he retired, and that they didn't exactly fall into line with the coroner's findings. Anyway...' He rubs his hands together as if he's getting rid of crumbs. 'He liked his hunches, did Malc.' DI Lambert glances across at the woman and grins. She remains deadpan.

'It was awful what happened,' I say, not sure if I'm meant to speak. 'My poor sister.' These few words feel safe enough.

'We understand how upsetting this must be for you and your family and I'm sorry for your loss last year. Hopefully this little... *wrinkle*, shall we say, can be ironed out easily,' the woman says, finally speaking. 'I'm DC Rachel Powell, by the way.' She crosses her legs so that one of her feet sticks out beyond the table legs, and I see that she's wearing black trainers.

'Thank you,' I reply, thinking it's safer to say as little as possible until I'm asked a question.

The two officers lean in close, conferring over a couple of things in the file. DI Lambert takes a few sips of his milky coffee and tells me that they're going to record the session, reminding me that I'm being interviewed under caution but that I can leave at any time. They introduce themselves, stating the time, date and place of the interview, the reason we're here – possible new evidence regarding the Rafe Lewis case – and then they repeat my rights, telling me that anything I say may be used in a court of law as evidence against me. I'm now wishing I'd accepted their offer of the duty solicitor.

Keep calm, I tell myself. *You've done nothing wrong.*

Apart from hiding what could be crucial evidence... another voice screams in my head and, for a moment, I'm worried that I've said what I'm thinking.

'Please state your name and date of birth,' DI Lambert says to me.

'Elizabeth Alice Holmes. Date of birth twenty-fourth of July 1984.'

'Right, let's get started,' DC Powell says with a smile. 'If you can just give us a quick reminder in your own words of the events of Saturday the twenty-seventh of August last year.'

'That was the day of my sister, Shelley's, wedding,' I begin. 'The service was planned for 2 p.m. I was her maid of honour. She had three other bridesmaids. She was marrying Rafe Lewis. They worked together.' I stare at my fingers clasped on the table in front of me, unsure how much detail they want. 'We were getting ready for the wedding at Shelley and Rafe's cottage. It was a bit of a squash, but we were having fun.'

'When you say *we*, who was that?' DI Lambert says. From the corner of my eye, I see DC Powell jotting down notes.

'It was me, Shelley, the bridesmaids – Laura, Ann and little Eesha. She was six. And my mother was there, too.' I take a breath, hoping they don't ask too much about Mum. Describing her under normal circumstances is hard enough. I don't want to explain how she was intent on making the whole day about her, soaking up the glory for all the planning and organising she'd done. And she'd not held back when it came to voicing her disapproval of Rafe, either.

He seems so aloof and detached all the time, darling. Are you really sure? It's not too late to call things off was one of the gems she'd whispered in Shelley's ear as I was zipping up my sister's dress. She didn't think I'd heard, but I had. I'd wanted to yell at her that Rafe wasn't in the least aloof, apart from with her, but I'd bitten my tongue, not wanting to cause a big row. And I knew that Shelley could handle Mum's barbs. We were used to her, after all.

'We were running a bit behind schedule,' I tell the detectives. Then I smile. 'Shelley is a stickler for timings and plans, and had everything written down on a chart. When we were going to eat breakfast, what time we were each to have a shower and do our hair and make-up. Shelley wasn't on call for work that day, of course, but just as she'd changed into her wedding dress, she had a farmer phone her in a bit of a panic. One of his horses was in a lot of pain after an operation, and all the other vets on duty at the practice were either busy or uncontactable because they were guests at the wedding.'

'Did your sister attend the call-out?' DC Powell asks.

I nod, rolling my eyes. 'Yes, very much against my advice, I might add. She took off her wedding dress and threw on jeans and a sweatshirt, telling us she wouldn't be long. She was gone for about forty minutes. She'd already had her hair done, and when she returned, she had hay stuck in it.' I roll my eyes at the memory. 'That's how devoted she is to her work. Rafe was the same.'

'Did she sort out the animal's pain?' DI Lambert asks.

'I assume so,' I reply. 'I didn't really ask. I was more preoccupied with getting her back into her dress and fixing up her hair. She smelt of horses though, I remember that. I sprayed a load of perfume on her.'

'And where was Rafe at this time?' DC Powell asks.

'He was getting ready with the best man, George Reid. George had rented one of the Airbnb barn conversions on the edge of Little Risewell for him, the groom and a few of the guys. He's not from the area. He and Rafe met in London some years ago.'

I remember Shelley telling me she didn't approve of Rafe's choice of best man, that she'd never seen eye to eye with George. 'He's a spoilt brat living the party lifestyle,' she'd said. 'All trust funds and cocaine.' George and Rafe had apparently bonded over a shared love of dogs, with George being involved in fundraising for Battersea. 'Or rather, he gets his parents to donate a shitload each year,' Shelley had informed me, resigned to opposites attracting in this particular friendship. 'Anyway, Rafe doesn't get to see him very often these days,' she'd said. 'So I suppose I can tolerate one day of best man duties.'

'It says on file that Rafe had been out on his stag do the night before the wedding on Friday the twenty-sixth of August.'

'Yes, that's right,' I reply. 'It was meant to have been the previous weekend, but Rafe had to cover on-call shifts at the practice, so they postponed it.'

The detectives nod in agreement, as though they already know this.

'Can you tell me who was present at the stag night and where they went?' DI Lambert asks, tapping his pen on his teeth.

'I think there were about five or six of them, including Rafe and George. A couple of them were from around here, and the others were from out of the area. I don't know all their names. As I said, they were all staying at the Airbnb barn. Rafe was originally from New Zealand and only moved to Oxfordshire a few years ago. He did his training in London, then moved to Edinburgh for a while before settling in the Cotswolds. That's when he met my sister.'

I take a sip of water, hoping the detectives don't notice my shaking hand.

'As for where they went,' I continue, 'I believe they took a taxi into Oxford and went on a pub crawl. George had organised it. Nothing too outrageous as that wasn't Rafe's style.'

'Do you know if any drugs other than alcohol were involved?'

'Drugs?' I say, incredulous. 'No, I very much doubt that. Rafe was as straight up as they came. A real health freak.' Though I suddenly remember what Shelley had told me about George and his cocaine habit. 'Rafe ate healthily, he ran, played rugby and he rarely drank alcohol, so I don't think you'd find him taking anything. Not even a joint.'

The two officers look at each other, with DC Powell

frowning as she glances at the file. 'The pathologist's report shows that illegal drugs were found in his system.'

'*What?*'

'And naturally, alcohol was detected,' DI Lambert adds. 'To be expected on a stag night.' He pores over the file, running his finger down the page, mumbling as he reads. 'Details about the undiagnosed heart condition... urine analysis... blood results...' He glances up, looking at his colleague. Then he turns to me. 'Do you know if they had a meal out?'

I shake my head. 'I don't know.'

'It says in the report that the only thing found in his stomach was a quantity of pre-cooked fruit,' he tells me. 'Various berries, according to the notes.' Then he shrugs and closes the file.

THIRTY-EIGHT

I stare at the detectives, forcing myself to stay calm, even though my nerves are shredded.

'I just can't believe that Rafe took drugs,' I say, not wanting to think about what else he just told me. Shelley never mentioned any of this, though I now realise that she must have known the details contained in the pathologist's report. All she revealed to me was that Rafe had died of a heart attack because of a genetic condition. I wasn't able to attend the inquest hearing because I'd gone back to London long before it took place, but Shelley was present, and I trusted that she'd told me the truth. 'Surely there's been a mistake.'

An image of the fruit crumble that Mum served up for Owen last weekend flashes through my mind, me swiping it onto the floor in a panic... and then it morphs into my mother's corsage lying on the floor beside Rafe, the pool of blood around his head where he'd hit it on the flagstone floor...

DI Lambert raises his bushy eyebrows. 'I know it must come as a shock, especially for someone who never normally took illegal substances. But the report states that alcohol, cocaine, ketamine and also fentanyl were detected by the lab.'

'No way...' I shake my head, unable to take it in. A whole cocktail of drugs, making me wonder if there was a mix-up with the results at the laboratory. 'But... I thought Rafe died of a heart attack?' I try to remember exactly what Shelley had told me after the coroner's conclusion was reached. 'That he had an undiagnosed heart condition and that had caused his death?'

Though I've since wondered what triggered the heart attack. He'd lived his entire life without any symptoms.

'That's correct,' DI Lambert informs me. 'The pathologist's report states that it was the high levels of fentanyl that depressed his respiratory system and lowered oxygen levels. In turn, this stressed his already compromised cardiovascular system, leading to cardiac arrest. It seems that no further forensic toxicology investigations were undertaken at the time, probably because the cause of death had been determined. Or due to lack of funding.' The detective rolls his eyes, muttering the last part.

'I'm truly shocked,' I say, not sure what to think. 'Rafe was such a clean-living guy.'

'Do you think he was the type to succumb to peer pressure on a night out?'

'I... I very much doubt it.' Though I'm beginning to doubt everything now.

'Detailed statements were taken from the others present on the stag night and their stories were all consistent. They said the evening began with a few pints and some shots, a lap-dancing club—'

'But Rafe would *never* go to a place like that.'

DI Lambert shrugs. 'As I'm sure you know, alcohol lowers inhibitions and makes people do things they wouldn't normally do. In their statements, the others admitted to taking cocaine at the club, provided by the best man, George.'

Shelley's suspicions about George were right. He wasn't a good friend.

DI Lambert then speed-reads a section of the file, dragging his finger down part of a long report. 'One of the group said that by this point Rafe was very drunk... willing to try cocaine... more drinking, followed by another club and dancing.' He looks up, making a sympathetic face. 'Apparently, during the evening Rafe got separated from the others. They eventually found him, but he'd been missing for over an hour. He was discovered passed out in an alley behind the club, having previously gone off with a couple of shady characters, according to other witnesses. This was confirmed by the club's CCTV. Dealers, apparently, and they'd sold him ketamine. Drugs tests were performed on the others at the stag, and they only showed cocaine, not the ketamine.'

'*Ket*? Rafe? No way. Absolutely no way. I can't even believe it about the cocaine, let alone the rest.' It's now clear why Shelley never told me about any of this – she wanted to protect Rafe's memory, knowing how ashamed he would have been to have it made public.

'I'm sorry to deliver this news, Miss Holmes. I thought you were aware.'

I shake my head.

'Street ketamine is sometimes cut with fentanyl. It happens all too often, sadly, and what people don't realise is that it's incredibly easy to overdose. In the wrong quantities, it's lethal. Especially for someone with an underlying heart condition. The pathologist's report suggested that further drugs were also taken the next morning. Not surprising, given he must have had a horrific hangover.'

This is not what I was expecting to hear when they brought me here, although I feel slightly ashamed by the relief that sweeps through me. If it was the drugs that killed Rafe, then maybe Mum didn't have anything to do with his death. And maybe the berries were just that. Berries that he'd either had for breakfast or eaten in a dessert the night before. Nothing toxic to trigger a heart attack. My thoughts are making a leap, my mind conditioned to be in overdrive when it comes to my mother.

But I still don't know how her corsage ended up on the floor at the cottage after she'd gone to the church. Something isn't right.

'Anyway, moving on,' DI Lambert says, as though he has better things to be doing. 'I understand that concerns arose when Rafe didn't arrive at the church for the wedding, having told George that he had to attend to something first. He'd assured the best man that he'd be at the church in plenty of time.'

'Yes, that's right.'

'Do you know what it was that he had to do?'

'No, I do not.'

'According to the best man's statement, George later realised that Rafe had taken the wrong shoes to the Airbnb. They weren't his black dress shoes, apparently. He believes he'd gone back home to get them, along with matching socks, once he knew the bridal party had left the cottage. Apparently, it's bad luck to see the bride before the wedding.' DI Lambert gives me a small smile.

Worse luck to see the mother *of the bride*, I can't help thinking.

'That sounds plausible,' I say, remembering Rafe's bare feet. I imagine how awful he must have been feeling – hung-over, weak, shaking. The stag night was never meant to be the night before the wedding.

'After Shelley arrived at the church, naturally worried and upset about where her fiancé was, I understand that's when you and George went looking for Rafe, with you deciding to check Shelley and Rafe's cottage to see if he had gone back home?'

I think back – it's all such a blur. At first, we weren't too concerned, thinking perhaps he'd got last-minute jitters and was maybe taking a few moments to himself. Then I began to worry that Mum had said something to dissuade him from marrying Shelley. I'd put nothing past her.

'Yes, that's correct. Shelley had given me her house keys to look after, so I said I'd go back and check. George was going to drive around the wider area to look for him.' Although I'm now thinking he was probably still over the legal limit for alcohol. 'I borrowed Mum's car to go up to Shelley's cottage.'

'And what did you find when you got there?'

My heart speeds up at the memory.

'The front door was open,' I begin, 'which was odd as I remember locking it when the cars came to fetch us earlier. The bridesmaids, Mum and I were in a separate vehicle to Shelley. She and Dad were in the Rolls-Royce together, as he was walking her down the aisle. I went into the cottage and called out Rafe's name. I thought he might be having a moment. Last-minute nerves. But there was no reply.'

I sip my water again, taking a breath.

'The living room was empty and so I went through to the kitchen and...'

My mind is suddenly crystal clear with what I found. At first, I thought Rafe must have dropped something, that he was on the floor trying to pick it up. But then I quickly realised he wasn't moving, that he was lying prone, his arms splayed out and his legs twisted to one side. His skin had a bluish tinge to it and there was a pool of dark blood congealing around his head from where he'd hit it falling.

'...and that's when I found Rafe lying on the kitchen floor.'

I cover my face and screw up my eyes, letting out a sob as I try to erase what else I'd seen lying beside him, right next to the blood. What else I *did*. I can't possibly tell the police. It's too late for that.

'OK, thank you,' DC Powell says. 'You're doing great. The reason we brought you here today, Miss Holmes, is because we want to ask you if you remember seeing this anywhere.'

From behind my hands, I hear the sound of rustling and something being put on the table, followed by DI Lambert mentioning evidence being presented, followed by a reference number. 'For the benefit of the recording,' he adds.

Slowly, I drag my hands down my face, uncovering my eyes, taking a deep breath to compose myself. When I look down at the table, there's a clear plastic evidence bag lying in front of me. I stare at it for a moment, trying to work out what's inside.

The blood in my veins turns to ice.

Some of the petals are missing, and the rose is now crispy and brown, but there's no doubt that the evidence bag contains my mother's wedding corsage.

THIRTY-NINE

It's Jared who's waiting for me in the reception area of the police station once the interview is over. Feeling punch-drunk and broken, I fight back the tears when I see him standing there, rattling his car keys in his hands, a frown on his face – which breaks into a look of relief when he sees me.

'Lizzie, oh my God, are you OK?' He strides over to me, his hands on my shoulders as though he's reclaiming lost property. It takes all my strength not to fall against him and break down. Instead, I give him a quick nod.

'I'm fine. Let's get out of here,' I say, heading towards the entrance.

Having been grilled to within an inch of my life by the detectives, I need to get as far away as possible from this place. Another six-month stint in Dubai is looking very attractive right now.

I take a deep breath of cool evening air as we walk to Jared's car. 'Who told you I was at the police station?' I ask as he opens the door for me.

'Get in first, then I'll explain,' he says, his expression serious again. Once inside, he puts the keys in the ignition and turns to face me. 'Try not to worry, Lizzie, but... but there's been an accident. I'm afraid it's Owen.'

'Oh my *God*, what's happened? Is he OK?'

'He's in hospital,' Jared says. 'An ambulance came.'

'An *ambulance*?'

'Your mother phoned the emergency services after... after Owen fell down the stairs. She was the one to find him.'

I remain silent for a moment, thinking, wondering, imagining how that could possibly have happened. I feel sick. *What did she do to him?*

'Is he OK? Was he hurt badly?' I can hardly stand to hear the details. I *knew* something like this would happen. I should never have left them alone together, but then I didn't exactly have much choice when the detectives took me to the station.

'I don't know much more than that,' Jared says, starting the car, 'but I'll drive you to him straight away.'

'How did you find out?' I ask as Jared pushes the speed limit, racing through town.

'I called round at Medvale to see you earlier,' Jared says. 'When I arrived, there was an ambulance on the drive and Owen was being carried out on a stretcher. He was conscious, but they had his head in a brace as a precaution. He managed to whisper to me where you were, asking if I'd come and get you. He was more worried about you than about himself.'

I bury my face in my hands. 'Oh, *Jesus*... poor Owen. And Mum was there?'

'Yes, she looked deathly pale and upset. I'd only called round to find out if you'd spoken to Danny's parents. Gav said his Mum had told you where they live.'

It doesn't seem possible that only this morning I was at the bungalow, talking to Mary about her sons. And only yesterday afternoon that Dad had dropped his bombshell on me. I grab the door handle as we speed around a corner.

'Did you find them, Danny's parents?' Jared asks, concentrating on the road.

I try to push my fears for Owen aside as I concentrate on telling Jared about my visit, how Mary had seemed willing to talk to me, but John was gruff and defensive. 'It was so sad,' I say, filling him in on Danny's suicide and their estranged son, Joseph – though I don't go into detail about the abuse he reported. I'm certain it's tied to Mum and her leaving her job. But right now, I'm too worried about Owen to focus on all that, hardly daring to think how he could have fallen down the stairs.

Twenty minutes later, Jared drops me at the hospital entrance and goes to park the car. I run past the ambulance bays, imagining Owen being stretchered inside, praying he's not in too much pain. There's a short queue at the A & E reception, and when I eventually reach the front, the woman tells me where to find Owen. Not knowing what to expect, I head through the double doors and venture past the triage area and on to the bays. A couple of nurses walk briskly past, and I stand aside as a porter wheels a very sick-looking old man down the corridor.

'Excuse me,' I ask a young nurse, who's standing at a desk, typing something into a computer. 'I'm looking for my fiancé, Owen Foster. He was brought in by ambulance. Do you know which bay he's in?'

While the nurse looks flustered and rushed, she still gives me a smile and switches screens to run a quick search. 'Ah, yes. He's in majors,' she says.

Majors? My frown makes her explain.

'This area is for minor injuries. Go that way for the major injuries unit. He's in bay seven,' she adds as I rush off towards another set of double doors, even more worried about what's happened as I wait for another porter wheeling an ultrasound machine to come through first.

'Bay one, two... three...' I say, hurrying past the cubicles.

Most have the curtains closed, but several are open showing patients of all ages lying on beds. And then, around the corner, I spot bay number seven. I take a deep breath before peeling back the curtain and stepping inside, unsure what to expect.

'Oh, *Owen*...' I whisper, my eyes fixed on him as he lies on the bed, a single white sheet draped over him. He's flat on his back in a hospital gown with various machines beeping around him, but I can't help the gasp when I see the other person sitting in the chair next to him, her hand clutched tightly around his. '*Mum*... what are *you* doing here?'

She glances up at me, a smug look spreading across her face. 'Well, someone had to be here with him, didn't they? I heard you'd gone off gallivanting about with that Jared person. Although you were lying, weren't you? He came looking for you just after the accident, so where *were* you, Elizabeth? No, wait, stop!' Mum holds her free hand up in my direction and shies away from me, screwing up her eyes. 'I don't want to know your sordid lies. The fact is, you weren't here for your fiancé and that's unforgivable. I could hardly let him come to hospital alone, could I?'

I take a deep breath, closing my eyes for a heartbeat before going up to Owen, standing on the opposite side of the bed to where Mum is sitting. Owen must have told her the cover story I suggested – that I'd gone off with Jared to view the house he's buying – and while she now knows that's a lie, she doesn't seem aware that I've just spent a gruelling couple of hours down at the police station. It takes even more strength to put out of my mind what happened while I was there – being presented with my mother's corsage in an evidence bag.

'Owen, darling, how are you feeling?' I lean over him, speaking softly, stroking his hair. Then I gently lift up his arm, loosening his hand from my mother's grip and curling my fingers around his.

'Lizzie?' Owen replies weakly, opening his eyes. He stares

up at me and it doesn't take a doctor to see that he's heavily dosed up on painkillers.

'I'm here,' I tell him, rearranging the sheet over him. 'Are you in pain? Where does it hurt?'

'Yeah, a bit,' he says, wincing. 'It's my neck.' He raises his free hand to touch the base of his skull, pulling a face.

'Did they X-ray you? Have you broken anything?' I notice that there's no brace on him now so I'm praying it's good news.

'No... no breaks, thank goodness,' he whispers, closing his eyes again. 'Still waiting for... brain scan results.'

'OK, just rest if you can.'

'Conc... concussion,' he says, touching his temple.

I lean down and give him a kiss on the forehead, noticing that he feels clammy and cool. 'I'm going to find a doctor and see if they can tell me anything,' I whisper to him, but it's Mum who replies, her tone of voice sending shivers down my spine.

'Stop fussing, Elizabeth. He just had a little tumble, that's all.' Mum looks at me, sitting quite still as her eyes lock onto mine. I've seen that look so many times before – smug and self-satisfied, with no words needed to convey what she's thinking. 'No harm done.'

I prise myself away from her glare and leave the cubicle, almost colliding with a hospital cleaner, who is busy emptying a waste bin. As they tie up the bag, I spot a bouquet of fresh flowers still in the cellophane, perhaps thrown away because they're not allowed in the treatment area. I can't help staring at the red roses, a few scarlet petals falling out of the wrapping and onto the floor, trodden on by the cleaner as he puts in a fresh bin liner.

'Do you know what this is?' DI Lambert had asked me. I stared at the crispy petals of the corsage sealed in the plastic evidence bag. They were now a deep, dark red, the colour of dried blood.

'I... I'm not sure.' My brain was scrambling to come up with a reply that was honest but that didn't incriminate me. There was no doubt in my mind that it was my mother's corsage, yet I had absolutely no idea how it had come to be in their possession. The last time I'd seen it was when I shoved it in one of the boxes before Dad put them in the loft. And then it had gone missing.

'Take a close look. Take your time,' DC Powell had then said. I knew they were both watching me intently – the woman with her arms folded tightly across her shirt, one leg hooked up over her knee, her black trainer thrumming out a beat on the table leg. DI Lambert was sitting back in his chair, sipping on his coffee as they waited for me to answer.

'I think they're flowers,' I'd said. My answer reeked of me trying to hide something – and they'd have been right to think that.

'Do you know where they came from?' DC Powell asked.

'Umm, no. Maybe... maybe a florist? They look as though they're wired together. See?' *Jesus*, what was I thinking? I'd even pointed to the dark-green wire that tied the stems together. My mother had had a terrible time getting the pearl-topped pin to hold the flowers on her jacket.

'Do you think it might be a wedding corsage?' DI Lambert then said. His tone was slightly patronising, indicating he had better things to be doing.

'Oh,' I'd replied. 'Yes, yes it might be.'

The detectives had then gone on to grill me about the types of flowers that Shelley had ordered for her wedding. Stupidly, I claimed I couldn't remember. Instead, I'd said, 'It was my mother who'd dealt with all that. She... she played a big part in organising the whole day.'

'We've been in touch with Martha's Flowers, the florist used for the event,' DC Powell had then said, sliding a piece of A4 paper from her file. 'Here's the order made on the ninth of May last year.' She runs her finger along one line, already highlighted yellow. 'We believe this is the item in question, a single red rose corsage with cream freesias, see? It was the only one of this particular style on the order.'

I'd nodded, reading the invoice. 'Yeah, I think someone had a corsage like that. It's possible. The whole day is a bit of a blur. Sorry.'

'Excuse me!' someone says now, striding past me – a nurse pushing a blood pressure machine into a cubicle. I step aside, my head spinning. And then I catch sight of a doctor going into Owen's bay, so I follow her in.

'Have you got the scan results?' I ask her, rushing up to Owen's side as the doctor picks up a clipboard attached to the end of the bed. 'I'm here, love,' I say, taking Owen's hand again. He seems more awake now and has raised his bed to a semi-sitting position. A good sign, I hope. He smiles at me, which almost makes me melt from relief. 'How did the accident happen?' I whisper to him while the doctor is busy reading Owen's notes. 'What on earth caused you to fall?'

Behind me, I'm aware the doctor is now talking to a nurse, who's also come into the cubicle. They're saying something about monitoring... pain relief... concussion... discharge... but my main focus is Owen, especially when he turns his head slowly towards my mother, his eyes locking onto hers.

FORTY

I took the doctor at her word when she said that Owen shouldn't be left alone for forty-eight hours in case any further concussion symptoms develop, which means that I barely slept a wink. All through the night – or rather the remainder of it after we'd got back gone midnight – I'd kept checking on him to see if he was breathing, making sure I heard the soft in–out wheeze as he'd slept. I'd also felt the temperature of his skin and, a couple of times, I'd put my fingers around his wrist to make sure his pulse was steady and even.

Now, as light begins to seep in behind the curtains of the bedroom – the bedroom I was trying to escape from yesterday afternoon – I feel exhausted, tearful, beaten down and ready to give up.

I'll never forget the way Owen looked at my mother in hospital when I asked the reason for his fall. But the moment to confront her about what she'd done had quickly passed as the doctor started talking about scan results and Owen's discharge.

She'd given him the all-clear, saying there was no sign of any bleeds or damage to his brain or skull, and his X-rays were fine. Thank God. She warned there'd be a bit of bruising and stiffness for a few days and had given him some painkillers, sending him on his way with an information sheet about concussion.

After Jared had dropped us all back at Medvale, the first thing I'd asked Owen as soon as we were alone was, 'Was it Mum? Did she push you down the stairs?'

Owen had just stared at me, releasing a sigh that told me all I needed to know. I'd closed my eyes as my worst fears were confirmed.

'I don't think she *meant* to hurt me, love. It's... it's all a bit hazy, really. I was fetching our stuff from the bedroom to take down to the car, and then your Mum was suddenly behind me on the landing.'

'What are you doing, Owen?' he told me she'd said. 'You're not leaving, are you?' He went on to describe how upset she'd seemed, how he'd tried to keep her calm, saying that I would explain everything to her once I was back. 'Then she grilled me about where you were, and she really didn't like it when I pretended to her that you were out with Jared. She muttered a few rude words under her breath, but there was this... this *look* in her eyes, Lizzie. It scared me a bit, to be honest.'

I'd taken a breath, knowing exactly the look he meant, and I was quite able to imagine the vocabulary she would have used. 'So... did Mum push you?'

Owen had hesitated, as though he was unsure what to say – the truth, because he hated lying to me, or a fabrication so it was easier for me to swallow. In the end, I told him to tell it like it was.

'No... no, I wouldn't say she *pushed* me, exactly. I'm sure it was just an accident. I was struggling with our stuff, and I think she was about to take something from me to help. Though...'

'Though *what*?'

'It's nothing. I probably just imagined her hands on my back. She'd never have done it on purpose. I'd smoothed things over after the cellar incident, and I thought we'd been getting on all right. But anyway, the next thing I knew, I was tumbling head-first down the stairs. Then everything went black.'

'Oh, *Owen*...'

I'd buried my face in my hands at the thought, almost igniting with anger. To me, it seemed cut and dried that my mother had indeed shoved him down the stairs. To Owen, it was an unfortunate accident and Mum had only been trying to help.

While there was no way we could leave Medvale when we arrived back from the hospital late last night, looking at Owen lying next to me in bed now – a purple bruise blooming around his left eye, him still sleepy and sore – I'm not sure it's wise to leave today and be holed up in a hotel either. But there's no way I feel safe staying here.

'What if I finish packing the car and find us a hotel?' I ask.

'I... I'm not sure I feel quite up to that yet, love. Perhaps we could consider it tomorrow?'

He's right. I'm knee-jerking. Besides, where would we go after that when Betty's cash runs out? Even if Shelley lends us the money, there are no flats to rent, and I haven't had a chance to check the agents' websites in the last day or so, which makes me feel even more stuck here, beholden to my mother.

I grab my pillow and shove it over my face, digging my fingers into the feathers and letting out a silent scream.

Suddenly, I stop. A noise. A tapping at the door. Without disturbing Owen, I slip out of bed, reaching for my dressing gown to see who it is – though of course it can only be one person.

'Mum?' I whisper, opening the door a crack. I peek out, seeing her standing there holding a tray and wearing a contrite expression. 'What do you want?'

'I thought you might like breakfast,' she says, holding the tray out towards me. There's a pot of tea and two mugs, some toast, butter, jam, as well as two pots of yoghurt and a bowl of mixed berries. 'But if you don't want it, I can go—'

'No, Mum, wait.' Our eyes lock for a moment. In mine, she probably sees suspicion, exhaustion, mistrust and fear. Within hers, I see... *nothing*. She's empty and cold, almost making me wish I *had* told the truth to the police about the corsage yesterday. Then I remind myself that if I'd done that, *I'd* be the one in trouble. And I can't risk that, not with a baby on the way.

'Do you have any idea who may have sent this wedding corsage to us?' DI Lambert had asked wearily in the interview room. 'Or why? It arrived anonymously. Our CCTV shows a teenager on a bike dropping it off at the station's main entrance. Unfortunately, their face is hidden behind a hood and scarf, and we only managed to track the bike a certain distance with the town cameras. Then they went out of range. But we suspect they were asked to deliver it by someone else. It wouldn't be the first time that sort of thing has happened.'

I'd pulled a puzzled face, shaking my head. 'No, I have no idea at all.' That was the truth, at least.

'It came with a brief note.' DC Powell opened the folder and took out a plastic wallet with a piece of A4 paper tucked inside. She slid it across in front of me and I saw what appeared to be a colour photocopy of the original note – a few words scribbled on a scrap of brown envelope. Parts of the diagonal flap were visible in the photocopy, and the edge was jagged and ripped.

'*Rafe Lewis case. She's a murderer,*' I'd read out loud, pulling another puzzled face, although a bone-deep chill ran through me. The writing was boxy and childish, the slightly uneven capital letters looking as though they might have been disguised. 'Oh my God, that's awful. What do you think it means?'

But I knew exactly what it meant – that I wasn't the only one who suspected my mother of doing something terrible.

'We were hoping you might be able to tell us,' DI Lambert replied.

I shrugged, staring at the dried-up flowers in the bag again. What was I supposed to tell them – that yes, I'd found my mother's corsage and then hidden it to protect my sister, my father, *myself*? There'd been enough trouble in our family over the years, and I knew that if Mum did have something to do with Rafe's death, then it would tip my father over the edge. As it turned out, that's exactly what happened anyway – although now I'm wondering what else Dad knows.

I glanced up at them, my mind swimming with the events of that day.

'Maybe it fell off someone's outfit and ended up on the floor next to Rafe?' I suggested, desperately wanting to tell them who it belonged to, but without implicating myself.

The detectives looked at each other. 'Whose outfit do you think that might be?' DC Powell asked.

'I... I...' My mother's name was stuck in my throat, waiting for me to spit it out. But I couldn't. The moment I said her name was the moment I got arrested. 'I don't know, I'm sorry. So many people came and went that afternoon, it probably dropped off without anyone realising. Someone must have picked it up and kept it all this time.' It wasn't the best response and I know I looked nervous as hell, and neither did it explain the accompanying note or why it had been delivered to the police station in the first place. But it was something for them to chew over given it was clear they wanted answers from me.

DC Powell jotted something down in her notebook, while DI Lambert had a slightly uncertain expression on his face.

'Thank you,' DI Lambert had finally said in a resigned and exasperated tone. 'Though... one thing you said puzzles me,' he'd added, a stern look sweeping over his face again.

'Yes?' I replied, gripping the edge of the table.

'Why did you say the corsage was lying next to Rafe Lewis's body? No one has mentioned that detail before.'

FORTY-ONE

I watch as Owen sips his tea. He's sitting up in bed and I'm pleased to see that his colour is gradually improving, though he's got a nasty bruise blooming down the left side of his face, varying in colour from grey to purple to green.

'And you're sure you don't have a headache now?' I ask for about the fifth time.

'Barely at all,' he says. 'I was lucky. It could have been a whole lot worse.' He tucks into some of the toast Mum brought up, though I've put aside the bowl of blueberries and raspberries just in case.

'And you're sure you'll be OK while I nip out to the garage?' I've already been up and down the stairs half a dozen times, ferrying our belongings from the Volvo back up to our bedroom after our failed escape. I also filled him in on what happened yesterday at the police station, though I didn't mention the corsage.

'What a pair we are, me in hospital and you being grilled by the cops,' he'd said, shaking his head. Then he'd winced, clutching at his sore neck. But we'd each found a small laugh within us about our situation, because it was that or utter despair. Then I'd told him that if we're forced to stay here with Mum for the time being, then there's something I need to do.

And by *forced* to stay with my mum, I mean our situation now feels exactly like that – as though we're prisoners. While Owen is under doctor's orders to rest for a few days, the detectives strongly urged me to stay in the area in case they needed to speak to me again. And that was only because I'd let slip about the corsage being found beside Rafe's body. They'd decided a few more enquiries would be needed.

I flick the garage light on, hoping that I'll find what I need. If not, I'll have to make a trip to the hardware store.

Dad was always a stickler for keeping everything neat and organised in his workshop – all his tools hanging on their correct hooks on the wall, with various cupboards and chests containing equipment that he's used over the years for DIY projects around the house.

I scan the handwritten labels, clearly printed in slightly crooked capital letters, directing me to the drawer I need – the one containing bolts and latches. Inside, I find an assortment of slider bolts, mostly small and the kind that would go inside a bathroom door, but underneath these, I find the perfect metal fitting – a steel hasp to be used with a padlock. And in another compartment, I find some chunky padlocks, each with a matching key. I can't help smiling at how ordered everything is, silently thanking Dad for making my job easy. I grab his cordless drill from its charger, plus a few screws, and head back to our bedroom. I don't want to leave Owen alone too long, even though he insists he's fine.

'What the *hell* are you doing, Elizabeth?' Mum says fifteen minutes later as I'm putting in the final screw, having drilled into the outside of our bedroom doorframe. I jump at the sound of her voice behind me.

'Securing our belongings with a lock,' I tell her without looking up. 'Don't worry, I'll fill in the holes when we leave, but Mum...' I turn round to face her, 'surely you can't blame me for doing this? You stole my engagement ring. You stole money from Owen's suitcase. You rifled through our boxes and found my pregnancy book. How much more do you think I can take before...' I force myself to stay calm, even though I need her to hear this. 'Before I *crack*?'

Mum is silent, the only sound the small swallow she makes. She nods her head. 'Fine,' she says curtly. 'Do what you have to, Elizabeth.' She points at the lock. 'And I'm sorry you think I'm a thief, but I need you to know—'

'Mum, stop,' I say quietly. 'I'm done with excuses and denials. All I want now is for Owen to get better and us to find a place to live.'

'And your wedding,' she whispers hopefully, tilting her head sideways. 'Reverend Booth has arranged for you to meet with a special member of the clergy, the marriage surrogate, on Monday. He is able to issue the common licence, and don't worry, I'll pay the fee, and once that is sorted, then the wedding can—'

'Mum... again, *stop*.' I don't even have the energy to bark at her. 'I need some time alone, OK? Just me and Owen. Please, will you quit fussing and organising and taking over? I honestly can't deal with it right now.'

'OK,' Mum says, turning to go. 'I understand.' As she heads downstairs, she lets out a throaty sound that, to me, sounds a lot like a growl.

FORTY-TWO

The rest of the day passes in a haze of sleep, cups of tea and eating the lunch I made for us. Owen and I lie on the bed together, chatting about everything from vague plans going forward, to the various things we did when we were in Dubai. Reminiscing about when we met seems to take the painful edge off our predicament now. It's what we both need.

'I'd love to try windsurfing again,' he says, flicking through some photos on his phone. 'I don't think I was very good at it, but we had fun, right?'

'We did indeed,' I say, gazing longingly at the pictures. I zoom in on one photo – a selfie he'd taken of us both on Kite Beach after our lesson. My hair is covered in sand and my nose dotted with freckles, and there's a glint in my eyes that I haven't seen in a long while. I can't help thinking that I look so much happier and healthier in the sunshine. The time that Owen and I spent together in Dubai, getting to know each other, realising that our souls chimed, our values and ambitions clicked, the way our bodies fell into a natural rhythm... it was so precious. I want that feeling back – carefree, adventurous, living in the moment.

It had been all about us.

Now, it's all about Mum.

I have no idea how we went from that to this – the pair of us holed up in my childhood bedroom in my mother's house – me fearful of her intentions, and Owen recovering from a serious injury caused by her.

'We'll get back on track, Lizzie,' Owen says, sitting up, rubbing his neck. 'If it helps put your mind at rest, I've finally had assurance that the money will come through this week, so we may not even need to borrow from your sister.'

I can't help the snort. 'Honestly? I'll believe that when I see it,' I say. 'I wish you didn't have to work for that wretched company any more.'

'Don't you worry,' Owen replies confidently. 'I've got my finger on lots of different pulses right now. I had a few productive meetings in London earlier in the week. I've got our little one to think of now, after all.' He places a hand on my stomach, and I snuggle up against him. 'It's all going to be fine.'

I sigh, knowing things are far from fine.

'It's worrying me that after everything, my mother is still forging ahead with plans for our wedding. I think we have some... some practical decisions to make, love,' I say, knowing we need to be on the same page. Out of habit, I fiddle with the two engagement rings on my finger. 'It's meant to be happening a week tomorrow.'

I pause, waiting for a reaction, but there's nothing. I feel so selfish even bringing it up, because I know how much Owen wants to get married here in Little Risewell.

'*Meant* to be? Are you saying you don't want to marry me now?' He sounds disappointed as he shifts round to look at me.

'No, no, of *course* I'm not saying that.' The hurt in his voice cuts straight through me, so I slide out from under the covers and sit cross-legged on the bed beside him. It's almost impossible to explain without blurting everything out, and there's no way I'm doing that. 'My little bump and I want to marry you more than anything else in the world,' I say, taking a deep breath, knowing this is the point at which I either change tack and go along with Mum's wedding plans, or pull the plug on the whole thing and risk upsetting Owen.

'I sense there's a *but* coming.' Owen looks up at me, one arm hooked behind his head, supporting his neck. The sheet is wrapped around his middle, his bare chest exposed. There's still a bit of a tan from Dubai, still a little reminder of the good times – though the bruise on his face reminds me of the bad.

'Not in the sense that I don't want to marry you. It's so very far from that. But what you need to understand about my mother is... things she did in the past... I'm worried that...' It's no good. The words still won't come.

Owen smiles – a warm, soothing, knowing, comforting smile. 'Love, I got the measure of your mum long ago,' he says, surprising me.

How can I tell him that he can't possibly have an inkling of what she's really like? That what he thinks he knows barely scratches the surface?

'I understand that she's volatile and unpredictable. I also know that she gave you and Shelley a hard time growing up. And that your dad suffered because of it. But things are different now, OK? I'm here. I'll protect you and our baby. Emotionally *and* physically, though heaven forbid that should be necessary.'

A hard time... I repeat his words in my head. I don't even have the energy to tell him how wrong he is, that if only my mother had simply given us all *a hard time*, things would have been very different. Pleasant, even.

'For what it's worth,' he says, 'I reckon that for all her faults, she's a good soul.' For a moment, Owen looks as though he's tasted something bitter, as if he's saying what he thinks I want to hear, but then his face relaxes. 'And since we're talking about the wedding, I want you to know that there is literally nothing else in the entire world that I'd rather do more than marry you next week. To think that we'll soon be Mr and Mrs Foster, having the ceremony in that beautiful church, our baby on the way – the thought fills me with a sense of happiness that I can't even begin to explain. My only regret is that my mum, dad and brother aren't here to see it.'

'Oh, Owen,' I say, clasping his hands in mine, looking at him earnestly. 'Me too. I want to marry you more than anything, I promise. But...' I trail off, my throat closing up, preventing me from saying what I really think. I must decide which is worse: getting married on my mother's terms or making Owen unhappy.

Something flutters in my chest – the same feeling I had when we first met. Anticipation and excitement, the promise of magic and positivity. The way we used to look at each other, knowing exactly what the other was thinking; the random little gifts we bought just to say I love you. It's been too easy to forget all that in the mire of Mum's presence, the weight of everything else.

'Since I lost my family, I've never felt that I ever belonged anywhere, not truly,' Owen says. 'So being here, in your child-hood home, surrounded by things that were dear to you...' A tear appears in the corner of one of his eyes, making him laugh and sniff from embarrassment. 'What I'm trying to say is that yes, despite all your mother's nonsense, I really want to have this wedding. I really want to have *you*. It's going to be fine, I promise. It'll symbolise the start of all things good again. These last few weeks have been tough, sure, but brighter days are coming. And they begin with us getting married.'

I stare into his eyes, seeing everything familiar, everything about him that I fell in love with. When I focus on that, I know there's nothing else we need.

'OK,' I whisper, the beginnings of a smile spreading on my

face. I can't help it as I bounce up and down, my excitement growing as I force my mother and all my concerns to the back of my mind. After Owen's accident, it's made me see how fragile life is. 'Let's do it,' I say. 'Let's get married in St Michael's church next Saturday. Let's have a big party in a marquee on the lawn filled with people we don't know.' I laugh at the thought, my smile growing bigger. 'Let Mum fuss and kick off with her drama and let everyone get pissed and let the roast lamb be tough as old boots. Let the vegetarians eat salmon and let the wedding cake taste like sawdust. Let the music be tuneless and cheesy, let the tent fall down, and let the heavens open with a thunderstorm so everyone gets washed away. And most of all, let Shelley be OK and let what happened last year stay in the past just for one day. Let me marry you in my beautiful dress in the beautiful church, and after that, I honestly don't care what else happens. Because no one can take that magic away from us, right?'

'Let them dare try,' Owen whispers, staring into my eyes and mirroring my smile as he pulls me close for a kiss.

FORTY-THREE

This morning's meeting with the reverend went seamlessly. I'd been expecting hiccups, but it had gone without a hitch at the marriage surrogate's office at the rectory in town. Besides, paperwork is the least of my problems. Owen and I had gone alone after I managed to persuade Mum that her time was better spent sorting out flowers or wedding favours for the tables. Anything to keep her occupied while we finalised our marriage licence.

Needless to say, she was thrilled when I told her I was looking forward to the big day – though I had to force myself to ignore the smug look she gave me when her dour expression twisted itself into something like a smile. She has no idea that I'm on high alert, watching her actions closely, preparing myself for whatever she might be planning.

'I can't believe it,' I'd said to Owen as we left the rectory. 'It's really happening!' I was trying to remain upbeat for his sake, but there was no way I could tell him about the adrenaline pumping through me, or how my mind was catastrophising every possible moment of our big day.

He squeezed my hand as we walked back to the car, giving

me a look that told me we were doing exactly the right thing – that nothing else mattered and nothing would go wrong.

'I must let Peter know,' I'd said on the drive back to Medvale. 'It's short notice, but I really want him to be at our wedding.' Plus, it's someone else who'll watch my back throughout the day – someone else to keep an eye on my mother. He knows exactly what she's like.

Owen had given me a sideways look. 'If you're sure,' he'd said. 'I mean... he threw some hefty accusations around, love. Are you certain he's the type of person we want to help us celebrate?'

But it hadn't taken much to convince him that Peter had simply been looking out for Mrs Baxter, and that I forgave him for assuming the worst.

'I'm not ruining our friendship over a misunderstanding,' I told him, promising Owen that I'd let Peter know that we had the money safe and would ensure its return to Mrs Baxter's estate. 'I'll visit Dad, too. Tell him our plans so that he can mentally prepare for Saturday. I want him to give me away.' I also wanted to make sure that he confessed to Shelley that he's been at Winchcombe voluntarily all this time, that he's been lying to everyone, but I kept that to myself. My excited chatter went on, Owen reaching out and giving my thigh a squeeze as I drove.

'I love seeing you so happy,' he'd then said, 'but do you think your dad will be up to that role? I'm sure your mum would step in if you needed her to.'

I'd shuddered at the suggestion, though I felt wretched for keeping such a big secret from him – *another* one. 'Dad's health has... it's improved loads recently.' I cleared my throat. 'I think it'll be good for him to give me away.' Then I'd changed the subject.

After I drop Owen back at Medvale – with him convincing me that, apart from a sore neck and bruised cheekbone, he's absolutely fine – I head over to Shelley's house to see who's home. I'm hoping that both she and Jared will be there. But before I pull out of the driveway, I call Peter from the car.

'I can't tell you what a huge relief it was to discover the money was safe,' I say to him, having explained how Mrs Baxter had given the money to Owen to pay into her bank. 'I think her memory was worse than anyone realised.' The line goes silent for a while, making me wonder if we've been cut off.

'Pete, are you there?'

'I'm here,' he says flatly. 'Though...'

'Though what? I will personally make sure every penny is paid into her account, so don't worry about that. Owen's got it safely in his bag.' *In a locked room*, I think to myself, but Peter doesn't need to hear about all the trouble with Mum, or how I still need to get the rest of the cash back that she stole from the envelope, which I'll be doing after the wedding. There's no way I'm poking the beast before then.

'Nothing,' he says after another pause. 'Just let me know when it's deposited, and I'll inform her son.'

Then I tell him all about the plans for our wedding, hoping he'll share my excitement.

'You're really going through with this, then?' It's not exactly the response I'd been expecting.

'Yes, we are,' I tell him. 'It's what Owen and I want. What we *need*,' I add, though I can't help my voice wavering. 'This last week... it's been a challenge, but it's shown me that the only thing I want right now is to be settled and happy with Owen. He feels the same.' Then I take a breath before telling him about my pregnancy, how we're over the moon. 'Getting married is about the only thing I have any control over at the moment, so that's what I'm doing.'

Unexpectedly, I feel as though I'm about to burst into tears. I screw up my eyes and swallow hard, trying to stop my throat closing up completely.

'Lizzie, darling, are you OK?'

'Yes... no... I don't know...' I whisper, not wanting to burden him, but I can't help it. 'Pete... I... I'm *scared*.'

There, it's out.

'Oh, my love, why? Tell me how I can help.'

'It's Mum. She's plotting something awful, I swear. I'm terrified Owen's going to get hurt, that she's going to do something dreadful to him. I just don't know what.'

Then Pete listens as I tell him everything that's happened since we've been here. When I'm finished, he waits patiently as the tears finally come.

'If you're set on going through with this then you can count on me to help. I'll be your ears on the ground, watching her like a hawk. Any threats or disaster, I'll avert them before you even know what's happening. Trust me?'

Something inside me loosens a little – one finger of fear letting go as I hear Pete's comforting words. 'Of course, thank you,' I say, blowing my nose. 'You're a good friend, Pete.'

'Anyway, your mother aside, I would not miss your wedding for the world. Text me all the details.'

Relief swoops through me. 'Bring Jacko, too,' I tell him before we say goodbye. And I head off to Shelley's feeling an ounce lighter than I did this time yesterday.

FORTY-FOUR

'You've just missed her, I'm afraid,' Jared says as I go into Shelley's cottage. I follow him through to the kitchen. 'I'll put the kettle on.'

'Cheers and congratulations,' I say, after he's made two mugs of tea, chinking my cup against his. 'Here's to your new home!' He's just told me that the vendor of Cherry Tree Cottage has accepted his offer, and Gavin has put him in touch with a local architect to get the ball rolling on plans.

'Thanks, Lizzie,' he says, seeming pleased. 'I just need to fill it with a family now.' The wistful look in his eyes doesn't pass me by.

'There's been no one special in your life lately?'

Jared lets out a laugh. 'Nope. Not unless you count a couple of relationships in LA that didn't go anywhere, but I guess my heart wasn't in it when I knew I'd be returning home to England. Fun while it lasted.'

'Maybe you'll meet someone at the wedding,' I say, giving him a wink. 'Though most of our guests are Mum and Dad's friends, so they'll have an average age of anywhere between sixty-five and eighty, so don't hold your breath.'

Jared smiles. 'I'm in no rush.' Though the sudden rise and fall of his chest as he lets out a sigh tells me that he probably is. And I don't blame him. Being in love, feeling safe and secure in the knowledge that whatever life throws at you, there's always someone who has your back, is priceless. Despite all my fears, I suddenly feel like the luckiest woman alive.

'And about the wedding,' I continue. 'I was wondering if you would do Owen a huge honour. Well, do *me* a huge favour, I suppose.'

'Go on,' Jared says, his interest piqued.

'Would you be Owen's best man?' I try to gauge his reaction, but he just stares at me from the other end of the sofa. 'He doesn't have any family coming to the wedding, and any friendships he's had over the years have fizzled out because he's moved around so much. It would mean the world to him to have another man by his side, someone to support him.'

Jared seems to be mulling it over and for an awful moment, I think he's going to refuse. 'Of course,' he says with his trademark smile – the one that makes his eyes twinkle. 'If it's what you want.'

I reach out and touch his arm. 'Thank you,' I say, but I can't help wondering if there's hesitation in his voice.

'I know what you're thinking,' I say with a nervous laugh. 'Shelley reckons I'm rushing things, too, but I've never been more certain about anything in my life.'

'We're just looking out for you, Lizzie,' he adds, which is telling. *We* must mean that he and Shelley have been discussing it. 'Where did you say Owen is from originally?' Jared asks. 'Are there no school or university friends he could invite?'

'His family were based further north, near Middlesbrough. His parents and brother died in a car accident. He took me to see their graves when we got back from Dubai. Imagine saying goodbye to three members of your family in one go. Awful.'

'That's shocking,' Jared says, looking pensive.

'He went to Leeds University to study physics but he's not really in touch with anyone from there now.'

'Physics,' Jared says, looking impressed. 'Smart guy.' Though by his expression, I can tell he's chewing everything over. 'Anyway, for Saturday, I have a couple of decent suits, so unless you have any objections, shall I wear the grey one? Perhaps with a cream silk tie?'

'Perfect,' I reply. 'Owen's hiring a morning suit.'

'Fancy,' Jared replies, though he still sounds pensive. 'Talking of old friendships, part of the reason I came to see you at Medvale on Friday was to show you something... hang on a moment.' He gets up and heads upstairs, returning with an old shoebox. 'Get a load of this,' he says, sitting down next to me. 'After I showed Gavin that old photo of us, he got a touch of nostalgia. He found a load of old school newsletters, clippings and class photos on top of a wardrobe at his mum's house. We had a drink to discuss potential plans for the house, and he brought this lot along. He said I could borrow it to show you.'

'Ooh, exciting,' I say, though I know there won't be any pictures of me because these are from St Lawrence's Grammar, not the comprehensive. 'Are there any photos of Shelley?'

'Certainly are,' he says with a grin. 'And muggins here. Some of Gav, too. The boy did good finding this lot.' He riffles through the stack and pulls out a special millennium edition of the school newsletter – a navy cover embossed with gold lettering on the front. 'We bookmarked a couple of pages.' Jared flips to a particular class photo with all the pupils lined up – the girls wearing blue check summer dresses and the boys in their white shirts and grey trousers.

'Oh my God, look, that's you there, isn't it?' I say, pointing at a face. 'Standing at the back, of course, because you're so tall.'

'Guilty,' Jared says. 'Christ knows what you saw in me. I was a lanky nerd.'

We stare at each other for a moment, sharing a look, then we both burst out laughing.

'You're still a lanky nerd,' I say, giving him a nudge. I turn a few pages, looking at pictures of highlights of the school year – everything from plays to class outings, to sports events and prize-giving day. I scan the names underneath, seeing if I recognise anyone from the village.

'Look, there's Danny Wentworth,' Jared says. 'In the school play.'

'You're right, it's him,' I say quietly, feeling a pang of sadness as well as guilt. I touch his face, though try not to fall back into the sad world of Mary and John. Not this week. Not until my wedding is over. I just want to focus on that. Then, depending, I might try to track down Joseph and see what he can tell me – a part of me still needs to know if my mother was involved. Though more importantly, I need confirmation that she *wasn't*.

Jared turns the page. 'Ah, the swimming galas. Now *they* were an event. God, I loved that outdoor pool. Butterfly was my stroke.'

I laugh, imagining Jared flapping his long arms wildly in the water. Then I stop, frowning and taking the booklet from him to get a closer look. 'Look, that's Danny's younger brother, Joseph, right there,' I say, reading the name Joseph Wentworth underneath a picture of three boys on a winners' podium. 'Looks like he won a bronze medal for diving.'

'He's the one you said doesn't speak to his parents any more?'

I nod. 'So awful for the family. It's as though they're stuck in a time warp in that bungalow, living in the past, unable to move on, almost like they're waiting for him to come back. Well, his mum is, anyway.' I haven't told anyone the full story of what I found out from Mary Wentworth, about how a female teacher groomed Joseph.

'His face is pretty clear,' Jared says, peering over my shoulder. 'There's definitely a resemblance to Danny. Crazy to think this was over twenty years ago.'

'I wonder if Joseph is on any social media,' I say. 'A reverse image search won't be much use because he'll look so different now, but I could search his name.'

'Are you going to contact him?'

I look up at Jared. 'Maybe. You know, just to see how he's doing.' I stare at his young, skinny body, his bright-red swim trunks, his face eager and keen as he holds out his medal, grinning at the camera. The picture is small, so I take a photo of it on my phone, zooming in, though it's still grainy. 'Definitely a resemblance to his brother,' I say, showing Jared.

'You do realise this is right up my street,' he replies, giving me a nudge. 'I'm involved with an AI crowd in Silicon Valley who could enhance this picture and even do an age progression on it. You never know, someone from around here might recognise him if you post it online.'

'Sounds like a lot of bother to me,' I say, knowing that's probably not going to give me the answers I need. 'But sure, if it's not too much trouble. Thanks.' If nothing else, it might help me narrow down all the many Joseph Wentworths that a quick search on my social media has told me there are.

FORTY-FIVE

When I get back to Medvale, Mum is in the dining room hunched over her sewing machine with swathes of white fabric bunched up in her hands. Her brow is pinched in a frown, and she's got several pins stuck between her lips as she concentrates.

'Hello, Mum,' I say tentatively, coming in and closing the door behind me. We've barely spoken since she found me putting the lock on our bedroom door – just a few words to inform her that we will be going ahead with the wedding. I didn't bother explaining that I was agreeing to it for Owen's sake – she does not deserve an explanation of any kind. Being here goes against all my instincts, and I'm counting down the hours until we can leave. In the meantime, I'm being careful not to rile her. Right now, while Owen is resting upstairs, I don't want to risk any harsh words between us disturbing him.

'Elizabeth,' she says, glancing up and taking the pins from her mouth. Her expression is stern and fixed, making my heart thump just like when I was a child and didn't know if a hug or a smack was imminent. Either way, I cowered.

'You still have the hedgehog,' I say, eyeing the pin cushion that I made at school when I was about ten. We were crafting

Mother's Day gifts and I'm pretty certain I was the only child who'd imagined sticking pins into their mother, rather than the felt creatures we were making.

'Of course I have,' she says, looking up. 'These little things mean so much to me.'

Slowly, I go over to her and pull out the dining chair beside her, sitting down. 'I always thought you hated stuff like that. You never put up any of my pictures or took much interest in what I did at school.'

'Didn't I?' Mum replies in a defensive voice. 'I... I don't really remember.' But there's something sad in her tone, too, as though working on Shelley's wedding dress, trying to convert it into something suitable for my big day, has made her pensive, perhaps forcing her to consider all her past failings. 'You know, I never thought I'd be doing this.' She holds up the fabric, a taut smile on her lips.

'We could just buy a new dress, you know, Mum. It's not too late to go shopping. Shelley certainly won't care. In fact, I think she'd rather *not* wear this.' I scan the fabric for signs of the bloodstain on the front of the skirt from where Shelley had knelt beside Rafe's body, sobbing.

Mum sighs, letting the fabric fall to her lap. 'To be honest, I don't really know what I'm doing.' I swear there's a wobble in her voice, as if she's on the edge of giving up but can't quite admit it. 'I was trying to make the best of a bad show.'

'Let me see.' If nothing else, maybe I can convince her to give up the project.

Mum stands and lifts the silk and lace fabric that, only a year ago, was a beautiful wedding gown that Shelley adored. She'd be horrified to see it now.

'Oh God, Mum, it's hideous. What the hell have you done to it?' I lift up bits of the skirt, seeing how she's tried to shorten the train at the back but has somehow managed to get one of the layers caught up in the side seam of the bodice. 'And what's happened *here*?' I say, pointing to the neckline that now has a piece of Owen's shirt sleeve stitched into it at an odd angle. 'It's a Frankenstein's monster of a dress.'

I stifle an incredulous laugh, remembering when I'd once laughed inappropriately as she was giving me a hiding for only getting the part of a star in the school nativity play. She'd had her sights set on me playing Mary. The laugh had come out of sheer terror when I'd seen the grotesque costume that she'd made for me as punishment.

For a moment, Mum is frozen – staring at me, piercing me with eyes the colour of black granite. I'm waiting for her to explode or lash out or slay me with cutting words. But then her eyes seem to melt, taking on a softer, silvery-blue shade, and that's when I notice her mouth curling into a smile. A moment later, she's cackling, dropping the dress onto the floor as she leans on me for support, rocking back and forth, unable to help the borderline hysterics.

It's weird, but I find myself clinging onto her and joining in the laughter – each of us unable to stop, though I suspect for very different reasons. I'm still waiting for the clout – even if it comes in the form of cutting words now that I'm an adult.

'Oh, Mum,' I say, feeling her bony shoulders beneath me. I can't even remember the last time we had physical contact. 'You're still in there, aren't you? The woman Dad loves.' Shocked by my own words, I cover my mouth as she pulls away from me. 'Sorry,' I mumble from behind my palm. 'God, I'm so sorry...'

'What are you talking about, Elizabeth?' Suddenly, she's not laughing. She wipes a finger under her eye, trying not to let me see that she'd almost been crying. She sniffs it all back. 'Don't listen to anything your father says.'

I stare at her, watching her believe her own lies, wondering what lurks beneath the icy veneer that I've so rarely seen behind.

'What happened, Mum? What made you so... so angry and hostile all the time? Why do you fight the world and everyone in it at every opportunity – including your own family? I know you weren't always like this.' I remember Dad's words.

Mum shudders and shakes her head, looking away. 'I don't know what you mean, Elizabeth. I think the stress of everything has got to you. Maybe you need to take a nap.'

'No, Mum, I do not need a nap.'

'I'm sorry if you don't like me, Elizabeth. That's a harsh thing to say and—'

'Don't twist my words. I want to know why you feel the need to attack everyone all the time. It's exhausting for me – for *everyone*. It must be utterly draining for you.' I can't believe I'm speaking like this when, as a child, I'd have run away at the first sniff of conflict – straight up to my room and under the bedcovers. And later, as an adult, I'd remove myself from the situation putting hundreds, sometimes *thousands*, of miles between us. But something is keeping my feet firmly planted on the floor, my arms folded across my chest as I wait for her reply.

'It's not attacking, Elizabeth, it's *defending*. And a good defence happens long before you give anyone the chance to get close to you. To *hurt* you. If that happens, then you've already let yourself down.' Mum thrusts her chin in the air.

It's like the fog is clearing around her – not completely, but my mother is showing a vulnerable side that I've never seen before. Something shaped her into the person she is today, yet I have no idea what that is.

'What happened, Mum?' I say, taking her hands in mine. She stiffens and tries to pull away, but I don't let go. 'Who hurt you?'

She shakes her head, looking away to the side despite our faces being close.

'Do you know how hard it is to watch everyone else's happiness around me when I have none of my own?' she suddenly says. 'To have learnt from such a young age that you're worth-less and unwanted and cause misery whatever you do, wherever you go? It became second nature to me, to be disliked. I became the person my mother believed me to be.'

'Oh, *Mum...*' I transpose her words onto myself – an easy swap to make – knowing how carefully I must now tread as I embark on married life, have a baby of my own. This cycle has to stop right now. Right here, with me. I will not teach this to my child.

Then I feel Mum's fingers toying with my engagement rings – both her mother's antique ring and the beautiful ring Owen gave me. She lifts my hand, holding it between us as she stares down.

'This is not your grandmother's engagement ring,' she whis-pers, hanging her head. 'I have no idea of its history.'

'But I thought you said—'

'You think a lot of things, don't you, Elizabeth? But have you ever stopped to think if you're *right*? Have you ever once thought there might be something else behind all the smoke and mirrors of my pain?'

'What? No, I—'

'I bought this ring a few years ago at an antiques market. The seller told me it's from the nineteen thirties. I have no idea if the stones are genuine or not. But I liked it. I imagined the kind of woman who might have once worn it. A clever woman, a kind woman, a woman with passion and an eye for beautiful things. A woman who loved her family and had a zest for life. A woman who loved and adored her child. Who loved and adored her daughter. Her *only* daughter... *Me.*'

'Then... then why did you tell me it was Granny's ring?'

'Because the woman I imagined this ring belonged to was the woman I wished your grandmother *was*. All the stories I made up about my imaginary mother,' she laughs then, shaking her head. 'They were a fantasy version of the real thing. Even now, I still do it. In my make-believe world, she left me this ring to pass on to one of my own daughters when they got married.'

I think for a moment, confused. I was young when my grandmother died, so don't remember her at all, and Shelley's recollections have always been vague, telling me that she only remembered one or two encounters with her at Christmas.

'But you always told me what a strong, wonderful woman she was. How you admired and looked up to her.' Then it occurs to me that Mum has rarely spoken of my grandad – a man I know little about. He, too, according to Mum, died when I was young. *Smoked too many cigarettes*, she'd once told me.

'Your grandmother wasn't strong or wonderful. She was the opposite of those things. She was cold, dismissive and loose with her fists. And she hated me.'

'No, Mum... that... that can't be true...'

Something inside me shifts, as though my mind is trying to slot this information into the framework of my mother's life. But it doesn't quite fit.

'What about Grandad?'

Mum instantly makes a 'pah' sound with her lips. 'Never knew him. Save when he came home drunk to beat up my mother.'

I gasp.

'Your grandmother was a typist, Elizabeth, but wanted nothing more than to be in the movies. She was certainly a looker and a talented actress, I'll give her that.' A sort of sneer takes over my mother's top lip. 'It's where she met my father, at an audition. He was working the lighting rigs.'

I never knew any of this. My own childhood had been so filled with dodging Mum's strange moods and unpredictable outbursts that I'd never considered what her own childhood was like. She'd always made out it was ordinary, uneventful, content.

'My father was considerably older than my mother, but that

didn't put him off. I don't know for sure, but I think he had a family elsewhere. He travelled a lot for work, going from movie set to movie set. They met at Ealing Studios in the nineteen fifties.'

'It sounds romantic,' I say, stunned by this news. 'As though there should have been a happy ending.'

'Well, there wasn't,' Mum retorts. 'My mother never made it as an actress, not in the career sense of the word, anyway. She was pretty good at putting on a show when she wanted attention. But never very good at *giving* it.'

Mum drops back down onto the dining chair, and I sit beside her.

'Then I came along. Your grandmother was a single parent in an attic bedsit in London with no support around her. It was the late fifties, soon to be the swinging sixties, but my mother never got to be a part of all that. And she resented every cell of my body for it. Sometimes, I almost feel sorry for her.' A pause as my mother wipes her eye. 'But mostly, I don't.'

'Mum...' I say, taking her hands in mine again. 'I had no idea.' It's a glimpse into understanding why she's so bitter, but it doesn't take the sting out of what she's put her own daughters through, how her anger has played out through Shelley and me.

'You don't even know the half of it,' she says, looking straight at me. 'Mostly, I coped, got on with my life. But when you and Shelley came along, it was like a switch inside me flicked, as if I'd been pre-programmed to turn into my own mother and there was nothing I could do about it. I tried to fight it, be different to her, but it was so hard. I simply didn't know the right way.' Then Mum hangs her head, a tear rolling down her cheek. 'I might not have always shown it, Elizabeth, but I am immensely proud of you and Shelley. You have both grown into the type of women that I once aspired to be. But unlike me, I know you will be the best mother to your child.' Mum takes a tissue from her pocket and blows her nose.

I close my eyes and take a breath, not having expected any of this when I came into the dining room. A part of me so wants to believe her, yet experience tells me that her aim is to make me feel sorry for her, to lure me onto my back foot for when she pounces. I grit my teeth, refusing to be manipulated by her any more.

'You know what?' I say, pointing at my imaginary grand-mother's ring. 'I think I'm going to wear this to my wedding after all.' My mother's head whips up, a surprised look on her face. 'It will serve as a reminder of everything you've just told me,' I say, though she doesn't know that, in my head, I'm think-ing: *a reminder of everything that I don't want to become.*

'Thank you, Elizabeth,' Mum says, leaning down and kissing my hand, giving me a glimmer of the self-satisfied smile that I know so well.

FORTY-SIX

'This one'll do,' Shelley calls out from behind the changing room curtain. It's the first dress she's tried on. 'Fits fine. Looks good.'

'Let me see,' I call back, figuring I should at least approve what my maid of honour is going to wear. 'Oh, wow, Shell. That *is* gorgeous,' I say when she comes out. The cream satin dress is simple but beautiful – delicate straps with a low cowl neckline. 'Love it with the Doc Martens,' I say, giving her a wink.

'Does that mean I can wear them on Saturday?'

I pull a face, giving her a slow shake of my head. Then my sister ducks back inside the cubicle. 'I'll be quick. I've got Tuesday's small animal clinic later and need to go home first.'

'Cool,' I say, thumbing through my phone while I wait – Instagram this time, in the vague hope of finding the right Joseph Wentworth.

'Who's Mum got to do your wedding photographs?' Shelley asks as I drive us back to her cottage. 'I'd recommend the guy Rafe and I had, but I've not been able to bring myself to look at the pictures he took yet, so I have no idea how they turned out.'

'You have wedding photos?' I ask, puzzled, because of course they never actually got married.

'Yeah, a few. The photographer sent me the ones he'd taken last year, but they're just from the first hour or so of the day. My brief was for the shots to be as candid as possible, capturing precious moments without people realising they were having their picture taken. None of that posed stuff. It's not my style. He began with people arriving at the church, that kind of thing, but then that's where it ended. No more were taken.'

'Oh, Shell,' I say, reaching out and giving her hand a squeeze. 'That's so hard. But I like the candid idea,' I say, making a mental note to tell the photographer Mum has booked. 'Do you think you'll ever be able to look at your pictures?' I ask, parking my car outside her house. She clutches the shopping bag against her – the dress and a new pair of cream ballet flats that, thankfully, she paid for. 'There might be some photos of Rafe.'

'Maybe,' she says. Then, once we're inside and she's put the kettle on, she adds, 'Perhaps you could have look at the pictures for me? See if you think they'll... you know, upset me. The photographer emailed them to me about a month after Rafe died.'

'Of course, Shell,' I tell her, watching as she opens her laptop. She searches for the photographer's message and downloads all the attachments. Then she gets on with making the tea as well as some lunch for us both. 'OK, let's see what's here,' I say, opening the files.

Each picture takes a few seconds to download, but by the time I've finished looking at the first couple, the other fifty or so pictures are fully resolved. I flick through them one by one, suddenly transported back to that day. 'He's certainly done a good job of following your instructions,' I tell Shelley as she busies about in the kitchen. 'He's caught people's expressions so well.'

The first few are of guests arriving at the churchyard, everyone dressed smartly and looking happy. I recognise some faces, though most I don't. A dappled light falls over the gravestones in the background as the sun filters through the yew trees around the church. 'There's a great shot of Tina and her girls,' I tell Shelley, and she dares to give a quick look at the screen. Tina is one of her oldest friends, who now lives in Birmingham with her family.

'I don't even remember seeing them on the day, but they all look lovely in their outfits.' She quickly turns back to making lunch again.

'There are some pictures of the guys arriving. The best man and all that crew,' I tell her, just so she's prepared for seeing George – though, of course, Rafe isn't with him in the photos. While Shelley has never divulged the full story to me about what the pathologist's report contained, I imagine that her feelings towards the best man are hostile. The cocaine he'd stupidly brought along to the stag night may not have been laced with the drug that had killed Rafe, but he was the one who turned the evening messy, lowering Rafe's inhibitions and kick-starting the hellish night out.

'I don't want to see those,' Shelley says predictably. 'Just like I never want to see *him* again, either.' On the drive to the department store to get her dress earlier, I'd gently explained what had happened at the police station, how the detectives had asked me to go over the events of last year again because they'd been sent some old flowers in an envelope that they believed were to do with the wedding.

'They asked me all the same questions the day before,' Shelley revealed, shocked that they'd turned up at Medvale to take me to the station. I downplayed how awful it was, steering her towards the theory that whoever had sent the flowers was probably just someone playing a sick prank, and the police involvement was simply a routine follow-up and she shouldn't be concerned.

'The thought of everything being dragged up again makes me want to get away from here,' she'd said, which surprised me. 'Just leave everything behind and start again somewhere fresh. Do you know how I spend my days now? Working, visiting Dad, trying to make sure Mum is vaguely happy as well as keeping the pair of them separate. Oh, and sleeping. That's it. This is not how I envisaged my life would be a year ago.'

'Oh, *Shell*,' I'd said. 'I wouldn't blame you if you did bugger off somewhere. Though I don't recommend taking a leaf out of my playbook. Your troubles just go with you.'

I scroll through a few more photos on her laptop, pausing on one or two to get a better look – a little girl in a lilac dress standing coyly beside the ribbon- and flower-festooned churchyard entry, a pair of older men in suits looking up at the sky, broad grins on their faces, and a few of Shelley and Rafe's work colleagues as they walk into the church. A woman's hair blowing in the breeze, a basket of petals, a sharply focused close-up of the hand-made sign: 'Shelley and Rafe's Wedding' hanging on the church gates.

But it's the next few pictures that make me catch my breath.

The first is of the white Jaguar with yellow ribbons decorating the bonnet that ferried me, Mum and the bridesmaids to the church. These pictures have been taken from inside the churchyard, just as the car pulled up on the lane, our happy faces visible in the back. While all the pictures are stills, viewed in order they play out as a kind of moving scene.

I shudder, realising this can't have been long before Rafe's death.

The next few are of us chatting as we head into the churchyard, the occasional glance at the photographer. Seeing myself in my satin dress – my hair in waves, my little silk bag hanging on my wrist, my pale-pink lipstick – it makes it feel as though it was only yesterday. I look at myself, wishing I could turn time back. I knew nothing of the horror to come.

'There are some of me, Mum and the bridesmaids arriving,' I tell Shelley. She's still at the worktop with her back to me. She nods, head down. Makes a little noise in the back of her throat.

When these pictures were taken, Shelley would have already left here in the Rolls-Royce, heading to the church with Dad beside her. I imagine how, after they'd arrived in Little Risewell, Shelley must have been getting more and more concerned as the driver was told by George at the church gates to circle the village time and time again, her anxiety increasing with each minute passing.

And then I see it – a photo of Mum doing her best mother-of-the-bride pose with pouting lips and doe eyes, taken just before she goes inside the church. It's a head-and-shoulders shot of her in her peach jacket with matching fascinator – with the blood-red corsage pinned to her lapel.

Proof that she was wearing it at the time we went into the church.

And behind her sharply focused face, I see the vague, blurry outline of me and the bridesmaids heading through the old church door.

I study the next few photographs – other guests arriving and filing into the church, close-ups of them greeting each other and chatting, laughing. Then I stop on one particular shot – a wider scene of the churchyard with about half a dozen guests milling about. Most are already inside.

I frown, noticing that my mother is in the background, walking back towards the church gates. I stare at the photograph, trying to remember if she'd come outside again once we'd all found our seats. It's possible, I suppose. I remember I had to take little Eesha to find a toilet, asking the verger if there was one we could use. He kindly showed us through the little community hall at the back, unlocking the cubicle for us.

Was that when Mum slipped out of the church unnoticed?

She certainly looks as though she's on a mission in the picture, her right leg scissoring forward as she's caught mid-stride. And the next photograph shows her in the background again, this time out on the lane. It looks as though she's talking to someone. A man.

I enlarge the photo, squinting to make sure I'm correct. Yes... yes, right there. She's standing in front of a man who's much taller than her, though not dressed for a wedding – old green jacket, grey hair beneath a tweed cap, boots.

When I enlarge the next picture, the photographer thankfully standing near the lane by the church gates again, Mum is much clearer in this one. And so is the man she is talking to.

I cover my mouth with my hand, stifling the gasp that wants to come out.

Because the man in the photo is John Wentworth – Danny and Joseph's father.

Then, a few photos later, Mum is back in the churchyard. And the corsage is missing from her jacket.

FORTY-SEVEN

Dad is sitting by the window in the living room at Winchcombe Lodge when I arrive, having afternoon tea with two ladies, both around his age. One of the women is crocheting a pink and green square, and the other is staring straight at my father, her eyes glassy and unmoving as he looks out of the window at the gardens beyond.

'Hey, Dad,' I say, bending down to give him a kiss. 'Hello,' I direct at the women, giving them a smile. 'I love those colours,' I say to the crocheting lady, pointing at her wool.

'For the baby,' she tells me, and, for a stupid moment, I think she means mine.

'Your grandchild?'

She stares back, giving me a puzzled look, her head tilted to one side. 'No, dear. No. *My* baby.' She beams up at me. Then her bony hand sweeps down her stomach, rubbing her lower belly. 'He's due any day now, so I best be quick with this.' She gives a tinkly laugh then goes back to her crocheting.

'Fancy a change of scene?' I ask as Dad drains his teacup, hoping he'll pick up on my code – *Let's go somewhere private.*

And indeed he does because he grabs a finger sandwich

then stands up, biting into it as we walk along the corridor back to his room. 'Hello, Lizzie darling,' he says, once we're inside and the door is closed. 'How's my fair lassie today?'

'Fine, Dad,' I say, frowning at him. I want to forgive him for lying to me, to feel nothing but relief that he's OK, but it's going to take time. 'There's something I want to ask you.'

Dad gives me a quizzical look.

'Owen and I are getting married on Saturday at the church in Little Risewell.' Just hearing those words makes me excited and terrified at the same time. 'I'd like you to give me away. There's a special car booked for us to travel in. It's all been arranged.' I don't tell him that it's Mum who has done all the arranging. I don't want to put him off – though after my last visit, I can't help thinking that, despite everything they've been through, he still loves her.

'Not a repeat performance of last year, I hope,' he says, easing himself down into his armchair.

'*Dad*... don't say that.' But my stomach still churns. I'm trying, but failing, to put what I saw in the photographs at Shelley's house out of my mind – that Mum was talking to John Wentworth outside the church shortly before Rafe died. I'd give anything to know what they were discussing – and more to the point, *why* they were even talking to each other. I can't imagine that John would want anything to do with my mother.

There was no timestamp on the pictures, therefore no way of telling how long Mum was gone for when she left the church – or how she found time to rush to Shelley and Rafe's cottage before returning to the church. All I know for certain is that she came back without her corsage, and I found it beside Rafe not long after.

'So will you come to my wedding?' I ask Dad. 'It would make me so happy if you gave me away.'

Dad beckons me over, so I go and sit on the edge of the bed, where he reaches out for my hands. He stares down at my fingers. 'Two rings?'

I explain about my lost engagement ring and Mum's replacement – telling him the story about her mother's ring that isn't her mother's ring at all.

'I do miss her, you know. Your mum. Even her bad bits. I miss how things *used* to be. And don't think I don't know that Shelley does her best to keep us apart these days.' He laughs, but in a sad way. 'I can't blame her, though. She's been through a lot and doesn't need more grief from us. Your sister is a peacekeeper.'

'She's *brave*, that's what she is,' I tell him. 'When did you last see Mum?'

Dad's mouth opens as if he's about to speak, but nothing comes out. He closes it again, rolling his eyes upwards as if he's thinking. 'I'm not... not sure.'

I can tell he's lying by the way his chin quivers and his jaw tightens. '*Dad?*'

He sighs, his shoulders dropping. 'She comes to see me sometimes, OK? But don't tell Shelley. I don't want her upset.'

'I had no idea.'

'Shelley thinks the last time I saw your mother was at Easter. And it's true... she did visit me then.' Dad bows his head, making me think there's something he's not telling me.

'Dad, what is it?'

'Those pills I told you about, Lizzie,' he whispers. 'The ones I hadn't been taking.'

'What about them?' My mind is suddenly in overdrive again.

'I'd been coughing them out into my hand when the nurses weren't looking. They had no reason to suspect me of doing anything like that, so they never checked up. I didn't know what to do with them, so I kept them in an old sock, hidden behind the pedestal basin in my bathroom.'

'Oh my God, *Dad*! You can't just go leaving medication lying around like that. How many tablets were there?'

'A hundred, maybe more,' he says, staring at the floor. 'But the thing is...' He bows his head again, his face crumpling with anguish. 'I think... I think your mother found them. She used the bathroom one time, and then they were gone.'

'Mum *stole* your pills?'

Dad nods. 'No one else apart from you and Shelley has been to see me, and if the nurses had found the tablets, I'd have known about it. So it can *only* have been your mother.'

I shake my head, suddenly aware that my parents are probably more well suited to each other than I've ever realised.

'What did she do with them?'

Dad shrugs. 'Maybe she just threw them away. I don't know.'

I stare at him, slowly shaking my head, incredulous at what he's telling me.

'But... but I really think things could be different this time with your mum,' he continues, cementing my thoughts about their relationship. 'She promised me that she's changed her ways...' He trails off, his expression switching to hopeful. 'I've given her my heart and soul over the years, Lizzie. I want to come home. Give things another try. I can't stand to lose her now...'

Again, he trails off, and for that I'm grateful. With only three days to go until my wedding, that's all I'm focusing on now – as well as my new life with Owen in London and the baby growing inside me.

'You're determined to get married?' Dad asks in a way that makes me think he has doubts.

I nod, frowning, wondering what's coming.

'Then I'm happy for you, fair lassie,' he says, picking up my hands in his and giving them a squeeze. 'It's a fresh start for all of us.'

'Fresh start?'

'I've decided I'll be discharging myself very soon. It's time,' he says. I see tears collecting in the corners of his eyes. 'I'm tired of the lies and pretence, and it's no life for me here. Besides, the funds won't last forever. But... but I need a favour from you first.'

'Yes, Dad. If I can help, I will.'

He gets up and goes to his wardrobe, opening it up. Then he pulls out several pairs of his shoes, fishing about in each of them. Finally, he pulls something out. A sock. 'Will you take these away for me? Get rid of them?'

'*More* pills?'

He nods, a guilty look sweeping over his face. 'Take them before your mother gets hold of them.'

I sigh, closing my eyes. 'OK,' I say, thinking at least that's one thing we agree on.

FORTY-EIGHT

On the way back to Medvale, I take a detour through Long Aldbury to pick up some basic supplies from the cut-price store – just some shampoo and toothpaste. It's cheaper than the village shop in Little Risewell. I hate having to think about if we can even afford these things, but I reluctantly took the two twenty-pound notes that Owen gave me before I left Medvale earlier, reassured by him that it was fine. That we'll soon be able to pay it back into Mrs Baxter's bank account.

'I have an exciting video call scheduled with the bosses while you're out. We're fine-tuning the details of a new six-month contract, Lizzie.' He'd given me a tight hug. 'Absolutely nothing to worry about money-wise going forward now, and they've confirmed that my invoice is on today's list for accounts payable. Honestly, Gerry was spitting chips that it's still not been paid.'

Knowing that he had another secure contract in the pipe-line was what I needed to hear – as well as seeing him so much better after his fall. The couple of days rest have done him good. Things are finally coming together with his work... and hope-fully, soon, a flat. Though whenever I think of Mum, a surge of adrenaline wipes out any good feelings, leaving me nervous and terrified that I'm doing the wrong thing by going ahead with the wedding.

I park the car and head into Price-Beater, the cheap and cheerful shop in the village – although village is an understatement now. Long Aldbury is verging on a small town these days and even has its own school, which didn't exist when I was growing up.

'Oh, sorry,' I say, moving aside as a woman barges past. She's shorter than me, and older too, clearly on a mission with her head bent down over her shopping trolley. But something makes me watch her as she blusters her way to the dairy fridge, standing and staring at the milk cartons, grabbing one before casting her eyes over the cheeses.

'It's *Mary*,' I whisper under my breath, edging closer to make certain it's her beneath the headscarf tied under her chin. She picks up a block of cheese, reading the price label before sighing and putting it back in the refrigerator. Then she picks up another, smaller supermarket-brand packet of cheese and drops that into her trolley instead.

I follow her down the aisle and up the next – tinned soups and beans, packets of rice and pasta – watching her face as she scans what's on offer. She puts two small tins of value-brand beans in her trolley, followed by a tin of spaghetti hoops. Then she continues further up the aisle.

'Hello... Mary?' I say, approaching her. She turns abruptly, staring up at me. I get a scowl at first, but then a look of recognition sweeps over her face.

'Oh...' she says. 'The journalist.'

'Well, I'm not exactly a journalist.' I still feel bad for lying to her and her husband. 'Just someone on a... a fact-finding mission.' Hopefully that goes some way to neutralising my fibs, though Mary doesn't seem to pick up on it. She stares down into her trolley, shaking her head.

'When my boys were at home, they used to eat my cupboards bare. Locusts, I used to call them.' She laughs. 'But now, look. It's budget suppers for John and me.'

'I can imagine,' I say. 'Money's tight for everyone these days.'

Mary stares up at me as though she's about to say something but thinks better of it. 'I can't let John see what I buy,' she tells me. 'Thankfully he's never been a cook so is none the wiser when I put his plate in front of him. But if he knew the truth, that I'm forced to buy these value brands, all the cutbacks I have to make...'

She shakes her head, going on to explain when I frown.

'He's a proud man, I tell you, but we have virtually nothing left,' she says. 'I've always dealt with our finances, but our state pension barely covers the bills – heating, council tax, petrol for the car. It's not what you expect when you work all your lives, paying into a private pension you think will see you right for the rest of your days. Not what you expect at all.'

'I'm sorry to hear that,' I reply, seeing the struggle on her face.

'John doesn't know, you see.'

We stand aside as a frazzled mother wheels past us with a wailing toddler in her trolley, apologising her way up the aisle.

'John doesn't know?' My ears prick up, wondering what Mary would think of Shelley's wedding photographs – her husband talking to my mother outside the church last year. 'What about?'

'That all our money is as good as gone.' She shakes her head and has that same bursting look on her face again, as though she can't help confiding in me, a total stranger, because it's better than keeping all her worries bottled up. 'And it's all my fault.'

'Oh, Mary, that sounds really tough.'

'But what can a mother do when her son needs help? It's the only way I can make it up to him, for all the wrongs he suffered.

He's a good boy really. Well, he's a *man* now.' She finds a small laugh from somewhere, but it's clear her pain runs deep. I still have no idea what she's talking about.

'You do anything for your kids,' I say, surprising myself by reaching out and touching her arm. Mother to mother. Soon-to-*be* mother, at least.

'Our Joseph struggled after he left school aged sixteen. Nothing was the same after what that woman did to him.'

I flinch internally at what, I presume, is the mention of my mother.

'John believes that Joseph never contacts us, but he keeps in touch with me from time to time. A letter sometimes, a phone call or a text once in a blue moon, just to let me know what he's up to, where he is. He doesn't want his father to know. We were always close, me and my boy.' She smiles wistfully. 'It's true what they say though, about kids only ever getting in touch when they need something.'

Then Mary reaches into her trolley and replaces one of the tins of beans on the shelf. She laughs again – a resigned croak. She folds her arms around her beige raincoat, her feet wide apart as if in defiance against the world.

'It's got to the point now where I'm just waiting for John and me to die. Then Joseph can sell the bungalow and be comfortable. It's no use me sending him a few thousand pounds here, another few thousand there. In this day and age, that soon goes, especially with all the business ventures he's tried to make work. God love him, he's had loads of jobs over the years – warehouse worker, porter at the hospital, taxi driver – but nothing seems to last. It's the trauma, you see.'

'Oh, Mary, I'm sorry.' She has no idea how much I mean that. 'Do you know where he lives now? Can you go and visit him?'

'Last I heard, a good few months back, he was living in Bedford. He was delivering pizzas on his motorbike. The motorbike *I* gave him money for, of course. John would have a fit if he knew he was riding one. But it weren't Joseph's fault the bike got stolen. Then his roommate did a moonlight flit, so he lost the flat deposit I'd not long sent him. Several years ago, I lent him money to buy a café business, but then the pandemic wiped him out, so he closed for good. It's how it's gone for him the last few years. So much bad luck.'

Mary shakes her head, not even close to tears like I would be. She's just matter-of-fact and stoic about the litany of costly failures – failures that *she's* paid for, it seems. It makes me count my blessings and good fortune and feel very, *very* grateful for what Owen and I have. Even if our wedding is being funded by my mother.

'Over fifty thousand pounds of our hard-earned pension gone in the last ten years. I hate lying to my husband, but he has no idea that there's nothing left. He's getting suspicious, though. Our life's savings have been virtually wiped out.' Mary stares at the meagre contents of her shopping trolley again, shaking her head. 'So yeah, you do anything for your kids.' She lets out a laugh. 'Every night I pray that he'll turn up on our doorstep one day, wanting to come back home. I'd welcome him with open arms, my boy. The stupid thing is, I keep seeing him, everywhere I look. A random man on a bus. Someone on the television. In my dreams.' She shakes her head, tucking a loose strand of grey hair back under her headscarf. 'Losing my mind, I am, dear.' Another resigned laugh.

'Let me pay for your groceries, Mary,' I say, following her as she heads to the checkout. It's obvious the contents of her trolley won't come to more than ten pounds and, in a small way, it feels appropriate. I grab the couple of items I came in for, and she smiles up at me, grateful, as I hand the cashier my money once her shopping is bagged up.

Outside, it's started raining and she heads off in the direction of her street, a good ten-minute walk uphill. 'Mary, wait.

Can I give you a lift? My car is just here.' I point to the Volvo parked right outside the shop.

'Thank you, dear,' she says, climbing into the passenger seat. Once I'm in the car, buckling up my seatbelt, Mary glances at my hand on the steering wheel. 'Engaged to be married, are you?'

I smile, pulling out of the parking space and onto the road. 'Yes, I am. In fact, our wedding is this Saturday in Little Risewell church.'

'Lovely,' she says with a teary smile, staring out of the window as I drive to her bungalow. When we're there, she gets out of the car but ducks her head back inside. 'Not a word to anyone about what I told you, dear.'

'Of course,' I say, reaching over and giving her hand a squeeze.

'It's more than my life's worth if *he* found out.' And she flicks a look towards the bungalow before shutting the car door and heading inside.

FORTY-NINE

'Oh. My. *God*,' I say. 'It's absolutely *stunning*.' I can barely focus on Owen's laptop screen, convinced my eyes are playing tricks on me. I turn to look at him, our faces close as we sit side by side at Mum's kitchen table, the smell of her rabbit stew wafting from the oven while I go over and over the images on the letting agent's website.

'Right?' he says in a tone that's far too calm. 'I knew you'd love it.'

'Love it? It's even better than the flat we viewed before coming here. It's my dream home. But look, it says it was listed on Monday. It's Thursday now, so it's bound to have gone already. Have you phoned up about it?'

'Of course,' he says, again far too calmly under the circumstances.

'Wenlock Avenue... and it's right near the tube, it's got two bedrooms, a perfect kitchen, a private garden... wait – a private garden!' I clasp my hands under my chin, knowing we *have* to get this flat. 'It's so light, and comes furnished, too. I just love everything about it. But God, what if it goes before we get to view it? What did they say when you called them?'

Owen laughs quietly. 'You're such a worrier,' he says, going to the fridge. He returns with a bottle of Mum's champagne.

'I just know what the market's like,' I tell him. 'We've had too many disappointments.' I click refresh on the browser, waiting a second as the page resolves. 'Are you opening that?' I say, eyeing the bottle in his hand. 'At your own peril,' I add, knowing Mum won't like him helping himself. I toggle through the pictures again, mentally moving in to yet another flat we'll most likely lose. Then I jump – and I'm not sure if it's from the pop of the cork as Owen helps himself to Mum's Moët, or from my utter disappointment when I spot the LET AGREED banner now displayed on the listing.

'Cheers,' Owen says, handing me a glass of orange juice.

It's all I can do to raise my hand to point at the words on the screen. 'When did you last refresh this page?' I say, pretty much numb to the feelings of loss now. 'Look. It's gone already. Literally before my eyes.'

Owen still chinks his glass against mine, a strange, sly smile on his face. 'It has indeed gone,' he announces rather too gleefully. 'It's gone to us! It's *ours*, Lizzie.'

I stare at him, speechless and nervous. I do not want to raise my hopes if he's having a joke or has made a mistake – either of which would be cruel. 'What, wait. You mean the "Let Agreed" sign is referring to... to you and me?'

Owen nods. Sips his champagne.

'Oh. My. *God*,' I say for the second time in five minutes. 'Are you sure? This is *our* flat? But we haven't even seen it. I mean... what if...? How come...? But why...?' My questions spill out, without me even giving Owen a chance to reply. He laughs as I stutter and stumble my way through the shock and delight of what he's just told me.

'I did a sneaky viewing when I was last in London. I didn't tell you in case it came to nothing. I put down a deposit – the company finally gave me an interim payment which just covered it – and, by the looks of it, it's literally just become officially ours. What perfect timing!'

At this news, I fling myself against him, not caring if he sloshes champagne down me. Not even caring if Mum gives him a telling-off for opening it in the first place. She's tied up outside for a while anyway, directing and bossing about the marquee people as they erect the huge tent on the lawn.

'It's all really happening, isn't it?' I say, squeezing him tightly. 'Our wedding, the baby, a home of our own... even a new work contract for you after your meeting on Tuesday went well. Everything is finally coming together. And thank *God*.' I rest my head on his shoulder, feeling the security of his arms wrapped around my back. 'I'm sure I'm going to wake up at any moment, but for now, I'm enjoying it. In less than forty-eight hours, we will be Mr and Mrs Foster and I can't bloody wait.'

I close my eyes, soaking up the relief and happiness, but then Mary's worried face, her two poor sons, and the photograph of my mother minus her corsage outside the church flash behind my eyes in a grisly reel of reality.

But the moment is interrupted as I feel Owen's body shaking and, when I pull back, I see it's because he's laughing. 'Uh-oh, look,' he says, pointing out of the kitchen window. 'I think the marquee guys are getting a load of grief.'

I go over to the window, wishing I could hear what is being said, but judging by the look on Mum's face, her words wouldn't be for the faint-hearted. Three burly men are standing around her, one with a giant mallet in his hands, yet all of them look terrified.

'She's probably ordering them to move the entire thing three inches to the west.'

'I can only imagine,' Owen says, draping his arm around me.

I watch the scene outside unfold. 'You'll think I'm silly, but when we arrived, when all this talk of weddings and us staying here longer kicked off, I was really scared. I tried to hide it from you, but...' I pause, wondering if I should change it to the present tense – that I *am* still scared – but I decide there's no point worrying Owen, too. Especially as I can't prove anything.

'Oh, love,' he says. 'Why were you scared?'

I point out of the window. 'Just like those poor chaps are probably regretting taking this job, wondering if they'll be getting out of here alive, well... Well, I was concerned she'd do something to you.'

'*What?*' Owen sounds genuinely shocked. 'You thought your mother wanted to hurt me? *Why?*'

I swallow, unsure how to put it. 'She's always been over-protective of Shelley and me,' I say. 'And in her eyes, no man will ever be good enough for her daughters.'

But still the words don't come out – words that would very likely have him changing his mind about marrying me on Saturday.

'And that's why I love you, Lizzie,' Owen says, pulling me close. 'For sticking by me, even when faced with the evil mother of the bride!' He growls and makes a silly clawing gesture with his hands, but I nudge him in the ribs, hissing a *shhh* at him when I hear Mum coming back inside.

'I could honestly kill them all!' she says, blustering into the kitchen. 'The useless idiots have put the marquee door in the wrong place. They're going to have to change all the sides around now. I wanted it done by the end of the day so I can work out the table positions. The furniture has been delivered and is all stacked up inside—'

'You look like you need one of these, Sylvia,' Owen says, thrusting a glass of champagne at my mother.

'Oh,' she says, eyeing the bottle on the worktop. Miraculously, she says nothing except, 'Thank you. I do indeed.'

'We're celebrating,' he says, pulling out a chair for her to sit down. 'Let me show you why.' He opens up his laptop with the pictures of our flat still on the screen.

'I'll need my glasses,' Mum says, fetching them from beside the radio. 'I have a terrible headache. It's the stress. I need pills.' She goes to the cupboard and takes out a pack of paracetamol.

'That reminds me, I'll be back in a moment,' I whisper to Owen. I leave the kitchen, grabbing my handbag from the bench in the hallway on my way upstairs. Since I got back from visiting Dad two evenings ago, arrangements for the wedding have been full-on, so the favour I promised him has slipped my mind.

After unlocking the bedroom door, I go in and sit on the bed, grateful for a few moments alone. I rummage in my bag, looking for the stash of pills Dad gave me. I need to dispose of them, though I don't know why he didn't simply flush them down the toilet. He was probably concerned he'd get caught.

As I search, I can't help wondering what Mum did with the tablets that she stole from him when she visited. If she still has them, I can hardly bring myself to think what she's got planned. Then I scowl into my bag, tipping out the contents onto the bed – purse, tissues, keys, lipstick, pens, a spare phone charger... all the usual stuff I keep in there tumbles out.

But there's no sock. And there are no pills.

The realisation that they've gone missing dawns on me just as my mother calls out from downstairs.

'Food is ready, darling!'

FIFTY

'I can't tell you how much I needed this,' I say, rolling the dice. Then... 'Oh *no!*' when I see I've rolled a four.

I tuck into some of the food Shelley has prepared, not having eaten much at all today after the stodgy fish and chips I persuaded Owen that we absolutely had to have last night, convincing him it was a massive pregnancy craving. I didn't tell him that it was actually because the pills Mum had stolen were preying on my mind, and I didn't want to risk eating her rabbit stew – especially after coming face to face with the poor things on the roof of our car. And I've been angry at myself all day for leaving my handbag unattended in the hallway.

'Ahh... back to the beginning you go,' Jared says, making a show of moving my counter all the way down to the snake's tail.

'You couldn't not have a hen night of some kind,' Shelley says. 'Though it's more of a hen *and* cockerel night.'

'Cheers to that, cheers to that,' Lynda says, sitting cross-legged on the floor around the coffee table where we're playing board games. If I had to have a hen night, I couldn't have been happier with Shelley's decision to have a few friends round for some drinks and snacks. Though I can't deny that it feels unsettling – being in the cottage where I discovered Rafe, on the night before my own wedding. But, as I know Shelley has to do every single day, I try to put it from my mind.

'Cheers,' the others say, raising their glasses. Never have I wanted to join in a celebration more than right now – marking my last night of being single with Shelley and Jared, Gavin and Lynda. Jared offered to take Owen out on a stag night, but he declined, saying he was tired after a day of heavy online meetings and that he'd rather be fresh for the wedding tomorrow, especially after his fall a week ago.

It feels selfish, but I'm relieved he's not going out. After last year, it would seem too much like tempting history to repeat itself. Though of course it means that he's stuck at Medvale alone with Mum. I didn't want to leave them together, but Owen insisted he'd be fine, that he'd get an early night. For my own peace of mind, I'm texting him every so often with random messages – how the evening here is going, excitement about tomorrow, a photo of the spread Shelley has put out. Anything to prompt a reply that will tell me he's fine.

'Shouldn't you lot be letting me win?' I say, rolling the dice again when it's my turn. 'Given that it's *my* hen? So far, I've lost three games of snap, botched several "operations", and my buckaroo bucked after only two goes.' Shelley had picked up the second-hand children's games earlier this afternoon at a stall the local Brownies were having to raise money for the animal charity her practice supports.

'At least you're having fun,' Shelley says, reaching over and squeezing my hand. 'It's not all about the winning. It's about the playing.'

It's about the getting through, I think but don't say, as I don't want to be maudlin tonight of all nights. But that's what it's felt like since we've been back in Little Risewell the last two weeks – as though I've only just managed to get through the days.

'Thanks for organising all this and making such an effort,' I say, eyeing the food she's put out. 'It's just what I need.'

'Liz, I ducked into Marks & Spencer on the way home from work and grabbed a bunch of things to open and heat up. It's hardly an effort.'

'It means the world,' I say. 'I know how hard this is for you.' We exchange a sisterly look that no one else notices, only to be interrupted by a raucous laugh coming from Lynda.

'I won! I won!' she crows loudly, and I don't think I've ever seen anyone look more excited.

'Right, Jenga next,' Gavin says, grabbing the box. He and Lynda set it up on the coffee table with Lynda batting Gav's hand away every time he stacks the bricks.

'Get it straight, get it straight. Call yourself a builder, Gav. Call your—'

'Cheeky,' Gavin replies, grabbing his wife around the waist and sending the tower of bricks tumbling down before we've even begun playing. More laughter ensues as the couple roll around on the floor in hysterics.

'Please, dear God, let Owen and me be like them in ten years' time,' I say to Shelley. 'Those two are just the best,' I add, catching their infectious laughter. Then I notice Jared watching on, a small smile on his face as he sits perched on the edge of the sofa – pensive and thoughtful. 'She's out there somewhere,' I tell him quietly, nudging his leg. In return, he just nods, looking at me for a beat too long.

'Oh God, let's hope that's not a work call,' Shelley says, leaping up from the floor at the sound of her phone ringing in the kitchen. 'I'm not on duty tonight, and I told the other vets I'm unavailable because of your wedding tomorrow.'

'That's what she said about the work call on the morning of *her* wedding,' I say to the others when she's left the room, deciding not to finish the story. Somehow, on the eve of my own marriage, it doesn't seem appropriate to discuss anything that happened on Shelley's tragic day. But it's testament to her devotion to work that she changed out of her wedding dress to go and attend to the horse in pain. I was convinced she'd be late for church when, in fact, it was Rafe who never made it to the altar.

I've had two goes at Jenga when Shelley creeps back into the room, coming up behind me. She taps me on the shoulder and, when I look round, she beckons me with her head, frowning. I get up and follow her out to the kitchen.

'Everything OK? You look like you've seen a ghost.'

Shelley opens the bottle of tequila she bought in case anyone wants a few shots later, pouring herself a generous measure in a tumbler. She knocks it back.

'Honest answer is, I don't know.' She wipes her mouth on the back of her hand.

'What's happened?'

She eyes her phone lying on the worktop beside her. 'Remember the strange call I said I had?' she says. 'Well, I've just had another one.'

'What? Was it a withheld number again?'

She nods. 'Yup. The voice was growly and low like before, and kind of distorted, but I could tell it was a man this time. It was horrid. He said something about revenge and... and about someone being *murdered*. No, wait...' She touches her forehead, frowning and distressed. Then she pours another shot of tequila, knocking it back again. Her hands are visibly shaking. 'No, he said something about someone I *know* being a murderer.'

'Oh my God, Shell, that's awful.' I grab her phone to see if there are any other notifications, but there are none.

She closes her eyes and takes a deep breath. 'I'm a bit tipsy, so I'm trying to keep it fresh in my head. He kept talking over me when I asked what he meant. But that's it... yes, he... oh Christ, he was talking about a woman, Lizzie.' She clutches my hands, pulling me close.

'I'm here, Shell, it's OK. Take another breath.'

'I swear he said it was...' Her eyes flick to the door to make sure no one can hear or is about to interrupt us. She's shaking and slurring and barely making sense. 'I swear he said it was *Mum*. I'm certain he said her name. He said that she'd get what was coming to her, that he'd make sure of it. Then, when I asked who he was, telling him to stop calling me or I'd phone the police, he laughed and said I should go right ahead. And that I should... that I should tell them... tell them his name is John.'

FIFTY-ONE

I open my eyes, slowly waking up. Remembering. A smile blooms on my face as I squint, shielding my brow with my arm as I grow used to the sunlight streaming in the window of Shelley's spare room – Jared had kindly slept on the sofa.

Today, I am getting married.

But then I remember the strange phone call last night, how upset Shelley was, and, worryingly, how much more she'd drunk to blot it all out. My stomach knots up at the thought of it all. I'd so wanted to explain who I believed the caller to be: Mary's husband John – Danny and Joseph's father John – but I'd kept quiet. It would have meant recounting the entire story about Danny's suicide, what Mary had revealed to me about his teacher – very likely our *mother* – being the cause of his death, not to mention what she'd done to Joseph, and I simply couldn't do it. Not with the others present, and not with my wedding only hours away.

I'd locked it all away in my mind along with everything else, and there it would stay, at least until today was over.

I swipe back the duvet and sit up, reaching over and

opening the curtains of the little window. I couldn't have wished for better weather – a clear blue sky with only a few wispy clouds hanging overhead.

I check my phone to see if any more messages from Owen came in after I went to sleep last night, but there are none. He'd been in touch throughout the evening, so I'd not been too concerned, but in the cold light of day, I feel my anxiety notching up again. His 'last seen' online says 11.24 p.m. Anything could have happened during the night.

I jab at my phone screen to call him. I don't care if we're not supposed to speak or see each other before we meet at the altar, I just need to check he's OK. 'Come on, *come on*, answer!' I say when his phone just rings and rings. Eventually, it goes to his voicemail, so I leave a message for him to call me back.

Then I call Mum's phone.

'Good morning, darling,' Mum sings out after the third ring. 'Did you sleep well? I hope you're all fresh for your big day.'

'Yes, yes, fine thanks,' though that's not entirely true. When I did finally doze off, my dreams were filled with images of John's angry face as he smashed up my wedding cake and rampaged through the reception, terrifying the guests. Another dream – or, rather, nightmare – was of me standing at the altar getting married and, when I turned to kiss my new husband, I saw John standing there instead, his large mouth full of crooked teeth looming over me.

'Is Owen there, Mum?' I ask. 'I tried to call him, but he didn't pick up.'

'Oh, no, no. You know that's not allowed, darling,' Mum trills. 'Next time you see him will be at the altar.'

'Mum, this is important. Can you put me on to him?' I feel a swell of anxiety in my stomach.

There's silence down the line for a few moments. 'Not really, Elizabeth. It's not convenient.'

'*What?* Mum, if you don't put me on then I'm coming over there to speak to him. *Please.*'

Mum sighs. 'He's... he's in the shower. I can hear the water running upstairs. I'll pass a message on to him.'

'Fine,' I say, determined to keep my fears in check and not be the one to spoil the day. But I'm still concerned – a little nagging feeling at the back of my mind. Something's not right. 'Tell him to text me when he's out of the shower. Surely that can't be bad luck?'

'I'll tell him,' Mum says. 'Now hurry up and get ready, Elizabeth. You don't want to keep your groom waiting at the altar now, do you? I'll see you at the church.' And then the line goes dead.

It's just Shelley and me at the cottage now. Jared gave Lynda and Gavin a lift home just after midnight last night. He only had one drink early on, for which I was grateful, and, when Shelley and I get up, we find a note from him saying he's gone for a run and that he'll be heading straight round to Medvale. I console myself knowing that if anything is wrong when he gets there, he'll call me immediately.

'Thanks for this,' I say to Shelley, eyeing the spread of fresh-baked croissants and fruit, juice and coffee too. Though I don't feel hungry. With my imagination in overdrive and the onset of morning sickness, food is the last thing on my mind.

'You'll need something inside you to get you through the day,' she says, though I can't help noticing that she's already poured herself the remains of a bottle of prosecco from last night to go with her coffee. I decide not to say anything, knowing how hard today will be for her. 'Mum made the jam, by the way,' she adds, popping the top on a new jar. She reads the label. 'Hedgerow Jelly,' she says, rolling her eyes. 'Since she got wind of my hen do last year, she's been foisting home-made pâtés and soups on me. She foraged for the ingredients herself. Her way of making a point, I suppose.'

I stare at the jam, then up at Shelley. 'Have you tried this before?'

Shelley shakes her head. 'No. God knows what "hedgerow" means. Blackberries, I suppose. There are plenty out already.' Shelley dollops some of the dark jelly onto her plate before spreading some on a piece of croissant.

'And the other stuff – the pâté and soup, did you eat that?'

Shelley looks guilty. 'Don't tell her but I had a quick taste and, bloody hell, it was vile. So I chucked it out. Told her it was delicious, of course. But even Mum can't go wrong with jam, right?'

I'm about to reply when my phone pings with a message. Owen's name appears on my screen – *thank God*. 'Oh, he's *fine*,' I say, smiling, reading the message. 'He's sent a picture.'

'Why wouldn't he be fine?' Shelley says, sipping her prosecco.

I stare at the photo he's sent me – a spread of food on the kitchen table. Mum has made him bacon, eggs and mushrooms for breakfast, and beside the plate I see a toast rack and another pot of her jam.

'*Mother of the bride spoiling me to death*,' the caption reads. '*Love you xx*'

I stare at it for a moment, my mouth hanging open. Then I show Shelley the picture.

'Don't expect the niceness to last,' she says. 'Especially when she and dad are in spitting distance of each other later.' She shrugs, as though she's resigned to fireworks between them, and picks up a piece of croissant. 'I think it's because you're home that Dad's mental health has improved so much,' she continues, but my mind is elsewhere.

'I need to go,' I tell Shelley, suddenly standing up. But first, I swipe the croissant out of her hand, pick up her plate and scoop the whole lot into the bin. 'And don't eat this either,' I say, tossing the jam jar in, too.

'What the *hell*... Lizzie? Wait, where are you going?' She scrapes back her chair and follows me.

I'm still in my dressing gown but I grab my car keys from the sideboard and head for the door. But just as I'm slipping my shoes on, I feel Shelley's hand around my arm.

'Stop right there, Elizabeth Holmes,' she says. 'What the hell has got into you?'

My breath is coming fast and shallow, and I suddenly feel light-headed. Shelley's face spins around me and the floor falls away. 'It's Owen... he's... I think Mum's trying to...' But I still can't get the words out, not to my sister. My poor, beautiful, heartbroken sister who is being so strong for me and didn't deserve any of this – how can I possibly tell her everything, today of all days?

'I need to go,' I say, pulling free from her grip. 'I... I... we just need to get away. Owen and me. This was all a mistake. I have to go...'

'Oh, no you don't,' Shelley says, barricading the door with her arms. 'You are not leaving this house unless it's in a white dress in a Rolls-Royce with me by your side.'

'But Owen, he's eating mushrooms and jam, and there's the drugs and the tablets and... and... and what Danny did, and poor Joseph. And I swear that John is... but surely Mum would never dare...' All this escapes through breathy gasps. 'Oh God, I feel faint,' I say, leaning against the wall.

'Come on, you,' Shelley says, suddenly taking hold of me as I begin to slide down to the floor. She half carries and half supports me, getting me over to the sofa where she lies me down and puts my feet in the air. Within a couple of minutes, I begin to feel better as Shelley makes me breathe into my cupped palms, calming me down with her soothing words.

'Look, do you actually want to get married?' she finally says, staring down at me.

'Yes, but—'

'Right, well, let's go and do it then, because nothing else matters, Lizzie. Nothing bad is going to happen today, I'll make sure of it. Not even the mother of the bride can ruin today.'

FIFTY-TWO

Two hours later, I look at myself in the mirror. The woman staring back at me is nothing like the terrified, nervous, excited, anxious and exhausted person I feel inside.

'There. Bloody gorgeous,' Shelley says, flicking the big blusher brush lightly across my cheeks again. Then she tweaks a few strands of my hair, rolled into a loose chignon at the back and decorated with little yellow and white daisies.

In my hands I clasp a simple spray of cream roses and gypsophila, with delicate greenery hanging down. My sheer veil is arranged perfectly, attached to a silver clip under my chignon and trailing down my back, brushing over my bare shoulders. And my dress looks even more stunning now than it did when I tried it on in the boutique.

I sniff, choking back a little cough, trying to hide the smile that's growing on my face when I see what Shelley has done with my hair and make-up.

'Don't you bloody dare cry,' she says, slipping an arm round me and staring at both our reflections. 'That's got to be the best make-up surgery I've ever done.'

'Not a bad job for a country vet who spends her life rolling around in the hay with sheep and horses,' I say, grinning at our reflections. Shelley also looks stunning in her cream dress, her hair clipped up in a similar style to mine. 'Thank you, Shell. For everything. If Rafe is watching over us now, he'd be so proud of you.'

'Oh, he's here with us, all right,' she says, polishing off the last of the prosecco. 'By the way, he told me I should definitely wear the Doc Martens.' She goes to push a foot into one of her black boots, but I'm quick to shove it out of the way.

'Don't even think of it,' I say, laughing as she pouts, slipping her feet into the ballet flats instead.

Then I hear a car tooting from the lane below. When I look out of the window, I see a uniformed chauffeur standing there, waving up at me as he stands beside a gleaming white Rolls-Royce festooned with ribbons.

'Time to rock 'n' roll, sis,' Shelley says, coming up beside me. 'I've got your phone, keys and lipstick in my bag, OK?' She holds up the satin drawstring purse to show me, and I notice the sad look on her face. It's the same bridal purse she used at her own wedding last year.

'My fair *lasses*,' is the first thing Dad says when Shelley and I pick him up from Winchcombe. His eyes, proud and glistening, sweep up and down the pair of us and his arms are spread wide as he stands on the drive waiting for us. He's dressed in a grey suit with a pale-pink tie and his silver hair has been freshly cut and slicked into a neat style. There's a suitcase on the gravel beside him, which a male nurse picks up and puts in the boot of the Rolls-Royce.

'Are we on time?' Dad says, beaming as Shelley helps him get into the car. 'Driver, will you drop my bag at Medvale House after we arrive at the church?'

'Plenty of time, Dad,' I say. 'And don't worry, we've

arranged for your belongings to be taken home,' I add, glancing at Shelley. Last night, before the others arrived for drinks, my sister and I discussed arrangements for Dad, given that he's insisted to each of us that he wants to come home. We agreed that there's nothing we can do to stop him and Mum living under the same roof if that's what he wants.

'You *knew*?' I'd said to Shelley, shocked that she hadn't seemed at all surprised when I told her that Dad had admitted himself to get away from Mum, that there was nothing mentally wrong with him.

'Not as such, but I had my suspicions,' she said with a slow nod. 'I kind of guessed. It's just been so much easier for me to have him at Winchcombe, him and Mum kept apart.'

We'd ended up agreeing that we wouldn't breathe a word to Mum.

'To the church, driver!' Dad calls out from the back seat where we sit in a line. Shelley hands him a white rose button-hole, but his fingers shake as he tries to pin it on his jacket, so she ends up doing it for him when it keeps falling off.

Ten minutes later, we drive slowly into Little Risewell, having been stuck behind a grain lorry most of the way. They're known for corking up the roads around here at this time of year, but we're still on schedule. After we'd left Winchcombe, my hand had crept across the cream leather upholstery of the car seat, my fingers weaving around Shelley's, and that's where it's stayed since. She'd given me a look; a look that told me she was with me, right beside me, here to support me and take away my nerves. If only she knew what I was truly afraid of...

Shelley peers out of the window as we approach the church, her throat rippling with a tight swallow. 'Lots of people are here,' she says, her voice choked. The lane is lined with cars plus a few smartly dressed guests milling about in the church-yard, most of whom I don't know. A familiar scene, I think, remembering the photographs on Shelley's laptop. I know she's being brave just for me. Aside from burying her dead fiancé, I imagine this is one of the hardest things she's ever had to do.

'I'm going to drive around the village, miss,' the driver says, glancing at me in the rear-view mirror as he pulls away from the church again.

I catch my breath, tensing up at the sight of his eyes in the mirror beneath his chauffeur's cap. And, when I look out of the side window, I see Mum standing in the old wooden gateway leading into the churchyard. She's beckoning us on vigorously with her white-gloved hand, a finger tapping on her watch.

'We're just a tad early, no need to worry,' the driver adds, seeing my concern. I bite my bottom lip, glancing at Dad's watch for confirmation. Sure enough, it's not quite time.

I nudge Shelley, leaning in close to her ear. 'So how *long* have you known?' I flick my eyes at Dad, who's thankfully staring out of his side window. 'About Dad not actually being ill...?'

Her shoulders visibly drop. 'I told you, I didn't know for certain, Lizzie,' she replies with a tinge of guilt. 'It's nothing like the first time he was in hospital. After everything that happened last year, Dad needed a break.' Then I swear I hear her mutter, '*From Mum...*'

I watch Dad – his face almost childlike as he gazes out at the pretty green, the memorial stone, the village hall, the little newsagent's shop, and we even pass Medvale House on our village circuit.

'But you do realise, they'll never split up,' Shelley whispers in my year. 'Dad adores Mum, and Mum... she adores him, too, in her own way. They'd be lost without each other.'

I shake my head, trying to fathom how their relationship evolved – or, rather, *degenerated* – into this toxic love affair. Mainly so it doesn't happen to Owen and me.

As we head back round and up the hill towards the church, the driver slows the Rolls as two horses and riders pass by,

flicking a salute in reply to the man on the chestnut mare as
they trot past. Then we wait for yet another grain lorry to pass
through the narrow gap. Finally, as we draw closer, I hear the
church bells ringing – and I realise they're ringing for me and
Owen.

We pull up outside the church, and I notice that the lane
and churchyard are now empty, everyone having gone inside. I
slip my hand from Shelley's, crossing my fingers tightly and
closing my eyes as the driver turns off the engine. Then I close
my eyes in a silent prayer. *Please, dear God, let Owen be safely
at the altar.*

FIFTY-THREE

The driver gets out of the Rolls-Royce and opens the doors, helping me and Shelley out, with Shelley arranging my dress as we stand on the lane. There's a gentle breeze and the sun is shining as I gaze up at the beautiful village church, taking a deep breath. Despite all my fears, I must be the luckiest woman on earth.

'Lovely day for a wedding!' a voice calls out. We all turn around, and there's a woman standing about ten feet away on the lane with her dog – a little terrier on a long lead. I've seen her around the village before, and I think she knows Mum from one of her various groups. With that in mind, I'm surprised she hasn't been given an invitation, seeing as Mum has corralled most locals for the event. Perhaps that's why she's hanging around, to make a point that she's been left out.

'Beautiful day, indeed,' I say, giving her a smile and a wave. But I notice that the woman has a slightly sour look on her face. A sneer, almost, and it sends an unwelcome chill through me.

'Come on,' Shelley whispers to me. 'Let's head into the churchyard. The photographer is waiting, look. That woman hates Mum. She's from the WI and they clash over everything. I've treated her dog at the surgery, and all she did was moan about Mum.'

I take Shelley's advice, feeling slightly sorry for the woman, and turn to go into the churchyard, grinning when I see a camera aimed at us.

'Wait, you've dropped this,' the woman calls out, rushing over to us. She bends down to pick something up, handing it to Dad. 'Your buttonhole flowers fell off when you got out of the car.' Her tone is almost snide-sounding. 'Don't want a repeat of last year, do you?' she adds, crossing her arms and staring at Shelley.

'What do you mean?' I retort, feeling myself bristle.

'You know, when your mother's corsage fell off her jacket.'

The blood roars in my ears. Am I hearing her correctly?

'I always come up here and watch the weddings when I know there's going to be one. It gets me out the house,' she adds in a way that tells me she's probably lonely. 'By the time I found the corsage, your mother had stomped off inside the church, after that angry man had finished yelling at her in the street. Threatening her with all sorts, he was. I wondered if I should call the police, but he eventually went on his way again.' She makes a self-satisfied face and pauses, almost as if she's waiting for a reaction. 'Anyway, I gave the corsage to the groom instead, dear,' she directs at Shelley. 'He flew past the church in such a hurry, looking like death and rushing to get somewhere. He grabbed it off me and didn't stop to speak.'

My brain is spinning at a hundred miles an hour. So is *that* how the corsage came to be up at the cottage?

'Rafe?' I hear Shelley whisper as it registers with her that this woman was probably one of the last people to see her fiancé alive. 'You gave my mother's corsage to Rafe?'

Angry man? I'm thinking.

'Yes, dear,' the woman says, clearly enjoying this moment. 'I hope it found its way back to your mother.' And with that, the woman sneers again and turns to go, raising her hand in a wave and chatting away to her dog as she heads off.

'Strange,' Shelley says, fiddling with my hair to tuck back a loose strand. 'I've no idea what she was talking about.'

'Very strange,' I say, making sure Dad doesn't hear the concern in my voice as I try to work it out.

If Rafe took the corsage up to the cottage, perhaps he was intending to bring it back to the church for Mum after he'd swapped his socks and shoes. Though of course, he never made it. And it's possible that John just happened to be passing and collared Mum when he saw her, giving her a stern dressing down. But as I walk up the path towards the church, I force it all out of my mind. I'm about to marry the love of my life and I want to savour every moment.

'It looks so beautiful,' I say to Shelley, gazing up at the wooden archway festooned in flowers. 'The florist has done an amazing job.' Then I spot all the white petals scattered along the path leading to the church door, and I'm suddenly aware I'm being photographed from all angles. It's as if I'm in a fairy-tale dream and nothing feels real – the world swirling around me.

'Nice and natural, that's it,' the photographer says. 'Just ignore me, pretend I'm not here.'

'OK,' I giggle, squinting in the sunlight. I grip Shelley's hand again. 'This is it,' I tell her. 'I'm really getting married. I'm actually doing it. But oh God, Shell, I also feel really, *really* bloody sick.' The feeling comes out of nowhere, so I grab onto her hand, and then Dad comes to my other side, sliding his arm around my shoulders. I look back through the gateway, seeing the Rolls drive off, wondering if it's too late to run out and flag the chauffeur down, have him take me to the nearest airport.

'I think I'm going to puke. I can't do this...' I say, my breathing quickening. 'What if Owen doesn't really want to marry me? What if he's just doing the right thing because of the baby? What if—'

'Lizzie, *no*,' Shelley says calmly. 'Steady breaths.' She grabs both of my hands, squaring up to me. 'Look at me.'

I do as I'm told. Shivering and shaking, my breathing all over the place and my heart beating like a sparrow's, I stare into my sister's eyes.

'Do you want to marry Owen?'

'Yes, I do!' I say, my teeth chattering. Suddenly, I'm freezing, goosebumps breaking out on my arms. I have an overwhelming urge to laugh hysterically.

'Right, then let's get you inside that church.'

'OK,' I say, nodding as I compose myself. Then I burst out laughing as Dad links his arm through mine and leads me towards the church door.

'Oh my God, oh my God, I'm really doing this. I'm really getting married!' The photographer follows us, the shutter on his camera clicking over and over as he captures the big grin on my face. Shelley follows on behind us, her little silk pouch on her arm, a spray of flowers to match mine in her hands. I glance back at her and mouth '*thank you*' and she smiles, blowing me a kiss.

'Don't worry, fair lasses,' Dad says as we step inside the cool dark porch before we enter the main church. He turns to look at me. 'Everything is going to be grand.'

An usher stands at the door, his hand on the old iron latch ready to open it. I have no idea who the young man is, but I take a deep breath, composing myself one last time, holding my chin up, making sure my back is straight and my arm is linked firmly through Dad's as I stare straight ahead.

'OK, I'm ready,' I say, before putting on a big smile.

The door opens wide, and I'm faced with a church full of guests all craning their necks around to see me. The organ strikes up the 'Wedding March' and I take the first step towards the altar, my eyes frantically scanning around the front pews.

But Owen is not there.

FIFTY-FOUR

I stop, completely frozen. I feel Dad tugging on my arm, Shelley's hand in the small of my back. 'Go on,' she whispers. 'Keep walking.'

I can't. Owen is not in his place. He is not in the church.

At the front, I see Mum in her pew to the left of the aisle. She stands up, with everyone following her lead and standing up, too.

Where is Owen? My eyes scan around – but there's simply no sign of him. I cannot see Owen.

Jared is there near the altar, positioned the other side of the aisle to Mum, grinning at me when he sees us enter.

But Owen is not beside him. *Oh my God, where is he?*

Whispers ripple among the guests. I see frowning faces and smiles of encouragement, everyone wondering why I've stopped.

Images of Owen lying on the floor at Medvale, all alone and bleeding to death, flash in front of my eyes. I picture a pool of blood around his head, his legs splayed out, his face contorted with agony.

I gasp. How can I walk down the aisle when my fiancé is not here? I can't do this.

'I need to go,' I whisper to Shelley, turning my head slightly as we stand just inside the church doorway. 'I need to find Owen. He's not here. Oh my God, Shell, I think he's... I think he's been—'

'Stop it!' Shelley hisses at me through a fake smile. 'What are you talking about? Pull yourself together, for God's sake.' I get a sharp prod in the back.

'Come on, fair lassie,' Dad says in a low voice. 'Let's go get your man.'

Slowly, I turn and look down the aisle again, feeling overwhelmed from all the faces staring at me, my vision blurry. The organ music resounds throughout the church, and I see the flowers at the ends of each pew marking my path to the altar.

And then I notice someone standing up... right at the front beside Jared. Someone who was bending down low and hidden behind the pew.

A huge smile of relief spreads across my face when I see that it's Owen.

He was tying his shoelaces... his bloody shoelaces!

I begin walking down the aisle again, grinning and looking at our guests (whoever they all are), getting closer and closer to the altar. Everything is going to be fine, I tell myself, trying to calm my pounding heart.

Owen catches my eye and smiles at me – that warm, loving, kind smile I know so well. And nothing else in the world matters any more as I approach my groom, my father proudly giving me away at the altar, passing my hand over to Owen before taking his seat beside my mother.

But then, behind me, I'm aware that someone is shuffling, changing places and, when I glance around, I see it's Jared quickly moving across the aisle to sit next to Shelley. And I can't be certain, but I swear I hear him whispering to her.

Did Lizzie get my message?

'Dearly beloved,' Reverend Booth says in his loud, deep voice after the organ music has subsided, smiling at the congregation as he stands in his formal white robes, a leather book spread open in his hands. 'Let me extend a warm welcome to all of you here today...' He continues with his greeting, telling everyone how delighted he is to be marrying Owen and me on this beautiful September day... but I don't hear his words, not properly. I'm more focused on the whispering behind me – between Shelley and Jared.

I turn around slightly, trying to see what's going on. There's a strange expression on Shelley's face, and a puzzled one on Jared's as Shelley opens her little silk bag, pulling out a phone. *My* phone. Like Owen, she knows my passcode – I've had the same one for years, the day of the month I was born on, followed by hers – and I watch as she unlocks my phone with shaking hands. She gives me a quick glance, a quick look. An *unsettling* look.

I turn back to Reverend Booth, wanting to enjoy his words, but I'm worried now. What is so important that it has made Shelley check my phone?

'So we are gathered together here today in the sight of God, as well as in the face of this – delightful, I might add – company to join together this man and this woman...' The reverend smiles warmly, clearly relishing his moment. But I'm distracted and glance at Shelley again, who's now got her hand over her mouth and is conferring with Jared.

'...In holy matrimony, which is commended to be honourable among all men. As this couple know, it is not by any means to be entered into unadvisedly or lightly, but rather reverently, discreetly, advisedly, wisely and solemnly...'

Suddenly, Shelley is on her feet, sliding past Jared and

making her way towards me. She's half ducking down and trying to appear inconspicuous, though judging by the few whispers around me, people have noticed that she's now at the altar beside me. She puts a hand on my arm, but I stare directly at Reverend Booth. Whatever it is, I do not want to know. Nothing will stop me marrying Owen.

'...Into this holy estate these two persons present now come to be joined...' Reverend Booth continues, but I can't concentrate. Shelley is tugging on my arm, holding my phone in front of my face.

'Lizzie, you need to see this,' she says in a terse whisper, trying to pull me to one side. I stand my ground. 'Lizzie, *please.*'

'*What?*' I hiss back at her, aware the reverend has now stopped speaking.

'Please, just look at this email Jared sent you earlier. There are pictures. It's important.'

I look at the reverend and he gives me a nod, so I quickly glance at my phone screen, expecting some disaster about the catering or the DJ cancelling for this evening. I'm aware of Owen standing beside me, clearing his throat, shuffling about impatiently as I take my phone from Shelley to look at whatever has bothered her so much.

At first, my mind doesn't latch onto what it means or whose face is staring back at me from the picture. I mean... I know *who* it is – it's a photo of Owen. But it's also *not* Owen. I simply can't get my brain to understand or unravel the photograph of what appears to be a man standing on a prizewinners' podium... a man that looks exactly like the man I'm about to marry. And yet the others around him are young boys. Owen's face looks wrong on the much younger body, as if it's somehow been manipulated or generated by a computer and pasted back onto the wrong person.

Or generated by AI.

'There's another picture, too. Look.' Shelley swipes my

phone screen, pulling up a mug shot of the same face but zoomed in. This one also looks computer-generated, but the likeness to my fiancé is uncanny.

I look up at her, my mouth hanging open. No words will come out. And suddenly, Jared is beside me, ushering me away from the altar a few paces.

'Lizzie, this is from my contact in Silicon Valley. Remember I asked them to age-progress the image of Joseph Wentworth? Their technology is cutting edge, used by the US government and the FBI. I only got their email this morning because of the time difference. I've been trying to reach you.'

I nod, desperately trying to work out what it means. Then I'm shaking my head. 'There's a mistake. Something isn't right. This isn't real.' I hear my words, but I don't truly believe them.

'Lizzie?' comes Owen's voice beside me. 'Everything OK?' A hand slides around my waist, gently pulling me back towards the altar.

'Yes, yes... sorry,' I say, looking up at him, frowning. I take one last look at my phone screen before handing it back to Shelley. Then I step in front of Reverend Booth again, giving him a little nod to continue.

But something is not right. As the reverend begins talking again, my mind churns with confusion.

Owen... Joseph...

Surely not. How can that even be possible? My mind races, trying to work it all out, piecing together what I know about Owen. The little I know about Joseph.

'Therefore, I ask...' Reverend Booth continues solemnly. 'If any person can show just cause why this man and this woman may not be joined together in holy matrimony, let them speak now or forever hold their peace.'

Silence.

Someone coughs.

Something rustles.

More silence.

Then a voice echoes throughout the church – crisp and clear. One single syllable.

'No!'

A woman's voice.

'Stop, no! *Wait.*' The same woman's voice ringing out, echoing around the entire church.

Someone gasps. Whispering and shock rippling through the congregation.

'This wedding cannot go ahead,' she says, this time sounding choked and tearful.

I turn around to look at my mother, her expression one of shock as our eyes lock, each staring the other down.

But the woman speaking is me.

FIFTY-FIVE

'*What?*' Owen whispers. 'Lizzie, don't be silly. What on earth's wrong with you?'

I turn, looking up at him, frowning. 'Sorry... I don't know... I... can't do this,' I say more calmly than I have any right to be. 'Who *are* you?' I step away from him. Owen reaches out for my arms, trying to stop me from backing away.

'Elizabeth?' comes my mother's voice, suddenly beside me. 'What's got into you? Do you know all the trouble I've gone to arranging this wedding? Just calm down!'

'Mum, don't,' I hear Shelley say as she comes up to warn her off. 'Come and sit down.'

'Get off!' Mum says, shrugging out of Shelley's grip. 'Elizabeth, get a hold of yourself and let Reverend Booth continue with the ceremony.'

'Your mother is right, Lizzie,' Owen says in that smooth way of his. 'You just have the jitters. It's normal.' He shoots Mum a look. 'Isn't that right, Sylvia?'

Mum is hesitant in her reply, mainly because Shelley has shoved my phone in front of her face and is forcing her to look at pictures of... of Owen... of *Joseph*... as a teenage boy, and then as an adult – the man standing beside us now. The changing expression on her face says it all as Shelley whispers something in her ear.

'Oh...' she says, slowly looking up at him. 'Oh... oh my *God*.'

Suddenly, there's a noise from the back of the church – someone saying, *excuse me*, followed by a commotion and footsteps. When I look round, I see Mary Wentworth standing beside one of the rear pews, staring down the aisle at us. Despite her small stature, she commands a large presence, her hands squarely on her hips, her staring eyes ablaze.

'Joseph,' she calls out in a surprisingly loud voice for a small woman. 'What have you *done*?' She marches towards us.

'This is all ridiculous,' Owen says. 'Who is that woman?' He jabs a hand down the aisle at Mary.

Reverend Booth clears his throat. 'Would you like me to continue, or perhaps a private moment in the vestry is appropriate?' he suggests, but no one answers him.

Mary is standing right in front of Owen now, glaring up at him. 'You've gone beyond the pale now, son,' she barks. 'I slipped in at the back to see this young woman get married. She's been very kind to me, though I had no idea who her mother was. And never did I imagine it would be *you* she was marrying. What the hell do you think you're doing? You're meant to be in Bedford. Or was it Germany? Or maybe you're destitute in London this time, I can't quite remember. Is this how you've been spending my money?' Her expression is a mash-up of desperation and anger as she lunges at him, slapping him on the arm. 'Bleeding your father and me dry.'

'Someone get rid of this madwoman,' Owen says. 'I've never seen her before in my life.'

'I am your *mother*,' Mary spits up at him. 'The lies, the cons, the sob stories you've fed me. All of it pure deceit. My God, the pity and sympathy and kindness I had for you, son. Always down on your luck. Always one step away from homelessness and destitution. All your mad business ideas, and every single time I bailed you out. Thousands of pounds sent to your various business bank accounts over the years. I felt so sorry for you after what happened to Danny. But now... now you're marrying *her* daughter?' She jabs a finger at Mum, shaking her head. 'Is that how you repay me?' Mary's cheeks burn scarlet from anger, though there are also tears in her eyes.

'How dare you!' Mum spits back at Mary, squaring up to her. 'However, I agree that it seems your son is indeed a liar of the most despicable kind.'

'Mum, please, sit down. Let Lizzie and me deal with this,' Shelley says, trying to guide her back to her seat. But Mum is having none of it. Jared positions himself between Mum and Mary, trying to defuse the situation.

'Maybe that was all lies, too,' Mary continues, thumping Owen in the side with her fist. 'All the accusations about *her* when you were at school?' Another glare at Mum. 'I hate the bones of her for what she did to my Danny, causing his suicide, but if you lied about the abuse, Joseph, then you're more of a monster than I ever could have imagined.'

'Jared, as my best man, would you please get this crazy, delusional woman out of the church so the ceremony can continue?' Owen says.

For a moment, my fiancé sounds calm and rational and just like the man I know and love – but there's something in his eyes, something black and empty and... and something *frightened*... that makes my heart race.

The photographs I've just seen – a young Joseph transformed by AI into a man that looks so like Owen it's uncanny – make everything fall into place, not to mention Mary's fervent claims that this is without doubt her son, the son who's conned her, who's made her send him so much money over the years, eating up hers and John's life savings. I think about the shocking amounts she told me she'd given him when we were in the shop in Long Aldbury. Does Owen's unpaid invoice really mean that poor Mary, his ageing mother, has simply run out of money?

'Owen, please, tell me none of this is true,' I say as calmly as I can manage, though it's hard to keep my voice steady. 'I mean *really* tell me. No accusations of madwomen or lies. Just look me in the eye and tell me that you're not really Joseph Wentworth. That Owen Foster has always been your name and you are the man you say you are – the man who is the father of my baby, the man with the high-flying job in Dubai, the man who I've built my entire future around these last six months.' My voice quivers and I'm on the verge of tears.

'*Dubai?*' I hear Mary scoff behind me.

Owen stares at me – though his eyes also dart around the crowd now gathered at the altar. My mother, my father, Shelley, Jared, Mary, Reverend Booth... and even Peter, plus several other men from the congregation who have come up to us, presumably in case things turn nasty. Owen looks hemmed in, fearful, cornered – and angry as hell.

'Owen?' I say quietly, taking his hands in mine. The church is completely silent as everyone waits for his reply. 'Who *are* you?'

It all happens so quickly – Owen grabbing me, me stumbling sideways against him, losing my balance as I trip on my long dress. He catches me before I hit the stone floor, yanking me up by my arm and hurting my shoulder. I cry out in agony, which chimes precisely with my mother's scream and Shelley shouting, and Jared booming at Owen to let go of me.

'Get away!' Owen yells, his voice deafening in my ear. 'Get back, all of you!'

That's when Owen bends his arm around my neck, the crook of his elbow directly under my chin, choking me. I grab his arm, trying to pull it away, but it's locked solid around my throat. Already, I'm finding it hard to breathe.

'Let her go, now!' Jared yells, lunging forward with his arms outstretched, ready to wrestle Owen. Peter approaches along-side him, but Owen drags me backwards down the aisle, my feet half stumbling and half scuffing as he hauls me towards the church door. Then, in the corner of my eye, I see something shiny and bright being brandished in the air. It's a knife. A switchblade that I've never seen before. Slowly, he brings it up to my throat.

FIFTY-SIX

'I swear, if anyone calls the police, she's dead,' Owen spits, his voice distorted by anger. I feel the cold metal of the blade pressing against the side of my neck, knowing he's only one cut away from slitting my artery. He drags me closer to the church door, fumbling with the old iron latch behind his back, opening it wide with his free hand.

'Elizabeth!' I hear Mum scream. 'Stop it! Let her go!'

Someone tells her to keep quiet, and I see that Jared, Dad and Shelley are tracking us down the aisle towards the door while keeping a safe distance so as not to antagonise Owen further.

'Owen, don't,' I beg, my voice coming out as a croak. I tug at his arm clamped around my neck, trying to loosen it, but there's no hope of me overpowering him. 'Think of our baby, please...' I cry, trying not to let the full force of my tears out. 'Just... just let me go and then you can walk free... no police...' I cough, finding it hard to breathe again as he tightens his chokehold. 'We can forget this ever happened.'

'The baby is your problem,' Owen spits in my ear. 'I never wanted the wretched thing in the first place.'

I try to twist around, to make eye contact with him in case I can appeal to the softer side of him that, until a few minutes ago, I believed he had. There must be a shred of feeling left inside him towards us as a couple, as a family. Surely it can't all have been an act.

'Owen... *Joseph*,' I say, keeping my voice low so no one else can hear. 'Wait... *please*. Let's get away, just the two of us. We don't even have to get married, if you don't want. We'll leave this mess behind, leave my mother, go where no one will find us. Whatever she did to you at school, then I'm so *so* sorry...' I lie. 'I believe you, OK? I... I totally understand that you want to hurt her back, get revenge. Is that what this is about?' I cough again, barely able to speak. 'We could go back to Dubai. Just me and you. What do you say?' All I need is for him to release me enough to make a run for it.

'Fucking shut up,' he growls in my ear, giving me a shove. 'And you, keep back!' he yells at Jared, who is closest to us out of the group.

'OK, OK, mate, keep calm.' Jared stands still again, his palms up, showing he means no harm. 'Why don't you just let Lizzie go, then we can talk about this? The best man and the groom chatting it out together, eh?' Jared sounds calm and in control, but his negotiations cause Owen's grip to tighten as he yanks back my head, exposing more of my neck. 'Steady, now,' Jared says, backing away again. 'No one need get hurt.'

'Son, wait,' Mary calls out as I'm being dragged backwards through the church door. Owen stumbles on the step and I manage to angle my head, catching sight of Mary just a few feet away as she follows us outside. 'Don't do this, son. We've had enough tragedy in our family. Come home, why not? Come back to your mum and dad, and we'll make things better for you. We'll look after you until you get on your feet. Don't hurt this poor woman. What do you think our Danny would say if he were here?'

At the mention of Danny, Owen – or *Joseph*, as I now know he is – hesitates. His arm loosens slightly, as if he's considering his mother's words. Then I hear a low growl resonating in the back of his throat, the pattern of his breathing changing to shorter, sharper breaths.

'No...' he rasps. 'Don't you dare bring Danny into this... I'm doing this *for* him. Don't you understand, you stupid woman?'

'Joseph, no... he wouldn't want this—'

'You don't know *what* Danny would want! It's that bitch teacher's fault he's dead. And you and Dad should have protected him! I should kill the lot of you.' He glares behind his mother, where I catch sight of my own mother, pushing past everyone to get outside.

Someone inside the church screams – I have no idea who – but a second later, Mum is standing beside us, breathless and red-faced.

'If you know what's good for you, you'll release my daughter right now! You were a loose cannon back then at school, and you're no better now. Spreading vicious rumours about me, reporting me for things I never did to punish me for your brother's suicide. I have my faults, I know that, and yes, I made a grave mistake when I mistaught that class. But there's no way on God's earth I *ever* hurt you or groomed or abused you, nor would I hurt anyone in that despicable way.' My mother lets out an angry, frustrated sob then spits as hard as she can at Owen, hitting him clean on the cheek. I feel the spray of it on my own skin. 'If anyone caused your brother's suicide, it was your bullying father pressuring him, not me.'

'Lying bitch!' Owen shouts, lashing out with the knife. Mum jumps backwards. 'You destroyed my family, and now I'm going to destroy yours. All the planning this has taken – finding a dead family's graves, changing my name, hunting your daughter down, even following her to another fucking country, worming my way into that pool party, my fake career, convincing her to marry me—' He lets out a demented laugh, sending chills through me.

'Owen, stop... *please*...' I cry, barely able to get the words out, his arm is so tight around my neck. I feel a shove in my back and Owen's hot, frantic breath in my ear as he brings the knife up to my throat again. 'I can't... breathe...'

'Shut up!' he yells at me, turning back to my mother. 'Do you know how hard I tried to ruin you years ago at school, making up those lies about you?' he says to her. 'Sure, I was just a kid, and no one believed me. It was swept under the carpet, and you got a fucking comfortable retirement out of it. But things are different now...'

He shoves me again.

'...I've never forgotten what you did. Every day I feel the impact of my brother's death. It's taken years of planning, of watching you, preparing your slow demise. I've been biding my time, waiting for the perfect moment. And until *he* interfered, I was all set to enjoy a long, slow torture, forcing you to watch me destroy your daughter's life piece by piece, and then yours.'

Owen glares over at Jared, who's still standing near us, his eyes wide and alert. 'And there'd have been nothing you could do about it. Shame, as I'd only just got started.' He shakes his head, making a tutting sound, pressing the knife harder against my skin as if he's about to make the fatal cut.

FIFTY-SEVEN

I hear a choked whimper – but it's me. 'Owen, stop, please...' I beg again, but he ignores me, holding the knife firmly against my skin. One wrong move and it's over.

'And as for the stupid sister...' Owen laughs, turning to Shelley, who's standing beside Jared, her face contorted from worry. 'What I said to you on the phone last night, it was true. Your mother *is* a murderer. She's the reason Danny is dead.'

'That was *you* calling?' Shelley says, her voice incredulous. She's shaking her head, trying to piece it together as her eyes flick down to the knife at my throat. 'Why?'

Owen tenses, giving his mother a hard glare. But when I twist round and look up at him, instead of blackness I see something else in his eyes – a look I've become familiar with over the last few months.

'After Danny died,' he says, 'all I ever wanted was for my father to make everything better, avenge my brother's death and see this woman pay for what she did,' he says, jabbing the knife at my mother. 'My mother was suffering, I was suffering. I was just a kid, and I'd lost the brother I adored. But instead of aiming his anger at *her* or the school and the authorities, my father targeted *me* with his wrath.' Owen catches his breath, almost choking as he spits out the words. 'At one point, he became so violent towards me, I was close to joining my brother. Close to taking my life, too.'

Owen closes his eyes for a second, fighting back the emotions that I know want to escape. I feel his arm tighten around my neck again as he sucks in a breath, composing himself. And that's when I finally recognise the look in his eyes – it's the look of a boy who's not been able to move on. The look of someone who's stuck in the past, wedged neck-deep in trauma. When we first met, it had seemed like an endearing boyish charm. But now I see it for what it is – pure pain. Pain that is now spewing out.

'I wanted everyone to know what that woman did. That's why I phoned you. I wanted to do what my father should have done back then – and I figured by pretending to be him, by telling everyone the truth, was a good start. Especially the night before my wedding. I do a good impression of him, don't you think?' he smirks. 'An angry bastard. He always was.'

I can't believe how wrong I got all of this.

'Enough!' Mum shouts, lunging forward, but Jared holds her back.

'Calm yourself down, *Sylvia*,' Owen says in a voice that makes me feel ill. It's him... but it's *not* him. As though he's possessed. 'By the way, don't forget to return the money you stole from that stupid old woman – sorry, the money *I* stole from her then put in your purse. You do realise that your dreadful behaviour has made this easy for me. And I can't believe you all thought I was commuting to *work* in London, when I was mostly hanging out in City pubs.' Another laugh, making him sound demented and absolutely nothing like the man I fell in love with, the man I trusted. 'It just means I have to get this over with more quickly now – long-overdue payback. Vengeance for my brother.' Then he leans forward and gives me a wet kiss on the cheek. 'Shame, as I was almost growing to like you, Lizzie.'

'You're mad!' Mum screams back at him. 'A psycho—'

'Want to know something else before I kill her?' Owen says, looking around the crowd that's gathered, his teeth bared above me, a terrifying look in his eyes.

But, before he can finish, Mum suddenly lunges forward, stopping abruptly when Dad catches hold of her sleeve. 'Sylvia, no, for Lizzie's sake, don't! Leave it to the police,' I hear Dad say as he casts a furtive look at Peter. They're all standing about six feet away. No one dares do anything while the blade is pressed against the side of my throat. They cling onto each other for support, while I stand caught in Owen's vice-like grip, shaking and trembling.

'I've phoned the police,' Peter suddenly calls out, 'they'll be here soon!'

But I wish to God he'd kept quiet.

'Big mistake, Peter. But I should have guessed it would be you,' Owen growls back. 'I never liked you, which is why I blocked you on Lizzie's phone. I knew you'd cause trouble.' He drags me closer to the churchyard gates leading to the lane, and I feel his body tensing up behind me. I've no idea where he's taking me as he won't have prepared for this turn of events. He's acting on raw emotion.

'Please... Owen, let me go,' I beg. 'You're hurting me and... I... I can't breathe properly. It's going to harm the baby... please, let me go...'

'Keep quiet,' he orders, shoving me again, his eyes darting around. He's feeling trapped, on a knife edge, and he doesn't know what to do next. If he hears police sirens approaching, I fear for my life. I've never seen him like this before; love must have blurred the early-warning signs – but it's clear he's lied about so many things. He probably hurled *himself* down the stairs. To think I was afraid of my mother all this time, when the real monster was right in front of me.

Then I feel his grip on me loosen for just a moment as he twists around to open the latch on the churchyard gate leading to the lane.

'*Now!*' someone yells – Jared – and several bodies lunge at us.

Before I can make sense of anything, I'm falling sideways, my head hitting the wooden gatepost as I go down.

There's a struggle around me – grunts and fists flying – then my mother hurtles past me, launching herself at the tangle of bodies and limbs that has stumbled out onto the lane. I scramble to my feet, tripping on my dress but righting myself again. People are screaming and shouting, and I can't tell what's what until I get my balance.

'Mum!' I scream. She's struggling with Owen, who's thrashing about, whipping the blade through the air as he tries to fight off Jared and Peter, as well as fend off Mum's attack. I've never seen her so ferocious.

Suddenly there's blood spraying through the air. I don't know whose it is at first, but then I spot the gash on Jared's cheek from a single swift swipe of the blade, followed by a line of red seeping through Peter's shirt as his shoulder is stabbed. The pair of them fall away, crying out and doubling up in pain from their wounds.

Then it's just Mum and Owen wrangling together – Owen grabbing her around the shoulders, trying to pin down her thrashing arms. Mum kicks at his legs, hoisting up her knee sharply to his groin but missing as he doubles forward to avoid the impact.

They stumble backwards onto the lane, my mother clinging onto Owen's jacket for all she's worth with one hand, while her other hand makes a grab for the knife. Never, in my entire life, have I seen such a selfless and brave act by my mother, throwing herself into the fray to keep him away from me.

But then, in slow motion, I see it playing out before my eyes – the outcome if I don't do something fast... the horror of what is about to happen.

'*Mum!*' I scream, my throat burning and hoarse.

The grain lorry thunders down the hill from the direction of the farm just as Mum and Owen are careering into the middle of the lane.

'Mum!' I yell again as instinct takes over. I charge out onto the lane, launching myself at Owen, trying to separate my mother from his grip. The shadow of the lorry looms over the three of us, the deafening sound of its horn blaring.

Half a second – that's how long my final stare with Owen lasts.

My fingers are gripped tightly around his wrist, the knife shaking in his hand, while my other hand is squarely against his shoulder, our faces close, each of us panting. Afterwards, when I think back, I swear I felt his final breath on my cheek. The whisper of a kiss goodbye.

But then he's gone.

Knocked sideways from me as the lorry hits him, crushing him under the front set of wheels... then the next... then the next. It takes the lorry until the bottom of the lane to come to a stop, having dragged Owen along under its tyres.

I stand quite still, my mouth wide open, everything silent and unreal. Then I screw up my eyes and collapse to my knees when I see the trail of blood spread all the way down the road.

FIFTY-EIGHT

The police have gone. The ambulance and medics have gone. Owen... or rather, *Joseph*... has gone.

My happy future has gone.

It takes all my strength to hold my head up, to stare at the fireplace opposite as I sit on the sofa at Medvale. I am still wearing my wedding dress – I can't even find the energy to change, despite Shelley trying to coax me. I bow my head and look at the beautiful skirt – torn and smeared with blood from where I ran up to Owen, dropping to my knees beside him.

'Help!' I'd screamed. '*Please*, do something!' His face was a mess, raw and skinless from where he'd been dragged. His body twisted and broken as he lay on the tarmac in the shadow of the grain lorry. Someone hauled me up and away from him, pressing my face into their shoulder so I didn't have to look. Jared.

I've been so determined to find Joseph Wentworth this past week, to ask him if his claims about my mother were true, I never thought for one minute that I'd been sleeping in the same bed as him for the last six months. And now he's dead.

'Hey, drink this if you can.' Shelley hands me a mug. I sip.

Warm, sweet tea. My hands are shaking so much, I can hardly hold it. I refused the diazepam the medics offered me earlier, even though they said it was safe for my baby. But I didn't want to risk it. Shelley curls herself around me.

'I'm so sorry this has happened to you, my darling sister. We're here for you. Your family.'

Mum and Dad are in the kitchen. I keep catching the occasional word of their conversation, what they told the police, their disbelief. Mum's self-righteousness is audible even from another room. *I knew it... never liked him... wretched family...*

Then Dad's soothing, quieter, patient tones as he falls back into the familiar role of people-pleaser, enabler, the man who appeases his wife. The clattering of utensils as, between them, they make a meal that no one will want to eat.

'Poor Mary,' I manage to whisper, staring into my mug. 'Two sons dead.'

'They've both been lost to her for a long time, by the sound if it,' Shelley says gently. 'None of this is your fault, Lizzie. You were taken in by that man. The only thing you're guilty of is love.'

'That'll teach me to let my guard down,' I say, shaking my head, sipping my tea. 'Never again.'

'You mustn't blame yourself.'

The rational part of me knows this is true, that I couldn't have prevented any of this. And that's the part I need to focus on because I can't expect Shelley to prop up my grief, not when hers is still scaffolded around her.

But somehow, like that scared, frightened little girl who blamed herself for everything, who wanted to take away her mother's pain and make it her own, I *do* feel responsible for what has happened. And it makes me want to run away. Flee to the ends of the earth to escape the gnawing agony that I feel inside. But nowhere on this earth would be far enough.

I glance out of the window – it's just starting to get dark.

Owen and I were supposed to be having our first dance about now. I can't even stand to look outside, to see the decorated marquee sitting in the middle of the lawn. After the police had surveyed the accident scene, taking statements from everyone, and the ambulance had taken Owen away, we'd come back to Medvale. Mum had rushed around telling the catering staff to pack up and go, wrapping up my wedding with as much efficiency as she'd organised it. For the *second* time.

An hour ago, DI Lambert and DC Powell had visited, having heard what had happened. 'I'm so very sorry for your loss, Miss Holmes,' he'd said, his eyes flicking between us all. I saw his mind in overdrive, incredulous that something so similar had happened twice in the same family.

The police constables who'd taken our statements earlier told us there would be an inquest, a full investigation into the circumstances surrounding Owen's death, but I'd just sat there numbly, answering their questions, telling them everything I knew through a muffle of tears and tissues.

I'd barely been able to lift my head when DI Lambert mentioned my mother's corsage again. Everything was pressing down on me. 'In light of today's developments, do you think it could have been your fiancé who sent the corsage to the police station with the note? Of course, we'll continue with our enquiries.' While they were here, they took away the pearl-topped pin, saying it would also be kept as evidence.

After the detectives had gone, my numb brain tried to process his theory. It was certainly possible – Owen had been up in the loft when he tried to find room to store our stuff, after all, and I remember thinking that the box had been opened. Clearly he'd hoped to find something that would incriminate my mother by coming here to stay in her home. But coming to terms with Owen only wanting to marry me to destroy my mother is almost more chilling than coming to terms with his death. I'm not sure I'll ever get over what he did.

My phone had rung almost immediately after the officers left. Shelley had answered it for me, listening to the caller as she rummaged around in her handbag for a pen, pulling out a bit of old envelope to write down a number.

'That was Jenkins & Jones, a letting agent in London,' she'd told me after she'd hung up. 'Something about a flat that might be of interest to you. I told her it wasn't a good time, but she kept talking, going on about how a let had been agreed with a family who had been moving to London from the States, but that it's literally just fallen through. I took down the address and their phone number, just to get rid of her.'

'Thanks,' I said, not even wanting to think about flats right now. I took the piece of paper from her anyway, though my mind was too preoccupied to concentrate – Owen's death was still only a few hours ago, his blood still on my gown. But I did a double-take when I saw the address that she'd jotted down. *Wenlock Avenue* – the same flat that Owen had claimed to have rented for us – his lies stringing me along into a future that was never going to happen. Pure coincidence and good fortune for him that the 'Let Agreed' sign happened to appear on the property site at just the right time. The interim invoice payment was no doubt a lie, too. It seems that nothing truthful had ever come out of his mouth.

I sip my tea, though it's virtually cold now. Minnie comes into the room, winding her way around Shelley's legs before rubbing against mine. Then she jumps up on my lap, kneading my wedding dress with her front paws as she settles down, oblivious to everything that's happened. From the other room, I hear Mum and Dad bickering – rather Mum telling Dad what to do, her voice shrill and overbearing. Dad suddenly appears in the doorway, his expression resigned and stoic.

'More tea for you, fair lasses,' he says solemnly, carrying over a small tray. He sits down beside me, handing me another mug.

I manage a smile. 'Thanks, Dad,' I say, not really wanting it. I'm more interested in finding out why he was so certain I shouldn't get married, that I should run far away and never come back. When I ask him, he thinks for a moment, finally taking my hand in his.

'Hear that?' he says, and I listen. But there's nothing, just silence. I frown, shaking my head.

'Wait a moment,' Dad says, sitting quite still beside me. 'It'll come.' Then, right on cue, there's a shriek from the kitchen, a bang, followed by a few swear words, then Mum yelling and sobbing before she falls quiet again. 'That,' he says.

'Mum?'

'No, *marriage*. I was scared for you, Lizzie. I shouldn't have said anything, it was wrong of me, and your experience didn't have to be like mine. But as it happens, my concerns weren't unfounded.' He sucks in a sharp breath. 'Even when you and Shelley were children, I handled everything so badly, taught you to run away rather than deal with things. Like *I* should have dealt with things.' He hangs his head.

'So you're getting a divorce?' Shelley asks in that forthright way of hers.

'Good God, no. I love the bones of your mother,' Dad says. 'But you don't have to be me, fair lasses. I'm not running back to Winchcombe again, that much is certain. Your mother and I will work things out in our own way. I'm not saying it will be easy, but we will try. That's all I can do.'

We all sit in silence for a while, hearing the occasional noise from Mum in the kitchen, which, strangely, makes me feel safe, at home. It will take time to come to terms with everything that has happened, and I know Mum will always be *Mum*, but she helped save my life earlier, putting her own life at risk. No one expected the mother of the bride's duties would include that today.

Soon, she joins us in the living room. 'There's something in the oven for later, but Lizzie, dear, you look white as a sheet. You need to keep your blood sugar levels up,' she says, fussing around me. 'Here, I've brought you these.'

She puts another tray on the coffee table, filled with scones that she always keeps in the freezer, the butter dish, some cream, plus a pot of her hedgerow jam.

'And I want you to know, darling, it most certainly wasn't me who hid your engagement ring, however much I disliked it. To think I nearly fired Preston over it.'

I nod, having already figured out it was probably Owen who planted it in Mum's bedroom. 'Preston?' I say, looking up. 'Why?'

'No need to worry about that, darling. But I must phone my friend back and tell her it wasn't him, after all. When we were in the bridal boutique, I confided to her on the phone that I was going to get rid of him. Now, eat up, darling. I don't want you passing out.'

'You'll have to convince Lizzie your jam isn't poisoned first,' Shelley says to Mum.

'*Well*,' Mum replies with a frown, taken aback, but quickly realises that, under the circumstances, she won't make a scene. 'I didn't want to say when the police were here earlier, but goodness, I could have poisoned an entire village with what I found on the drive the other day.'

Mum then chastises Dad about how he should have been more careful with his medication, but no one is listening. We're all lost in our own thoughts, processing what's happened.

'The sock was lying right beside your car, Elizabeth, on the gravel. It must have fallen out when, I presume, your father gave it to you to dispose of. I did the same a few months ago when I found all his untaken pills. I couldn't leave them hidden in his bathroom.' She shakes her head and tuts, as though it's a perfectly normal thing for a family to be dealing with. Then she puts some cream and jam on a scone, before handing it to me. 'Eat up now, darling. It'll do you good.'

I stare at it for a moment, not feeling the least bit hungry. But, just to be on the safe side, and when Mum's not looking, I slide the plate back onto the tray.

EPILOGUE

TWO MONTHS LATER

The seatbelt lights go out and Shelley relaxes. She's never much liked flying, but she intends on dulling the twenty-four-hour flight to Auckland with a few drinks, some mindless movies and sleep. Anything to get her through to the other side. *It's only for a year*, she tells herself, suddenly stricken by homesickness as she overhears a New Zealand accent from the man beside her, reminding her of Rafe. *A year's placement at a veterinary practice on the other side of the world... You can do this... It'll help you forget... Do you good...*

And that's what she needs – some good being done in her life. Even if she has to run away to get it. Or perhaps it's escaping the bad. She's not sure.

Lizzie drove her to the airport earlier, promising that if she's still in Auckland after the baby is born, she'll bring her little niece or nephew for a visit. 'It'll be a chance for me to run away without actually running away,' she'd said, jangling the cottage keys at Shelley. 'No need to worry, I'll look after your place as though it's my own.'

'You've never *had* a place of your own,' Shelley had joked, giving her sister yet another hug before she headed through security.

'Which is why I'm so grateful to you for trusting me with yours. Jared is staying on, and even when he moves into his new house, he won't be far away. Any property disasters that I can't deal with, he'll help me. Or I'll call Gavin. I've got real friends now. And while you're away, I'll get back on my feet. Get some work, have my baby, find myself without looking in all the wrong places.'

More hugs, more tears. More smiles. And Shelley hadn't failed to notice the warm look in her sister's eyes whenever she mentioned Jared. It happened every time his name cropped up. There was just something about those two.

'FaceTime is our friend, right?' Shelley said. 'I don't care about the time difference. You call me whenever you feel lonely or sad, OK?'

'Same to you,' Lizzie replied. They each had a deep understanding of the other's grief, the tidal waves of emotion that gripped them periodically. One minute they'd be coping, the next they'd be flattened and needing to talk it through.

'I know the police and coroner are satisfied that Owen's death was a terrible accident,' Lizzie had said more than once during their late-night chats these last few weeks. 'But... I've played it over a million times in my head, and each time it feels more and more like... like it was...' It was at this point she'd always hesitated, not quite able to say the words. 'I've just got it in my head that it was *Mum* who pushed Owen into the path of the lorry. I feel awful for even thinking it.'

'Shh, it's OK,' Shelley had replied, holding her sister tightly. 'You can't keep playing it over in your mind, Lizzie, or you won't survive. Trust me, I know.'

But Shelley had been thinking the same thing. She'd seen what happened. She'd noticed it, too. In those bright, sharp, focused, dreadful moments as her sister, her mother and Owen had fought in the lane outside the church, something *had* happened.

She remembered how Lizzie's head had turned, spotting the lorry coming down the hill, her expression changing as it careered towards them. She'd since thought it was only her who'd observed the sharp shove her mother had given Owen. Instead of pulling him back to safety, she'd pushed him into the road, knowing what would happen. Their mother had killed Owen.

Shelley had no plans to tell anyone what she'd witnessed. Just as she'd never tell anyone that she'd found her mother's corsage buried in a box in the attic of Medvale House a few months ago when she was searching for one of her old veterinary books.

She'd kept it, not knowing what it meant, though when DI Lambert came sniffing about, she'd panicked. The bored-looking teenager in town had gladly taken her twenty pounds to deliver the corsage to the police station, along with an anonymous note that would hopefully distract the detective for a while, throw him off any scent he might be about to pick up.

No; she'd keep their mother's secret safe, just as she'd been keeping her own.

While Lizzie's loss was still raw, Shelley's had dulled a little over the past year. Though she'd always remember the morning of her own wedding as though it was today – still as clear in her mind now as it had been then.

The seemingly endless journey in the Rolls-Royce to the church, her initial excitement changing to worry, anxiety, concern... circling the village, puzzled looks from the driver... the reverend's soothing words as everyone searched for Rafe... Lizzie phoning her, sobbing, telling her to get home fast.

Then the familiar smells of home... Lizzie hysterical... Rafe's body lying on the kitchen floor... the stab of pain in her knees as she dropped down beside him... her hands racing all over her fiancé, searching for signs of life, shaking him, stroking him, the disbelief. Lizzie rushing out of the back door to throw up... the sound of police sirens approaching the cottage... All of it in sharp, brilliant focus.

And that's when she'd seen it. Her senses on fire. Everything alert. It was stuck to the sole of Rafe's bare foot. Looking back, it seemed to take ages for her brain to work out what it was, where it had come from.

But in reality, it had taken less than a second.

How could she have been so *careless*?

And in that same, single second, while her sister was outside, she'd replayed her entire morning. The laughter, the excitement as she, Lizzie and the bridesmaids got ready, doing their hair and make-up, the adults sipping champagne. Even their mother had been on good form.

Then the phone call from the farmer. Her head was already giddy from drinking alcohol on an empty stomach. Her nerves adding to the effect, her poor judgement. 'Sure, I'll be there shortly,' she'd said to him. One of his horses in severe post-operative pain. Even driving was risky after what she'd had, but she wouldn't enjoy her wedding knowing that an animal was suffering.

'Shelley, for God's sake, it's your wedding day. You're not on call,' Lizzie had pleaded. 'Get someone else to go!'

'I'll be there and back in half an hour,' she'd insisted, changing into her jeans and a sweatshirt, grabbing her vet's bag and racing to the farm – only a ten-minute drive at most. She'd take it steady, even though her head was swimming.

Somehow, despite all her training, all her good sense and years of practice, all her experience and knowledge, she'd made a mistake. She'd since blamed it on the alcohol, all the distractions of the morning, as well as rushing and not wanting to be late for her own wedding, but she was the one who'd done it. She was the one who'd made that fatal error.

Shelley had never quite worked out how she'd managed to mishandle the disposal of the equine fentanyl patch so badly. She recalled the first one she'd applied hadn't adhered properly – her fingers fumbling, the horse restless and agitated – so she'd tried again with another.

There were strict guidelines for administering the medication, as well as for its safe disposal, and she knew the protocol well. But she'd already broken the rules by having the patches in her possession in the first place. The medication was usually locked away at the practice, but she'd been in a rush after her last on-call visit, and hadn't had time to return them and sign them back in. Just this once, she'd decided to do it after the weekend. No one would notice. It was her wedding weekend, after all. The patches would be safe in her bag, locked in her house. She'd had no idea she'd have a reason to use them when she was called out to the farm.

Shelley had looked up from where she was kneeling beside Rafe's body on the kitchen floor, the pool of blood dark and congealing around his head. The dose of drugs in the clear, sticky patch was for a horse – and lethal for Rafe, especially given his drug-taking on his stag night, as well as his undiagnosed heart condition. She could hardly believe what she'd done. How careless she'd been. The mistake she'd made.

Had the patch got stuck somewhere – on her bag, on her clothing, fallen out of where she thought she'd disposed of it safely? She couldn't be certain. All she knew was that she'd done something wrong, that she hadn't noticed her error and the patch had somehow ended up on her kitchen floor after she'd got back. And Rafe had trodden on it with his bare feet.

It was during that same single, interminable second that she raced to get some tissue, ripping the patch from his foot, flushing it down the toilet before anyone saw. What would happen after that, she had no idea. A single second wasn't long enough to work all that out.

But her mistake had killed Rafe. She was certain of that.

'Gin and tonic, please,' Shelley says as the drinks trolley comes past. The man beside her asks for the same in his New Zealand accent, and she passes his over to him.

'Cheers,' he says, giving her a smile. 'Going home?'

'Maybe,' Shelley replies. 'Depends if I like it there or not. You?'

The man thinks about this for a moment, giving Shelley a smile. He's about her age, the type she'd probably look twice at if she was on a night out, if she was in the mood – neither of which she has been for a very long time.

Then he nods. 'I think so,' he says. 'I'm Alex. I'm a doctor. I did a year's placement in London, but it's time to go back home now. You can't run away forever, right?'

Shelley laughs, raising her plastic glass in the air. 'Oh, I think you can,' she says.

Especially when you've killed your husband...

A LETTER FROM SAMANTHA

Dear Reader,

Thank you so much for taking the time to read *Mother of the Bride*. I do hope you found it as thrilling to read as I did to write. If you'd like to be kept up to date with all my new releases, you can click on the link below for book news (you can unsubscribe at any time).

www.bookouture.com/samantha-hayes

Getting married might well be one of the happiest days of your life, but there's no doubt that it can also turn into one of the most stressful – especially if there's a mother of the bride like Sylvia desperate to take over the day.

The potential for heightened emotions leading up to the 'Big Day' was too rich a vein not to tap into for a psychological thriller. And throwing my bride-to-be into a situation that was way out of her comfort zone was perhaps a cruel card to deal Lizzie, my main character, but a necessary one for her journey. After all, she's used to running away and avoiding her family and conflict at all costs.

Lizzie truly believes that she's finally found the love of her life in Owen, and once the couple are back in England and forced to stay at her family home, she grows increasingly fearful of her mother – and the danger she's put her fiancé in.

With a traumatic and unpredictable childhood, Lizzie

struggles with relationships, and this got me thinking... What if the current danger wasn't her mother at all? What if the real danger is the man she believes will *save* her from her troubled past – the one person she should be able to trust completely? With the added tragedy of Rafe's death still recent and raw, life suddenly becomes a boiling pot of emotions for Lizzie, making her blind to the *real* threat in her life.

If you enjoyed reading *Mother of the Bride* and following Lizzie's journey (by the way, in my imagination, she gives birth to a lovely baby girl!), then I'd be so very grateful if you could leave a quick review on Amazon to let other readers know about my book. It really does help spread the word.

And meantime, I'm getting stuck into my next novel – another psychological thriller to keep you turning the pages!

With warm wishes,

Sam x

[f] facebook.com/samanthahayesauthor

[X] x.com/samhayes

[O] instagram.com/samanthahayes.author

ACKNOWLEDGEMENTS

Huge thanks and gratitude to Lucy Frederick, my amazing editor, for all her hard work on this book – it's been an absolute pleasure working with you! Big thanks and gratitude to my equally amazing and usual editor Jessie Botterill – welcome back! And massive thanks, too, to Sarah Hardy and the entire publicity team at Bookouture for working so hard to promote my books. To Seán for his eagle-eyed copyediting and to Jenny Page for proofreading – thank you so much! Plus, my sincere thanks to the entire team at Bookouture for continuing to believe in me and publish my books.

And of course, big thanks to Oli Munson, my wonderful agent, and the whole team at A M Heath.

As ever, I'd like to say a heartfelt thank you to the dedicated book bloggers, reviewers and readers around the world who take the time to shout out about and review my books. I appreciate it more than words can say.

Finally, much love to Ben, Polly and Lucy, as well as the rest of my family.

Sam xx

PUBLISHING TEAM

Turning a manuscript into a book requires the efforts of many people. The publishing team at Bookouture would like to acknowledge everyone who contributed to this publication.

Audio
Alba Proko
Sinead O'Connor
Melissa Tran

Commercial
Lauren Morrissette
Jil Thielen
Imogen Allport

Data and analysis
Mark Alder
Mohamed Bussuri

Editorial
Jessie Botterill
Imogen Allport

Copyeditor
Seán Costello

Made in the USA
Monee, IL
31 May 2024

59201360R00204